Born in Ch… …onnell/ Malcolm R… …Market Drayton, Prestwick, Port Elizabeth and Cornwall. He studied medicine and then art before going to Sweden to teach English. He married in 1962 and settled in Hertfordshire soon after. He worked in publishing before becoming a freelance hack and graphic designer. Since 1974 he has lived in Ireland (the spiritual home of all writers in English) and has concentrated on historical novels under a number of pen-names. His elder daughter is a molecular biologist; his younger daughter works in publishing.

Malcolm Ross's romentic novels of nineteenth-century Ireland, *Hell Hath No Fury*, *A Woman Scorned* and *All Desires Known*, are also available from Headline, as are his Cornish sagas, *On a Far Wild Shore*, *A Notorious Woman*, *An Innocent Woman*, *A Woman Alone*, *A Woman Possessed* and *To the End of Her Days*.

Also by M. R. O'Donnell

Hell Hath No Fury
A Woman Scorned
All Desires Known

For I Have Sinned

Malcolm Ross
writing as

M. R. O'Donnell

[redacted]

KNIGHT

First published in 1994
by HEADLINE BOOK PUBLISHING

First published in paperback in 1995
by HEADLINE BOOK PUBLISHING

This edition published 2000 by
Knight an imprint of Caxton Publishing Group

10 9 8 7 6 5 4 3 2

ISBN 1 84067 199 8

Printed and bound in Great Britain by
Mackays of Chatham PLC, Chatham, Kent

Caxton Publishing Group
20 Bloomsbury Street
London
WC1B 3QA

PART ONE

The Name of the Daughter

1

Had the little wee man gone away? Salome could not be certain. When you're only seven years old there are lots of things about which you cannot be certain. True, he was no longer calling out, 'Little girl?' and endlessly repeating that he didn't want to harm her. And when she looked through the knothole in the wood, he was no longer in sight. But there was a sort of noise out there that could be someone breathing and other noises that could be someone going about on tiptoe. Not that it was easy to pick out vague noises like that amid all the hustle and bustle on the quayside. She was lucky to have found the empty packing case, really. Samson was an awful long time fetching Mammy to come and rescue her.

She began counting to a hundred once again. Surely this time it would work?

Samson, still down on the quayside, saw his Mammy standing at the farther end of the gangway for the steerage passengers. She was peering anxiously downward – straight at him, or so it seemed to him in his guilt, even though he realized she'd hardly notice him in all that jostle. And anyway, the people around her were arguing and shaking their fists. She was blocking the way. Daddy was beside her, shouting at one of the seamen.

Suddenly the little boy was afraid. The Da would surely whip the skin off his back if he told them what he and Salome had done – or Salome, really. She was the divil. It was all her fault. The Mammy would never believe it, of course. Her darlin' little Salome was a saint on wheels. But it was Salome who had spotted the gangway for the quality and bet him they could get down there and come back up the steerage gangway a second time. It was Salome had led the way under the rope with the sign that read FIRST-CLASS PASSENGERS ONLY PAST THIS POINT. And it was Salome had stuck her tongue out at the little wee man and got him to chase them. But, of course, the Mammy would never believe any of that.

Samson turned from the wrath to come and raced back up the gangway for the quality. At the top a man in a white coat tried to stop him, but he ducked under the outstretched arm and raced among the startled and outraged passengers toward the rope with the sign that, on this side, read simply STEERAGE.

One of those passengers, Paul Delaroux, said to his wife, Georgina, "The little rascal! He can't be more than eight or nine."

"Sign of the times, darling," she replied coolly. "We must learn that bits of glorified string with notices hung from them are no longer enough to restrain our Irish peasantry."

Several people around them turned and looked at her askance. The trouble with Georgina – *one* of the troubles with Georgina – was that one never knew whether her tongue was in her cheek, and, if so, how deeply. Her tone seemed to be one of hearty contempt for what she called 'our Irish peasantry', yet there was a merry glint in her eye and a fleeting lilt at the end of one or two words, enough to suggest a certain glee that the Irish giant was at last waking from its troubled slumbers. She was English by birth, which ought to have put her firmly into one camp; but on the other hand, she was also a Roman Catholic, which would put her – though rather less firmly – in the other. And then again, she was neither fiercely patriotic nor devoutly religious . . . so where did that leave one?

Not that young Samson was troubled by such ambiguities; he was, in any case, well beyond earshot before Georgina spoke. Now he was leaping down the companionway three steps at a time, hastening bravely toward a punishment he knew would be swift and terrible. People cursed his haste and tried to cuff him as he sped past them. His feet did not drag until the last dozen paces or so.

"I assure you, ma'am, no little girl and no little boy have gone back . . ." one of the seamen was saying – or trying to say.

"But didn't three people see them shlip under that rope?" the Da objected.

"Would you stand aside in the name of God and let the rest of us aboard?" shouted a perspiring man with a roly-poly wife and fourteen children at his heels.

"All I want is to go back down there and satisfy meself they're not left behind," his Mammy pleaded.

"And I'm giving you my *personal* assurance . . ." the sailor tried again.

And all the while, from farther down the gangway, came cries of anger, frustration, and dismay: "What's the hold-up? Who's that eejit?" . . . and worse.

Samson could not believe that their little prank – down one gangway and up the other for the second time – could lead to all this turmoil. His courage began to ebb.

It deserted him entirely when the Da spotted him and gave out a roar that rang around the whole of Queenstown. "Samson! Come here you bold monkey!"

He took one look at his father's purple face and, with a cry of "Mammy!" fled to the sanctuary of her embrace.

She took a pace toward him, freeing the gangway once more. Behind her, like bubbles in an uncorked lemonade bottle, the perspiring man, his roly-poly wife, and their cartload of children – and all the complainants behind them – came flowing up the incline and erupted onto the deck.

"Is that one of them?" asked the triumphant sailor, nodding at Samson.

"It is, so." Finbar McKenna began fingering the buckle of his belt.

"Not now!" his wife snapped. "You know how it robs him of speech." She shook her son and tried to make him look her in the eye. "Samson! Tell me the truth now – as God is your witness. Did you and your sister go beyond that rope?"

He licked his lips. "What rope?" he croaked, not meaning to lie, really, just playing for time. If the Da would go away a moment, he thought he might be able to confess the truth to her.

"*That* rope!" She pointed up the companionway, which was too thronged with people for the barrier to be visible. "There's a rope slung across the deck up there with a sign on it saying for first-class passengers only. Did you and your sister shlip under it?"

"We did not," he assured her. And it was, indeed, the literal truth, for, though Salome *had* slipped beneath the rope, he had vaulted over it.

"Even if they did, they could never have got down the first-class gangway." The sailor managed to finish his sentence at last. "Amn't I after telling ye? 'Twould be against regulations entirely."

Samson wanted to tell him how they'd managed it when the officer was distracted by the lady with the ostrich feathers who'd fainted for half a second when she reached the deck and then demanded a glass of iced water.

"Where's Salome?" his father asked.

The boy buried his face in his mother's bosom. "Hiding," he mumbled.

"What?" he roared.

"Hiding!" his wife snapped back at him. She wanted to be angry with her son but knew from long experience how tongue-tied it would make him – and there just wasn't time for all that. "Where?" she asked Samson, in as gentle a tone as her agitation would allow.

"Were you playing hide and seek?" his father put in. "Is

that it?" He was also making a valiant effort to master his rage.

Samson nodded, not wanting to risk a spoken lie. Anyway, surely Salome would soon realize she was safe by now? Then she'd come out and skip up the gangway, just like she said. Wasn't it her idea in the first place? Would it be his fault if people didn't stick to their own ideas?

"What?" his father asked, beginning to let his anger show again.

"He said yes," his mother cried, furious that he would not curb himself and let the boy calm down. "So – she's hiding somewhere here on this boat. Is that it? Lord, such a time to go playing games!" She held the boy at arm's length and tried once again to see into his eyes.

He stared at the deck and shrugged. "Sure she could be anywhere," he mumbled, artfully laying the foundations of a future defence. "Anywhere at all."

"Well, you make sure she isn't," his father put in. "Go and find her – and bring her to me."

"Finbar . . ." His wife laid a restraining hand upon his arm. "Go aisy, now. Don't be putting the fear of God into them."

He forced a smile. "Away with you!" he said, giving his son a playful cuff.

They waited by the rail but the boy had still not returned by the time the crew raised the gangplank to the steerage. Then Finbar McKenna let out a mighty oath that he'd skin the pair of them and went off in search of either.

Deborah McKenna's renewed agitation touched the sailor who had earlier barred her return to the quayside. "Look ma'am," he said, "isn't it all but deserted down there now? And wouldn't you see any wee shlip of a colleen in a pretty dress?"

"She was in plain gingham," Deborah told him.

"Wouldn't you see her, even so, and you her mammy? And didn't the gossoon say she was hiding here aboard ship? And anyway, the first-class gangway is still in place. If she's down there at all – which is impossible – she has that way still."

Deborah leaned against the rail, trying to accept his reassurance, trying not to cry, and wondering why such a terrible sense of foreboding oppressed her; and all the while her eyes quartered the quayside, up and down, back and forth, looking for the smallest patch of blue gingham that would prove them all wrong.

She wanted to join Finbar and help him turn the ship upside down but she dared not leave the rail nor take her eyes off the quayside for one moment. Suppose little Salome *was* down there somewhere, hiding – perhaps as a game, perhaps in genuine fear of something . . . And suppose she crept out at last when she thought the coast was clear? Who would notice her then? Who would put two and two together and say, 'Aha! There's a little girl who should be on that ship!'

She turned to the sailor. "Don't let them leave until we're sure she's aboard."

"I'll go and speak to the officer meself, missiz," he promised.

She would have felt even less reassured if she had seen how he raised his eyes skyward once his back was turned to her.

Down on the quayside the heat of the July afternoon, reflected back and forth between the shed and the great iron cliff of the SS *Knysna*'s hull, grew more oppressive by the minute; inside the packing case Salome was beginning to wonder how much longer she could stand it. She put her eye to the knothole yet again and moved her head this way and that to see whether or not the little wee man had returned. Her two previous inspections – between each of which she had counted to a hundred – had revealed no sign of him; she promised herself that if there was still no sign of him this third time, she'd risk flying out of her hiding place and making a bolt for the gangway.

But it was not to be. The little wee man, having made one careful search of the quayside, was about to start all over again, this time even more carefully.

He did not dare let that pretty little colleen go free to inform on him, even though he'd barely touched her – as yet. They'd never believe him, no matter what he said. And this time he'd get two years – *and* a flogging. Two years was just about bearable but the flogging would kill him. They flogged Jamjars Quin last time he was inside. Fifty strokes of the birch – fifty times God-knows-how-many cuts from a bundle of whippy quicksets. The poor fella had never been the same man since. And that was just for ringing a horse. For *this* offence they could make fifty seem worse than five hundred. There'd be places where the skin would never grow back. He had to find the colleen and silence her.

When he shuffled away Salome closed her eyes and began another slow count to a hundred. At twenty they lowered the first-class gangway to the quay but she did not see it. She had still only reached fifty when the lines and hawsers fore and aft were slipped from the bollards and pale water began to open up between the ship and the land.

Out on the quayside Marion Culham-Browne gave way to the tears that had threatened to overwhelm her ever since Maude O'Brien had walked up the gangway – and out of her life for ever. Or at least for the next five years, which was just as awful. She waved her damp and inadequate little hanky at the departing boat but could no longer be sure which pale blur above the rail was Maude. She went on waving until the vessel was well offshore and the pale blurs had themselves coalesced into one long smear.

Then she was startled out of her misery by a shriek from somewhere behind her. She turned to see a little girl in a blue gingham frock hurtling toward the quayside as if she intended taking a flying leap out into the bay. And hard on her heels was a grotesque little man who bore an extraordinary resemblance to Mr Punch. Marion's first impression was that the fellow was chasing the girl; then she realized that he must, in fact, be trying to stop her from carrying out her obvious intention of leaping into the sea. A moment later she herself had intercepted the child and, almost bowled over by her momentum, swept her up into the air, carrying her around full circle. "Whoo! You'll make me giddy!" she cried, hugging the skinny little thing tight in case she broke free again.

Marion almost yielded to tears once more. To hold a little girl in her arms again – a girl of just this age – was more than she could bear. She even had the same jet-black hair and the same smoky grey eyes – it was uncanny. "Is that man your Daddy?" she asked.

The slim, pale lady smelled nice. And she had a voice like an angel. Perhaps she was an angel. Her hug was so loving and warm that all Salome's fears were lifted; somehow she just *knew* she was safe once more.

Marion had to repeat her question; she was surprised at the speed with which the child had gone from the extreme of agitation to this astonishing calm.

"No!" Salome said, shivering with rekindled fear as she glanced at the man.

Marion turned to him and asked in much more peremptory tones than she would otherwise have used, "You! Were you chasing the child?"

"Oh God, indeed I was not, your ladyship," he replied anxiously. A second later he wished he could have bitten his tongue off.

Of course, what he ought to have said was that the colleen was his niece and a bold little creature she was, too, that had him kill't with the worry the way she'd run and hide and think it great gas to see him searching high and low. Had he said that, he could have walked off with her under his arm.

But it was too late now.

"Be off with you then," Marion ordered. "I don't care for the look of you at all." She glanced around the quayside, obviously searching for a constable.

Mr Punch took to his heels.

She smiled reassuringly at the child, whom she still clasped tight in her arms. "That's the way to deal with such blackguards," she said.

Salome chuckled and tightened her grip around the angel's neck in case she tried to put her down. "How old are you?" the angel asked her.

"It's my birthday today," she replied.

The angel closed her eyes and stopped breathing. "And you are seven today?" she asked, almost in a whisper.

Of course, an angel would know things like that. Salome nodded. To her surprise a large tear rolled down the angel's cheek.

"This is more than uncanny," Marion said aloud but to herself; she clutched the little girl even more tightly and began to sway, twisting now right, now left, with a soothing rhythm. For Rachel, too, would have been seven today if she had lived – little Rachel with her jet-black hair and her smoky grey-green eyes. Marion had been struggling *not* to remember it all day long. It was surely more than uncanny.

"Is that ship coming back?" Salome asked.

The angel nodded. "In three months, darling. First it's going to the Cape and then onward to India. And then it's going to turn around and come back."

Three months meant almost nothing to Salome; but the fact that the ship was coming back gave her all the reassurance she needed just then.

"Why d'you ask?" the angel prompted.

For as long as she lived, Salome was unable to say why she did not reply with the plain truth. In later years she came to accept that she must have had an intuition of some kind that Mrs Culham-Browne did not want to hear the plain truth. She accepted this explanation although she knew it was absurd – for little girls of exactly seven years old simply do not have intuitions of that kind.

2

Few indeed were the hours of sleep that Deborah McKenna snatched over the next three or four days. When the *Knysna* cast off, she was still fairly sanguine that little Salome was aboard, hiding somewhere, as her brother had explained. Her mood then was more of anger than alarm; and her anger only increased as a search of the more obvious places drew a blank. She might have exploded in full-blooded fury if Finbar's rage had not exceeded her own. He was utterly beside himself. The things he'd do to that wretched colleen the moment he got his hands round her neck! The leathering he'd give her would take the skin off her backside. She'd pass the voyage on one serving of bread and water a day. After they reached the Cape she'd never hide again, not if the entire Zulu nation was to come charging at her over the veldt.

Samson heard these threats and shuddered. Luckily both his parents seemed to have forgotten his role in Salome's disappearance. He was not old enough to realize the truth; for they could not imagine that he would *not* have told them she was down on the quayside if he had known it. Therefore he had not known it. Therefore he could not be blamed. He looked after his other young sister, Martha, while his parents carried on with their frantic search. And Martha, to show that a little girl of four did not really need looking after, officiously minded her younger brother, David, who was only one.

As so often happened, Finbar's excessive threats of punishment induced a countervailing caution in his wife.

Angry as she was, she realized that it was precisely the fear of such dire suffering that might be keeping young Salome in hiding. Even as her blood seethed, a calmer voice counselled that the pair of them were simply prolonging their own agony. The child would never reveal herself while their passion raged like this; she'd wait until it turned to alarm – when they'd be at their wits' end, and only half kill't with joy to be reunited with her – and then she'd come out all tears for an orgy of hugs and kisses.

When Debbie said as much to Mrs Rourke, who was helping with the search of that small part of the ship to which they had access – the part at the back where there was a steady falling of soot from the funnels – the woman was amazed. "Imagine!" she said. "The minxeen that could wrap ye round her little finger so!"

It made Debbie think. Was Salome really so good at it – getting her own way by playing on people's feelings? Compared with other children her age? Perhaps she was. Perhaps little Martha was, too – which would make it seem normal. Mrs Rourke would know more about it, her having eight of her own, five of them girls, poor soul!

"I suppose she can," she admitted ruefully. "Half the oul' fella's anger is that he knows she can do it, even to him. I've seen the tears of pity and disgust on his face even while he's plying the leather to her."

"Imagine!" Mrs Rourke repeated. Her own private view was that a child with such skills needn't be sought out of hiding quite so frantically as the McKennas were seeking their Salome; like fruit left to go oversweet, she could usefully stew in her own juice until she'd come out of her own accord. And even then she should only meet indifference, which would be far harder to charm away than this hot anger. However, she would also have conceded that the bearing of a dozen children, eight of whom had survived, would give a woman a different slant on things; so she held her peace and matched her outward concern to poor Mrs McKenna's.

Their search ended in a large locker, large enough to walk into, on the deck beneath the padded cell in the after-deck housing. The discovery of the padded cell had, in itself, been quite a shock – almost as if they had found a room with a gallows set up ready for an execution. It had never occurred to them that people could go mad in the middle of the ocean just as readily as on dry land. And what would you do with them if you had no padded cell? To Debbie it seemed an obscure kind of omen – a warning of the fate that might overtake her if she didn't calm down and take Salome's hiding (she still would not call it disappearance) more steadily.

The large locker beneath the padded cell was packed with lifejackets. Some were like men's coats, made of white canvas and with wads of cork sewn into the lining all round. Others were like small overstuffed pillows, stitched together by two broad shoulderstraps; their underarm strings were tied in neat, uniform bows. And there they all lay in great heaps, providing just the sort of concealment any child would adore.

Debbie, having convinced herself that Salome could not be hiding anywhere else in steerage, fell upon them with a cry of triumph. "Come on out, you little divil!" she cried, forcing herself to sound gay so as to lull the little girl's fears. "I know full well you're in here somewhere!"

Mrs Rourke said nothing until much later, when they had restacked the lifejackets as best they could. As they rose, dusting their hands and smoothing down their aprons, she said, "What would they be doing with all them things at all?"

Debbie stared at them morosely, no longer seeing a child's hiding place among them – just a heap of kapok, cork, and linen. Like the cell above, it was a reminder of things she would rather not face. A padded cell to prolong one's madness. Padded jackets to prolong one's drowning.

For
Jo and Des Kampff

who were there
in bad times and good

"It's since all that spleen they gave out after the *Titanic*, I suppose," she said. "The captain could stand up and say they carried three lifejackets for every man, woman, and child aboard."

"Begod, isn't that the truth!" Mrs Rourke chuckled at their cunning – also to mask her growing conviction that Salome was, in fact, nowhere aboard the *Knysna*. It was a fear she did not yet feel able to articulate to her poor friend.

Mrs McKenna closed the locker door before the piles could disintegrate and come spilling out again. "We must have missed her," she said despondently.

"It could be your man has her found," Mrs Rourke offered.

But Finbar himself came clattering down the companionway at that moment, with an arch on each eyebrow and nothing in his hands. "Well?" he asked. There was little hope in his voice. He, too, was gripped by the same fear as Mrs Rourke and, like her, he shrank from voicing it yet awhile. "What's behind that door?" He nodded toward the locker to distract himself.

"Nothing but a whole raft of lifejackets," Debbie told him.

He would not believe how thoroughly they had searched it, until he, too, had pulled out half the contents of the locker and, drawing the same blank, stuffed them all back in again.

Before he had quite finished, an officer, spying them from the top of the companionway, came down it three steps at a time, shouting, "You there! What the devil d'you think you're doing? Get away from that locker!"

The three of them vied to explain.

"One at a time!" he shouted over their clamour. "You! Fellow – what's your name?"

Finbar told him and went on to explain. As his words began to sink in, the officer's demeanour underwent a subtle change. Long experience of steerage emigrants who boarded at Queenstown had led him to suppose that these three were up to their usual devilry – looking for places to hide moonshine liquor . . . that sort of thing. On the last voyage one old woman had even managed to smuggle a goat aboard and had hidden it in that very locker. But this story of a missing child was different; it smacked of danger to the Algoa Line, the owners of the *Knysna*. True, these particular specimens looked too poor to make much trouble, but there again his experience led him to set little store by that. Irish families were large; their clans larger still. Somewhere in the family tree there'd be a lawyer-kinsman whose McKenna blood might be stirred enough by this same tale to take up the cudgels – or the shillelaghs – on their behalf.

"You should have said something before we lifted the gangways," he told them.

"Lord but I said nothing else!" Debbie protested. "And that sailor of yours – the useless one *he's* turned out! Isn't he after swearing blue in the face ye'd not sail a yard until my wee girl was found!"

The officer rubbed his chin. This was more ominous still.

"I heard him meself," Mrs Rourke put in, though she had, in fact, been claiming a bunk in the female dormitory at the time. "With these two ears."

"We asked could we search in the first class," Finbar added. "And he said 'twould be done for us and ye'd not sail without she was found and brought to us."

Debbie decided to chance it. "Will your honour unlock that door now, sir? And let us through?" she asked, nodding at where the corridor was barred beyond the foot of the companionway.

"Of course not!" he snapped. "That's out of the question." Then, remembering it might pay to be gentler, he added, "You wouldn't even know where to begin. Tell me, is your daughter a . . . what's her name, by the way?"

"Salome." Finbar glanced at his wife, deflecting the blame for this pretentious name upon her.

"It's biblical," she replied defensively, speaking equally to the man and Mrs Rourke.

"Sure 'tis a grand name altogether," the woman said. Then, to the officer: "Your honour was after asking about her – is she . . . what?"

"Oh yes. Would you say, Mrs McKenna, that Salome is a gregarious little girl? I mean outgoing? Friendly?"

"Oh God but she'd talk the jawbone out of an ass, sir," Debbie replied.

"She'd tell the world how to build a clock," Finbar confirmed.

The man smiled reassuringly. "There you are then! I'll wager she went through and hid somewhere in the first class, and someone's found her in there and has set a plate of sticky buns before her and she's having the time of her life. So I'll tell you what. Why don't you go and have another quick look through the steerage – just to be quite sure she's not slipped your notice – and I'll organize a proper search of the rest of the ship, eh?" His smile broadened. "We know *all* the places a body might hide herself, even a body as small as that."

Then, pausing only to get a description of Salome out of them, he left them to it and hastened forrard.

The first thing he did, however, was to get a wireless signal ashore, giving Salome's description and requesting the Queenstown harbourmaster to make a thorough search for her along the quayside and through its surroundings.

3

The wireless station was not actually in Queenstown harbour. It was housed for the moment next to the gun battery on Spike Island, about a mile offshore. When he received the message from the *Knysna*, Pat Clancy, the operator on duty that afternoon, realized he must telephone the harbourmaster at once. He rang the exchange and then picked up the earpiece. Sally McMahon, who was looking after the switchboard *and* the meat counter in the general store, was in the middle of serving Lady Redmond's housekeeper and, though Lady Redmond hadn't paid her bill for the past three months, Sally didn't dare just leave her standing there while she took care of whoever might be calling.

Pat Clancy replaced the earpiece and rang again but his hope dwindled. The line was probably wet again. Funny how they could lay a cable to America and keep it going all these years but the one to Spike Island would break down every month. At last he gave up. In half an hour his tour would end and he could cycle down to the harbour himself.

When the housekeeper left the general store Sally reminded her of the bill outstanding and that terms were strictly nett monthly. The woman pursed her lips and replied she had every good reason to know it – probably meaning that she herself hadn't been paid for even longer. Sally watched her all the way up the street, just to let her know that the sands of tolerance were running out on her ladyship. By the time she returned to the switchboard the little red marker behind the wireless station's porthole had stopped swinging.

Sally sat down and, noticing that Mrs Walshe was still talking to Mr Carmichael, she plugged herself in and listened eagerly. She did briefly wonder who might have been trying to get the exchange – but, if it was important, they'd surely try again in five minutes. They must know she couldn't be in two places at the one time.

So, what with one thing and another, it was several hours before Clancy finally reached the harbourmaster's office. First he met Francey Sullivan who wanted to know was he going to the dance at the cross on Saturday – a thorny question that required a pint or two of Murphy's to tease out the answer. Then Rose McMichael and Mary Kelly, two bold lasses from the shellfish packers, had shouted insults that his sense of honour had obliged him to answer with a pleasing half-hour of banter and a couple of shared cigarettes. And then . . . but why go on? Suffice it to say that several hours passed before the young blade found himself hammering uselessly at the locked door of the harbourmaster's office. He found a blunt pencil in his hatband and a crumpled envelope in his waistcoat pocket and left a rather befuddled message stuck in a crack of the wood.

Next morning the harbourmaster, Mr Wellbeloved, read: "Rashers Did ye find a little fair colleen answering Cycle Clips to the name of Salome being about Tin of Beans seven years old left behind Matches when the Knysna sailed Razor Blades yesterday they want to know Collect Boots from Repair?"

"Who left that?" his assistant asked when he saw it.

"Who d'you think?" the man replied contemptuously. "*Did* we find a little girl left behind after the *Knysna* sailed yesterday?"

"Not as far as I know, sir. Will I find out?"

Twenty minutes later he returned, saying, "One of the lads, Pius O'Connor, says he saw a grand lady hand in hand with a ragged wee girl, sir."

"And?"

"That's all. He just saw them in passing, you might say."

"Did he recognize the lady? Or the little girl?"

"Divil a one of them, sir."

The harbourmaster pulled a face. "Not much to go on, is it? If they did leave a little child behind, I don't think we can allay their fears with a vague tale like that. What d'you think?" He set little store by the answer to his question, whatever it might be, for he knew well the Irishman's eagerness to tell you black was white if that was what you wished to hear.

"Whatever you think yourself, sir," the man replied.

"Then I think we'll just say no." Wellbeloved turned the crank on the telephone and lifted the earpiece. Several cranks later he was speaking to Sally McMahon – or, rather, listening to her explanation as to why she hadn't answered earlier; he also learned that Mr Carmichael had sent Mrs Walshe a box of chocolate bonbons for which she was very grateful. She, Sally, wouldn't tell everyone that, of course, only she knew Mrs Walshe was a cousin to Mrs Wellbeloved.

A short while later he was connected to the wireless station. Toddy Hogan, the operator on duty, told him Clancy wouldn't come on until six that evening. He said not to worry – just send a cable to the *Knysna* to say no little girl had been left behind on the quayside when she sailed.

There followed a brief discussion as to who would pay for the transmission since the original request from the vessel itself was not logged in the 'Reply Paid' book.

So, by the time that was all sorted out and the reply safely transmitted to the *Knysna*, she was halfway across the Bay of Biscay – a hundred nautical miles beyond the point where, even if the reply had been positive, the captain might just possibly have considered turning back. And by then, of course, Debbie and Finbar McKenna were beside themselves with worry and grief.

4

Marion Culham-Browne – normally such a sensible woman, one who always knew what to do for the best in any crisis – was so excited by her discovery and rescue of little Salome that it took some time for her to return from the clouds and face the truth of the situation. The *Knysna* would surely still be within wireless range. The child's parents would just as surely be out of their minds with worry by now. She simply must get a reassuring message to them.

The thought opened the door to further blasts of cold realism. By then she and Salome were in a cab on their way back to Cork City, where they would take the train to Nenagh and the branch line to Simonstown. In this she was following her initial plan – which had sprung fully formed into her mind the moment she realized Salome had been accidentally left behind. Her intention was to take the child home to Cloonaghvogue and look after her until arrangements could be made for her to join her parents in India, or the Cape, or perhaps the Gold Coast, for the *Knysna* called at all those places. But now it began to dawn on her that such a simple, attractive scheme was really not possible. She ought at once to have taken the girl to the harbourmaster's office. True, the *Knysna* had been passing out of sight beyond Roche's Point when she had discovered the child – and the captain would almost certainly not have put about for one small steerage passenger. But they could have telegraphed a wireless cable and put the McKennas' minds at rest, at least to the worst of the possibilities that must by now be torturing them.

And then . . .

Her spirit sank yet further as all the sensible, *proper* actions suggested themselves.

She glanced across the cab at her little charge, who, now that she knew the ugly wee man was gone and the big ship would be coming back for her, was calm and self-contained once more. In fact, she was sitting there, swinging her legs and gazing out at the bustling city streets and all the grand buildings in a contented sort of wonder.

You can't! Marion told herself. *When the moment comes, you won't be able to do it.*

But she was a woman who knew her duty. She knew the right and proper thing and she framed herself to do it.

"Tell me, Salome," she asked, "are you a Roman Catholic?"

Salome knitted her brows. She had heard the words before but wasn't quite sure what they meant. She hadn't liked the smell in the cab when they first got in but the smell of the kind lady had soon filled it and now she was much happier. "I don't know, please ma'am," she replied.

"Can you say your Hail Mary?"

Salome smiled. An easy one to answer. "Hail Mary full of grace . . ."

"Very well!" Marion held up her hand to stem this distressing flow of words that were now more odious to her than ever.

Salome felt awful now. She did so wish to please the kind lady and she'd only been trying to show how well she could say her prayers; but all it seemed to do was distress her. "I do be forgetting it sometimes, ma'am," she admitted hopefully.

That was better. The lady laughed as if she'd said something funny and reached across to pat her hand. "You'll do, my dear," she said.

But behind her immediately good humour Marion felt bleak once more. Her duty now was plain. She must find a Roman Catholic priest and hand this little girl into the care of her own people. And yet . . . and yet . . . she shuddered to think of it. A grim picture of the presentation convent and orphanage in Simonstown came before her mind's eye.

Tomorrow! she promised herself. The poor child had suffered enough hard knocks for one day.

She rapped the handle of her parasol against the roof of the cab. "Take us directly to the Royal George," she commanded.

The servants at the Royal George Club were well trained in the art of appearing unsurprised. But the sudden reappearance of Mrs Culham-Browne, hand in hand with an angelic-looking little waif, put them to quite some test.

"Have they trouble on the line, ma'am?" asked Old Michael, the head porter and the man around whom all the workings of the establishment revolved. His inquisitive stare, directed entirely at Salome, put the question that was really on his mind.

"Not at all," she assured him. "This young lady and I will have the room Miss O'Brien and I shared last night." She went on to order tea and cake for herself and a glass of milk and a bun for the child.

Only slowly did it dawn on Salome that *she* was 'this young lady'. When her Mammy called her young lady it meant she'd been bold and deserved a smacking. Sadness filled her again when she thought of her mother – and the Da, of course, and the others. But it was too great to comprehend all at once. And the living moment was too full of incident and novelty to give her sorrow scope.

Flahertie, one of the club maids, came to unpack the valise she had packed only eight hours earlier. "That's a wee colleen we've not seen before, ma'am," she said gaily.

"Yes," Marion agreed. "Or I mean, no, you haven't. She's . . . I'm, er, taking care of her for a while."

"And would you just look at the roses on her cheeks! Has she a name at all?" She squatted and smiled close-up into Salome's face.

"I'm Salome McKenna." The little girl glanced awkwardly up at her benefactress. She was already old enough to understand the mistress-servant relationship, of course, but she was uncertain as to where she herself now stood in its complex spectrum.

"Imagine!" Flahertie pinched her cheek jovially and resumed her duties. She remembered that Mrs Culham-Browne had brought her own little girl here last winter, for her Christmas treat in Cork; she could hardly avoid noticing the resemblance – and was, indeed, about to remark upon it when she remembered the tragedy that had carried the little one off.

Marion, having sipped her tea and taken a well-bred bite of her cake, said, "Will you stay here and keep the child company, Flahertie? I have one or two telephone calls to place." It was not really a question so she did not pause for a reply. Instead she bent over Salome and asked her if she'd like to stay with the nice young woman. "Would you like to do me a drawing, perhaps?" She opened her travelling notecase and took out a sheet of paper and a stub of a pencil, just right for a tiny hand. "Draw the big ship you saw today and we can send it to your Mammy and Daddy. I'm sure they'd like that, eh?"

If there was ever a moment when Salome became utterly captivated by the strange, kindly, nice-smelling lady, that was it. If someone had asked her what the bestest thing she could be doing while she waited for the lady to place her telephone calls, she could have racked her brains for ever and still not have thought up anything half so wonderful. It stunned her into a smiling, grateful, eye-popping silence and she fingered the paper as if it were holy.

As she went downstairs to the telephone kiosk behind Old Michael's desk Marion wondered, fleetingly, why she was taking such elaborate care to appear so casual about Salome. When Flahertie had asked the child's name she had wanted to interpose herself between them, and give her name as Sally, and tell the maid to be about her business. What had prevented her was the almost instantaneous thought that, in any subsequent inquiry, the girl would be able to say, 'Herself behaved in a quare fashion altogether!'

In any subsequent *inquiry?* The words jolted her, particularly the last. Clearly, part of her mind was beavering away in secret, making plans the rest of her mind would not yet even contemplate.

First she rang her husband, Gordon, at their home, Cloonaghvogue Castle in County Keelity. Martle, the butler, took the call and informed her that 'Himself' had just returned from a poor day's fishing and was at present in his bath. She left a message that she was not feeling quite up to the train journey and so would be spending a further night in the club. Her second call, to the harbourmaster's office, went unanswered. The telephonist said she knew where she might get the quare fella himself (probably meaning she knew his favourite bar) but Marion thanked her and said she'd try again in the morning.

Well, hadn't she done her best, she reassured herself as she returned to her room.

Meanwhile, Carmel Flahertie had been gently but skillfully probing the little girl's origins and story; she had the bones of it well before Mrs Culham-Browne returned – mainly by dint of discussing the drawing Salome was making. And an amazing little drawing it was, too, for a child of seven. Not that the Algoa Line would have recognized the *Knysna* from it, but it was more than the perfunctory six lines and a squiggle of smoke that most of her contemporaries would have produced.

For Salome it was a labour of love, for hadn't the sweet lady said they'd be sending it to her Mammy and the Da. The pink tip of her tongue almost licked her lips raw as it followed the gyrations of the pencil, making its deliberate marks on the paper. That was a gangway. That was a mast; she felt sure there had been two but she couldn't remember where the other one was. That was a sailor's hat. That was the sun. The crowds were difficult, though, so she just did a lot of dots and some scribble. And then, with her tongue shivering in concentration, she drew two tiny circles on the deck near the back, added dots for eyes and slits for lips, and wrote 'Mamy' and 'Da' above them. Then she frowned, remembering that's where the other mast was, but too late now. Actually, the writing would excuse her why she left the mast off!

Happy again she grinned up at Miss Flahertie to see did she understand.

"Aren't you only brilliant!" the maid said.

Salome considered her drawing a moment and answered, "Yes."

"You're the little artist of the world, so you are. But you've left off one thing, you know."

"I know. The other mast. But . . ."

"No! Divil take the other mast. Something much more important – the most important thing of all."

"What?" She stared at her creation in panic.

"Yourself, of course! You're too modest for your own good."

"I was in a wooden box," Salome explained, relieved it was nothing worse.

"A coffin?" the maid asked nervously.

"No! Square. Like a little tiggeen with no windows. Will I put it in?"

"You've space enough in that corner."

While the child distracted herself with the effort of drawing squares, Flahertie said idly, almost as if musing aloud: "I wonder why a brave wee colleen like you would go hiding herself away in the dark like that?" From the light in Mrs Culham-Browne's eyes she suspected the woman had something to do with Salome's failure to join her own family on the boat. Women of that class didn't just go around picking up waifs and strays off the streets and quays – or, by God, they'd find work to fill all twenty-four hours of the day!

The pencil had stopped moving; Salome's eyes were shut.

"But you had good reason, I'm sure."

"He was a nasty wee man," Salome said at last.

Now it was Carmel Flahertie's turn to close her eyes. This revelation was the very last thing that would have crossed her mind, and, of course, her mind made the worst it could of those six words. For the love of God – a child of seven! Talk about something else. "And weren't you great to outwit the blackguard!" she exclaimed admiringly. "Tell me now, I want to hear – when's your birthday, I wonder?"

Salome grinned proudly. "It's today!"

"Ah, g'wan!" The maid frowned warily. "Are you coddin' me? What month is this? You'd surely know that if this *is* . . ."

"July," the girl replied. "The third of July. The three of the seven. I'm seven today but *thirty*-seven *every* year!" Samson had told her that when they woke up this morning.

Carmel laughed. "Haven't you the oddest notions! Well, I suppose it is your birthday after all – and I suppose you never thought it'd turn out so full of excitements and marvels!"

Salome smiled and shook her head. She wanted to go on drawing, but something new; the ship was finished and she didn't want to spoil it. She turned a pair of hopeful eyes toward the writing case, which the lady had left open on the bed.

Carmel saw it and guessed at once what the child wanted. It gave her an idea but first some imp of mischief made her say, "And wasn't it the greatest wonder of all that 'twas Mrs Culham-Browne herself that found you – and not any old lady who'd have handed you straight into the hands of the nuns."

Salome stared at her, jaw gaping.

"D'you not know what happened her? Did she not tell you?"

Salome shook her head.

"Lord, 'twas the saddest thing. She had a little girl of her own, just the age of yourself, with straight black hair, the same as yours, and the pale green eyes, the way yours are, too. And didn't she bring her here to Cork for the pantomime last Christmas, and didn't they share that very bed! And" – she closed her eyes and swallowed hard – "didn't the poor wee colleen up and die on her in the spring!"

Salome suddenly realized she'd been holding her breath all this while; now she breathed in hard and let it out in a barely controlled shiver.

Carmel, afraid at the degree to which her tongue had run away with her, now tried to wrap it all up quickly and be done. "Don't tell her I said so or she'll half-kill me. Promise?"

Salome blinked and nodded.

"Only I thought you ought to know. You've lost your Mammy for a month or two, and Mrs Culham-Browne has lost her daughter for ever. So you're each in a good way to help the other, d'you follow? You're sure you won't let on I told you?"

The little girl shook her head vehemently.

"Good lass! And now – seeing as it really is your birthday – I'd best be away and bring you a present. Would you like that? I have just the thing for you."

Salome's eyes gleamed; happiness kept her tongue-tied. This was surely a day she'd never forget.

Outside, Carmel saw Mrs Culham-Browne's head, then her top half, then the all of her, coming up the stairs. She was deep in thought and seemed reluctant to approach her bedroom. She had almost arrived there before she realized the maid was standing by the door in the half-light. She frowned. "I thought I told you to stay with the child!" she snapped.

"Sure I'm only after popping my head out, ma'am," the maid replied soothingly. "She's as content as the larks on Mount Leinster with her drawing of the ship. 'Tis her birthday, did you know?"

Marion softened. "I did, as a matter of fact. Her seventh. This very day – the same day as . . ." She hesitated, staring away over the maid's shoulder. Then she returned to her with a smile, as if she imagined she had completed the sentence. "Why d'you mention it?"

"Because I have the very present for her, ma'am."

"Oh?" Marion's smile became a little wary.

" 'Tis an empty sketching book a lady left behind a few weeks ago."

"And the club hasn't returned it to her?"

The maid licked her lips and gave a conspiratorial glance all around as, lowering her voice, she murmured, " 'T'was Lady Orden herself, ma'am."

"Ah!" Marion asked no more. Lady Orden – Miriam Southey, as was – had done a bolt last month with a penniless subaltern in the Inniskillens. People understood it, of course – she was only twenty-three and Orden was in his sixties. In fact, Marion understood it better than most, for she was a mere thirty-two to Gordon's fifty-one. Miriam and her paramour were said to be living on bread and cheese and kisses in Paris, where they were trying to make a living as painters. No one spoke about her now. What was there to say?

"An empty sketchbook, eh? How big?"

"Ah!" The maid licked her lips uneasily. "When I say empty . . ." She hesitated and then, changing tack, went on, "Wait till I show you, ma'am, by your leave." And she hastened away to fetch the thing.

Marion breathed in deeply – not quite knowing why – and went into the bedroom.

"See, ma'am!" Salome held up her drawing.

Marion, who had prepared a face of conventional admiration and a cry of conventional encouragement, stared at the drawing in an amazement that was wholly genuine. "But . . . Salome! That's beautiful, darling," she exclaimed at last. "So intricate! How d'you remember all those things? Even the ventilator there, look! And Mammy and Daddy – oh!"

"It's for you," Salome decided suddenly, holding it forward.

"Oh no. It's to send to your parents. I told you."

"I can do another. I done this for you."

"Not done – did. I *did* this for you. Are you sure?"

The girl shrugged; one lie was enough. "Miss Flahertie's after going to get me a present. For my birthday."

Marion frowned in jocular accusation. "So she said! I *wonder* how she knew?"

"I'm after telling her," Salome admitted.

Marion laughed and tousled her hair. "Yes, well, that possibility had already occurred to me!"

The maid returned at that moment, carrying a slim volume, measuring about six inches by nine. It was bound in imitation leather and had the word SKETCHBOOK printed in blotchy gold ink on its cover. She handed it to Marion, hoping it would pass muster.

"I knew the lady slightly," Marion told her. "I find no difficulty in believing this was hers."

However, the paper was of good quality – and so were the few sketches her ladyship had had time to make. But Marion saw why the young maidservant had hesitated, for they were all nudes, male and female, drawn from the life. At least, they were not after any statue or painting that Marion recognized; and she was an avid subscriber to the *Art Journal* and *The Studio*.

"Will I rip them out or what, ma'am?" the other asked anxiously.

Marion turned them to face her. "Why? Do you see anything there that is *not* part of God's own creation?"

The maid wet her lips and shook her head.

"Or anything *other* than as He made it?"

A further shake of the head.

"Well then, let's not throw it back in God's face, eh?" She snapped the book shut and passed it over with an encouraging smile.

Salome watched the exchange intently, understanding little of what was said yet taking it all in regardless. She wiped her hands vigorously on her pinny before she dared accept it. She opened the book at a blank page and marvelled at its whiteness, touching it with reverent fingertips.

"What d'you say, Salome?" Marion prompted.

"Thank you," the girl whispered.

"That book belonged to a lady who is now an artist. If you use it well and study hard, you may be an artist one day yourself," Marion added.

Salome turned the page and saw a drawing of a shameless she-divil. She shut the book with a snap and glanced fearfully up at the kind lady – only to find her shaking her head and staring down with eyes full of disappointed pity. Salome understood she had done the wrong thing, but it was too late now.

That night she fell asleep the moment her head touched the pillow. The lady was trying to tell her a story but she was just too tired to keep her eyes open a minute longer.

Later, when it was quite dark and the roar of the city had fallen to a hush, she woke again, aware now that the lady was lying in bed beside her. A moment later she froze and tried her best not to breathe even, for the lady was *crying!* She couldn't bear it when grown-ups cried. She'd seen her mother crying once and it upset her so much she hadn't been able to speak for a day.

Then she remembered what the maid had told her – and suddenly she understood. And then she didn't mind the crying so much because at least there was a reason for it.

And then she saw a way she might help. And repay the lady for all her kindness.

So she turned and slipped her little arms around the lady's neck and whispered, "Don't cry now. I'm here! I'm here!" – the way her own mother comforted her at moments like that.

And then the lady was laughing and crying all in one breath: "You *are*, my dear. God bless you, so you are!"

"And you won't hand me into the care of the nuns?"

There was a long, almost explosive silence before the

reply came; it was almost a whisper. "If you don't wish it, darling, then I won't."

And then Salome cried a little bit, too, before she fell asleep all over again.

5

Well-meaning people told Debbie that no harm could have come to Salome – not with such a throng of people on the quayside. If the child had been injured or anything like that, the authorities would surely have sent a wireless message to the ship. Anyway, there'd be a cable soon explaining everything. Salome wouldn't be the first child to get separated from its parents and be left behind when an emigrant ship sailed. Everyone, it seemed, knew someone who knew someone whose family could recall such a thing. There was always a happy ending in which the child came out on a later boat. Hadn't the captain of the *Knysna* himself promised that the company would find the wee colleen no matter where she might be, and he'd bring her out in style on the very next voyage – and that would be in only six months. Lucky little Salome! She'd remember it as the year she sailed from deep midwinter into full midsummer – unlike the rest of them, who were even now sailing from summer into winter. And anyway, hadn't Debbie got the other three childer and a husband in full vigour to count among her blessings?

It was all true, of course, but it only heaped her spirit the more; for it seemed almost a sacrilege to feel so cheerless when she had so many comforters and so many blessings for which to be grateful. And yet to count those blessings when her darling little girl might be lying at death's door in the poor-law hospital, or crying herself to sleep each night in some cheerless home for waifs and strays, seemed like blasphemy against a power that was even stronger and more ancient than religion itself. In such circumstances grief became a necessary anaesthetic against the determined jollity of the steerage.

The loss affected Finbar, too, but in a different way. People thought he was a hard man. Debbie herself had thought so, too, when she met and married him. Indeed, that had been part of his attraction, for she knew herself to be too soft for her own good. Over the years, though, she had come to suspect that he was one of the softest and most sentimental of men. More – she suspected that he knew it, too. Or something inside him knew it, and feared it, and drove him to be the 'hard man' he showed to all the world. It was as if no measure existed between an inch and a mile; if he yielded the one he'd slip the other. He'd rather go about saying that children were 'aisy got' than show the slightest chink of grief in his armour.

These mysteries were some comfort to her during many a long, lonely vigil at the ship's rail. It consoled her to think that she was, in a curious way, even stronger than Finbar because she could admit to her sorrow without fearing that it would destroy her selfhood. She loved best of all to stand alone at the very stern of the *Knysna* and let the boiling fury of the wake mesmerize her.

Once, before her marriage, she had worked at the steam laundry in Limerick, where the clothes were turned in the vat by a big paddle driven off a pulley; the power of it had frightened her but now she realized it had been a mere child's toy compared with the mighty propeller spinning away beneath the *Knysna*'s stern. This monster transformed the ocean into an element she could hardly recognize. She had seen rushing waters before, of course, for all her life she had lived on or near the Shannon; but when an entire river is running in spate, no particular part of it can be singled out as remarkable. But the *Knysna* pushed out massive surges of water, each the size of a large room and jetting backwards as fast as the eye could follow. And then, only a dozen or so yards behind the vessel, they'd meet the more placid waters of the Atlantic, against which each thrust would pile up in a boiling white eruption of salty foam that turned the sea beneath it black by contrast. A yard or so later it would half-settle to a seething fury, creating a patch of water where you'd think a thousand invisible fish were thrashing and writhing just beneath the surface. Beyond that again it calmed down to a mottled hithering and thithering of lacy bubbles on a surface that was, all of a sudden, amazingly calm. Last of all, less than a hundred yards from the frenzy and the turmoil of its birth, was a broad swathe of idle water stretching beyond the limit of easy discernment. You could live all your life beside the Shannon and still not see water in so many different moods.

Many a time she would stare down into the chaos and imagine what it would be like to drop herself in among it. You'd be sucked down into the depths, of course, and probably never bob up to breathe the air again. One of the sailors told her that the violence you could see on the surface was as nothing compared to what was going on underneath, where the waters were closing back in again around the keel of the ship that had parted them up at the bows. The swirling and the skirling going on down there would leave the biggest whale in the ocean giddy. She could just picture herself in that maelstrom, arms stretched high, skirts ballooning out, spinning and turning cartwheels at the mercy of those mighty currents.

The temptation to experience it – to leap over the rail and end her suffering – was strongest in those moments when she felt the most powerful apprehension that Salome was already dead. Sometimes the random ordering of the foam would assume the girl's features, smiling up at her, calling her home; at other times the mewing of a gull had the timbre of Salome's shrill cry, saying, "Yes! Yes! Now!" It began to frighten her to realize how close she came to acting on these delusions.

Then, on the third day out, when the pain of her loss was turning into a dull ache, deep in her spirit, an albatross decided to join the ship's complement. He (everyone agreed it was a he, though on the flimsiest ornithological knowledge) found an aerial niche where he could stretch his wings and simply glide on the slipstream; this point in space lay about a dozen yards astern and level with the promenade deck, which was for first-class passengers only. For hour after hour he simply hung on the air, giving no more than the occasional twitch of one or other wing to bring himself back to that magical point where travel was free. The only time he moved from his station was when the galley staff threw their 'gash' overboard – rich pickings from half-eaten first-class meals. For his benefit they would jettison it as far to the side as possible, to keep it clear of the wake. The moment he saw its splash he would peel away to that side and swoop down to pluck up some choice morsel before it could sink, barely dipping his webbed toes into the foam. Then, with slow, graceful sweeps of his wings he would rise and come wheeling back among the eddies of air, his movements growing ever more effortless until he was back on station, simply hanging on air again.

His attachment to the *Knysna* roused great excitement among the passengers, for the seamen claimed it brought good luck; he was an omen of a calm and uneventful voyage. On the fourth day almost every first-class passenger hastened to the back of the promenade deck before breakfast to see if he had survived the night. Amazingly, he had. And, indeed, it *was* amazing to think that throughout the long, lonely watches of darkness, that massive body, like a preposterously overgrown seagull, had simply glided along, gently falling down an invisible gradient in the sky – a gradient which the vessel's movement constantly renewed and raised in precisely compensating measure. On the deck below the steerage passengers were doing the same.

And that was how Georgina Delaroux, who might otherwise never have met Debbie McKenna (though they slept, as it happened, a mere twenty vertical feet apart), came to notice her. "D'you see that woman down there?" she asked her husband, Paul, before breakfast on the fifth morning. They were standing at the stern rail, which, for the moment, they had to themselves.

"She'll hear you," he warned.

"I don't think so. I called down to her yesterday evening but she didn't respond."

"Anyway, what about her? All I can see is the top of her bonnet." It wasn't entirely true, for he could see the top of her bosoms, too, which was a jolly sight more interesting; he took advantage of Georgina's question to extend a survey that would otherwise have been guiltily brief.

"I think that's the poor woman whose little girl got left behind at Queenstown."

He chuckled. "How can you possibly know a thing like that?" He squinted down again at the unsuspecting Debbie, as if seeking evidence to confirm or refute her assertion.

"I just know. She spends hours each day simply staring at the sea. I can just imagine how she feels, poor woman. Are we allowed down into the steerage, I wonder?"

He withdrew from the rail and became serious at once. "I wouldn't get mixed up in matters like that," he said.

"*Like* that? I mean – there can't be too many things in this life that are *like* that."

"What good could you do?" Her persistence was beginning to worry him. When he had said "*I* wouldn't get mixed up . . ." he meant it more or less as a command. A wise husband didn't openly command his wife these days, but a wise wife knew when the prohibitions were being handed out nonetheless.

"I could talk to her. Nobody else does, or not for long.

Her husband comes – and goes away. Her children come – and go away . . ."

"Perhaps she prefers it so." He took her firmly by the hand. "Come on – I'm starving. Race you to the dining room!"

After breakfast and the usual ablutions he was so convinced she had taken the hint that he did not even bother to check on the reading room, where he was sure she had her head buried in a trashy tale by Hardy or Galsworthy or some other ghastly modern.

In fact, Georgina was at that moment retying the rope that bore the sign saying, on her side, STEERAGE, and, on Debbie's, FIRST-CLASS PASSENGERS ONLY PAST THIS POINT. Cautiously she approached the stern rail.

The woman was still there; had she taken breakfast, even? Had anyone brought her a bite to eat?

"Mrs McKenna?" she asked hesitantly. She had learned the name from one of the stewards after Paul had left the table.

The woman turned round, slightly startled, saw a lady, and bobbed an awkward curtsey. "Ma'am," she replied.

Georgina very firmly held out her hand. "I'm Mrs Delaroux. I happened to be standing up there, and I saw you down here – and I felt sure somehow that it *was* you – and . . . well, I just wanted to say how very sorry I am over what happened." She smiled encouragingly but not too jovially.

Somewhat bewildered, Debbie took the proffered hand and shook it awkwardly, mumbling that it was very kind . . . everyone had been very kind.

"If only there were something one could *do*," Georgina went on. "I mean . . . when one knows such a dreadful thing has happened . . . the moment I heard about it, I found myself thinking back to the moment of our departure from Queenstown, cudgelling my brains to think did I *see* anything? Anything at all?"

Debbie raised her eyebrows hopefully, feeling certain the woman must have something to impart; else why bother to come down here? This was no idle outpouring of well-meant sympathy.

Georgina saw it and realized what vain hopes she was rousing in the other's heart. She shook her head at once. "I didn't, I'm sorry to say. But the point I'm making is that one feels one jolly well *ought* to have noticed something. One had no right to be so heedlessly gay at such a time – cutting the ties with the old country . . . setting off for a new life in a new land – all that sort of thing. One had no right to such gaiety when a tragedy like yours was i. the middle of . . . unfolding. You know what I mean." She smiled apologetically.

But Debbie was not so quick to let her hopes be dashed. "And you're quite sure you saw nothing, ma'am?" she pressed. "Not the smallest little thing?"

"Well . . ." Georgina larded her voice with all the doubt she could muster, to let the woman know she was not to get her hopes up again. "I saw no sign of your daughter but I believe I did see your little boy. I gather he had been down on the quayside with her?"

She saw it was news to the woman. "Where did you see the gossoon, ma'am, if I may be so bold? On the quay or on the ship?"

"On the ship." Georgina was pleased to be able to add something new about the affair and she went on to explain how Samson had dashed up the first-class gangway and almost bowled her and her husband over. "He came down those stairs there," she concluded, pointing toward the companionway she herself had just used.

These new bits of the puzzle fell into place for Debbie while the young lady was speaking. "The bold little divil!" she said. "And him letting us think the pair of them were in hiding here on the ship! Didn't we hunt her high and low until the land fell out of sight!"

"You mean until now you haven't been certain whether she was aboard or ashore when we sailed?"

Debbie shook her head. "Not certain for sure, ma'am. Those last two days I came to pray she *was* ashore, for if she was aboard, she could hardly be still . . . among the . . ."

She could not complete the thought aloud but Georgina touched her gently on the arm to show there was no need. "So, in a way – a rather bleak way – my news is some sort of comfort to you? I mean, it does make it far more likely your little girl – Salome, is it? It makes it far more likely she was ashore."

Debbie turned and stared again at the ever-lengthening wake, a smooth highway across the choppy seas.

Georgina followed her gaze. "If only it were as solid as it is smooth!" she sighed. "One would gladly walk every inch of the way back to Queenstown. And beyond – to hell and Connaught, as they say. It's being imprisoned here in the middle of the ocean that's so unbearable."

The words struck a chord in Debbie, who turned and stared at her in amazement. This unknown lady understood! Of all the comforting words that had been spoken to her since their departure – from Finbar, the captain, Father Claffey, Mrs Rourke . . . and dozens of others – none had shown the first glimmer of understanding as to how she truly felt. Until now. "You have the truth of it, ma'am," she said. "The God's truth. I'd crawl on hands and knees, so I would, if someone but told me Salome was there."

Their eyes dwelled in each other's until the shared emotion became too raw to bear. And yet they could not part now. Each was moved to turn again to the rail and stare out at that hypnotic fury of white foam and black salt water.

"Has no message of any kind been received from Spike Island?" Georgina asked gently.

"Spike Island, ma'am?" Debbie responded.

"The island just offshore from Queenstown – with the

gun battery, remember? And the iron masts. Those were masts for the wireless-telegraphy station – which is where any message would come from."

Debbie nodded but did not answer the initial question.

"We must be well beyond their range by now. I expect there'll be a message when we call at Freetown."

Debbie nodded. "The captain's after telling me that, too, ma'am. But I think it's best to hope for nothing."

"Without actually falling into despair."

"You have the way of it, ma'am."

The silence between them was easy then. After a while Georgina said, "There is just a chance *I* might be able to help, too."

The hope that suddenly glowed in the woman's face wrenched Georgina's heart. "It's little enough, mind," she warned, "but you never know. I have a cousin in the constabulary at Castlemartyr, which, as you may know, is but a hop-skip-and-jump from Queenstown. I'll send him a cable from Freetown and follow it up with a letter. Assuming, mind you, that there's no news already waiting for you when we get there. Whatever may have happened to Salome, he'll get to the bottom of it – rest assured!"

"You're very good, ma'am." Debbie risked touching the lady's forearm briefly as a sign of her gratitude.

"It's little enough," Georgina responded. "And meanwhile . . . if it would help to talk about it with someone . . . well . . . I'm around." She laughed. "I mean, I can't get away!"

Debbie sniffed rather saltily. "If you do write your cousin in the peelers, ma'am . . ." she ventured.

"Yes?"

"Well, I'm thinking – there'd be no reply until after we reached the Cape."

"Not for many months after, I'm afraid. But remember, we're keeping him up our sleeve as our very last resort – just in case . . ."

"No, it isn't that, ma'am," Debbie interrupted boldly. "It's just . . . well, we – McKenna and I – we'd have to be near you out there."

A thoughtful look stole over Georgina's features. "Indeed," she said slowly. "You're quite right."

6

When the train came to a rest against the buffers at Simonstown station, the silence and stillness filled Salome with a sense of peace. She closed her eyes and leaned back into the soft upholstery of the first-class carriage, and she thought it would really be rather nice if this could go on for ever. Marion was on the point of reaching out and tapping the child on the knee, saying, "Come on, darling – time to be going!" when the tranquillity of the moment touched her heart and stayed her hand. There was something so vulnerable, so utterly trusting in the way Salome half-lay there with her eyes closed and a seraphic little smile on her lips. It forced Marion into making a silent promise to the girl, to do everything . . . to *be* everything . . . the actual words were reluctant to form but the intention was unwavering.

She stumbled over the words because the thought that lay behind them – the monstrous, unthinkable thought – had still not taken shape in her mind. She could feel it there, dark and formless, just waiting for moments like this to creep a little closer, nearer the light of reason, which it threatened to extinguish. Every now and then her mind would turn toward it, see it, or, rather, glimpse its outlines, and hastily shy away again. Sometimes she'd catch herself thinking of Salome's mother and father and saying, "After all, they abandoned her at Queenstown . . . or as-good-as . . ." Then she'd be afraid to pursue the argument further. Reason told her what a childish point it was – and morality joined in, too, of course. But the dark, shadowy thoughts would not go away. They lingered on, biding their time, as if they knew that, sooner or later, reason would shrivel and morality yield.

"Home?" she said at last, making it both exclamation and query in one.

Salome opened her eyes and stared out of the carriage window. The scene was new to her, naturally, yet it revealed much that was familiar, too. The row of lime trees that flanked the station approach was like the elms near the courthouse in Ennis, her home town in County Clare. (Ennis was only twenty miles west of Simonstown as the crow flies but, thanks to two large lakes and several even larger landowners, it was more than sixty miles distant by what for want of a better word could be called 'road.') The dour gray pebbledash and moss-stained stucco on most of the visible walls was familiar, too. And even the porter, who was presently unloading the evening papers from the luggage van, looked vaguely like Mr Cassidy at Ennis station. Salome smiled and echoed her benefactress: "Home!"

Marion said, "I hope you'll think of it like that, dear."

There was a clattering and banging from the station approach. A large upright motor car, built more on the lines of a boat than a carriage, lurched along beneath the limes and ground to a sudden halt halfway up. Its cloud of attendant dust engulfed it briefly before the light breeze carried it onward to annoy the departing passengers and ruin the salads set out in the open-windowed still room at the temperance hôtel.

"That's our carriage from Cloonaghvogue, believe it or not," said a rather tight-lipped Marion. "Now comes the really *adventurous* part of our journey!"

She did not appear in the least surprised when Gorman, the chauffeur, jumped down from the driving seat and immediately lay flat on the ground behind the car so as to roll himself beneath it.

Salome scanned the sky, thinking it might be raining; but there was scarce a cloud to be seen. She glanced up at Mrs Culham-Browne.

"I expect he's *mending* something," she explained, laying sarcastic stress on the word.

The porter who looked like Mr Cassidy trundled past with his trolley. "I have your luggage here, Mrs Culham-Browne, ma'am," he called through the little window, which they had opened for ventilation. "Will I bring it down to your carriage beyond?"

"If you'd be so good, Flynn," she told him.

Salome thought it a very gracious answer, so much softer than a plain *yes* or anything else that might have occurred to her. She stored the phrase away for future use – "If you'd be so good . . ." Storing away Mrs Culham-Browne's sayings was something she'd found herself doing quite often over the past twenty-four hours, ever since her path had become entwined with that of this kind and beautiful lady.

As they walked up the platform behind Flynn and his rumbling trolley, Salome became aware that she was attracting rather more attention than she was used to. Indeed, she was used to attracting almost no attention at all. Marion, by contrast, as the wife of one of the largest landlords in south County Keelity, felt nothing out of the way until Salome slipped a hand into hers and clutched tightly. Then she saw one or two bystanders nod in a knowing fashion among themselves and she realized that word of her adventures in Cork had already reached the town. She herself was Irish, of course, and had lived here all her thirty-two years, and yet she was still capable of wonder at the sheer speed with which tales about people and their latest doings could spread among the populace.

The only person she had spoken to about Salome was Martle, the butler at Cloonaghvogue. And all she told him was that she'd come across a little girl who'd got left behind when the *Knysna* sailed and that she'd be looking after her until the next sailing. And Cloonaghvogue was all of ten miles south of Simonstown. Lord alone knew what bush telegraph had carried the tale back here with such dispatch – nor what form it had assumed during its journey. Half of these people so busy nudging one another and pretending not to stare were probably convinced that she'd dashed up the gangway at the very last moment and snatched the wee colleen out of the arms of her doting mother. "Poor soul!" they'd be telling one another. "Wasn't she driven mad with her own bereavement?"

Marion knew that the loss of her daughter, Rachel, was in some way connected with her eagerness to take Salome under her wing. To deny it would be to give the idea a greater power than it deserved; better to admit it freely and then pooh-pooh it as being of little weight. It was of no real importance, anyway.

The ticket collector tipped his hat and let them through. His attitude suggested that asking to see her ticket would be like accusing her of not having one. It was a kind of inverted patronage that annoyed Marion, who thrust the two bits of card belligerently at him; he pocketed them with a smile, but never a glance at what might (or might not) be printed upon them.

"One day," she said as she led Salome away down the approach, "I'll hand him two slips cut from a shoebox. That'll teach him."

Salome couldn't quite see what lesson the man was to learn, though she could see it would be cheaper from Mrs Culham-Browne's point of view. Then she recalled that her little doll, Maggoty Meg, was in a shoe box on the big ship. She wondered if her Mammy would remember and take her out and play with her, otherwise she'd get awful lonely. The thought of Maggoty Meg being so lonely brought on another brief battle with her tears, which, however, she was proud to win quite swiftly. She was getting quite good at it now.

The porter dragged his trolley to the back of the waiting car, where a pair of boots was being waggled in response to some heroic exertion beneath it. "Is it yourself, Gorman?" he shouted at the boots.

"Well it's not the man who invented rust," came the reply from among the springs and axles. "Just wait till I catch *him!* I'll bury him in the stuff, so I will – and I'll know where to go looking for it!"

The exertions finished and he levered himself out like a crab trying to walk forward. " 'Tis the exhort, ma'am," he explained as he rose to his feet and dusted himself down. In one hand he clutched a ball of horticultural twine.

"Exhaust," she corrected him. "What about it?"

"Doesn't it lose its footing every two miles and fall to the ground."

"And you keep tying it up with string!"

"Sure what else." He flourished it proudly.

Briefly she levelled her eyes in his. He was probably waiting for her to ask why he didn't use wire. He would certainly have a ready answer, even if the thought of wire had never occurred to him. "How long has it been 'losing its footing'?" she asked instead.

"Those three days, ma'am."

She realized it was by no means certain that the disadvantages of using twine for tying up a hot exhaust tube would have occurred to him yet. She gave up. "Very well. The sooner we start, the sooner we'll finish." She mounted the running board and stepped directly into the rear seat, for there was no door.

"And is this the wee colleen?" Gorman asked, picking Salome up and swinging her into the back in one easy sweep. The words 'about whom we've heard so much' were strongly implied. Aloud he added, "There's scarce a pick on those bones."

"We'll soon put that right," Marion assured him, instantly regretting that she had let herself be wheedled into any sort of an answer.

The man put his face close to Salome's and grinned. "Aren't you the darlin' of the world!" he said.

"Yes!" the girl modestly agreed.

Looking into those mysterious, grey-green eyes, Gorman wondered how long the quare fella, Mr Culham-Browne, would be able to hold out; he'd made it plain enough to everyone at the Castle how annoyed he was at his wife's impetuous gesture – but that was before he got his own sights upon her.

All the way out of town he kept up a steady flow of news, as if his mistress had been away a month or more. Some of it was decades old, though still news to Marion. Gorman knew everyone in Ireland, or so Miss Kinchy, the housekeeper, liked to claim on his behalf; sometimes it seemed no exaggeration at all. He certainly knew the names of the occupiers of each house they passed, or of each house he chose to make comment upon. This one was away 'up the Cut' – that is, in gaol – for being too hearty in charge of a horse; that one had a run with the bailiff only yesterday; another had successfully carried four gallons of poteen past the sergeant under a rack of turf last spring.

As one story succeeded another Marion realized she was being tested in a subtle way. Nothing would ever have stopped Gorman from talking; he'd talk the cross off an ass's back, as the saying goes. But he wouldn't have been telling quite *these* tales if Rachel were still alive and was now sitting at her mother's side. They were not absolutely suitable for a young girl's ears – yet nor could you say they were entirely unsuitable, either. They straddled that vaguely in-between territory with masterly balance. Gorman was gauging the strength of her protective – in other words, motherly – impulse. She steeled herself not to protest, not to give him the satisfaction of finding out.

And then her mind veered off on a different tack. Why should a child Salome's age (all right, Rachel's age, as it would have been) *not* hear such tales of human weakness and misdeeds? Hadn't she, Marion, bitter enough cause herself to regret the ignorance in which her parents had reared her? Was it likely she'd have married a man almost twice her age if she'd known a little more about the world and its ways? How often she'd looked at Rachel and made a silent promise to tell her everything, absolutely everything she knew, 'when you're a little older'. It occurred to her that this was that rare event in life's merciless round: a second chance to get it right.

She put the thought from her at once, comforting though it was, for it suggested a more permanent liaison between her and Salome than her conscience would yet allow her to savour. To distract herself she gazed fondly down at the little girl and wondered what sense she was making of it all. What a bewilderment of novelty and strangeness she must have endured those past few days, ever since saying farewell to her home in Clare 'for the last time', as she must have thought. Did there come a moment when novelty itself turned into a new kind of normality and ceased to be a wonder? She certainly seemed to be taking it all very calmly now. Not once since the train had left Cork, four hours ago, had she asked if her mother had got the wireless message yet, though she had asked it half a dozen times that morning. At first Marion had tried to explain how much easier it would be to set out the whole situation in a letter to the Algoa Shipping Line and that the wireless was a hazardous means of communication at the best of times – or even at the worst of times, as the passengers on the *Titanic* had learned at such cost. But the explanation seemed beyond the child so Marion replied only vaguely, saying things like, "We must wait and see what comes back."

Suddenly these pleasant speculations were shattered.

They were about three miles out into the country by now and there came a loud clang followed by the most awful sustained clattering noise. Gorman braked sharply, almost hurling Salome off her seat; then, muttering near-substitutes for curses, he sprang from the car, clutching his ball of twine, and strode to the rear of the vehicle. There, again, he lay flat on his back and rolled himself beneath it with many a long-suffering groan.

Salome said it was a good thing his clothes were the colour of the dust or his mammy would give him socks. Marion laughed and the chauffeur called up from below to know what crack he was missing. Marion put a finger to her lips and explained in a whisper to Salome: "He knows how provoking he's being and he's only desperate to make me talk about it – this nonsense with the ball of string." She jabbed a finger at the floor. "But we shan't give him that satisfaction, shall we!"

The girl grinned and shook her head. She had no idea what Mrs Culham-Browne meant but she was beginning to realize that life was an unending battle of wits between *us* and *them* – and that by some miraculous translation she was now included among the *us* portion of mankind.

After a further three miles they caught their first glimpse of Cloonaghvogue Castle, whose tower dominated the countryside. Marion pointed it out to Salome, saying, "There's your home for the next few months, my dear. I expect Mister Culham-Browne is up among the battlements now, spying out for us with his telescope."

At that moment the twine burned through and the exhaust fell off again. This time Gorman remarked that there was little peace for the wicked as he vanished beneath the car again.

Salome glanced questioningly at Marion, who shook her head stubbornly in reply and went on talking about her husband's telescope. "It's very powerful," she remarked. "You can see Jupiter's moons through it, you know. And you can watch the shadow creeping across the face of our own moon."

Salome said she'd heard tell there was a man in the moon.

"There is," Marion assured her. "You can see him quite clearly through my husband's telescope."

This time the twine lasted them all the way home. As they went through Cloonaghvogue village, a mile short of the castle gate, Marion took over Gorman's running commentary and produced a sort of *vade mecum* of selected cottages and their tenants. Almost every dwelling boasted at least one person who worked at the castle or on the estate – housemaids, laundresses, menservants, hedge trimmers, gamekeepers, and general labourers. There was even 'a little woman who runs up my husband's everyday clothes'.

What good that did to the clothes Salome could not guess but she had the clearest picture of the little woman – something like an organ-grinder's monkey, about two feet tall and dressed in old-fashioned skirts like all the Little People; and she'd go lepping and scrabbling up the shiny cloth every day, getting a toehold in his pockets and buttonholes with the shiny toecaps of her little toy boots. Salome couldn't wait to see her at it. Her mother always did be saying that landlord people lived in a different world.

Gordon Culham-Browne was not up among the battlements. Indeed, he avoided the battlements during daylight hours because the crenellations, being tall enough to hide a man of ordinary height, only emphasized how ludicrously short he was when he stood between any two of them. He had to scrabble among the stones with his toes and lean out dangerously to see anyone on the drive at the foot of the tower; he was sure people laughed to see him do it. So Culham-Browne was standing in a much more imposing position, at the head of the dozen or so stone steps that led up to the massive oak door. Two wolfhounds – the gentle giants of the canine world – stood at his side, reminding everyone of a joke once coined by one of the gamekeepers: that he should fetch a saddle for the master to ride something of a convenient size. That man was now an ex-gamekeeper – so 'ex-', in fact, that he had been forced to move house to Canada before he found someone who'd employ him. And to complete the picture of himself as monarch-of-all-he-surveyed, the master of Cloonaghvogue cradled a shotgun lightly over his arm. The men were cutting the lower lawn for hay and he was bagging the rabbits as they fled.

"That's Mister Culham-Browne," Marion told Salome in as neutral a tone as she could manage; she had been reared on neutral tones so she managed very well, leaving the little girl with no idea what to do with the information.

"He looks . . ." she began shyly, not knowing how to go on. She didn't want to say 'tiny', but she could well understand why he'd want a woman of the Little People to do the necessary gymnastics with his everyday clothes.

"Grand?" Mrs Culham-Browne came to her aid.

Salome looked at him and, though she saw nothing you could call *grand* about the man – apart from the setting in which he'd arranged himself – she responded with an enthusiastic, "Yes!" And thus she entered the conspiracy by which Marion's body and soul had sustained a life together for the past seven years, since her marriage to that man.

Her heart no longer fell at the sight of him. That response had made the first few years of her union miserable, until she had realized it led nowhere; he was impervious to it, so the only one it hurt was herself. Now she could journey up this drive – his beautifully manicured gravel drive – without feeling like a convict after a day's outwork. She could look at him without cringing, too, even secretly, inside herself. After all, life had so many unpleasant duties – from the cold dip each morning to the nightly tot of her housekeeping accounts. Each one could be coped with after a little practice; and marriage with C-B was now ranked among them.

There were compensations, too. The cold water, miserable at the time, left the body feeling wonderfully invigorated; and her nightly tot of figures (while C-B enjoyed his nightly tot of whiskey – a witty play on words that always amused him) could fill her with the most virtuous glow when it came out right first time. The compensations for being Mrs C-B were less immediately related to the raw experience of being Mrs C-B, but they were great for all that. Her social position in the county was not to be sneezed at for he was master of the South Keelity Hunt, a justice of the peace, and virtually held powers of life and death (or at least of life-here or emigration-there) over thousands of souls. And though he was careful with money he was never mean about it; her allowance was greater than her father's entire income had been in the days of her spinsterhood. (Now *there* had been a real imprisonment for you!) C-B might damn her for spending shillings on something worth mere pence, yet she could spend a hundred guineas and more on something of true quality and receive nothing but praise for her sagacity – as long as she did not do it very often, to be sure! And so, in short, she had learned in her girlhood the ancient art of taking the rough with the smooth and had now perfected it in the matrimonial bond with C-B. Her heart no longer sank when she saw him playing cock-o'-the-walk like that; but it did not exactly leap up to behold him, either.

The two huge dogs came bounding down the drive to greet them.

"Stay, you curs! Back, I say!" C-B called after them, though even he knew how useless it is to issue commands of any kind to that particular canine breed. They paused, glanced uncomprehendingly at him, and then continued doing precisely what they felt like doing anyway.

Salome looked down in dismay as they bounded along beside the car, tongues out, jaws slavering. She tried to curl herself small as she clung ever tighter to Mrs Culham-Browne's protective arm. Marion laughed and told her they were the two biggest softies in the world. "If you let them, they'd only lick you to death," she said.

Salome half-relaxed her grip but continued to eye them warily.

"Be brave about it," the other warned as they drew nearer the front steps. "The one thing my husband abhors is a faint heart." She herself leaped down ahead of Salome and took the brunt of their boisterous welcome, allowing them greater licence with their saliva and their wet noses than she would normally have tolerated. "Come on, dear!" She stretched a hand up to encourage the girl.

Salome leaped down at once, determined that whatever other failings she might unconsciously reveal, a faint heart should not be among them.

It was the first time Marion had heard her giggle in that way. The two hounds, taller than Salome when they raised their heads, butted her with their noses and batted her with their tails, licking her and whining all the while; and, of course, the child overcame her fear and dissolved in an almost uncontrollable fit of giggling. Marion had heard the odd chuckle from her and even one or two polite laughs, but the giggling was new. And it was so reminiscent of little Rachel that it shocked her, leaving her momentarily dumb.

She shot a glance at C-B and saw that the similarity had struck him, too. In fact, during the last week of their daughter's life, before the appendicitis had carried her off, she had stood almost at this very spot, here at the foot of the stairs engulfed in a rowdy milling of wolfhounds – who had set her giggling in just those tones. Marion saw a rare glint of softness cloud her husband's eyes before he took a grip on himself (as he would put it) and snapped, "Stop that pandemonium, girl!"

Salome froze. The hounds continued to fret around her but she held her breath and stared fearfully up at the master of Cloonaghvogue, the little wee man with the big coldness in his eyes.

"Not a good beginning," he growled at her, at the dogs, at his wife.

7

Two weeks after Salome's arrival at Cloonaghvogue, the *Knysna* made her first landfall in Africa. She steamed into Freetown harbour one morning and dropped anchor with a great green splash. For most of the passengers – especially those in steerage – it was their first close-up view of the great continent, though once or twice over the past few days they had seen a vague blue smudge of it low on the port beam. It was daunting, to say the least.

Everyone had heard of the jungle, of course; they knew it was hotter, greener, lusher than anything you'd experience in the thickest Irish woodland on a broiling summer's day. But even the most vivid description cannot prepare one for the actual experience. Most potent of all was the heat – or *heats*, rather, for the heat in the air seemed quite separate and distinct from that of the sun. The hot air was like a living creature, invisible but with a will of its own; it could insinuate itself through every little opening in a person's clothing; it felt like snakes of fire, wriggling up the sleeves, pushing in around the collar, lapping at the ankles. And once inside it itched and tingled, making the flesh crawl as if with microscopic biting insects.

Old India hands in the first class and a few world-roaming navvies in steerage pretended not to notice and went about saying they'd known far worse; but the sweat gathered on their lips and brows and spread its dark tentacles round the folds of their shirts and blouses no less obviously than it did for all the rest. Up on the boat deck the quoits and shuffleboard languished in the noonday sun.

The sun!

What had become of the dear old sun? The benign god of the temperate north was here transformed into a pitiless devil; worse, it seemed to have swollen until it half-filled the unbroken vault of the sky, which it bleached to the palest azure. Even beneath the wide canvas awnings that shaded the decks – there was no escaping its blinding light nor its baleful reach. Out at sea, though the same devil sizzled in the same tropic skies, it had all been so different. There, in the shade of the awnings, the ship's motion had wafted a steady breeze to lull the unthinking voyager; but here, riding at anchor on the slick green water, the canvas went over to the enemy and served only to gather the heat and re-radiate it into every little cranny.

Nor was escape to be found below decks, either. Again, out at sea, the ventilation funnels had scooped enough air to keep a cooling draught going, day and night. Now, with the air as slack as the waters all about, the iron hull pinged and cracked at the heat, which made even the shadow side of the vessel quite uninhabitable.

"Jaysus!" commented one old farmer to Finbar as they leaned against the rail, wondering how they'd manage to stay alive until sunset brought some minor but blessed relief. "They must have the praties up and ready for harvest before they've half-done with the sowing!"

"Isn't that the truth," Finbar agreed.

They were staring at the luxuriant growth that clad the hills all around the harbour; it was so lush that the few visible houses seemed to be drowning in upward-flowing cataracts of green. A seaman had told him there were several thousand dwellings dotting the hillsides, all within a mile of where they lay at anchor; but almost every one of them was smothered in forest green. A mere handful of buildings – grandiose colonial piles in gleaming cut stone – huddled the waterfront to mark the port and distinguish these hills from thousands of others along that coast.

"You wouldn't envy *them!*" Finbar nodded at the shore pinnace, threading its way among the fishing boats and merchantmen. It was making for the passenger jetty, where it would land a motley of colonial administrators, planters, and traders. "I'd want a fortune to get off here and stay, so I would."

"D'you think they'll not be getting one?" the old fellow countered.

"If Africa doesn't get them first." Finbar waved a finger at the landscape; in cooler climes it would have been his whole arm. "That's the part they call the white man's grave. One of the lads is after telling me he rested a suitcase for five minutes, and didn't the termites eat the bottom out of it – and half the soles off his shoes into the bargain!" He saw Samson picking a way toward him along the deck and gave the lad an encouraging smile.

The farmer chuckled. "Now here are the lads to envy today!"

His sharp eyes had spotted a small flotilla of bark canoes being paddled out toward the *Knysna*. All were manned by lean black men clad only in loincloths. Their white-toothed smiles were visible from a quarter of a mile away and their glistening bodies seemed perfectly at ease in the full glare and heat of the sun. Finbar saw the incongruity of it all – the suffering white men, lords of creation, groaning and sweating their way ashore, while these lithe, smiling sons of the continent – the supposed 'subject people' – came bustling past them in the opposite direction, as easy as calves on the callows.

The occasion for their happiness was soon apparent, for their canoes were laden with fruit, carved ornaments, bead trinkets, chained monkeys, brightly printed cottons . . .

indeed, anything that might catch the eye or tempt the appetite. And it was all on offer at less than half the price it might command back home in Ireland. The sailors threw nets over the side for them to scramble up with their wares.

"Look at that lad, Da!" Samson slipped his hand into his father's and peered out over the railing, on which he could just rest his chin. "The one with the funny hat."

"Where's your Mammy?" Finbar asked.

"She's tending the babby. She sent me to say she'll soon be done."

Word of the approaching armada had spread and was bringing people from all over the ship.

The 'funny hat' was an old-fashioned stovepipe hat, quite green with age. The grinning African who wore it wore very little else – just a white celluloid collar and a loincloth. When he had approached to within twenty-odd feet of the vessel, he laid down his paddle and rose rather precariously to his feet. Exaggerating his wobbles to make a joke of it, he raised his hands in a begging gesture. Someone up in the first class who knew him of old, or recognized his type, threw down a silver threepenny piece. In a flash he dived after it, catching it a mere fathom or so down, leaving his hat floating. His trick then was to return to the surface at some speed, aiming his head directly at the hat and impaling it on the frizzy cannonball of his skull as he broke out into the air again. He dropped the coin into a leather pouch attached to a fishing float, which was, in turn, tied to one end of his canoe. This brought a round of applause and three more coins to dive for.

"One at a time!" The cry went up from the promenade deck, where the providers of the silver were gathered.

But 'Top Hat', as one of the officers called him, darted like a fish, this way and that, catching all three before the green gloom of the harbour waters obscured them. The applause this time was tumultuous and then, of course, the cry was, "Three at a time!" and a coin-throwing committee was swiftly formed, with a captain to select the throwers and synchronize their efforts.

Samson, ever the anarchist, took a precious penny from his pocket and threw it between salvoes of silver from the deck above. Top Hat looked at it and, instead of diving after it, left it to sink while he waved a scornful hand at his audience. "No copper!" he shouted up at them.

This naturally caused a stir of resentment. There were cries of, "Damn the fellow's cheek!" and for a while nothing but copper coins were thrown for him. But he folded his arms and stood his wobbly ground, looking more than incongruous in his top hat, celluloid collar, and loincloth, and he let the dull brown coins sink unhindered into the murky green. In the end he won, of course, and the shower of more discernible silver resumed. It continued until boredom set in on the promenade deck; by then the leather pouch was almost dragging the fishing float beneath the water.

"He must have gathered up a small fortune in the last fifteen minutes," Paul Delaroux said to Georgina at his side.

Finbar, directly beneath them, could not help overhearing. "Begging your honour's pardon," he called up to them, "but 'twas one pound six shillings and sixpence by my reckoning."

Delaroux laughed. "The devil it was! How can you know that?"

"There was eighty-three silver coins dropped, sir. And if sixty of them was thrippneys and the rest tanners, that would be one pound six and six."

"Well, well, well!" Delaroux brushed his moustaches upward – a sign that he was intrigued. "I daresay you're not far out."

"I hope you didn't mind my interruption now, sir," Finbar added. "I meant no disrespect."

"Of course not – indeed, no!" The suggestion prompted

Delaroux to be slightly too effusive in his denial.

For a moment there seemed nothing further to add. Then, more to fill the awkward silence than anything, Delaroux went on: "Forgive my asking, but aren't you Mister McKenna? Wasn't it your little girl who . . . you know?"

"It was, sir." Finbar smiled broadly to show they could take all expressions of sorrow and regret for granted.

"Go down and talk to him now!" Georgina whispered to her husband.

"I'm not ready," he whispered back. "I've not made my mind up yet."

"And you never will unless you talk to him. At least you could do that."

He drew a deeper breath and squared his shoulders to ask aloud, "May I come down and have a word with you?"

"And welcome, sir," was the immediate reply.

Both Georgina and Paul came down the companionway; he untied the rope barrier and left it for some menial to rehang; the steerage crowd watched them with listless curiosity.

"Is Mrs McKenna about?" was Georgina's first question.

"She's after feeding the youngest, ma'am," Finbar replied. "She'll not be long now."

"I want to go ashore with her as soon as that pinnace comes back. I want to see what can be discovered or arranged about . . . you know."

"I know, ma'am. And grateful it is we are to ye both . . ."

She waved off the rest of his thanks. "Away with you. Ah – there she is now." She flapped a handkerchief to attract Debbie's attention and set off along the deck, walking with a tortured sloth beneath the baking canvas awning. Samson let go his father's hand and followed her; the sacrifice of his precious penny still rankled with him. To be spurned by a near-naked fuzzy-wuzzy, of all things! He was going to *hate* Africa. He just knew it.

"And I thought Dolan's bakery on a July afternoon in Scarriff was hell on earth!" Finbar commented as he and Delaroux settled by the rail. "What wouldn't I give now to be let climb into one of his ovens and cool off beside the baking loaves!"

Delaroux laughed – and used the opportunity to look the man over at close quarters. Georgina's idea was to offer him the post of manager on her uncle's farm, which she and he were about to inherit. Her impulse had, of course, been mainly charitable, but the more Paul thought about it the more he realized there was practical merit in the idea, too.

And the more he saw of Finbar McKenna, the better he liked him. He was plainly a cut above – indeed, several cuts above – the average purchaser of a steerage ticket. On a larger vessel than the *Knysna* he'd doubtless be in the second class.

Delaroux took out his snuffbox and offered Finbar a pinch. "You're for the Cape, I gather," he said after they had sniffed and relished the bite of the powder.

"We are," Finbar agreed.

The natives were now swarming over the decks, proffering fruit, spreading their wares. Their presence helped to dismantle the barriers that would otherwise have separated the two white men.

"Anywhere in particular?" Delaroux asked.

"I have a cousin in Cape Town itself – manager of an ice factory – and an uncle at a vineyard at a place called Graaf Rienet, which is like in the middle."

"I know it. I've been there. You'd like it, I'm sure – a little jewel of a town on the Sundays River at the foothills of the mountains that divide the lower from the middle Karroo."

Finbar nodded. He knew the man had some purpose in this apparently casual encounter, so he didn't want to suggest his future was all cut and dried. "It's not certain I'd go to either, mind," he said.

"Well, you're a wise man to say so, Mister McKenna," the other replied. "It's a land of opportunity ahead of us out there."

"And is it going back to Graaf Rienet ye are?" Finbar prompted.

Delaroux chuckled. "No! Between you and me, there are reasons I'd not be greatly welcomed there. The fact is, Mrs Delaroux's uncle has a farm just down the coast from Port Elizabeth. Ostriches, mostly . . ."

"Ostriches!" Finbar was surprised enough to interrupt. "Ah, for the feathers, of course."

"And the meat. Anyway, he's wishful to retire next year, and so – as it's her inheritance – he thought it best for us to overlap with him and pick up the rudiments at least."

Finbar nodded. "Ostriches," he murmured. "I never saw one of those to talk to, but they look fierce awkward in their pictures."

"I hate the brutes," Delaroux responded with obvious feeling. "Fierce is the *mot juste*, I may tell you. Fierce. Vicious. Unreliable . . . I've seen them open a man's side from his ribs to his knee – before you could shout stop!"

"Jesus, Mary, and Joseph!"

"It took more than prayers to save his life, I can tell you. And he was doing nothing to annoy or harm the creature. He just came rather incautiously within range at an evil-minded moment."

"Well now, a bull could be just as evil in that way," Finbar put in. "Especially a dairy bull. I wouldn't mind an Angus or a Hereford but a dairy bull is a divil." And he went on to give one or two examples out of his own experience.

"You're a farming man yourself, then?" Delaroux prompted.

"Sure I had the secure tenancy of a few acres and I fought

the banks and the lawyers for the ownership of a few cows. You could be sweating and toiling all your life just to keep them fellows happy. So the missis says to me, says she, 'We might as well be sweating and toiling on our own account as theirs.' And that's how I'm standing here – sweating *without* the toil!"

Delaroux laughed again. "You never spoke truer than that!" he said, offering a second go at his snuffbox.

Finbar, sensing that some minor probing on his own behalf was now in order, sniffed up the powder and said, "It's not your heart does be lepping up at the thought of the ostrich farm, then, Mister Delaroux?"

"Nor my lights, nor my liver!" the other agreed dourly. Then, brightening, he added, "But it's occurred to me I might take on a manager to run that side of the enterprise – which would leave me free to try and farm a bit of it. *Our* sort of farming, I mean – milk, vegetables, eggs . . . hens' eggs, of course!"

"And it's near the town, you say? Port Elizabeth?"

Delaroux nodded. "Food for the town." Then, with a light laugh, he added, "Food for thought, too, eh?"

8

Marion lay back – no longer with a sigh; she spread her legs – no longer with distaste; and she let C-B in – no longer with any sort of feeling at all. By long habit she began to explore the cracks in the plasterwork of the ancient ceiling, trying to discover if they were getting worse. God but you'd think she knew them by heart now – backwards, forwards, upside down, and mirror-reversed! How many hundred times had she lain here, committing them to memory like this? She closed her mind to the thought, knowing that even the wildest underestimate would depress her.

That crack by the swag where the flower was missing was a bit worse, surely?

Portia Dacre said she actually enjoyed it with Jim after a year or so . . . after the first baby, really. "God," she said, "when he first waggled that awful *thing* of his at me, I nearly took fright and died! There should be a statue of them in that condition in every market square to warn us – instead of those titchy worms they can hide under half a figleaf in the art galleries."

Portia had a laugh like a basket full of fruit; but she didn't know the half of it. She had fondly imagined she was making Jim out to be such a brute on their honeymoon. Marion had not dared reveal the full horror of *her* experience. 'Waggling that awful *thing*' was only the beginning. Jim had surely never boasted that a Napoleon had ten times the potency of men twice his size. (C-B never spoke of 'a small man', always of 'a Napoleon'.) Nor would Jim have spent the rest of his honeymoon month proving it – until he collapsed one blissful night and had to be taken to hospital for three blissful weeks. Portia would never have understood. All Marion had told her was that C-B had been a bit of a glutton. And as for the rest of the truth . . . well, how could she even have begun to tell it? "Actually, I rather enjoyed it, to be honest – once he'd stopped 'waggling that awful thing at me' and put it where it belonged. I quite enjoyed that. But then, like an utter BF, I let him realize it. And of course he was absolutely horrified! His *wife!* His pure and saintly wife – enjoying it like any common hoor! Where would *that* sort of thing lead to? So, naturally, he did what any true-blue gentleman would have done – he made sure I stopped enjoying it. I leave the details to your imagination."

How could she have said that to Portia?

In fact, come to think of it now, she probably *could* have said all that to her friend. Quite easily. And more. It was just that she didn't realize it at the time.

"I didn't realize it at the time!"

That was the legend they should carve on her gravestone: *Here lies Marion Culham-Browne, who never realized anything at the time – nor, indeed, at any time when understanding really mattered.*

Poor lamb! she added sarcastically to herself. *She obviously never ran short of self-pity!*

She let out a single involuntary laugh.

"Lie quiet, can't you!" C-B snapped.

He lay still a long moment, gathering his concentration. Then he began again. She had counted the number of thrusts once: four hundred and sixty-two. She had tried other counts on other occasions, to get a good average, but she always started thinking of something else halfway through. A third of the way through, actually.

Lately her favourite diversion had been a fantasy about replacing herself with some kind of replica.

It all began when she fell to wondering why he needed her there at all. Suppose they could get a really good sculptor to make a perfect replica of her in some kind of rubbery material, and introduce water at blood heat through a system of tubing . . .

And from there her fantasy usually meandered down many a pleasant byway until his thrusting and grunting was done. The questions were endless. Would the replica have to breathe convincingly? Would it need a system of speaking tubes so that it could answer when spoken to? To which class of maid would fall the task of washing out the 'visiting cards', as C-B called them, next morning – and would the same class of maid prepare the replica for use each night? How would C-B cope with those nights when all the grunting and thrusting petered out into nothing – something that happened increasingly often these days? Knowing him, he'd probably keep a little supply of starch or wallpaper paste, and a syringe to place it inside the replica, to let the servants understand that the Napoleons of this world *never* lose their potency.

Sometimes she was hard put to it not to laugh when these fancies flitted through her mind.

Sometimes she wondered if she was mad. And sometimes she didn't – she only wondered when the madness had descended upon her.

She could regain her sanity at any time, however, by reflecting on the impossibility of it all. Even if one could find the right sculptor and lay hands on the right material and solve all the other technical and social problems, it still wouldn't work. C-B didn't require a dummy at all; he merely required a wife he could train to behave like one. He wanted a woman full of thoughts and feelings to lie beneath him in a kind of living death. Because what he really desired was to know that his will prevailed.

He *wanted* her to hate these almost nightly couplings. He made them as intrusive and degrading as possible so that she *would* lie there, seething with resentment. He wanted to be sure that his will triumphed over her feelings – and the stronger her feelings were, the greater was the triumph of his will.

She did not realize these things until very recently, but that, she also realized, was why she had long ago stopped caring one way or the other. To resent his demands was to give him what he craved. Her indifference was *her* triumph over him.

She did not think C-B understood himself in this light at all; he hardly ever paused to think about anything, least of all his own inner workings. A long time ago someone had primed him with all the responses he'd ever need, to every conceivable situation life might throw at him. And now, as any given situation arose, it detonated the primed response without the need for his mind to intervene at all. It would never occur to him that her indifference was identical – in all its outward signs – with the sort of suppressed rage and resentment he required of her. And yet *something* within him must have twigged it. Surely that was why his most desperate efforts to leave his visiting card could sometimes peter out in failure? That unknown something inside him (her True Enemy, perhaps?) would dimly comprehend that she had managed to transform herself into the dummy of her fantasy – or the nearest a living woman could get to it: a replica of a replica! Then, of course, there'd be no point in going on. The True Enemy would throw a bucket of cold water over his mindless, rutting partner . . . the waggling *thing* would shrivel to a titchy worm . . . and C-B would mutter something about a chill coming on, or the Wine Blight, or getting the well seen to, or any one of the dozens of excuses he had devised to explain away his failing performance.

Tonight, however, was not one of those nights. She had been away in Cork three days and so he had three continent nights of visiting cards to 'leave in her hall' – which he eventually did with gusto.

"Come on, little lady!" he gasped as he rolled off her. "Up on your head!"

She groaned. She had supposed all that nonsense lay behind them. "Oh, C-B!" she pleaded. "We *tried* all that. We agreed it did no . . ."

"Three nights!" he cut across her. "There's three nights' worth in there. I really think it deserves a try. You *owe* me an heir."

She protested her tiredness no further. She slipped her nightie back on and, turning round in the bed, scrabbled her feet up the carved head of it until her botty rested against a horn-of-plenty cradled in a swag of pomegranates and grapes. Every Culham since 1610 had been begotten in this bed – until 1832, when the feckless Toby Culham, C-B's grandfather, had piled up such debts that only the fortune of the parvenu Brownes could rescue them. C-B's father was begotten here that very night on Cynthia

Browne. And then, thirty years later, the visiting card that grew into C-B himself was left in his mother Dorinda's hallway. And it all happened 'on this very spot', as the guides to historic places like to say.

Had Cynthia and Dorinda been compelled to lie in absurd positions like this? Marion wondered. Was the Culham-Browne seed so feeble and defective that those forces of nature which would normally reject it had to be cajoled into acceptance by such ludicrous stratagems?

The fault certainly lay with the Culham-Browne seed – or with the C-B seed, anyway. Dr Hooke had made that quite clear, though not to C-B himself, of course. Too frightened of him to tell him to his face. Scared witless. Preferred to leave it to the little lady to break the news to him tactfully!

So why hadn't she? Was she also scared witless? Or could she be saving it for the right occasion? The pregnant moment!

Yes, *that* was why she kept it from him, of course. Suppose that by some miracle he became temporarily fertile again. If he got her with child, he'd never believe it was his. She'd have the worst of both worlds. She'd tell him what Dr Hooke had said. He'd reply that she must have misunderstood. He'd never check back with Hooke himself, naturally, but he'd mock her for her silly little brain and its inability to grasp a few simple words from a Dublin quack – until the moment she told him she was expectant. *Then* he'd change horses and accuse her of going with some other man, quoting Hooke as his authority!

She hadn't been married to C-B all these years for nothing!

Actually, it wasn't too bad a life as lives go. At least it was consistent. You knew where you were. His range of responses to life was tiny (Napoleonic, let's say!) – and *always* negative. If you shut him out of your life and only pretended to let him in, you could get along very nicely. Much better than poor Tillie Porter. Harry would be nice as pie to her one moment and black as thunder the next – and no reason whatever for the change. That must be awful. No wonder Tillie was so interested in murder!

There was a gentle snoring at Marion's side. She rose at once and douched the filthy stuff from her – the only way she could sleep.

Perhaps she ought to find some other man to go with? As long as C-B fondly believed himself to be fertile, the possibility that the child was fathered by another would never occur to him. She'd have to find someone who looked like old Toby Culham because C-B would be on the qui vive for a family resemblance. A tall, handsome divil he was! She wouldn't mind. She must take a good look at his portrait in the minstrels' gallery – see if he reminded her of anyone.

If she gave C-B the son and heir she owed him, there'd be no limit to his gratitude. And thus an idle fancy became the beginnings of a notion of an outline of a possibility of a plan.

Besides, she thought just before she fell asleep, *Salome would adore a little brother to play with.*

9

Georgina took Mrs McKenna's arm to slow her down. How could anyone walk so fast in this heat? Of course, the answer was that a mother on her way to the Imperial Cables office, where there might be word of her missing little daughter, would run through the fires of hell itself to get there.

Mrs McKenna looked sharply at her, surprised that she, Georgina, wanted to slow down.

"Didn't Mister McKenna wish to come with us?" Georgina asked – as if that were her reason for taking her arm.

"He did," Debbie admitted reluctantly. "But 'twas meself asked him to stay with the gossoons and Martha."

Georgina noted that the boys were just 'the gossoons', but the little girl was always spoken of by name. She wondered if it had been so when Salome was around, too – or had it been 'the gossoons and colleens' then. "I think you've already decided there isn't going to be any cable waiting for you – haven't you," she said.

Debbie nodded morosely. "Or someone would surely have brought it to the ship. What sort of man would let parents grieve a minute longer than they needed?"

Most of the ones I've ever met, I'm afraid, Georgina thought, though she kept it to herself. "Maybe there's a rule against it," she said vaguely. "Anyway, if there's no word waiting, we're going to fire off a message of our own – aren't we?" She raised her voice brightly.

Debbie caught her eye, saw what was expected of her, and smiled a thin-lipped smile.

"Also" – now Georgina's tone promised a revelation – "see that ship there? The *Hengist* – the one they're loading with all those bales?"

"Yes?"

"Well, she's sailing for Bristol on this afternoon's tide. Captain McTavish told me so at breakfast. And he's arranged for her to carry a letter from me to my cousin Martin – the one I told you about, remember? In the RIC at Castlemartyr?"

"You'll be sending him a cable as well?" Debbie asked anxiously.

"Of course. But one can put so much more in a letter, you see?"

Whether she understood the point or not Debbie did not appear as delighted as Georgina had hoped. "What's troubling you now?" she asked.

Debbie made an awkward gesture. "You'd not mention the letter in the cable, ma'am? Or would you?"

"Why not? I hadn't given it any thought, to be quite . . ."

"Only, you see, if your man got a cable saying there's a letter on the way, too, wouldn't he likely think to himself he'd as well wait for the letter – and not do the half of what he'd do if he thought the cable was all that's in it?"

Georgina gave a small, self-deprecating sigh. "You're absolutely right, my dear. The point would never have occurred to me. But set your mind at rest. I shall say nothing as to the letter."

They hastened their steps, for the shield saying Imperial Cables was now clearly visible. The afternoon sun beat down with undiminished ferocity. Every now and then there was a suggestion of a breeze, but it was only a dust devil threatening to form. The two women were almost the only things that moved along the seafront. On the inland side of the street, beneath broad canvas awnings that displayed messages bleached and faded beyond all deciphering, men sprawled in cane and wickerwork chairs, sipping iced drinks and watching them with more lethargy than interest. Beneath the shade of a three-headed cabbage palm a donkey woke up with a start as the two women hurried by.

They looked pointlessly to right and left before they crossed the street. Georgina racked her brains for something bright to say and realized that the moment was too fraught for any words. Just as they crossed the threshold she murmured, "Here we go!"

The office was narrow and long, barely wide enough for the pair of them to walk side by side down to the counter. Behind it, amid defensive ramparts of folders and box files, sat an Indian clerk, a young fellow with a shock of dense black hair, glossy with macassar oil; he was staring into space, chewing some kind of aromatic seed, a small pile of which lay in the lid of a tobacco tin at his elbow.

He looked up in surprise just as Georgina raised her hand to strike the plunger on the desk bell. Then he scrambled to his feet and hastened to the counter. Debbie noticed that his steel-rimmed spectacles were glassless. For some reason it surprised her so much that it took the words from her mouth.

Georgina stepped in: "Have you a cable waiting here for Mrs McKenna" – she nodded toward her companion – "passenger in the *Knysna?*"

"McKenna, ma'am?" His eyes raked the ceiling, suggesting there were so many cables awaiting passengers on the *Knysna* that he could hardly hold them all in his mind. "No." He smiled wanly at them. "Sorry, no."

"Have you any cables at all – waiting for *any* passengers?" Georgina pressed him.

He shook his head and sighed.

" 'Tis what I thought," Debbie murmured.

Georgina persisted. "Has there been any cable for anybody on the *Knysna*, then? The captain . . . any of the officers . . . the doctor, the chaplain . . . anyone? Nothing concerning a little girl who was unintentionally left behind on the quayside when the ship sailed?"

The clerk took down a large ledger marked CABLES INWARD and laid it open, facing them. All this while they had been able to see through a glazed partition into the inner office, where a European in crumpled tropical ducks lay at attention in his chair, apparently asleep under a large revolving fan. This individual now sprang to life and came to the door between the inner and outer offices. "What seems to be the trouble, Raai?" he asked.

"These gentle ladies wish to know about cables for the *Knysna*, sir. I tell them none. And they ask again." He waved a hand at the ledger.

"It isn't that we disbelieved you . . ." Georgina launched into a further explanation.

Debbie meanwhile was running an eye down the list of

cables received over the past two weeks: Hellyer & Son, Cocoa Agent; Stavros Koulouris, Furniture and Machinery Importer; Helmut Wahl, Colour Merchant . . . they were all land-based and they all had agent or merchant or some such description after them. She just closed her eyes and stood there while the words of the others flew around her head, no more comprehensible than the buzzing of insects. Until this moment she had not realized – had not *dared* realize – how many expectations she had pinned on finding a cable awaiting her in this office. She had deliberately killed each little bud of hope as it burst open in her conscious mind; but somewhere inside her, Hope itself had survived.

She had not dared picture little Salome, either. In those few moments when an image of the child had slipped beneath her guard, there had always been the shadowy suggestion of someone else, holding her hand, taking care of her. Now, however, she could keep that image at bay no longer. It was as if the sun came out from behind a cloud in her mind's eye, throwing a pitiless brilliance on the scene – which was, of course, the quayside at Queenstown. But not as Debbie had seen it last, when, in happy innocence, she had assumed Salome to be hiding aboard. This was an imagined scene, half an hour after the *Knysna* had sailed, when the quay was a deserted higgledy-piggledy of ropes, bales, packing crates, and trampled paper ribbons. And there at the heart of it all stood one bewildered and lonely little girl, frightened out of her wits, crying, "Mammy . . . Mammy!" Forever.

Debbie closed her eyes, oblivious of the two fat tears that rolled down her own cheeks, and thought how often she had used the phrase, ' 'twould break your heart,' without once realizing what a precise and graphic description it was. The pain in her breast was unbearable. Now that she had at last dared to face this imagined scene on the Queenstown quay, she knew it would haunt her to the grave and beyond.

The piteous cry of 'Mammy! Mammy! . . .' endlessly repeated, would ring in the caverns of her mind for as long as she lived. "Oh, my little bird!" she sobbed.

Arms stole around her shoulders; a warmth she had not experienced since her own girlhood, when her mother had hugged her so, now rescued her from the ultimate pit of despair. The arms turned her back toward the door. "Come away now, back to the ship. We've done all we can."

As they stepped out into the street, in the shadow of the cable-office awning but facing the full glare of the westering sun, Debbie said, "I just know I'll never set eyes on her again."

"Of course you will!" Georgina responded, almost angrily. "And before the year is out, too. My cousin will find her, never fear."

Debbie shook herself and blinked rapidly, as if surprised to find tears in her eyes at all. "Sure we didn't send the cable yet."

"I did, you know. And I said nothing of the letter." Georgina gave a little cajoling sort of laugh. "So now it's all set in motion. The mighty machine of the Royal Irish Constabulary is set in motion. No one could have taken a little girl from that quayside without someone noticing – you know yourself what Ireland is like. You can't move hand or foot. The first thing that happens to an Irishman or woman when they reach heaven is the Recording Angel asks them to check his records and correct any errors they see."

Debbie laughed unwillingly. "Lord, but you're very good to me, ma'am. Except for you, I'd have thrown myself on that darkie's spike back there. I was the thickness of that fingernail from it."

"And would you double the grief of a fine husband and three lovely children? I don't think so, you know."

They were still standing outside the cable office. The door opened behind them and the manager said, "Oh, thank heavens! I had visions of having to run half a mile in this heat." He proffered a shilling to Georgina. "We miscounted, Mrs Delaroux. Castlemartyr is one word according to our gazetteer." He lowered his voice to a sympathetic drawl. "May I offer you a glass of water, Mrs McKenna?"

Debbie smiled wanly and declined his offer, somewhat to his relief. He went on: "I really ought not to divulge this but in common humanity I feel I must. There *was* a cable – for the *Knysna* – to the captain – from the harbourmaster at Queenstown." He let the news out in dribs and drabs.

"*And?*" The two women were on tenterhooks.

The manager sucked a tooth. "Not good news, I fear. It just said that no little girl answering to that description had been reported lost to his office."

"Description?" Debbie asked vaguely, still trying to absorb this blow.

"They probably telegraphed her description to Spike Island soon after we sailed," Georgina put in.

Debbie remembered the encounter with the officer then.

"It probably means," the manager went on, "that someone found your daughter and is taking care of her."

Debbie knew the man was only trying to be kind but she had faced this situation so often in her waking nightmares – and all its variations – that she could not bear her hopes to be raised on so slender a surmise. She drew a breath and forced herself to say quite calmly, "Or that she is dead."

The man was shocked but Georgina understood what desperation had driven Mrs McKenna to such an outlandish response. With smiles and gestures she managed to convey that the woman was not herself; the man dipped his head and withdrew.

"I shouldn't have said that," Debbie murmured.

"Especially as it's the least likely thing to have happened. We should go back at once and tell your husband."

"Maybe the captain's told him already. He was probably waiting for me to come ashore."

"Men – God bless 'em!" Georgina said bleakly.

They could not face stepping out into the sun again so they decided to brave the stares of the waterfront idlers at closer quarters. They began to saunter from one pool of shade to the next.

Debbie looked out across the harbour, fixing her eyes on the *Hengist*. Smoke was now starting to billow from her funnel; she was clearly getting up steam. "Say what you will," she murmured, "there's some things you just know without the need for thinking."

"Such as?" Georgina asked warily.

"Such as I *know* I should be on that boat out there, sailing for England tonight. I know I can't be. I know 'tis impossible. Yet I also know 'tis what I should be at. And if I don't, 'twill scald my heart for many a year."

"And suppose you did?" Georgina asked. "When you got to Bristol, what then?"

"I'd take the next packet to Ireland and the next ride to Cork, and I'd haunt every workhouse, every presbytery, every orphanage – God, I'd haunt every hedge and ditch – till I found her. And if I don't do that, 'twill lie like a curse upon me until the day I die." She stared at her friend with great, haunted eyes. "What can I do? What can I do?"

Georgina decided to take the greatest risk of her life. "If that's what you really want," she said, "I'll put up the money. You may go at once."

Debbie stopped in her tracks and stared at her. For a moment the words meant nothing; then their full impact struck home and she saw that this kind, generous, wonderful lady, who thought she was offering the greatest gift, was in fact, and quite without meaning it, taking away . . . *everything!* Until this moment the trap of her poverty, her utter inability to *do* anything about her lost little girl, had been the only balm she could give her grieving spirit. She could indulge in those brave, self-sacrificing fantasies – soothing her troubled conscience and freeing it to let her get on with the rest of her life – and all without the slightest fear of having to carry it out. And now, in one moment of thoughtless generosity, Mrs Delaroux had killed the possibility for ever. She had turned 'I would have done it but I couldn't' into 'I could have done it but I would not'!

Desperately she tried to remedy the situation. "God be good to you, ma'am, but I couldn't accept such generosity. How would we ever repay you?"

Georgina, seeing the die was cast, decided there was no turning back. "I'm afraid it's not completely disinterested generosity on my part, Mrs McKenna. I wish I were that sort of woman, but I'm not. No – I have my own reason for making this offer."

Debbie frowned. Her self-absorption and the luxuriant growth of feelings that went with it suddenly shrivelled and she became her old worldly self again, watchful and suspicious. Georgina saw it and heaved a sigh of relief – mentally, anyway. "Perhaps it's a little premature to be saying this but one can't always pick the best possible moment, can one? Mister Delaroux and I are going out to Port Elizabeth to manage my uncle's farm there – a little way down the coast, actually. Forgive me if I speak rather too bluntly, but I think I judge you correctly to be the sort of person who will never break the confidence I'm about to impart. The fact is, I know my husband rather better than he knows himself. I respect him. I admire him. I love him for his many virtues *and* for his few faults – but I am not blind to those faults. I'm sure you understand?"

Debbie, despite her mood, could not avoid a light laugh. "You could take the words off the tip of *this* tongue, ma'am!"

"And many another wife's besides, I'm sure. Well then, among Mister Delaroux's faults is, shall we say, an eagerness to be done with the present while he leaps all enthusiastic onto something new. The farm I mentioned is chiefly devoted to the rearing of ostriches. There is a lively trade in their feathers in Port Elizabeth – in fact, the grandest building in the town, or so I'm told, is the Feather Market. Anyway, if my misgivings prove correct, my husband will throw himself heart and soul into the ostrich-farming business. It will suddenly become the one thing he's always wanted in life. There'll be no talk out of him but the history of ostriches, the breeding of ostriches, the feeding, the rearing . . . before the first month is out, he'll be able to fill an encyclopedia devoted entirely to the wretched birds. Then six months later he'll remember what excellent game hunting there is up in the Karroo, or discover its equivalent in the bush around the farm, and then the business of ostrich farming will quickly become the most irksome chore imaginable."

Debbie could not help wondering if the man was the same way with the women in his life. How long had they been married? Was there something very pointed – worried, even – in this wife's assessment of her man? "Does he not know it himself, ma'am?" she asked.

Georgina nodded. "I believe he does, deep down. I think we all know how we really are, deep down, but we don't usually like to face it – especially when we're forced to it by someone else."

Her smile and her words were innocent enough yet Debbie felt there was a hint that the woman now realized what her offer of funds had done to lay Debbie's soul bare to herself – a hint of an apology, even.

"So," Georgina continued, "to spare his blushes I've put the situation to him in a rather more flattering light. I've reminded him that he can never look at anything without immediately seeing half a dozen ways to improve it – which is true, though it's not the truth that's important in this case. Anyway, I've suggested to him that the danger is he'll throw himself body and soul into ostrich farming for about six months, only to realize there'd be more profit in some other kind of farming. Dairying and poultry, for instance. Or market gardening for the town. I suggested that we'll need a good reliable manager to keep the main business going while we experiment with the improvements his restless and inventive mind is sure to wish for."

Her smile was sad rather than conspiratorial – sad that such underhand stratagems were necessary.

"And you think McKenna's the man?" Debbie asked. "Your reliable manager?"

"You tell me, my dear. I'm sure you know him as well as I know Delaroux."

Debbie had a sudden vision of themselves – Finbar, her, and the children – standing in a clearing in the jungle (for she imagined the whole of Africa to be one unbroken stretch of green such as she saw all around Freetown harbour), or leaning over a wooden stockade, staring proudly at a great flock of the giant black-and-white birds, many of which they had reared by hand, just like the hens at home in Clare. And she knew that Finbar was absolutely made for such work. "Sure 'twould be the crowning of him, ma'am," she replied with whole-hearted fevour. "Is that what himself and McKenna were talking about on deck this morning?"

Georgina smiled. "If they weren't, I shall want to hear good reasons why not! So, you see, my 'generous offer' has a great deal of self-interest in it. Now if that makes it easier for you to accept . . ." A lift of her eyebrows completed the sentence as she turned and gazed at the *Hengist*.

The flurry of activity at her side had ended. There were no more little bumboats waiting with bales for loading. Two of her mast derricks had been tied in the vertical and the third was swinging great baulks of timber to close off the cargo hatches.

"I'd say you have a few minutes to make up your mind," Georgina concluded.

10

Marion watched with approval as Salome tied her own shoelaces. It was something Rachel had not quite mastered before she died. In fact, her observation of the McKennas' daughter over the past few days had led her to the uncomfortable conclusion that her own dear child had perhaps been a little backward. A sneer nudged in at the edge of her mind – that it was only to be expected when one looked at her father – but she pushed it out again. There was no profit in starting up such trains of thought. And, anyway, who had allowed herself to be led to the altar by him!

Perhaps Salome was more than commonly bright? That was a more bearable notion – and one with more evidence to back it, too. Just look at the way she could draw. The keenness of her observation was better than that of many grown-ups. And the confidence with which she set it all down. And then there were the odd little remarks she'd make every now and then, something that just slipped out, showing how her mind never stopped working. She never seemed to stop – forever storing things away, making connections between this and that, connections others wouldn't notice unless you drew three lines underneath whatever it was.

For instance, they were walking through the wild garden on the morning after her arrival at Cloonaghvogue Castle, and Marion happened to point out some snowberry bushes, saying, "They're shade-loving plants."

A few paces farther on, Salome had mused aloud, "Maybe they don't really *love* the shade, ma'am."

"What makes you say that?" Marion was intrigued.

"Maybe they'd want to be out in the sun with the others," the girl explained, "but the others won't let them." After a further thoughtful pause she added, "Or it could be the others *can't* live in the shade, so the snowberries get it all to themselves."

Marion, who had recently read a life of Mozart, had wondered what it must be like to start teaching a child and suddenly to realize that, though it might know far less than you, it was actually streets ahead in intelligence; it had not occurred to her that she might meet the situation face-to-face – nor so soon, either. The responsibility of it frightened her a little. "Did you ever think of such things before, child?" she asked.

"I never had the cause, ma'am."

Yesterday she would have said, 'never had no cause'; but you only needed to tell her things like that once. Marion sighed. "Listen, I don't want you to go on calling me ma'am, like one of the servants." She longed to suggest *Mum* as a near-sounding alternative but she lacked the courage. "Call me Aunt Marion," she suggested. "D'you mind?"

Salome smiled and took her hand. Prattling happily she strolled down the path beside her new 'aunt' to where she heard some water gurgling invitingly among the trees.

Gordon Culham-Browne, who was out inspecting the vermin traps with Mangan, his head gamekeeper, watched them from a distance and had to force himself to hold his anger in check.

But not successfully enough. Willy Mangan saw it, followed his gaze, and said, "Is that the foundling-colleen herself, sir? Isn't it the missis has the heart of a Christian!"

His reward was a harrumph and the observation that a fox had clearly managed to spring the trap now at their feet – and all without being caught. "If you attended more to your duties and less to what doesn't concern you, we'd have more pheasants come the autumn!" he barked.

Mangan took the rebuke on the chin but he smiled inwardly.

Salome and her new protector followed the rushing stream down to a broad, tree-girt pool at the bottom of the valley. Essentially a natural feature, it had been embellished by several previous Culham-Brownes. Gordon's grandfather had bounded it by a low wall of cut-stone alongside the path. His father, more aesthetic than his son, had added a pair of lead statues, standing waist-deep in the water. The farther one depicted an adolescent Pan, goat-haunched and playing the traditional pipes with a wicked grin on his puckered lips. The nearer showed a wistful girl, half-child, half-woman, crouched as if rising from the water, and staring warily across the pool at the young musician. Both were nude.

The pair had aroused great controversy when they were first installed, and even now grown-ups who saw them for the first time were made uncomfortable by the overtones of budding sexuality. But locals had long since grown used to the pair; no one had ever seen anything untoward occurring between them; and in any case, a thin coating of limescale and lichen had by now added a touch of venerable age and made them less intrusive in that limestone landscape.

Salome saw nothing of all that, of course. She saw two actual people, so real and so still that for a moment they frightened her. "Did they . . . ?" she asked, unable to say the words. "Have they been . . . ?"

From the shrubbery on the far side of the path came a crackling of careless footsteps. They turned in time to see Gordon Culham-Browne emerging from the undergrowth. "Ha!" he cried. "Thought you'd be here."

Marion was seated on the smooth capstone of the wall. Salome shrank against her skirts. It occurred to her that this ever-angry gentleman was the one responsible for turning the two young people in the water to stone – like in the ogre stories her Mammy had often told. She was comforted to feel Aunt Marion's hands settle on her shoulders.

"Trap any poachers, dear?" Marion asked.

Salome looked at the statues again; perhaps they had once been poachers, too?

Culham-Browne ignored her question; instead he followed Salome's gaze. "Wondering how they got there, eh?" he exclaimed jovially as he closed the distance between them. He forced himself to tousle her hair in an avuncular fashion – but he was surprised to observe that the look of fear he had half-expected to see in her eyes was absent.

Salome, who would not have been surprised to be hit by him, was so relieved at his gesture that she smiled and even managed a little laugh.

It occurred to Culham-Browne that he could quite easily steal this little waif away from his wife's affections; he could turn this happy acquisition into a most bitter cup. "I'll tell you how they got there," he said in a tone that promised the most wondrous revelations. "It all began when that young girl came down here one gloriously hot summer's afternoon. And, seeing no one about and feeling rather hot, she slipped out of her clothes and went for a bathe in the cool water."

"Gordon!" Marion interrupted in a warning tone. She had no idea what tale he was going to make of it but his geniality filled her with misgiving.

He smiled at her. "It was before your time, my dear, but I'm sure you've heard the tale."

"I'm not even sure I want to," she replied guardedly.

He sat on the capstone, too, a few feet away from his wife, and held out a hand to Salome. Against her better instincts, Marion removed her hands from the child's shoulders. Somewhat against her will – but intrigued nonetheless by the sudden access of friendliness in this little man, who had been so gruff and chilling at breakfast – Salome edged toward him.

"So there she was in the nice cool water," he continued mildly, making it easier for her to complete the brief journey, "giggling and splashing, happy as a sandboy. Or perhaps we should say sandgirl in her case."

Salome put a shy hand on his knee and leaned against his thigh. She turned her clouded green-grey eyes upward, gazing at him in rapt attention. A shadow dimmed this moment of his triumph as he became aware that in the race to snatch away the affections of others he might not be the only contender in the field. Unable to take his eyes off hers he continued: "But then came the moment – the awful moment – when she felt sufficiently cool again and wished to come back out of the water and get dressed once more. Her clothes were here on the path, exactly where you're sitting now, so she hadn't far to come. But she took one step toward the edge of the pool and suddenly . . ." He behaved as if he were trying to suppress a yawn . . . but a yawn too powerful for him to resist. And then the urge became genuine and water filled his eyes.

Salome laughed delightedly and clapped her hands to her mouth in an unconscious attitude of prayer. Now she hung on every detail of the story. Marion watched in amazement; she had never seen her husband behaving like this.

"Yes!" He wove his involuntary yawn into his tale. "I can feel it, too. Can't you?"

"What?" Her lips formed an O of anticipation.

"Lethargy! D'you know what that is? Tiredness beyond tiredness. Lethargy! These" – he trailed his hand dramatically in the pool at his side – "are the waters of Lethe. D'you know what that is?"

She shook her head.

"Lethe is a river in the Underworld. Drink its waters and you'll forget everything that ever happened to you."

Salome turned from him and stared at the statue of the girl.

"Yes!" he said in a near-whisper. "You even forget how to walk!"

Her gaze turned toward the young Pan.

"He tried to rescue her, of course," Culham-Browne went on. "He came cavorting through the woods on the opposite side of the pool over there – saw her – realized she was in difficulties – and knew the only thing that could save her was the sound of his pipes. I expect you know all about the pipes of Pan, don't you?"

She shook her head and fixed her eyes in his once again; to him it seemed as if she had made the sun come out. Somewhere inside him a small voice was warning him not to fall under the strange spell of this little cuckoo in his nest; but the reward of her smile was too great a lure for him to resist. "Ah," he said, "if ever you hear them, little one, run a thousand miles rather than dance to their tune! But poor young thingummy there had no choice."

"What was her name?" Salome asked.

For a moment he was nonplussed; so many names occurred to him. Then, on an inspiration, he replied, "Nobody ever knew. She came from out of nowhere, you see, and before anyone could ask her a civil question . . ." He waved a hand dramatically toward the statue. "Oh yes, it all happened very quickly. And to young Pan, too. Of course, he's not *the* god Pan – just one of his young minions. Anyway, he stood on the bank over there and played his heart out for the girl with no name, trying to save her from being turned to stone."

Salome's eyes sought out a likely spot on the farther shore.

"Soon enough he realized he was doing no good. And the only thing he could think of was to get nearer to her, play right in her ear. So he started to wade across, piping away for all he was worth. And then the awful thing began to happen to him, too."

"He started turning to stone?" Salome asked in a hushed little murmur.

He nodded and gripped her by the arm, as if to say, *Be brave!* "Heavier and heavier grew his limbs. Slower and slower dragged his pace. Weaker and weaker grew his piping. Until . . . well – see for yourself. That's as far as he managed to get."

Salome stared at the young Pan in wonder. To be frozen in that attitude until . . . forever! All through the long winter nights, when the ice would lie thick on this water. And the long summer afternoons, too, when the whole world was drowsy with sleep. It was something so far beyond her mental grasp it made her mind reel. "He's smiling," she said quietly, more to herself than to him.

It was such an unexpected comment it left him at a loss for words. He glanced helplessly at his wife, who, on a sudden inspiration, answered for him: "He knew, you see."

They both turned to her. Salome let her hand fall from Culham-Browne's knee and took a step in his wife's direction. It was like a stab of treachery to him and he had to quell an impulse to grab her by the nape of her neck. The emotion disturbed him.

Meanwhile Marion was saying: "He knew that he was about to be frozen in one particular attitude for ever – and that she would have her eyes fixed on him, also for ever. What should his attitude be, then? Fear? Anger? Horror? Sadness? Well" – she, too, gestured toward the young demigod's statue – "you can see for yourself what expression he chose. And only just in time, eh!"

For a long moment the three of them kept silent, staring from one effigy to the other. For Salome it was one more instance of the charm and unpredictability of the world she was now privileged to share. Nearby, a somewhat bemused Culham-Browne was staring at Pan and thingummy in a new light; until this moment he had never thought of them as being anything more than a needless annoyance during the mayfly season. And Marion took her eyes off the statues to gaze at her husband, whom she was also seeing in a new light. Never in the six short years their own little Rachel had lived had he behaved in so kindly and genial a fashion to her.

11

It was a routine meeting. The constabulary at Castlemartyr was to lend the usual picket of three constables to help in policing the steeplechase at Cloyne on the last Saturday in August, which was in twelve days' time. The main contingent, as always, would be sent from Midleton, for Cloyne was in their district. It was a sought-after picket, for there was always good eating and good drinking and good crack at the event; so competition among the Castlemartyr constables was keen. The debate about whom to reward, which was inevitably also a debate about whom to deprive, was more protracted than usual; but the arrival of the sacred hour for luncheon brought it to a conclusion at last. It was with some relief that Martin Woods, Georgina's inspector-cousin, accepted Major Haston's invitation to sup with him at Mangan's, the principal hostelry in Midleton's main street.

He was a little surprised when the Major led the way upstairs to a private dining room but, as the man explained as soon as they were seated, walls have ears, especially in Ireland, and there were certain operational matters it would be unwise to discuss in any of the public bars downstairs. He waited until the curate had brought their meal and porter before he revealed what was on his mind.

The authorities in Dublin Castle, it seemed, had noticed a marked increase in the activities of the numerous clandestine patriot organizations that riddled the life of the country – republicans, anarchists, labour agitators, various anti-landlord factions, and that fringe of the Home Rule movement which believed in force. The government wanted reports from every district in all four provinces on the activities of these dissident bodies.

"It looks as though we're heading for one almighty war in Europe," Haston added. "So I suppose it's only prudent to make sure that England's back-door is bolted shut before the first shot is fired in anger over the water. The trouble is, they want this information in a hurry and there's only so much we can achieve by direct investigation. They live in a world of their own up there in Dublin. They don't seem to understand that asking direct questions is the last way to get anywhere in Ireland."

Martin saw his chance. "I believe I have the perfect thing here, sir," he said, producing Georgina's letter from Freetown. He passed it over.

Haston gutted it swiftly. "Another little-girl-lost," he commented.

"No, sir, it's the same one – but . . ."

"But we got nowhere last time. What was her name? Delilah?"

"Salome – Salome McKenna."

"Yes, well, there you are – how could anyone hide a child with a name like that!" He passed the letter back. "I'd bet all Lombard Street to a china orange she's drowned."

"Perhaps, sir." Martin was diplomatic. "But we have a great deal more detail here." He tapped the paper. "It gives us an excellent reason for reopening our inquiries. And an investigation into a missing child always brings out more enthusiastic cooperation from the populace than any other type of inquiry. We get nothing out of them when we're looking for poteen or stolen horses – as you know, sir."

Actually, it wasn't quite true, for the less inclined an Irishman is to assist the police, the more friendly and blathersome and hail-fellow-well-met he becomes.

Haston rubbed his chin thoughtfully. "New details, you say? For example?"

"Her exact height – forty inches. The fact that she's unusually skinny. That her dress was a blue-chequered pattern. Also that she's from around Ennis in County Clare. If someone has taken her in, they may try to get in touch with other McKennas in Ennis. And questions about a child speaking with a Clare accent here in County Cork might just jog memories where earlier questions about any old stray child have failed. But really my point is that once one has engaged people's attention – *and* cooperation – with sympathetic inquiries of this kind" – again he tapped the letter – "one can often pick up other little nuggets in passing. Touching on, shall we say, matters of interest at Dublin Castle?"

It was by now clear to Haston that his keen young subordinate intended to follow up his cousin's letter, come what may. Better, then, to swim with the tide and try to harness it to more important inquiries – in short, to take the bait being offered. He smiled what his sergeant called 'the iron smile on the velvet lips' and said, "Results on my desk before the last of the month, eh?"

Martin went directly from their luncheon to Mr Wellbeloved, the harbourmaster at Queenstown. The incident was by now five weeks old, during which time almost two dozen vessels had come and gone; the man could barely remember seeing the sergeant during the earlier inquiries, let alone Pat Clancy's message-cum-shopping-list. He played a straight bat and stonewalled every question. He had seen nothing. He could recall nothing. No one had reported anything to him. No trace of a missing child of either sex had been observed.

"And have you noticed any unusual boat movements in

and around the harbour recently?" Martin asked. He managed to imply that this was still in connection with the missing child but that the inquiries were now moving into more serious realms. "Any sort of boat at all – even one-man row boats? Strange lights at night? You know the sort of thing."

Wellbeloved hesitated and Martin knew the question had touched a nerve; the man was now trying to work out who could cause him greater trouble – the clandestine boatmen (almost certainly smugglers) or the constabulary. "Is it still to do with the wee colleen, Inspector?" he asked, playing for time.

"We've had some fairly firm information from other sources," Martin responded vaguely – implying that the populace was siding with the constabulary on this one, so that was where the harbourmaster's bread would be buttered, too.

But his ruse – to use the missing-child inquiry as a cloak for a more serious investigation into unlawful movements of any and every kind – now blew back in his face. Wellbeloved's assistant cleared his throat respectfully and said, "There was that sighting I told you of, sir – what Pius O'Connor seen the day the *Knysna* sailed."

The harbourmaster had entirely forgotten the matter; even now it rang no bell. But he realized his assistant was giving him the chance to avoid an immediate answer to the more awkward question, so, trusting that nothing too damaging would result from it, he said, "I have only the vaguest recollection of that incident. Tell me again what happened?"

Martin fumed inwardly, feeling quite certain that this was some on-the-spot persiflage to divert the course of his real inquisition, which, from the harbourmaster's point of view, had suddenly taken a most uncomfortable turn. However, his interest pricked up again when the assistant mentioned that this Pius O'Connor had apparently seen a ragged little girl being led away by a rather grand lady. The tale was too circumstantial – and full of unnecessarily verifiable detail – to be the usual bland lie that such people tell in order to run the constabulary out to sea without a compass. He didn't believe that the 'grand lady' took the child to a waiting coach and four, nor that it had an aristocratic crest on its door; but the core of the story – the lady and the waif – had the ring of truth.

"Is this O'Connor here today?" he asked.

Wellbeloved smiled. "He's in your custody, I believe, sir. Drunk and disorderly in Midleton last Saturday night. Seven days."

"So it's not the first time."

The other two exchanged rueful smiles. "Nor will it be the last."

"Which of the cabmen bring passengers out from the city?" Martin asked next.

"Lord but it could be any one of them, sir," Wellbeloved told him. Neither man tried to press the point that the lady had had her own gilded coach. The Inspector appeared to have accepted the gist of the story, so the details no longer mattered; if, on the other hand, he had treated it as a pack of lies, they would have told him the colours of each horse and which one had cast a shoe – and what the driver had for breakfast.

Martin decided he could get no further without having a direct word with the man O'Connor, who would be serving out his seven days in the lock-up at Midleton. On his way out of the port he dropped in on the Customs and Excise to see whether they were aware that Wellbeloved and his assistant were aware of clandestine movements of small boats within the port. They were; but it was good to have confirmation of their own suspicions from an experienced investigator like himself. Martin felt a little glow of pride. An 'experienced investigator'! Sometimes it seemed to him that no one could claim that title in this benighted land until he was ten years into his retirement and had had time to mull over all his mistakes.

Satisfied with the afternoon's work, he set off for Midleton, hoping that alcohol had not taken too great a toll of Pius O'Connor's brain cells over the past five weeks.

12

Eight days after leaving Freetown the *Knysna* put in at the Cape. She had steamed close to land several times on her journey south so it came as no surprise to anyone on board that the lush jungle of the tropics, even greener than the Emerald Isle, was here faded to drab olive and sage and half-bleached khakis. What did surprise all who saw it, however, was the extraordinary bulk of Table Mountain, which, from down in the bay, appeared to live up to its name in the most literal way; half-close your eyes and you could imagine you were looking at the silhouette of a table, spread with a cloth that reached down to the floor. But open them wide and you could not help marvelling at the vast scale of the thing. Huge and brooding, its eroded slopes, all furled like the sinews on the legs of a strong Irish hunter, invited exploration. Of course, everybody had to go up it, especially when they heard that one could now ride all the way to the top in a cable car. And, since the ship would be sailing again in thirty-six hours, the visit would have to be made that very afternoon.

Debbie, however, had other things to do; she avoided an argument with Finbar by inventing a second-cousin with whom her family, the Breens of Ennistymon, had lost touch. Clutching a scrap of paper, on which a kindly member of the crew had sketched the route to the church of St Francis Xavier, she followed a confident path through the cool, winter streets of the city.

Everything was so novel. To go from high summer to midwinter in a matter of weeks! She stared up at the watery sun and had to remind herself that *that* was north. 'South' here meant Antarctica, so southerly winds could shrivel the flesh off your bones. And then there were all these black faces and brown faces – and yellow ones, too; she had never seen such a mixture of peoples. They were really surprising close-to, where you could see the colour was real, not put on from a bottle like the darkie minstrels who played in Ennis last Christmas. And how respectful they were – always stepping off the pavement to let her pass, and always with a smile. And all these trees with leaves whose shapes she'd never seen before; how fat and succulent-looking some of them were. And all the flower beds, full of giant versions of the sort of plants she'd seen in little pots in the conservatories of the quality back home. And the strange calls of the birds, too – cuckoos that weren't quite cuckoos, and blackbirds and thrushes that sang like they'd followed an Italian opera troupe around, learning all the trills and slides.

Yet there were many familiar things, too. The people wore the same fashions as they did back home; the carriages looked the same – and drove on the same side of the road, which Mrs Rourke said they wouldn't, so she was wrong. The streets had the same macadam and the pavements had the same flagstones and the same kerbs. The dogs and cats looked the same – and behaved identically to the ones she'd always known.

Still, it was those very similarities that made the differences so stark. If *everything* was different, like in Mandalay or Timbuctoo or those places, you wouldn't find any one difference so remarkable. She remembered the first time she'd crossed the Shannon and saw people cutting turf from above, standing on the bank; the only turf-cutting she knew was when the men stood level with the bank and cut horizontally into it. How wrong it had looked to see the near-vertical gashes left by the slane in the uncut bank! It was the only difference between the 'wrong' landscape and the one with which she was familiar, but – for that very reason – it practically shouted at her.

She needed but a small step from this idle reverie to the thought that there was only one difference between her family on the afternoon they had arrived at the dockside in Queenstown and that same family now, here in Cape Town. But with this reminder came the realization that for the past fifteen minutes or more she had not once thought of her great loss; such blessed forgetfulness had not relieved her once during her waking hours, ever since that awful day.

She felt a sudden pang of remorse. She *must* hold on to her grief, her guilt. Until she knew her darling little Salome was alive and well cared for, she durst not indulge the luxury of oblivion and start enjoying her new life in this new land.

The church of St Francis Xavier was less than fifty years old but it was built to look five hundred. Debbie paused between the cut-stone piers of the entrance gate as if afraid to dent the immaculate white gravel of the drive; in fact, her eye had just been caught by the flash of sunlight off the cable car making what from this distance seemed like a snail's ascent of the mountain slope, away to her right, between two Lombardy cypresses. Finbar and the children would be on that, with Mrs Rourke to look after David for her, good woman that she was; she alone knew Debbie's real purpose in making this visit today.

She watched it awhile and imagined she could hear the hum of the wire cable. It looked so thin in the sunlight. What if it broke? They wouldn't have a chance. Then it would be all her family gone. All except Salome. It would leave her free to go back and search out her child. God forgive her the thought! She stepped onto the gravel and crunched her way toward the familiar comforting outline of an honest-to-God Roman Catholic church.

"Bless me, Father, for I have sinned."

The priest's mouth was the merest slit behind the grille. Outside a woman was demonstratively wailing her Hail Marys; Debbie could see it annoyed him. "Name your sins," he intoned.

"I abandoned my child back in Ireland, Father."

The man sat up. The intrusive penance from beyond was forgotten. "Tell me more about it," he said. From Kerry, she guessed.

As she unfolded her explanation she was annoyed to see him relax. "This is no sin," he interrupted. "You clearly believed your daughter to be on board."

"Yes, but . . ."

"Didn't your son tell you so? Didn't he say they were playing hide and seek *on board?*"

"Yes, but I should have pressed him on it, Father. Sure I *know* the gossoon does be frightened of his father and of telling the truth when 'twould anger the man. I should have guessed."

"Even so, my child, this is no sin – you must accept that from me as your confessor. *It is no sin* to think later of all the things that would have been better done earlier. Call it an error – a mistake, a fault, if you will. But a *sin* is something altogether more grievous. It is committed in full knowledge of doing wrong. It is done in spite of what your conscience tells you."

"Then why do I feel this guilt?" she asked bleakly.

"Ah!" The lips parted in a sad, unhumorous smile. "We can talk about that after – if you wish?"

"After?" she echoed in surprise.

"After you have confessed to me your real sins."

She produced a familiar list of venial slips and petty falls from grace and received a familiar dole of penances.

Absolved, she left the confessional in something of a daze, feeling cheated of the drama she had thought of as her right. She had come here, weighed down with the guilt of a cardinal sin – a burden that a few decades of the Rosary were not going to lighten by much.

Her bewilderment increased when her downcast eyes saw the dark folds of the priest's soutane and the scuffed toecaps of his old boots fall in beside her. "You have a priest on board the *Knysna?*" he asked amiably. "I'm Father O'Halloran, by the way."

She wondered if it was right to give her name, so soon after a confession that was supposed to be anonymous and without fear or favour. "Deborah . . . McKenna," she said uncertainly. "Missus."

"Ah." His tone implied it was of no importance to him. He waited for her to answer his question.

"He's called Father Claffey," she said.

"Would that be John Claffey, I wonder? I was at Maynooth with a John Claffey." He caught her expression and added, "You look dubious?"

"You'll forgive me for saying so, Father, but you could give him twenty years." She thought he would turn back then; when he did not, she realized that the whole thing was a ruse to walk with her and talk about her guilt, as he had half-promised.

She knew she ought to feel grateful – and was surprised she did not. Indeed, she even felt a hint of resentment at the man's intrusion. She realized then that she did not want the *man* – Father O'Halloran – to comfort her grief; she wanted the *priest* – the huge, anonymous, impersonal machinery of her church – to wash away her guilt.

Guilt was their business; the grief was hers. She felt ashamed to make such a distinction but she could not help herself.

"While we're on the subject of age, Mrs McKenna, may I be so tactless as to ask yours?"

"I turned twenty-seven, Father, on the day we left Queenstown."

"A birthday you'll not forget!" he remarked. "I'll tell you one thing I've noticed. Young people in their twenties go in mortal fear of what the world thinks of them. By the time they reach forty, they've stopped caring, thank God. At sixty – let me tell you from personal experience – we begin to realize that the world never held any strong opinion about us *anyway* – one way or the other." He paused.

"And when we reach eighty?" she asked.

"Ah! Well, that flows out of the discovery we make at sixty – that the world is a pretty uncaring sort of place at the best of times. Then at last we begin to worry about what God thinks of us. *His* opinion gains greater relevance with every day that passes!"

"Sure we must be a great disappointment to Him," she said, puzzled as to the point of all this.

He gave her a sardonic smile and gazed all about them in a conspiratorial fashion before he murmured, "I often wonder about that."

Now she was attentive.

"Oh, I know it's what we're supposed to believe," he told her. "We're supposed to live all our lives burdened down by the guilty knowledge that we are a grievous disappointment to Him. It's the cross we must carry for Him even as He carried a far crueller cross for us."

"And isn't it so?" She gaped at him. Her heart was beating fast and her mouth was dry; she had a feeling that she stood on the verge of an important revelation.

He touched her elbow, nudging her to resume their stroll. "As I said just now, I often wonder," he replied. "If I make a machine for cutting hay and it *doesn't* cut hay, do I say to meself, 'Well, *I'm* perfect. I know I'm perfect. Doesn't the whole world keep telling me how perfect I am! So let's kick the machine into Hell!' "

Again she stopped in her tracks and stared at him agape.

And again he nudged her forward with a smile. "Don't worry," he said soothingly. "I'm not being blasphemous – just playing devil's advocate. Of course God is perfect – that's my point. If He makes a machine for 'cutting hay' and it just lies around the farmyard until it's eighty years old doing everything else under the sun *except* 'cut hay', then I think it's a fair bet He designed it that way."

"But why?" she asked, meaning really that she couldn't see much point to this conversation, anyway.

"Ah!" he exclaimed. "If we knew *that*, we'd know everything. And we will, one fine day. Until then there's nothing but faith to lean on. D'you understand what I'm saying, Mrs McKenna?"

She licked her lips hesitantly; she wished he'd call her 'my child', or something.

"I'm saying that God has some purpose in separating you and Salome. Did they let you baptize her under that name, by the way?"

"Our own priest wouldn't – Father Henty. But I found one who agreed to it."

Father O'Halloran chuckled. "There's always one! Anyway, as I was saying, God is working out some purpose of His own, using you and Salome – be sure of it. The fact you and I cannot see it yet – and may never see it this side of the grave – doesn't mean it isn't there."

Still she hesitated; the thought was so seductively comforting. She hadn't been neglectful after all, he was telling her. It was just that God had put His finger in her mind and forced her into what, on any *other* day, would have been the most dreadful neglect. How nice! That way you could hardly ever sin at all.

They were approaching the road leading down to the harbour by now. They heard laughter behind them and turned to see the earliest group to visit Table Mountain that day now coming back to the ship – Father Claffey among them.

Father O'Halloran said, "Is that your Father . . ." and then realized he had forgotten the name. Debbie smiled at his unmasking; she thought of suggesting 'Father Caughey' or something close to Claffey, just to see would he take the bait, but in the end she named him correctly.

"Of course," he said with a rueful grin. "I'll forget my own name yet. And you're quite right, Mrs McKenna – I could give him *forty* years and still come out his senior."

She wondered whether to offer to introduce them, or did priests have their own ways? He obviously decided against an immediate encounter for he began walking again, keeping a good hundred paces ahead of the others. Taking her courage in both hands she blurted out, "You're like no other priest I've ever met, if I may say so, Father O'Halloran." Her ears burned hot and she added, "Don't be taking offence now . . ."

"None taken, I assure you, my child," he replied at once. "In what particular way?"

Seeing she'd as well be hung for a sheep she said, "In just about every way, Father. Telling me my neglect was no sin, for example."

"What did you expect, then?" he asked. "What did you think a different priest might have said?"

"Sure they don't bother whether *they* think it's a sin or not. I'm sure half the things we whisper to you in confession aren't really sins at all. But if we have it on our conscience, they'll absolve us of it – sin or no sin. What's it matter when the guilt weighs as heavy?"

He pondered this in silence.

Eventually she felt she had to fill it herself. "Also coming straight out of the confessional and talking to me like that. No priest I know ever did that to me, nor to anyone I know."

"You're annoyed with me!" he exclaimed in surprise.

"You wanted a familiar and comforting ritual and I gave you . . . what? Rational talk, be all the holy! You wanted bread and I gave you stones!"

She laughed at this exaggeration and said, even more boldly, "Don't be taking on so! It was nothing like that. I admit . . ."

He interrupted, not realizing she was continuing. "Since I *am* being so unconventional, may I ask if you had already confessed your neglect to . . . well, any other priest? There's absolutely no need to answer me, of course."

"I did." She swallowed heavily.

"And were you absolved of it?"

"I was."

"Then why . . ." He hesitated. "No. I'll pry no further. But it seems that absolution for a sin that *was* no sin does nothing to ease the guilt of it, eh?"

She looked up at him and met his gaze calmly. "Lord, but I wish we were staying longer in Cape Town," she said. "You see things so clearly, Father."

"Perhaps I'm not as unusual as you suppose," he replied. "I'm sure you'll find others like me where you're going. Port Elizabeth, is it?"

She nodded.

"This is a young country still, you know. Even the 'natives' haven't been here long. The *real* natives are the Hottentots and the Bushmen. The Zulus and the Xhosa killed most of them off and took their land – and now we've done the same to them. Don't be thinking the English rule this land the way they rule Ireland. Here *all* the people – the white people, I mean – are on the one side. Even the Boers will come round to that before long. We hang together or, as the man said, the natives will hang us separately." He frowned. "Why did I start telling you this? Oh yes! The whites stick together – we're all gentry here! A priest may behave like a little Napoleon back home but he'd get short shrift from his gentrified flock if he tried it on out here! That's what I wanted to tell you."

"There's the *Knysna*," she said, for want of anything better.

"A fine, sturdy-looking vessel," he replied. "The other thing I want to tell you is this – if you're lucky, you may find God's purpose in all this before He calls you to Him. Perhaps the nuns have Salome in their care this moment. Perhaps the inquiries you and your friends are making will re-establish contact between you and perhaps she will travel out later to be reunited with you. Then you and Mister McKenna will understand how precious she is – and your other children, too. And that would be God's purpose – to strengthen your family. But perhaps you will never be reunited – or not until she has grown up. It could be that God has chosen her to be a nun in the order that is now her temporary guardian. Who knows? Thirty years from now you may meet her in this very city, doing noble work among the poor and dispossessed – and God knows they need it! Then you'll understand."

She did her best to imagine that happy outcome. Her mind's eye put the shade of a saintly-looking nun on the farther side of the road and she called it Salome and told herself what wonderful work the girl was at; but she knew that even then she would not understand. Oh yes, she'd understand *more*, but the heart of the matter would remain as opaque as ever – namely, why she had to endure all this pain so that God might ensure that outcome? If only He'd asked her, she could have told Him so many easier ways.

She smiled at the priest and said how grateful she was.

"God doesn't gamble with our lives," he assured her. "In fact, He doesn't gamble with anything."

Sure He'd hardly need to! she thought – but again she kept her peace.

13

Culham-Browne swilled his whiskey round in the glass, round and round and round, following the movement with his eyes. Marion, absorbed in repairs she was making to Too Small, Rachel's old teddy bear, watched him warily out of the corner of her eye; he was building up to some kind of outburst. She could feel it. Sometimes, she thought, life at Cloonaghvogue would be calmer if it had been built on the slopes of Mount Etna.

"Is someone watering it again?" she asked when he had swilled it round for the twentieth time and still not tasted it.

"Say?" he barked.

She breathed in and out rather heavily, only just avoiding a sigh – for fear it would provoke him. She said nothing.

"We'll get a second cut off that grass this year," he put in.

"We've had almost two weeks of brilliant sunshine by day and rain at night," she said. "It's uncanny."

He remembered there was some part of the world where they could predict the weather like that – rainclouds massing after tiffin every day – you could set your clocks by it. But he couldn't remember where. Worse, he'd forgotten, until this moment, that he'd ever known of such places. He was used by now to forgetting this and that but the experience of forgetting that he had already forgotten something was novel and alarming. He stared at the whiskey and the words *pickle your brain* ran across his thoughts. Old Doc Hooke had a brain in a bottle in his surgery. Pickled in alcohol. It came from some house in Tipperary where Bram Stoker wrote *Dracula*.

How could one remember trivial, useless little things like

that and forget important things like . . . like . . .

Forgotten again!

He slung the whiskey into a clump of willow-leaved hebe at the side of the terrace – and instantly regretted it.

"Watered?" she asked again.

He glanced guiltily toward the open french window. "Walter?" he asked. He was pretty sure no friend of theirs was called Walter but perhaps that was another of those things he had forgotten – or forgotten-forgotten. He didn't want to reveal such a lapse by directly challenging her. "Where?"

This time she did risk a sigh, but she held Too Small at arm's length, suggesting that *it* was the cause of her perplexity. "It's the shape of the head," she murmured. "No matter where you put the eye it looks wrong." She kissed the creature coyly and added, "Accept it, little thing – you were born to be boss-eyed." On a happier tone she added, "And I don't suppose Salome will mind."

"Hah!" C-B grunted. "The divil she will!"

"Don't swear, dear," Marion said mechanically, knowing it would infuriate him. She herself swore quite frequently – and with words a lot worse than 'divil' – and they both knew it. Her reprimand would make him so angry he wouldn't even know where to begin. She wondered why she did things like that. But in her heart of hearts she knew why – because the alternative between them was warmth, love . . . *intimacy*. Even the word could make her shudder.

Anger and good breeding conspired to redirect his spleen against the little cuckoo in their nest. "That child has become an obsession with you," he fumed. "I really don't consider it healthy. If it persists . . ." He hesitated.

She raised her cool green eyes and stared at him calmly, challenging him to flesh out his threat.

He met her gaze and felt his stomach fall away inside him. How, with all the animosity that had now grown up between them, all the spite, the bickering, could he still love her so passionately – desire her with this intensity? But it wasn't love, another voice inside him said; it was old one-eyed Polyphemus down there, cock-o'-the-walk.

"If it persists . . .?" she prompted him icily.

"How much longer are you going to be?" he snapped.

The slow traverse of her gaze settled on the clock over the stables. "It's only nine, dear."

That bright little 'dear' was like the stab of a bodkin. She knew what he meant. She knew what he wanted. And she knew he'd never say it out loud, not in so many words. You could understand why gentlemen let their wives get on with the garden parties and At Homes and sought solace elsewhere; but as long as her eyes, her beauty, her youth could stir him like this, there *was* no 'elsewhere' for him. He was as yoked to her as if they were mutually bound by chains of Toledo steel.

"I said I think the child is becoming an obsession with you," he repeated.

Marion did not rise to it. "You're probably right, dear. But then she's hardly been here six weeks . . ."

"Eight," he snapped. "Eight weeks, all but two days."

She waved a hand, as if shooing off a fly. "Whatever. The novelty will pass. The wonder will dim. This rosy glow will fade . . ."

These were the sort of wet blankets he had so often cast over her past enthusiasms; it amused her to throw them back at him now, especially since they implied that, even if her obsession (as he called it) was unhealthy, it was also self-curing. Time would kill it off – so she could indulge it without fearing it might swell into madness.

"You know yourself now," she added, "the worst thing to do with obsessions is to thwart them."

She had not meant to refer to his obsession with her but that is how he took it. He turned on his heel and went back indoors to replace the whiskey he had jettisoned – leaving her angry with herself for not picking her provocations more carefully.

Then her anger became more generalized. Why should she have to pick her provocations at all? Why could she not be more friendly to him? Why could two civilized people, brought up in the same beliefs, sharing, by and large, identical attitudes, not live together in a more civilized manner? Why these endless dog-fights? Why could they not behave in private as they did when they were 'on parade', as he called it? She was sure none of their friends imagined there was the slightest division between her and C-B.

She had a vague intimation, too fleeting for her to pin down, that it had something to do with closeness, physical propinquity . . . territory. Apropos dog-fights, there had been a minor squabble earlier that evening between Rory and Ranter, two of the wolfhounds. Ranter had turned over in her sleep and had lain half-across Rory; normally they were the best of friends – indeed, Rory had sired two of Ranter's litters, and you can hardly get more friendly than that! But her unintentional trespass had been too much for him this evening. And when two massive hounds like that fall out, even a minor squabble is frightening to behold.

Territory . . .

She lost the thread of her thought. Only the aftertaste of her annoyance lingered.

14

Salome opened the eye farthest from Miss Kinchy, the housekeeper, and let it linger happily on Too Small, who had entered her life that afternoon by way of recompense for the loss of Maggoty Meg. Aunt Marion said she wasn't to mind his boss eye but – apart from the fact that she had no idea what 'boss eye' meant – she could see no difference between the two X-shapes of wool (which is what the eyes were, really).

Miss Kinchy, who could see the far side of Salome's head in the looking glass, noticed her inattention and despaired for her immortal soul. But she was also a kindly, roly-poly, motherly sort of a woman who would have loved to marry and have children of her own, and to raise them in the fear of God and the mercy of Mary. Now, at the age of forty-three, she realized her chances of seeing that dream come true were vanishingly small, so she must make the best of what God in His mercy set before her. "Oh child!" she said sorrowfully, interrupting her prayer. "If even I can see you letting your eye wander about the room – coveting worldly goods like that – d'you imagine the Dear One above can not?"

Racked with sudden guilt, Salome clamped her eyes so tightly that she soon saw stars and strange coloured lights shooting behind her eyelids. She wondered was it a glimpse of heaven?

"Who didn't we include in our prayers yet?" Miss Kinchy asked.

"Maggoty Meg and Too Small," the girl replied. "Is it Too Small or Tooth Mall?" She had only lately grasped the distinction between a proper ess-sound and a lisp and so she liked to be careful.

"Never mind," the housekeeper scolded, "keep your mind on your devotions now. We didn't pray for your little brother, did we?"

"Oh no!" Salome wet her lips and began: "God bless . . ." Then came a moment of panic. She had forgotten her brother's name! Samson? No, that was the older one.

"D-d-d . . .?" Miss Kinchy stuttered a hint.

"David!" The relief was enormous. "God bless David and make him grow big and strong."

"And good."

"And good."

This was the first occasion on which Miss Kinchy had been asked to hear Salome say her prayers; she wondered whether the mistress (who was at a charity dinner that evening) had difficulties like this in making the girl concentrate – with her chatter flying off at all angles all the time and saying things that would puzzle you round the clock till you suddenly woke up to what she had meant. Now, finally, came the bit she was most nervous about – the Lord's Prayer in the Church of Ireland version with all that extra business about, 'Thine is the Kingdom, the Power and the Glory, for ever and ever.' They never spoke those words at Mass, so she was sure they were part of the Protestant heresy. Could she in good conscience permit the child to say them? Could she say them herself if the child stumbled?

It did not help matters that the Culham-Brownes were so tolerant. Himself had paid for half the new presbytery back in 1905, to mark his wedding to Herself. And hadn't his father, Kelso Culham-Browne, built the entire chapel for the RCs after the famine times? And you'd always see him at a funeral, bowing his head respectfully during the Rosary even though you knew he'd consider it the prayer of the Antichrist. So it was hard not to be tolerant back. But, on the other hand, Father Hines had kicked Seamus Hogan, whose mother was Protestant, for standing *outside* the Protestant church during his sister's funeral – and kicked him so hard he'd left him lame for life. So what was the right thing to do, at all?

Salome began to gabble the Lord's Prayer.

Miss Kinchy made her slow down but, being still perplexed by the conflict between tolerance and faith, did not listen to her words: "Our Father, charting heaven, Harold be thy name . . ." which was what the child had made of the new, unfamiliar Protestant version. Only when she reached, "And deliver us some evil, amen!" – and sprang joyously to her feet – did Miss Kinchy take notice.

"Here, you haven't finished, child," she remonstrated.

"I did, so, ma'am," Salome assured her, snatching up Too Small and hugging him so hard that, had his eyes been real, they would have popped right out of his head.

"What about," the woman steeled herself to utter the heretical words: "For Thine is the Kingdom . . . ?"

Salome stared at her blankly and then said, "Oh . . . yes!" like one who has forgotten something newly learned.

The hair bristled on the back of Miss Kinchy's scalp. "For the love of God, colleen – did you never say those words with your Mammy?"

Salome shook her head.

"For Thine is the Kingdom, the Power and the Glory . . . You never spoke them?"

Again she shook her head. "But I like them, honestly," she offered placatingly.

"Nor even heard them before?"

"Oh, yes – in church here at Cloonaghvogue." She was desperately insistent.

"I believe you. Don't fret, now. I do believe you." Miss Kinchy's mind was racing. It had never occurred to her that Salome might be a Roman Catholic. 'Salome' wasn't any sort of a name she could imagine any sort of a priest permitting for baptism. And she *looked* so Protestant, too. Not that Miss Kinchy could have said what she meant by that, but anyone who saw Salome all dressed in Miss Rachel's Sunday frocks and white gloves, and going off hand in hand with Herself to church, would have to agree; anyone seeing her would say, 'That's surely a wee Protestant colleen.'

Guiltily she looked over her shoulder before, with bated breath and lowered voice, she said, "Say me a Hail Mary, then? See if you can remember."

Salome screwed up her eyes and rattled it off the way she'd always heard it: "Hail Mary full of grace blessed art thou among women and blessed is the fruit of thy room Jesus."

Miss Kinchy pursed her lips to correct the single mistake and then thought better of it. Time enough for that. At this moment it was far more important to digest this astonishing discovery.

Should she tell Father Hines?

Of course she should!

And yet she hesitated, already knowing – by some intuitive process that baffled reason – that she would not tell her priest. She was too fond of Herself – and too admiring of what she had done – to sow the seeds of what would be a bitter dissension in the parish. Father Hines was a terrier when it came to things like that. He'd not deny the tolerance and generosity of the Culham-Brownes, yet he'd not permit it to stand in his way when it was a matter of righting a wrong. He'd turn over every stone in every parish in Ireland to track down Salome's kinsfolk. And then he'd raise a legal fund to fight for her custody, to restore her to her own people and to the faith of her forefathers. God forgive her, but Miss Kinchy could not bring herself to destroy so many lives, just for the sake of righteousness.

Casting around for some small article of faith on which she could hang this monstrous decision, she remembered that Father Mee SJ had preached at her last retreat that in *certain* circumstances, *certain* Protestants might, by the infinite mercy of God, be let into heaven – if they were indoctrinated before the years of understanding and had lived good lives by the light of their faith. He excluded Methodists, Baptists, and Nonconformists in general, but not Church of Ireland Protestants. True, Father Hines had later preached a sermon after Father Mee left, saying he had been in error and that *all* who did not worship the Virgin went straight to Hell for all eternity. But he couldn't get over the fact that Father Mee was a Jesuit and knew more about the faith than a mere secular priest like himself.

So if Father Mee said Salome might be saved, though reared a Protestant before her years of understanding, that was all she needed to know.

"Tell me a story?" Salome begged.

"What story?" Miss Kinchy was flustered.

"A pome, then – *please!*" The amazing grey-green eyes stared up at her.

"I don't know a pome," she confessed. "Except I know one that's a riddle, will I tell you that?"

Salome grinned and snuggled down between the cool linen sheets, still hugging Too Small tight against her.

"I'm long, lean, and lustrous though I have but one eye," Miss Kinchy intoned. "Back and forth o'er the field, just see me fly! This way and that I lepp o'er the gap. Yet ever I leave my tail in the trap. Who am I?"

"Miss Kinchy," Salome replied confidently.

"No! Of course I'm Miss Kinchy – I don't need to ask *you* that. I'm pretending to be someone else. Or some*thing* else. What can it be? Listen again." And she repeated the riddle to the child.

"I like pretending to be someone else," Salome told her when she'd done. "Will I tell you who I like to pretend to be?"

"I asked you a question first – my riddle. You can't answer it, can you!"

"What's lustrous mean?"

"Shiny. Gleaming like a new . . . well, glittering, anyway."

"I like to pretend to be Rachel," Salome said.

Suddenly the riddle and its answer were forgotten. Miss Kinchy sat bolt upright. "Sure how would you know about her? Does Mrs Culham-Browne be telling you about her?"

Salome shook her head. "*You* could, though. Tell me a story about her, please?"

The eyes made it impossible to refuse. Miss Kinchy had once heard Himself muttering something rueful about 'those eyes' and now she understood what he had meant. "Wasn't she the darlin' of the western world," she began.

"Make her *good*," Salome urged happily. "Make her the bestest little girl ever."

"I don't need to, colleen." Miss Kinchy suddenly saw the chance to palm off some valuable moral and social lessons under the guise of this 'story'. In truth, Rachel had been no better and no worse than any other little girl of seven, but she now became such a paragon of all the virtues – even to 'plucking the very snails from the mistle-thrush's beak!' – that Salome herself, notwithstanding that she had begged to be so entertained, grew bored and sleepy. She dropped off just when the housekeeper had started listing the number of little dens Rachel had made for all the wild animals in the garden.

She smoothed the sheet at Salome's neck and straightened up Too Small (who, to her way of thinking was more tipsy than boss-eyed). Then she leaned over and planted a feather-light kiss on the little girl's unfurrowed brow. She thought of the family she herself would now never have and an incipient tear sprouted in her eye.

And then she knew what really lay behind her decision to say nothing to Father Hines – nor to anyone else, either – of the dreadful secret she had learned that evening.

15

Algoa Bay is almost as far as you can get from the tropics – and therefore as close as you can get to Antarctica – in the whole continent of Africa. In high-summer January, when the grass burns yellow and the heat is a living devil, you might not suspect it, but on the day when the *Knysna* dropped anchor there, Sunday, 27th July, 1913, none could doubt that the Ice Continent, itself in the grip of winter darkness, lay only a few horizons away to the south. A mockingly bright sun hung low in the northern sky, casting deep blue pools of shade across the town and port of Port Elizabeth, built on the steeply sloping hillside above the only natural harbour for a hundred miles and more. Even then, it had required a jetty and breakwater almost three hundred yards long before steamships the size of the *Knysna* could berth there.

As if to emphasize the special character of the place the hill, barely a mile long, descended to a rolling coastal plain on either side. The dense cover of thorns, shrubby trees, succulents, and sere grass – known collectively as 'the bush' – made the huddled buildings seem quite incongruous.

To the McKennas, standing at the rail among the dozens of others who were to disembark here, it was a forlorn sight indeed. They had thought their native Ireland a wild enough place; visitors were always telling them so. But at least there was a network of roads to hint at order and communication, and a reticule of stone walls and ditches marked the brand of Arable Man on even the most inhospitable hillside. By contrast, this Port Elizabeth, though its fine stone buildings seemed as grand as any they had seen in Cork or Limerick, looked like the venture of a lunatic. How could this huddled outpost of a grand civilization survive with nothing about it but this cold, parched, inhospitable bush?

Georgina Delaroux came down the companionway from the first class and joined them. "What d'you think, eh?" she asked brightly.

Debbie glanced at her and gave a hopeless shrug.

"Is that what they call farming country?" Finbar asked dourly. "What class of things would grow there, at all?"

"Where is the farm?" Debbie asked brightly, thinking that her husband's glumness made him sound rather surly.

Georgina stretched an arm over Debbie's shoulder and

sighted along her pointing finger. "Count the headlands. One, two, three . . . that one's called Skoenmaakerskop – shoe-maker's head. Then there are two more out of sight. And then you can just see the tip of another – almost lost in the haze. That's called Saint Francis Bay and the farm we're going to is just there."

"What's it called again?"

"Oppgedroogtefontejn." She parodied the Afrikaans gutturals.

"Sure I'll never get my tongue round all that," Debbie told her.

"Nor me. I propose to call it Fountains, instead," Georgina said firmly. "It means 'dried-up fountain', you know."

"You said."

"I suppose whatever fountain dried up can be made to flow again," Finbar put in. "It all depends on why it went dry."

"Mister Delaroux believes it to be a good omen, anyway." Georgina spoke with finality, as if her husband's opinion were all that mattered. "However, I just wanted to point it out to you before we steam farther inshore and it passes out of sight. We'll meet up on the quay and have a slap-up luncheon at the hotel before we set off." She crouched down, eye to eye with Samson, and smiled directly into his face. "Cheer up, Sunny Jim! We'll find her yet – and bring her out to join us – never fear!"

The little boy smiled wanly but was not to be so easily comforted. "I thought she was on board with us," he said. "Honest."

"Of course you did!" She tousled his hair and, with a brief smile of commiseration at his parents, left them at the rail. The headland of Fountains, as they were now to call the farm, was already masked by the nearer coastline.

As they drew in to the quayside, Debbie found herself scanning the faces among the waiting crowds; it was a moment or two before she realized she was looking for Salome. She had prayed so long and so devoutly – and so sincerely – for a miracle that, although she did not expect one to happen, she would not have been altogether surprised to see a man in the livery of the Algoa Line standing down there and holding her little girl by the hand. They could have found her within an hour of the sailing. They could have put her on the next boat, a faster one that didn't stop at Freetown. There could have been a mix-up with the cables . . .

Of course it *would* be a miracle to leave a child behind on the quayside at Queenstown and find her waiting for you here on the quayside at Port Elizabeth, three weeks later. But it was the sort that could happen – not like flying without wings or bringing the dead back to life. She found her Rosary in her pocket and fingered the beads once again: "Hail Mary, full of grace . . ."

Finbar, who knew well what she was at, touched her elbow gently; they had three other children to look after – specifically at this moment, to bring ashore all in one piece.

The quay was narrow and the gangway had to be pitched steeply. The men were compelled to bring their families ashore and then go back for the wanted-on-voyage luggage.

"Third time on Africa!" Samson cried as he leapt the last yard from gangway to quayside; the guilty misery of ten minutes ago was effaced by this new excitement.

"Third time lucky," his father added.

"Over here, McKenna!" Paul Delaroux, who had been ashore for ten minutes already, called from a little way down the quay.

The McKennas set off to join them. As he drew near Finbar explained that he had to go back for their bags, but Delaroux said 'one of the boys' would do that after lunch. "Don't let 'em see you doing unnecessary manual work," he advised when he was close enough to lower his voice. "Skilled work, yes, but not simple hod-carrying." He dramatized their new relationship by clapping Finbar on the shoulder and saying, "Welcome to democracy – we're all democrats here!"

Debbie glanced uncertainly at Georgina, who nodded back and smiled brightly, as if to say, 'It's all true!'

Little Martha let go her mother's hand and, planting her feet wide apart, held out her hands, like one struggling to find her balance. "The land is swelling!" she cried.

For a moment none of them understood what she meant; then her elder brother exclaimed, "Yes! She means the ground is going up and down like the swell of the sea. And it is, so it is."

Debbie stood still a moment and closed her eyes. A smile spread across her face. "They're right!" She opened her eyes and clutched at the air to steady herself.

The others tried it and soon all were agreed that when you stood quite still – and especially when you shut your eyes – the solid land seemed as turbulent as the rolling ocean had seemed steady, only an hour or so earlier. Paul Delaroux tapped his forehead and said, "It's all in here." Looking straight at Debbie he added, "The mind and body can adapt to anything in time."

Georgina darted a swift glance at Finbar and found him watching Paul with intense but inscrutable eyes; she had an intuition that here was a man with a powerful capacity for jealousy – something of which Paul, with his easy-going, even flirtatious, ways, should be warned.

A Native policeman on the dock gate waved them out with hardly a glance. They walked up a short, gently sloping street, between impressively grand buildings of a commercial nature, and emerged into a neatly kept market square.

"Would you look at that!" Finbar pointed away to the east. "Isn't that as grand as Union Street in Cork itself!"

"Except it runs straight," Debbie said.

"The Feather Market . . . the Post Office . . ." Paul gave them a brief orientation course. "We have no deliveries out to Oppgedroogtefontejn . . . sorry! No delivery to Fountains. We have to come in here a couple of times each week and open our box."

Debbie looked inquiringly at Georgina, then at Finbar. "I don't suppose . . ." she said hesitantly.

"Sure, who knows we're taken on at Fountains?" he reminded her gently.

"Even so," she persisted.

"There might be something with poste restante." Georgina agreed with her. "You never know. We could drop by on our way back – while the men see to our baggage."

The road from the port continued across one side of the market square and then rose steeply up the hill upon and around which the town was built. A chill southerly breeze funnelled its way between the tall buildings and soughed through the bare-branched trees, hustling them onward. They had covered a third of the distance to the crest when Paul turned into a side street to their right. Here they discovered that the central part of the hill was a large open space, mostly grass, covering perhaps twenty acres – or ten morgen, as they must now learn to measure it. Paul led the way up a diagonal footpath that brought them to the brow of the hill at the centre of the green. "You can see the whole town from here – or at least see how it's laid out. This green, by the way, is called the Donkin Reserve, given to the town by Sir Someone-or-other Donkin in memory of his wife, Elizabeth. Hence *Port* Elizabeth. It's all written up on a plaque on that obelisk." He pointed out a large stone pyramid at the centre of the green. "To the east of the town it's mostly Malay fishermen. From Malaya," he added when he saw the word meant nothing to them.

"Would you believe!" Debbie murmured.

"It's a real hodge-podge of peoples here," he assured her. "Malays, Indians, Chinese, Zulus, Xhosas, Bantu, Dutch, French, English – and us. A Tower of Babel – you'll see!"

On the farther side of the open green stood one obvious hôtel – their present destination. It was flanked by rather grand houses whose gardens were full of stately cedars and wellingtonias, planted almost a century ago and now well on their way to maturity.

"Wasn't it a great notion to keep all this green between the houses and the town," Finbar said admiringly.

Paul sniffed. "I'm not too sure of that, McKenna. Look!" He turned and swept a hand across the view behind them.

They were only halfway across the green but already the town, or the commercial part of it, was out of sight below the brow of the hill. Only the tops of the masts of the vessels in port gave any indication of commercial activity down there. For the rest it was just grass and the endless expanse of the Indian Ocean, most of which simply vanished in the chill winter haze.

"How easy it must be," Paul went on, "for all the grand people in all these fine houses to forget the commercial life of the town. Out of sight, out of mind, as the man said."

"Sure where's the harm in that, sir?" Finbar responded.

"Harm is it! We all know – or know *of* – families who made their money in trade and manufacturing, whose children turned their backs on their origins, and whose grandchildren were back at the factory lathe or shop counter. England's downfall – and Ireland's curse. They shouldn't hide from commerce as if it were something squalid."

Georgina wanted to tell him he no longer had any need to justify his decision to become 'a working man', as he put it – to make a joke of what he felt as a shame. Not out here in the Cape, and most certainly not to the McKennas, who wouldn't understand his scruples anyway.

At the hôtel they ran a gauntlet of more than a dozen Native 'boys' – doormen, porters, pages, and waiters – all in starched white tunics and white gloves, which had the curious effect of making their black faces almost disappear. They fascinated Martha, who still could not decide whether or not to be afraid of them. One stooped and picked her up, jogging her on his hip and clucking his tongue as if to start a horse. She laughed in delight, for it was a favourite game, all the way to the dining room. When he made to put her down she squirmed in protest and then, with a cheeky glance at her mother, solemnly wiped her finger down the side of the man's face. She inspected the tip of it and then stared at him, slightly puzzled.

He grinned at her and shook his head slowly.

Then, without protest, she let herself be set down.

They all went off to wash and brush up before settling down to the most ambitious buffet lunch they had eaten in many a month – indeed, in the McKennas' case, for many a year. Some of the food was familiar – mulligatawny soup and cold roast beef and bubble-and-squeak. But there were dishes of Indian and Chinese provenance there, too, some hot, some merely spicy. Finbar was so conservative in matters of food that Debbie did not even try to persuade him, so she was greatly surprised when Georgina said to him, "You really ought to try one of these," and popped a spicy little sausage on a wooden pin between his lips – and he ate it with relish and even went for more.

Paul, watching Debbie as she watched this tableau, and seeing her eyes narrow and harden, wondered how firmly she was wedded to this man of uncertain temperament. It must be hell for her, he thought; one moment he'd be gentle as a loon, next he'd fly off the handle and lay down laws that no one could follow. He was a man to keep on the right side of, that was certain – but also a man who, with the proper handling, could be led in almost any direction without his being aware that the choice wasn't his.

The future, he thought, looked promising.

16

The southern winter had gone and spring was well advanced. Rains had briefly justified Georgina's renaming of the farm as Fountains but now, in November, the intimation of summer was on each dawn and the lusher vegetation had already traded the adolescent brilliance of its green for something quieter and more mature.

"The curious thing is we average thirty-six inches of rain a year in these parts," Uncle Harry pointed out. "That's as much as some regions of Ireland – but where's the green to go with it? Riddle me that, ye Trinity scholars!"

Uncle Harry, who was Georgina's father's brother, fascinated the children, who were by now his courtesy nephews and niece. He was full of odd little quips and sayings and he knew all about the bush and even the ostriches were afraid of him a little; but the main focus of their fascination was a large 'canker' – as he called it – on his cheek. Every now and then, when it got too big, he took out a knife and pruned it. Then he drank whiskey and went to sleep while the bleeding stopped. He cut tasty little slivers of biltong with the same knife. Mammy said they were to refuse it politely, for fear they'd catch cankers in their tummies, but it was so delicious and Uncle Harry offered it with such an understanding wink – as if he were saying, 'Sure we all know what fussers the women are!' – it was hard to obey her command.

"All that rain must go somewhere," Finbar said.

The old man jabbed his finger earthwards a couple of times and gave a sage wink. "*He* gets it all! Not that it will cool *his* flames by one degree. Isn't that a waste, now."

"Some of it must linger somewhere," Georgina put in.

"Or I'd have no walk before breakfast," Debbie added in support. Her first chore of the day was to go the half-mile between the house and the clifftop, descend the zigzag path that meandered across the slope of it, and look at the level of the water in the little concrete reservoir. If it was above a certain mark, she went on down to the foot of the cliff and started the hydraulic ram. This handy little device required no other energy than the head of water in the reservoir, two-thirds of which went to waste in order to pump the remainder up to the farm. If the level was below the mark, she still started the ram but she had to stay by it twenty minutes and then stop it again. That hadn't happened yet but they said it would in January, quite often – unless they found a better supply before then, which was the point of their present earnest conversation.

"Yes." Paul added his pennyworth. "That reservoir is filled from a spring, surely? It's the point where some natural underground reservoir overflows."

Harry laughed, not unkindly. "So all we have to do, you think, is buy some blasting compound and smash out a hole, following Alph the sacred river back until we come upon the caverns measureless to man?"

Paul shifted uneasily. His wife's uncle did not mean to mock, he felt sure, yet his effortless parade of knowledge and common sense often had that effect. He glanced at Finbar, who always relapsed into silence when the 'oul' wan' started playing Socrates; he wished he had the same capacity, except that he'd never learn anything unless he challenged old Harry and made him come out with what he knew. "Why not?" he asked. "It might be only a few yards inside the cliff."

"And then again it might not. In fact, Mrs McKenna already *knows* it's not. I'll go further and say she already knows it's a fair distance inland."

Everyone stared at Debbie, amazed that she had kept this knowledge to herself. But she was well used to his manner by now. A couple of months ago, when they first settled into the little community at Fountains, she'd have risen to the bait and expostulated she knew no such thing; now she merely smiled and told him she'd been keeping it a secret for she liked to slip into it for a wee swim on her way back from the cliff each morning. She flashed him a brief grin as if to say, 'So there!'

Harry wagged a reproving finger at her and said to the others, "She thinks she doesn't know, but she does!"

Two months earlier he'd have addressed the remarks directly to her but now she had the measure of him, he knew better; so they had both learned something.

"I'll prove it," he said, turning to her. "D'you recall the heavy rain we had in August, when it rained nonstop for two days?"

She nodded warily. No harm so far.

"And what was it you said to me when it ended?"

Debbie had to think. She had said so many things for he seemed to enjoy talking to her in his provoking, bantering, humorous manner.

"About the water level in the concrete tank?" he prompted.

"Oh yes. Didn't I say I was amazed it had gone up so little. After two days with the whole of God's heaven wide open like that."

"And it comes out by the pipe at what rate, would you say? A bucket a minute?"

Debbie shook her head. "Less. 'Twould take longer than a minute to fill a bucket."

"But less than two? Very well. When the real drought is on us, you'll still find it flowing at almost the same rate. A bucketful every two minutes, let's say. So what does that tell us? Suppose the measureless cavern is just ten feet behind the cliff face?" The comic arches of his eyebrows punctuated the question.

"Then 'tis seeping out by way of a very narrow crack,"

Debbie replied. "But isn't that unlikely?"

He waved an impresario's hand toward the others. "Didn't I tell ye? And if the main body of the water is a fair way inland – under this house, for instance?"

"Then 'tis a long, twisted, narrow way out. But that's more likely, I'm thinking."

"And so am I, Mrs McKenna!" He beamed at the entire company. "In short, the fact that we have one lone spring on the whole farm, and it hardly varies with the rainfall, has always suggested to me that we have a large underground cistern of water somewhere, which is well contained inside impervious rock."

"Have you ever tried to find it, Uncle?" Georgina asked.

He jerked a thumb toward Paul and Finbar. "There are some things three men can do that one can not."

They started the very next day – not, however, by hiring a rock-boring rig but by going down to the wetlands beyond the hydraulic ram and cutting twigs of hazel, one for each man . . . "And one for Samson," Harry insisted.

Back at the clifftop he directed them to spread out and start walking slowly inland, keeping as near abreast of one another as they could among the scrub and the dry, eroded gullies of the ostrich 'pasture'.

Samson concentrated hard on his dowsing twig, holding it just the way Uncle Harry had shown him. He was certain, however, that he was going to be a failure at it. God had not let His countenance shine favourably upon him ever since he'd left Salome behind in Queenstown. She kept appearing to him in dreams – or a girl everyone else called Salome kept appearing, though he could see it wasn't her. He took Maggoty Meg to bed with him every night and pretended she turned into Salome, which she sometimes actually did. Then he'd talk and talk to her – tell her everything – in his quietest voice. It was the only speaking he could manage nowadays without stammering all the time. His father said if he didn't stop stammering, he'd be sent away, but he never said where.

He stumbled over a root and fell headlong into the dust. There was a sharp pain under his jaw where the dowsing twig was jabbing into the skin. He pulled it away and felt himself gingerly. No blood. Not even a scratch. He forgot it at once.

His eyes refocused about two inches beyond the tip of his nose and he found he was staring down into an ant-lion pit, miraculously undisturbed. Even as he watched, a black ant slithered into it and began its fruitless climb up the sloping sides – succeeding only in scrabbling down the fine grains of sand so cunningly spread there by the maker of this conical trap. He watched in fascination as the first grains of sand rolled to the bottom; what a frightening place the world would be if you were as small as that! The ant-lion, alerted by the thistledown touch of the sand, came swimming – the only word for its curious motion – out of hiding, pounced on the unfortunate little insect, and carried it back below ground, where its death throes continued to disturb the surface for a brief while.

There was a sudden stinging pain on Samson's backside and then his father was shouting at him for being such an idle, shiftless, good-for-nothing. In the middle of his howling and his pleas not to be hit more Samson heard Uncle Harry's voice saying sharply, "Don't move! Either of you!"

Finbar started to protest, saying that Mr Williams had no right . . . but the rest of his words died in his throat. In the deafening silence that followed Samson raised his eyes, only to find himself staring straight into the beady, almost glass-looking eye of a full-grown cobra, its head about a foot off the ground and its hood magnificently deployed. It was too beautiful to fear.

Everyone had warned him about snakes and they all went about in high leather boots in the bush, but this was the first he had actually seen – apart from darting shapes that someone told him after had been snakes; this was the first that had stood its ground. He watched its feathery tongue dart in and out, drawing attention to a mouth that seemed pursed in a startled whistle.

"Stay quite still," Uncle Harry added.

There was a metallic click. He must have drawn his revolver. Samson longed to turn and see it.

"Ya little hoor!" came his father's angry cry.

He cowered from further chastisement, but for once his father did not mean him. He took one almighty kick at the snake, missed, and was lucky not to bring himself tumbling down.

The cobra darted its upreared head to one side and then struck out at the leg that remained planted on the sand. It reckoned without hardened leather and steel-ringed lace-holes, though, which deflected it to the ground. Then, more by fortune than by judgment, Finbar, in trying to regain his balance, managed to bring the heel of his other boot down on the creature's head.

"Good man!" called Harry from behind.

The creature's tail lashed about furiously, throwing up dust and catching Samson a mighty blow on the ear – which at last galvanized him into scrabbling backward, out of range of the thing. Uncle Harry was shouting, "For the love of God keep him pinned whatever you do!"

He was stuffing his revolver back in its holster with one hand and drawing his knife from its scabbard with the other. He fell to his knees at Finbar's side. Paul, who had been way over to the right, came running up at that moment, just in time to see his wife's uncle sever the cobra's head with one firm stroke of his knife. "You're all right now," he said, calm again.

Finbar leaped back as if the severed head had powers of its own to pursue him. The tail went on writhing in the sand. Samson was surprised to see so little blood; the severed end of it soon acquired a heavy coating of dust. "Is it dead?" he asked, approaching it in renewed fascination.

As if to answer him the cobra head wiped its eyes with a curious 'wrong-way' swipe of its nictitating membrane and stared at him, bright as a button.

"Snakes never die till sunset," Harry told him.

"Not even if you cut them in a hundred pieces? Not even if you cut them in a *thousand* pieces?"

Harry laughed. "Would you hark at the boy! Listen!" He stared solemnly into Samson's eyes. "You could burn them to nothing, if you wished, but the very *ashes* wouldn't die until the sun went down. So there, now!" He produced a small flour bag from one of his voluminous pockets and, picking up the carcass, dropped it inside and tightened the drawstring.

"Are you going to bury it?" Samson asked.

"Yes!" Uncle Harry chuckled and patted his belly. "In here."

The boy looked up at Finbar, hoping for some clue as to whether he should believe this reply or just laugh at it; to his surprise he saw his father just standing there shivering, eyes closed, face pale as chalk.

Uncle Harry clapped him on the shoulder. "Bravely done, man," he said, "but foolhardy in the extreme, let me tell you."

"The boy," his father murmured, almost as if he wished Samson not to hear him. "It'd have got the boy."

"Don't tell *me!*" Harry replied, but Finbar didn't take the hint – or, if he did, he failed to act upon it. The most he could do was smile feebly at his son and look away.

Samson thought his heart would burst with all the wild, contradictory feelings that now contended for occupation there.

"Dear God – look!" Harry bent down and clamped his hand round Finbar's left leg, the one the cobra had struck at. "Hold still. Just squat down and have a dekko at this."

Paul and Finbar went down on their haunches together. Samson, still fascinated by the writhing *thing* in Uncle Harry's pocket (not to mention the thought of eating it later), joined them just as the tip of the old man's knife pointed out a drop of fluid nestling in a little indentation in the leather. "There's enough there to stop your heart in its tracks," he said.

"Venom?" Paul asked, taking the knife and scraping off all he could. He held it up for Samson to look at.

"Curiously enough," Harry went on, "the Kaffir doctors collect it and mix it with mealie flour for treating *feeble* hearts. A little goes a long way, as the bishop said."

"Does it work?" Paul asked skeptically.

"Of course it works! *Anything* works if you believe in it firmly enough." He rose again. "Come on! We've got an underground lake to find." He saw Samson gazing in renewed fascination at the severed head, still staring back with its beady eyes. "D'you want it?" he asked.

The boy gaped at him, unable to believe his luck.

Harry took his knife back, lifted the head on the point of it, and wiped it off in a forked branch of a nearby Kaffir thorn. "Now," he said, "we'll come back at sundown and – if the kommetjiegatvoel hasn't passed this way and stolen it – we'll bring it home."

"What's a comicky . . . – what you said?" Samson asked.

Harry laughed uproariously and said, "A very special bird with a very amusing anatomy. I tell you – he'll get the shock of his life if he tries his usual tricks on *that!*"

And with that enigmatic 'explanation', which left the other men as mystified as the boy, they resumed their attempts to dowse for the lake they weren't even sure existed – not within the boundaries of the farm, anyway.

It was a slow, uneventful stroll until they came within sight of the house. Then Samson gave a sudden yelp. The bush here was sparse and they all turned to see what creature of the wild might be threatening his life this time. He stared guiltily at his father, expecting yet more curses and sneers at his inadequacy, but, to his surprise, his father's gaze was questioning rather than critical. "It just lepped out me hands!" he shouted, pointing to his forked twig, not really expecting to be believed. " 'Clare to God," he added lamely.

Uncle Harry came running to him. "Pick it up," he said excitedly. "Show me."

The moment Samson had the twig in his hands it began to twist and writhe as the snake had done under the heel of his father's boot. He watched it helplessly, not knowing whether to be horrified or elated.

"You're not messing, now?" Finbar asked sternly, but his rising tone at the end betrayed his uncertainty.

"Indeed, I'm not, Da," he replied.

"You could see that with half an eye," Uncle Harry added, stabbing his own hazel into the ground as a marker. "Walk boy – quick – in case she goes lame on you! Show us how big a lake we've got." As Samson almost ran to obey he added, "Steady as she goes – a measured pace is better by far. The elephant outlives the impala." To Finbar he added, "He has the gift, all right."

"My father had it, too," Finbar said, raising his own twig hopefully. When nothing happened he shrugged.

Paul joined them and tried his luck, too – also without success. "Many are called but few are chosen," he murmured ruefully.

They set off in pursuit of Samson, who, now that he, too, had accepted the reality of his powers, was almost skipping along.

"Steady the Buffs, boy!" Harry boomed. "This is serious business, not a church picnic."

The lad settled down and, after he had covered a good furlong and a half, was disappointed to find the rod beginning to wilt between his hands. "I'm losing the power," he called out anxiously, faltering also in his stride.

"Balderdash!" Uncle Harry replied as he drew level. "You're losing the water, that's all. Turn about and go back." He gouged a deep rut in the soil with the heel of his boot.

Sure enough, when Samson had retraced a dozen or so paces, the hazel began to go wild again. He laughed, as if he had not fully believed it all until now. When he had covered about half the ground, his Uncle Harry made him turn left, away from the house, and walk until he came to the eastern edge of the water – or whatever it was that made the rod leap and twist in his hands.

The moment came distressingly quickly.

"I knew it!" Uncle Harry cried. "Didn't I say it? Well, I don't believe I did, but I surely meant to. That house of ours is sitting right on a lake of water big enough to drown every hippo in the Cape!"

That, however, proved something of an exaggeration, for Samson's dowsing rod fell slack a good hundred yards shy of the gate that preserved the garden from the ostriches and mules. By now a small group of Natives, who worked on the farm and lived in rondaavels near the kraal, had gathered to watch, it being the break for their midday 'samp' and a smoke of Indian hemp, which they called, in Afrikaans, 'dagga'. The little black children were already imitating Samson, picking up any old bit of stick and trying to make it leap and twist like his. It made him feel immensely important.

"Well!" Uncle Harry pretended to sound like a man fighting back severe disappointment. "It's still one hell of a lake, man!"

Samson saw his mother emerging from the house, attracted, he imagined, by the commotion outside. "Mammy, Mammy!" he cried, running to her. "I have the gift! I can find water! I found it with this!"

But she continued to stare over his shoulder; she did not

even notice he wasn't stammering – though excitement usually made it worse. She was watching the point where the road to the farm emerged from between two large acacias, about half a mile away. The dust already told her that Mrs Delaroux had left the main highway. "She has a letter from Ireland," she murmured.

"How d-d-d-d'you know?" Samson asked, crestfallen.

"I just know it in my bones." She smiled wanly and glanced at him at last. "Call it *my* gift."

17

Debbie was right about Martin's letter; it was dated Sunday, 14th September, 1913 and it ran:

> Dear Georgie and Paul,
>
> I think you left the oul' sod in the nick of time. This must have been one of the most disappointing summers anyone can recall – certainly the biggest washout I can remember. Fortunately we had one fine spell for the Cloyne steeplechase last month, which has contented the populace and lightened our task. More and more I appreciate why the emperors of old pacified the mob with bread and circuses.
>
> But to business. The powers that be are taking the possibility of war in Europe very seriously. This time it'll be us against Germany. Last time it was France – so much for a 'Century of Progress'! The response is the same, though. England must bolt her back door. Last time it was against Bonaparte's invading armies; this time they fear the armies will be indigenous, so the bolted doors will be in Mountjoy, Kilmainham, Grangegorman, and every local

lock-up in all thirty-two counties. You may imagine how hard we are working, even now.

I was able to light two candles with the one taper, that is, to use my inquiries into Salome's disappearance as a cloak for my inquiries into the forementioned seditious elements – and I made good progress on both. To put you out of suspense at once: I am as certain as one can be of anything in this life that the little girl Salome is alive and well.

My earliest investigations were naturally at all the orphanages and workhouses in the area. When they drew blank, I turned to Queenstown harbour itself. They had already conducted a most thorough search of every nook and cranny, the day after the Knysna sailed; thank heavens, it proved fruitless. I instituted another, using my own men this time. We, too, were glad that we failed to turn up the smallest sign of her. I can vouch that not a shoe, not a handkerchief would have escaped notice. Local people, who know the run of the tides at every time of year, searched the foreshore where a body might be expected to wash up – and, indeed, the bodies of two drowned men and an adolescent girl of around sixteen were found on various days, but none of any child.

However, the harbourmaster, a man called Well-beloved, and his clerk recalled a singular incident on the day the Knysna sailed. Thanks to a series of misunderstandings and mishaps, they did not receive the cable from the ship until the morning after. They made immediate inquiries of their own and, as I said above, conducted a thorough search of the place. Though they found no actual evidence, their activity prompted a casual labourer by the name of Pius O'Connor to volunteer that he had seen 'a grand lady' departing hand-in-hand with 'a ragged wee colleen' the day before – immediately after the

Knysna sailed. He claimed he had actually seen the pair of them climbing into a carriage with a crest on the door but under further questioning from me he admitted it might have been a common hackney. He denies describing the little girl as 'ragged'; he says she was 'dressed very plain in blue checks' – which accords with the details in your letter.

He also says he saw this same woman berating one Charley Fox, a gentleman well known to us, for he has two convictions for indecent exposure and would have been prosecuted for a worse offence involving a little girl if the parents had permitted the child to give evidence. Word of my investigation must have reached him, however, for he has decamped – to Belfast, we are told. I have circulated his description there and have good hopes of tracing him. He bears a remarkable resemblance to Mr Punch!

Inquiries among the hackney-carriage fraternity produced one Eamonn Corcoran, who claims to have carried a lady, name unknown, and a little girl in a blue dress to the corner of Hart Street and Tivoli, at the eastern edge of Cork City. I am always suspicious of cabmen who can recall details of one fare among dozens after a lapse of several weeks, but I am more inclined to believe this Corcoran fellow. He remembered the pair, not only because he thought them rather ill-matched, but also because – he said – there is no obvious destination around there. I am also more inclined to believe him because, oddly enough, he imparted this little nugget of information with a decidedly shifty look!

In fact, there is a very obvious destination in the Tivoli district, namely, the Royal George Club, which is precisely where a 'grand lady' might wend her way. But poor Corcoran, knowing where his main interests lie, would not want to put his finger so directly on the place. The patrons of the Royal George are of that class which believes that the constabulary exists to keep down the seditious Irish, not to go meddling in the affairs of the quality. They would think ill of any cab driver who brought the RIC to their door.

This is almost a universal characteristic among those who wish to help us without becoming 'informers' – the vermin of Irish life. They salve their consciences by taking us halfway there, saying, in effect, 'There you are, Mr Peeler, if you can't go the rest of the way unaided, you're not worth your pension!'

Naturally, I made a few inquiries at the Royal George, but got nowhere. Nor did I expect to. Their bread is too well buttered. I'm sure one of the maids knew something, but the butter they put on her bread wouldn't melt in her mouth! I also inquired among the nannies who take their little charges down to the sands there in summer, whether any of them knew of a house in that district where they'd taken in a little girl around the beginning of July. Again I drew blank, but this time I believe for the very good reason that no such adoption has occurred in that locality. My money is on the Royal George.

All in all, then, here is what I believe happened. Salome McKenna was frightened by Charley Fox and hid herself from him. She was still there when the ship sailed. An unknown lady on the quayside, probably seeing off a friend, noticed the child and took her under her wing. Perhaps at first she intended to hand her in care of the orphanage but then, for reasons best known to herself, decided to look after her in person. I know one's instinct is to look for the most consoling explanation at moments like this, but I truly believe it most likely that Salome is now happily situated with a new family somewhere in Ireland, loved and cared for and in very comfortable circumstances.

I base this conclusion on a process of elimination. It is most unlikely that anything criminal has occurred. We should certainly have got some whisper of it by now, if not the full tale. It is even less likely that Salome has been taken up by a poor family; such people might have sheltered her a day or two but, the times being as hard as ever with the poor, they would have handed her into the care of the nuns, who, in their turn, would automatically have informed us. The rich, however, are a law unto themselves. All my inquiries point in that direction, though, for reasons stated, they end in a blank. I am sorry not to be absolutely positive but am glad to think the prospect is so heartening.

As I presume you will wish to show these words to Mr and Mrs McKenna, I shall start a new page with the rest of my news.

The remaining quarter-page was blank. Finbar looked at Debbie, who, having read the letter twice by now, nodded. He passed it back to Georgina, who said, "Oh no – you keep it. I'm sure that's what my cousin intended." She smiled sympathetically. "I don't know! It's almost more frustrating to get *so* close and still know nothing for certain, don't you think?"

Finbar nodded. Debbie drew a determined breath and said, "You'll be writing to him again, no doubt, Mrs Delaroux?"

Georgina said she would, of course. "If you want me to include a brief note of thanks from you . . .?" she suggested.

"Indeed," Debbie replied. "But I was also wondering – would you ever ask him if he has the name about him of the girl at that club whose mouth was too cool to melt the butter?"

18

Salome discovered something new every day, though most of it passed without notice, even by her. After all, it must be a very uneventful sort of day on which even the dullest seven-year-old doesn't discover at least one new fact about herself or the world. So she noticed only the biggest and most obvious things – like the day Miss Kinchy lifted her onto Rachel's fairy cycle and she *didn't* fall off after one crank of the pedals, or the day she knew right from left without going to the nursery door, where Mrs Culham-Browne had marked the jambs with R and L in indelible ink. (Miss Kinchy said the day she could tell right from *wrong* with the same ease would be even grander. Privately she thought there must be a door in heaven somewhere with its jambs marked Roman Catholic and Protestant but she said nothing as to that.)

The day Salome learned to cycle was one of the great days in her life so far. It had happened about a month after she came to live at Cloonaghvogue. That same evening, when Aunt Marion put her to bed, she described how wonderful it felt and then said, "But how did I know how to do it all of a sudden? Yesterday I didn't know and today I do, but I don't remember when it came to me. Do *you* know when?"

As with so many of Salome's seemingly simple questions, Marion was hard put to it to answer. "These things just seem to happen on their own, darling," she said. "There was a time when you couldn't breathe, and then suddenly you could. Can you remember that?"

Salome shook her head and waited; she didn't see the connection.

"And there was also a time when you couldn't talk, and then one day you just started. D'you remember *that?*"

Another shake of the head, but now Salome could see there *was* no connection. "You can start talking one word at a time," she pointed out. "But you can't start bicycling one" – she held finger and thumb an inch apart – "*that* much at a time."

Marion ruffled her hair playfully. "What a *quiz* you are, as my grandmama used to say. D'you think a great deal about such things?"

"Sometimes," Salome replied.

"What are you going to think about after I've kissed you goodnight and turned down the lamp?"

"Mammy and Daddy. And Samson and Martha and David."

Marion felt the stab of jealousy – and was instantly ashamed of it. "That's good," she forced herself to say with an encouraging smile. "You must never forget them."

"Did three months go by yet?"

Marion, who had forgotten the words she had spoken on the day the *Knysna* sailed, shook her head and said, "What three months is that, darling?"

"The three months you said – when Mammy and Daddy's ship will come back for me."

"Ah." A sadness filled her eyes.

Salome wanted to say something comforting but couldn't think what. "Will we get on the train again and go back to the seaside?" she asked.

Marion went on staring out of the window. "Is that what you'd like?"

"I liked the train."

"And what would you think about . . . Cloonaghvogue? After you sailed away on the ship, I mean?"

Salome's face fell. Until that moment it hadn't struck her that going away on the boat would actually mean having to leave Cloonaghvogue and all the wonderful things she enjoyed here – all Rachel's pretty clothes and toys and the front pew in church and Rory and Ranter – and now the fairy cycle, too. And Aunt Marion, of course, and Miss Kinchy, and . . . everything.

Marion watched the consternation as it grew in the child's expression. "I'm afraid it'll be some time yet before the ship comes back," she said vaguely. "It may even take longer than three months. I was just guessing when I said that. When *did* I say it, by the way?"

"That day when it sailed when you found me left behind."

"Oh!" Marion raised her eyes heavenward. "That day! I remember almost nothing about it, do you?"

Salome nodded but, not wishing to claim a better memory, held her tongue.

"Tell me," Marion challenged.

Salome giggled. "I thought you were an angel! My gardening angel."

Marion laughed. "You mean *guardian* angel. Well, you're half-right, anyway. I am a sort of guardian to you, aren't I! And I'll promise you this, darling: I'll go on being your guardian just as long as you want. If you want to stay here at Cloonaghvogue – even after that ship comes back – you can. It's for you to decide. You won't have to go away if you don't want to."

Aunt Marion tucked her in tight then and left her to go to sleep. The moment the nursery door was shut Salome whispered, "Poor little mite!" and felt a small hot tear sprout obligingly in her eye. It was by now something of a comforting ritual.

In the first few days she had only to think of her Mammy and Daddy – or even Samson and Martha and David – and the tears would spring unbidden to Salome's eyes and flow in spate down her cheeks. Yet in a curious way she'd almost admit to welcoming the tears – proof of the bonds that held them all together.

Then came a time when merely to think of them hadn't been enough; instead she had had to picture them on the big ship, anxiously crowding the rail, staring down into the confusion on the quayside, calling out her name in anguish. Then that also lost its power and she had to picture them actually sailing away, weeping and wailing at their loss. Then even that failed to work – until, one evening, in her imagination, she saw her mother holding up Maggoty Meg; and then the floodgates had opened once again. That was quite a powerful picture. It had worked for the best part of a fortnight – and, if she forgot it for a while and then suddenly remembered it again, it could still help her cry for one or two nights more.

And so it had gone on – this need for ever-more poignant images of loss and sorrow before the tears would come. Then something inside her began to question whether there was any need for tears at all. You couldn't call it an actual thought – just a vague sort of half-conscious drifting of her mind in that awkward direction. But it liberated something within her that was able to rise above her sorrow – indeed, above feelings of every kind. It was like having a third eye to see with, except that this eye had no tears; it just watched and stuffed everything away in its own cool thought-box.

This vague *otherness* within herself was another of Salome's discoveries. It is one that most youngsters make as they pass from childhood into adolescence, when they suddenly stop being able to take themselves for granted; circumstances forced it on her rather early. But, since she was less than half-aware of it herself, it was not something she could communicate to others. Yet they sensed it in her, for all that. "The colleen is old before her years," Miss Kinchy said, and no one contradicted her.

If this sense of otherness had come when Salome's mind was ready for it – at, say, thirteen – it would have produced an intellectual stirring. Instead, being precisely half that age, she perceived it in a more primitive light, almost as an invasion by another spirit. Not quite an alien spirit, though. She felt more as if another Salome, with a different upbringing and wanting different things, had moved in alongside the one she had always known. Sometimes when she was alone she tried to make a different face for herself – not a grotesque face, like you'd pull to make people laugh, just a little drooping of the eyelids and a tiny lopsided smile or something like that. Then she could feel more like the *other* Salome. Sometimes she did it in company, too, and nobody noticed the change. Or if they did, they didn't seem to find it in the least surprising. It didn't surprise her, either.

Some aspects of this other Salome she liked, some she didn't. Some she wasn't sure about. For instance, other-Salome *did* things to her but refused to take part in the consequences; she merely observed them. One night, when the image of Maggoty Meg in her distracted Mammy's hand was failing to provoke more than a tiny grizzle in the throat and a feeble shimmering in her eyes, the other Salome said, as clear as clear could be, "Poor little mite!" And suddenly the tears had flowed as copiously as on that very first night, when her whole world had collapsed around her. But even then, in the deepest depths of her revived sorrow, she was aware of its origin in those three clear words – and aware, too, that the Salome who had spoken them was merely watching the result with interest.

Other-Salome made it impossible for Salome to throw herself heedlessly into any fun that might be going; she was always there, watching, keeping a distance. That was the worst thing about her.

Neither Salome, however, was conceited enough to believe that their largely happy sharing of a common life made her in any way special. In fact, she hardly paused to think about it at all. Even if she had, she would have assumed it was all part of what they called 'growing up' – something that happened to everyone at around her age.

Those early, tear-provoking images of her parents at the rail or the orphaned rag doll being brandished aloft – being real, or real possibilities – had soon lost their power to make her cry. But the phrase *poor little mite!* – which had somehow risen from inside her – seemed to retain its power for ever. She needed only to whisper it once and the tears would flow. And they continued to flow in that transient nightly ritual for many weeks before she realized that the grief which once united her with her vanished family had somehow turned into something quite different; now it was the comforting promise of one more night's oblivion.

And thus the complex business of the healing of her soul continued in its unhurried, and unhurryable, progress. Summer at Cloonaghvogue was marked out in the blood of the feathered tribe, beginning on the first of August with snipe and woodcock, and progressing by way of wildfowl, grouse, and blackgame to partridge and quail, by which time September was on the threshold. Daily the silence of the countryside was shattered with volleys of shot and cries of triumph or disappointed rage; and the occasional sweet reek of cordite drifted into the garden where Salome played. Aunt Marion, who hated the murder of animals, as she called it, said it was a wonder no one was killed; after one of the beaters *was* accidentally shot to death she didn't rest on her laurels and say, 'I told you so!' Instead she took to saying it was a wonder *more* weren't killed. Evening after evening the huge oak table in the castle hall was laden with bloodstained feather bundles. Some of them were then hung up to 'go high' in the cool room at the base of the water tower; some were sent off to hotels in Dublin; a few were despatched in braces to relations.

September ended the close season on the king of all game birds – the pheasant. The coverts rang with the harsh clatter of its feathery alarm. It made the doom-laden silence after the shots rang out all the more poignant for Salome, safe with Aunt Marion behind the high garden wall. 'Sir' – C-B refused to let her call him Uncle Gordon – became one with the ogres in the fairy tales Salome read so voraciously, plundering Rachel's old library for a new one almost every night. One evening he came home, laughing hugely because an English guest had fallen on his own unbroken gun ('thundering eejit!') and was bleeding a little. But Sir didn't laugh because the man was bleeding, he laughed at his own comment on the affair, which he hooted through the echoing castle from battlement to cellar: "Fee, fie, foe, fum! I smell the blood of an Englishman!"

That proved his 'ogre-ous' nature for Salome and she kept out of his way as much as possible. When it wasn't possible, she just closed her eyes and froze – which made him shout at her until Aunt Marion told him he was a bully. "Just look him in the eye," she advised her little ward after Sir Ogre had stumped off to his slaughtering one day. Salome, greatly daring, tried it – and found to her surprise that it worked! Sir Ogre grew uncomfortable and cleared his throat and found other things to shout at, or about.

Then Aunt Marion said to wait until he'd had his evening whiskey and then climb on his lap before he could say no, and lay her head on his waistcoat. But she couldn't find the courage for that and Aunt Marion didn't press her.

Indian summer gave way to autumn, and the valleys and hillsides around Cloonaghvogue rang with the baying of hounds at cubbing. It was the time of year when, early in the morning on several days each week, the foxcubs were driven from their dens and spread across the landscape, nice and even – all ready for the bloodletting of winter. Some foxes were killed if the master thought they were too many for his country; but spreading, not killing, was the main business of cubbing; also to teach the hounds their duties. In November, proper hunting would begin, with the huntsmen in pink or black and the ladies in veils. But for cubbing they wore what old King Edward had called 'ratting clothes' – tweed hacking jackets and bowler hats.

No one was blooded, no brushes or paws were hacked off, no trophies carried home to add their stains to the hall table.

Salome found she enjoyed cubbing – a discovery she made on a pre-breakfast walk with Miss Kinchy, one crisp October morning with a hint of frost on the air. The rising sun, thinly veiled by cloud, cast a silvery sheen over field and copse, and the great shire horses, straining at the plough, breathed silver steam into their own long shadows. She could hear Sir Ogre, the Master, winding his horn and the music of the hounds as they gave excited tongue somewhere in one of the coverts up ahead; and then, as their path rounded the shoulder of the hill, the hunt came in view at last. There was no mistaking the place for the sky above was almost black with alarmed and furious rooks, put up by this invasion. And then they broke for a brief chase across the fields, with the master checking them all the way, letting the cubs gain not only ground but also the dangerous illusion that they could outrun a pack of hounds any day of the week.

"There's two of the divils!" Miss Kinchy pointed to a small break in the ditch on the far side of the field where she and Salome were standing. "Stand still and they'll mebbe not see us at all at all."

Two browny-red specks, lacking the fiery colour of their parents as yet, came streaking toward them over the newly ploughed furrows; halfway across one snapped playfully at the other's legs. "Would you look at that!" Miss Kinchy marvelled. "All the time in the world!"

By then the hounds were squeezing their way – or their two dozen ways – through the far ditch, milling around, tails going like flags, as they sought for a line to own – for Sir Ogre ran a tightly disciplined pack and God help the hound that led a riot after a hare!

"They know they're at play, too," Miss Kinchy said. "That's the laughter of hounds you hear. The music outa them when they're chasing for a kill would curdle the blood in your veins!"

Her eyes sparkled and her nostrils flared wide; and Salome, recruited by her excitement, understood that she was here attending at one of life's great thrills.

The two cubs had now drawn within an easy stone's-throw of where Salome was standing, doing her best not to move a muscle while not missing any of the excitement, either. They halted in uncertainty for a second or so, tongues drooling; she'd almost swear they were grinning. Then they parted and resumed their too-easy escape, one to the left, the other to the right. Salome, now freed from the necessity to stand motionless, turned and followed them, marking their trails and popping them in her memory so she could come back another day and find them again.

After a while she wondered why the pack had not caught up yet. She turned back, only to find they had been lifted halfway across the field, having done all that the hunt required of them that day, at least as far as that pair of cubs was concerned. The small field in attendance – the real enthusiasts, as Sir Ogre had called them – milled around just this side of the far ditch, which they had leaped for practice. There was the flash of silver hip flasks and cigar smoke drifted over the furrows, not as sweet as cordite but somehow more enticing, Salome thought. Nothing about the guns had made her want to join them. But hunting . . . ah! She could already feel the seductive pull of it.

Then to her terror she saw Sir Ogre skirt his pack and come cantering across the field toward them. As he drew near, Miss Kinchy grasped her hand. "Would he frighten us out of our wits!" she declared. "Stand still now, child, and don't mind the horse."

Salome fought an urge to cling to her ample skirts, knowing in some obscure way that *he* would count it a triumph. Over the last twenty strides, however, the smile she had taken to be devilish turned into something unusually cordial – for *him*, anyway.

He rode right up to them, deftly turning his hunter at the last moment. Tiny flecks of clay spattered her leggings and shoes. "Ho!" His gloved hand patted the gelding's lightly steaming flank; yellow foam fell from its bit; its eyes swivelled as if desperate to find something startling and its ears joined in that same fruitless hunt, for a serene peace had settled over all.

"Out for a walk, eh?" he said brightly.

Miss Kinchy curtseyed. Salome stared up at him – and he, for once, stared back. What is more, he was actually smiling. By some miracle they had found a little patch in their lives where they could meet without rancour.

"Like to join us?" he asked with a laugh.

The wonder in her eyes answered for her. Miss Kinchy made the expected mother-hen noises but he ignored her. Salome's response, so immediate and so intense, had taken him aback. "Well!" he harrumphed, embarrassed at having raised her hopes so high only to have to dash them at once. "We'll see . . . we'll see." Then with a spur to flank he was away in a hack.

After that he remained on cool terms with her but the edge had gone off his old irascibility; 'Sir Ogre' reverted to being plain 'Sir' again, though 'Uncle Gordon' was nowhere in prospect. Salome still lacked the courage to follow Aunt Marion's advice to sit on his lap and try to steal his heart – not that she repeated it, for she was aware that changes were in the offing.

Salome sensed it, too, though hardly in so conscious a manner. There was an extraordinary incident when she woke up one night – the stable clock struck one but that could have been half-past anything – and saw him standing in a shaft of moonlight at the foot of her bed, just looking down at her. She closed her eyes at once, in case he should see she was awake. She had meant to open them again, very slowly, but had accidentally gone back to sleep. When she awoke next it was still fairly dark but the moon had gone and so had he.

She had quite forgotten the incident of the foxcubs, or at least the vaguely implied promise he had made that morning before breakfast, until Christmas morning came – bringing with it the harbinger of a soft December day where rain and sun fought equally for mastery. She had just finished unloading the stocking that Santy had left by the mantelpiece, and was wondering could she eat the peppermint mouse, when Miss Kinchy came bustling into the nursery. She was full of blather, as Aunt Marion called it – telling her that Themselves had gone to Communion and she was to get up and be all washed and dressed by the time they returned – charging the air with so many words that Salome found no room for any of her own.

She was surprised not to be dressed in the pretty clothes they'd looked out yesterday. Instead she was put into her everyday walking-out clothes – boots, leather leggings, tweed coat and bonnet, and woollen mittens joined with a long string up one sleeve, across her shoulders, and down the other.

"Are we going for a walk?" she asked. The next question would be could they take the wolfhounds, which had been impossible during cubbing or on any morning the hunt had a meet.

"Indeed, we are not!" Miss Kinchy replied with a jolly sort of finality.

The Culham-Brownes always walked to church and back through the park; they did not believe in making unnecessary work for their servants on the sabbath, or any religious festival – especially when most of those servants kicked with the other foot. So Salome wondered why, as soon as she was dressed and ready, she was brought to wait for their return in the stable yard, rather than by the front door.

It seemed an interminable while before she heard the scrunch of their feet on the gravel of the drive round the side of the castle, but at last they came into view. Sir was sober as a judge in his morning coat and top hat but Aunt Marion, though no less sombre in her costume, was smiling all over her face. "Come!" she said, holding out her hand as she drew near.

Sir was already striding across the cobbles to one of the stable doors. Bewildered, yet already feeling little premonitions of excitements to come, Salome let her guardian angel lead her in Sir's wake.

The stable was disappointingly empty. But then it became obvious that it was not, in any case, their goal. Sir removed his hat while he ducked through the low door at the back; the other two followed him out into the paddock beyond.

"There!" he cried, waving a showman's hand – a gesture that was strengthened by the simultaneous appearance of the sun.

And there, in a morning turned suddenly gold, stood Alf Gorman, holding the reins of – and towering over – the most beautiful Shetland pony in all four kingdoms of Ireland and of all the lands beyond. Salome just stood there and stared at it, not daring to believe what every ounce of her understanding was urging on her as true – until Aunt Marion bent down and whispered it in her ear: "Yours, darling! He's your very own." She rose and nudged her husband gently in the ribs.

"Ah, yes!" He spoke as if his real purpose were merely to clear his throat. "Happy Christmas" – an awkward pause preceded the final word – "Salome!"

Happiness of this order left her paralyzed. It needed another nudge from Marion to make him stoop and lift her into the saddle. "Come on!" he barked. "Brace up, gel! Don't go all to bits now – it's only a pony."

But somehow she could feel there was no harm in him now. Even Miss Kinchy had once said his bark was worse than his bite and now she could see it was true. She *burned* with pleasure to be sitting so high in the world. For one awful moment she feared she was going to wet herself but she tensed every muscle and sat up tall and concentrated hard, trying to remember all the things she'd been told about ponies.

The creature tugged at the rein in Gorman's hand and stared up at her with one beady-bright eye. She wondered what his name was even as Aunt Marion told her: "He's called Hannibal."

"Hannibal!" She leaned forward and stroked his ear, hoping he understood she already loved him more than anything else in all the world.

Meanwhile, Sir, encouraged by her animation, said, "That's the ticket!" and began arranging her legs properly. She was too young to ride side-saddle as yet; that would come when she graduated to a Connemara. "Heels down, feet straight forward!" He pressed her calves against the pony's fat flanks. "That's where you tell him who's boss, right?" He placed a protective hand in the small of her back and said, "Walk on!"

Gorman led Hannibal in a series of small circles round a clump of pheasant bower that grew in the middle of the paddock; C-B stayed holding her for the first circuit and then stood proudly back to admire.

Marion watched him warily, not entirely able to accept his apparent conversion.

That evening, after a day of festivities, he was sitting by the fire, sipping his first whiskey and running his fingers idly through Ranter's coat, when he was ambushed by Salome, already in her nightie and dressing gown. With all the skill of a new-born horsewoman she jumped on his lap and whispered, "Thank you, Sir, for Hannibal."

"I say!" he murmured. And then, almost as if he were cross with her, he snapped, "Call me Uncle C-B, if you wish."

Suddenly shy of her own boldness, she hid her face in his

waistcoat and stuck a comforting thumb in her mouth. After a brief silence she withdrew it and said, "Uncle C-B?"

"Mmm?" was all he could manage in reply.

"When the ship comes back again . . .?"

"Yes?" He had no idea what she was talking about but he supposed it would become clear in time.

"When it does, I want to stay here with Hannibal. And you and Aunt Marion."

He was too surprised to speak – which was just as well because the sudden lump in his throat would have made it difficult, anyway.

At that identical moment – though it was an hour later by the clock – Debbie, who had gone down to stop the hydraulic ram for the night, heard a seagull cry in a voice that might have been Salome's. It pierced her to the heart. She had to stop and close her eyes and clutch the side of the reservoir for support.

"Darling?" she cried aloud. She could not help herself though she knew it was only a bird. Even the most bitter delusion was better than the ache of her loneliness, her deprivation of that dear little bundle.

She opened her eyes and saw nothing but the vast, empty ocean. The fast-sinking sun shone aslant the great rollers as they reared for one final charge across the rocky shelf that protected the thin strip of beach from the open water. So often did her own hopes rise, too; and so often were they dashed to extinction.

All that water!

All those millions of miles of water between her and little Salome!

"Come back!" she shrieked across the heat-hazed ocean. "My darling! Oh my little darling one!"

On the far side of the tank Samson, who had been waiting ten long minutes to spring out and shout 'Boo!', clenched his eyes tight and puckered his nose against the stinging of his tears. Then he began slowly and methodically beating his forehead against the concrete, as if to give his anguish some other cause – in fact, *any* other cause – but that.

PART TWO – 1916

In the Name
of God

19

Normally one Kaffir 'boy' could work a pair of mules, but these huge scoops were heavy when they were filled with sand and gravel, and the dam wall was getting higher by the hour. By midmorning it took three boys – or a man and two genuine youngsters – to encourage the beasts up the inner face to the top. There, after the scoop was flipped over, adding its burden to the top of the wall, they had to exert all their strength and skill to hold the creatures back, for they did not like the clang of the iron and they feared the flying handles would hit them in the hocks.

Samson, being twelve, was given the responsible task of noting the number of scoop-loads that were hauled to the top of the bank and dumped there. He also told Uncle Paul if any particular team was consistently dumping only half-loads. A meagre load every now and then was unavoidable. For instance, if the scoop hit a boulder as it trawled across the bed of the dam, the Kaffir on the handles had to jerk it up or aside pretty swiftly or he'd lose the lot. And, of course, there was no going back, because there were six mule-teams at work on the site and at any given moment three of them would likely be scraping up a scoopful across the bed. It was better to go on with half a scoop than to go around again – as long as it didn't happen too often.

Finbar's job was to stand in the heat and dust of the deepening basin and mark all the hidden boulders revealed by the scoops and then to organize gangs of boys to dig them out by hand. The liberated boulders were dragged on sleds and reburied in the base of the dam wall to make a sloping 'road' up which the scoops could be more easily hauled – that is, without trampling backward as much sand as they carried upward.

Samson thought it must be the most exciting day of his life. He knew from bitter experience just how much effort and muscle he put into digging a single shovelful of sand and how long it took to fill a wheelbarrow. To see the mules scooping up the stuff a whole wheelbarrow at one time was awesome. When they had started at dawn that morning the land in front of the rocky shelf (which would form the back and one side of the dam) was flat, sparsely dotted with little bushes and succulents. By noon, when they broke off for lunch, the dam wall was six foot high and he could no longer see over it. He remembered harvests in his childhood, back in County Clare, when dozens of men had worked to a common purpose like this; but the result had merely been sheaves of corn that even a child like himself could handle. This, by contrast, was real engineering, building on a grand scale – altering the entire landscape, using power that beggared the imagination. When Uncle Paul blew his whistle, the relaxation of that power was like something you could touch. The younger boys outspanned the mules and galloped with them to the drinking trough, which had been set up about a furlong away, so as not to distract them; the mules were so parched they would not have walked in any case, but the lads wanted to get back in time to watch the slaughtering of the sheep.

The Kaffir women had come out from the kraal an hour earlier and had got a good fire going by now, full of shimmering ash – and, incongruously, a branding iron for two of the mules, who lacked a mark. The women had also brought out the two sheep, which were now grazing, all unsuspecting, among the lower branches of a thorn tree, stretching up as if practising different ways of offering their necks for the sacrifice. Two of the men began whetting their knives. They took a swig of beer, swallowed most of it, spat the rest onto the stone, rubbed, tested the edge, rubbed again, grinning to themselves. Samson took up a good position near the sheep; he could see where they were going to be killed because the women were already spreading mealie flakes on pudding cloths to catch the blood.

His mother and Aunt Georgina had come out with his sister Martha and two of the house girls; they carried the baas's hamper, packed with cold chicken, hard-boiled eggs, salad, watermelon, sponspek, guavas, and lemonade. They stretched an awning between two acacias and set out camp stools and a folding canvas table. Samson watched them with contempt. With each fresh touch of civilization, he thought, they simply made themselves look more and more ridiculous. How beautifully simple it was for the Kaffirs. They made a fire and they sat around it, laughing, jabbering away with all those strange clicks and la-la singsongs that still made no sense to him. (Uncle Harry Williams wouldn't employ a Kaffir who could speak English; his master-servant dealings were in Afrikaans, which all the new immigrants at Fountains had had to learn, as well.) How natural they looked. How naturally they behaved. But his own people had all the appearance of aliens who would never acclimatize. They even had two girls with horsehair switches to brush away the ants.

"Samson, come away here," his mother called, "before these flies destroy your dinner on you."

"I just want to watch," he replied, not taking his eyes off the two men with the knives. *Come on, come on!* he urged them silently. *They're surely sharp enough by now?*

"Samson! I'll not tell you again," came the call from the aliens' camp.

"Coming!" he shouted, rooted to the spot, watching the sunlight flash off the steel.

A gang of half a dozen cornered the sheep, who – too late – realized something was afoot. They bleated piteously and kicked out in a frenzy as they were half-dragged, half-carried to the smooth stretch of bare rock set aside as their killing ground. But the knives were swift and merciful, and the kicking soon degenerated into the automatic twitching of an animal that has ceased to feel. Indeed, the two men worked so swiftly that Samson missed the actual moment; he was still held in fascination by their eyes. He knew that whenever he did anything a bit squeamish – like poking the squids out from hidey-holes in the rock pool where he and Martha and David went swimming – he would screw up his eyes and make the most awful grimaces. But these two Kaffirs remained quite expressionless as they did their fell work. It was as natural to them as everything else they did. He felt a flush of shame at his foreignness here and despaired of ever belonging.

"Samson!" his father called sharply – having considerately waited until the lad had seen what he had been so desperate to watch.

"Coming!" he snapped, still half in a daze; then, realizing it was his father who had spoken, added more respectfully, "Yes, I *am* coming." And he ran to the little patch of civilization in the wild, dry bush. Suddenly he realized how desperately thirsty he was.

Actually, he had to admit there were one or two things to be said on civilization's behalf. Ice, for instance – the magical availability of ice in this outpost of an outpost of the twentieth century. How invitingly it clinked in the tall glasses of lemonade! He gulped the lot down in one and held his glass out for more, chewing the ice and pretending it was gunfire inside his head.

"You're disgusting – d'you know that!" his mother said with a grin. She handed the glass to one of the maids to refill. The girl looked so longingly at it when she passed it back that Samson felt he ought to offer her a gulp. But, of course, you couldn't start that sort of thing or no one would know where it'd end. His mother didn't notice the girl's longing at all. "Now slowly," she said. Then, to Georgina, "Boys, eh!"

Aunt Georgina winked at him; she always did that when his mother ticked him off or said disparaging things. She made herself out to be some kind of refuge against his mother's anger, but Samson had never felt able to trust her absolutely. He sensed she had a selfish streak, deeply ingrained in her, which would make her least reliable when most needed.

Uncle Paul swirled his glass around, making the ice clink. "Hear that?" he asked. "I'll tell you a story about that. I spent a week in the Middle Karroo once – beyond Graaf Rienet – the hottest week of the year – in the company of a chap who could imitate that sound to perfection."

"Jaysus, 'twould drive a man mad," Finbar said. "I'd have killed him."

'Oh, I did, of course." Uncle Paul chuckled. He might have done so, too, Samson realized. You could never tell with him because he tried to make a joke of everything. Well, not an out-and-out joke, perhaps, but he tried to make out that everything had a mildly amusing aspect to it. Even when he took a sjambok to one of the Kaffirs for being too drunk or brawling, he never lost that light, supercilious smile at the corners of his mouth.

The coming of the ice machine was all thanks to Aunt Georgina. Last summer, their second at Fountains, she had threatened to move to Port Elizabeth if they didn't get an electric set. At first everyone said it was impossible, because of the war in Europe – the Great War, as people were starting to call it now. But then the son of the neighbouring farmer had been killed in the capture of de Wet at Bloemfontein and his parents had lost heart and sold out their entire farm, called Suidhoek, to Uncle Harry and Aunt Queenie; and Suidhoek already had an electric set, so it was dismantled and brought over to Fountains – just in time to stop Aunt Georgina from carrying out her threat. The McKennas had then moved up the coast to live at Suidhoek, minus its electrical conveniences.

A separate fire had been established for the white baases. It was called a *braaivleis*, which means 'cook-meat.' But it was burning too fiercely to cook anything other than 'societies' at the moment – and anyway, the boys were still butchering the two sheep carcases. Societies were lumps of raw mutton fat taken, in this case, from the sheep they had eaten yesterday, and steeped overnight in a curry marinade. Now they were tightly skewered in kebabs on long, straight twigs of a particular thorn tree, whose peeled wood turned bright yellow and imparted a pleasant tang to the fat. Now Cookie, the baases' cook, arranged them over the flames and soon the glorious aroma of roasting curried fat filled everyone's nostrils and made them all drool in anticipation. The melted drops fell into the ashes, where they flared and spat bright orange, leaving behind a flavour that would later soak into the chops.

By now both sheep were flayed. The lads were rubbing Chile saltpetre into the hides before rolling them up, ready for proper curing back at the kraal. The dogs were already brawling over the entrails. The women put the heads up in the branches of a tree, to stop the dogs from running off with them, as well. The two butchers were making quick work of cutting and jointing the carcase. The best chops were carried first to Cookie, who stripped them of their fat, ready to be marinaded overnight for the next lot of societies. Then she buried the lean meat and bone in the hot ash of the fire, raking the embers over them and sealing them instantly.

Samson trapped the last society between his teeth and pulled the thorn skewer free of it. The crispy coating yielded to his bite and a squirt of hot, aromatic fat coated his mouth. He surrendered to the intensity of his pleasure and chewed slowly to make it last. He eyed Martha's skewer enviously, for she had three left. She read his mind and half-turned from him, jutting a protective brown shoulder between him and her trophy.

"That was hard work this morning," he told her. "What did you do?"

"Helped in the house." Delicately she drew a society off the skewer and held it between the tips of her front teeth, as if she were afraid it might still be hot enough to burn her tongue; but the merry glint in her eye betrayed her real purpose as she deliberately held her face toward him and toyed at the morsel with the tip of her tongue. It annoyed him especially, because he knew she wasn't at all fond of societies. It occurred to him to offer her a bite of his chop, when it was cooked, in return for the last two on her skewer; but then he imagined himself holding a succulently braaivleised chop in his hands, scorched hard on the outside and all tender and juicy within, and he knew that the agony of giving her the run of her teeth on that would be even worse than this.

"You may have a shot with my gun if I can have one of those," he offered.

She held it out to him at once – and then snatched it back. "Two shots for both," she said.

Too late he realized he should have said one shot for both in the first place. She'd have accepted because she was mad-keen to get a shotgun of her own, which she would on her eighth birthday, just before Christmas. But that was almost nine months away, which might as well have been nine years to a little girl of seven.

"Done," he said.

But somehow the societies were not as appetizing as his sacrifice ought to have made them seem. Disappointed, he drifted away to be among the men until his chop was cooked.

"Do we want to go much higher, Mister Delaroux?" his father was asking. "We're almost level with the rocks now."

Uncle Paul shook his head. "It doesn't matter if floods spill back over the rocks. It'll all be contained behind them, still. It's a question of going deeper. We have to get down to the clay – which, by the drilling log, should be another couple of feet below where we are now. When that happens, the scoops will become useless. The boys can stack them over there while we open the sluice from the tank – you checked the valves?"

Finbar nodded. "First thing this morning."

"Good man! I reckon a foot of water on the clay should be enough to start with."

"And then?"

Uncle Paul chuckled and tousled Samson's hair. "This'll be the bit you'll really enjoy, young fellow," he promised. "The boys will walk the mules up and down, churning up the clay until it's thick and creamy – thicker than cream, in fact. Thick as Cookie's samp . . ."

His father pointed a warning finger at Samson and said, "You stay out of the water while they're doing that – or you'll get trampled underfoot."

The maid came round at that moment with a platter laden with braaivleised chops. The men let Samson choose first. He looked at the biggest but took the next-down in size. Uncle Paul slapped his hand playfully, as if he had done wrong; then he took the chop from him and gave him the biggest. "A growing boy should eat more than his father," he said.

Samson looked at his father for confirmation of this rule; Finbar responded with a terse nod. The McKennas' ambiguous status as both employees and friends always made him uncomfortable – especially when it came to the courtesy-uncle and -aunt relationship between the Delaroux and the children. Mind you, things were a lot better since they had moved to Suidhoek and he'd been given a hundred morgen to sharecrop with his employers.

"What was I saying?" Uncle Paul asked. "Oh yes. When it's all churned up to a thick creamy wallow, we'll take the mules off and dish out the shovels. Then we'll just throw the puddled clay up on the banks until we've got it all covered to a depth of about two inches." He sniffed. "That'll hold through to next summer, anyway – by which time it'll probably all have washed into the sand. But as long as we've got a fathom and a half of clay bed to draw on, we can puddle it every year until it's completely sealed." He ran a satisfied eye up and down the bank. "I must say, I never thought we'd get so far so soon."

Samson looked at the last morsel of meat left on his chop bone and realized with dismay that he'd been so absorbed in Uncle Paul's plans for the afternoon that he'd devoured the rest of it without a thought – certainly without relishing each succulent mouthful as he had intended.

But before he could develop his self-recrimination he was distracted by some excitement among the Kaffirs. In fact, his father spotted it first. "Jannie!" he shouted at one of the boys – in Afrikaans, of course – "take your foot off that thing!"

The other boys smelled it then and turned to yell the same warning in their own tongue.

Jannie stamped his foot in the sand and made rude but restrained gestures at his fellows. To Finbar he nodded respectfully and called out, "Dankie, baas! Baie dankie."

The words always made Samson think of the schoolboy joke: "Baie dankie? But why should I buy a donkey – I've already got two fine horses! Ha-ha-ha!" He was still unsure what had happened or what Jannie was thanking his father for. And then he saw one of the boys lifting up the hot branding iron. He sniffed it, looked at Jannie in comic disgust, and held his nose in a parody of revulsion.

"Jannie was standing on it," his father explained. "Imagine the soles of your feet being so thick you wouldn't even feel a thing like that. You'd smell yourself burning first!"

The other boys had already thrown and roped the two mules for branding. Samson ran over and was just in time to see the red-hot iron sizzle and bubble as it bit into the poor creature's hide, high on the flank. It left an ugly welt, shaped like an F in a larger O, derived from the proper name for the farm, Oppgedroogtefontejn – though their labours that day were about to consign that reputation to history. Part of him flinched in sympathy with the animal; the other part, however, exulted in the power that humans could exert over dumb beasts like that, for all their strength and cussedness. He couldn't deny it was nice to be on the winning side.

And so the work resumed. The women – the white women, that is – fled from the dust and noise; the native women packed away the lunch and doused the ashes – the first rule of the bush. And the men – of all colours, but chiefly the ochre of sand and clay – went back to scooping their way down to the clay, which they reached just after two o'clock. Samson was amazed that the mules he'd seen being branded worked just as hard, and as cantankerously, as they had that morning.

Then, while the Kaffirs made a pile of the scoops, Finbar and Paul rode away to the water tank to open up the sluice. Then they galloped back along the line of the pipe to watch it come out at the other end. This was 'Samson's water', because the drillers had sunk their well where he had divined it most strongly, and they had come upon a large natural cistern after going through a mere seven fathoms of overburden. And there they had placed the windmill pump, which had made the farm independent of the weather ever since.

The windmill filled a domestic tank near the house and the rest went to a much larger tank for the stock, placed high on a rock outcrop, almost a mile inland from the farm. The arrangement had worked well enough, except in prolonged dry spells with little wind. Then, although the underground cistern was still full of water (indeed, they had never drawn off enough to change its level at all), the tank ran dry and they had to connect the windmill crank to a mule-driven apparatus, which was depressingly cumbersome and slow. Hence the new dam. The windmill might raise no more than a bucket a minute but that added up to almost three thousand gallons between one dawn and the next!

The water came sluggishly at first but soon gathered pace and eventually gushed out in a thick stream of hot, green water.

"Will we be able to swim in this dam when it's full?" Samson asked excitedly. It was a possibility that had not occurred to him before he saw the projected size of the thing.

"For a year or two, anyway," Uncle Paul told him. "Until the turtles find it and make a home here."

"Are they dangerous?" He was not particularly worried. The bush held rhino, wild boar, elephant, bull kudus, baboons, porcupines, and every kind of venomous snake; one more 'dangerous' animal would hardly matter.

"They are if you swim skinny," Uncle Paul replied. "They swim up underneath you and bite your wang off!" He laughed and rode away to close down the sluice.

Samson winced and felt annoyed that he'd never swim there at perfect ease now; he couldn't think of anything worse than losing his wang like that.

The 'boys' became truly boy-like as they jumped and splashed in the ever-thickening liquid at the bottom of the dam. Even the mules enjoyed it and had to be goaded up several times when they lay down and rolled in the muck. Soon everyone and everything was a uniform pale khaki.

"Ho!" Paul shouted when he judged the mess thick enough for his purpose.

Reluctantly the men led the mules out between the rocks at the back of the dam, by way of a narrow defile through which, during the few weeks in the year when a river actually ran through the farm, surface water might be persuaded to flow. When they returned, they were surprised to find both baases and the young white master knee-deep in the ooze, ready to pass out shovels for the final operation of the day.

And then it was all hands to it, for evening was drawing on – and night follows sunset by a mere fifteen minutes in those latitudes. After an hour's steady puddling of the banks, just when Samson thought his arms would fall off with the exertion, he was sent to ride to the tank and reopen the sluice, keeping it flowing until he saw his father wave.

It was just the rest he needed, and by the time he got back only one small patch at the end remained to be puddled; the throng was so thick it left no room for him – for which he was, by now, grateful.

The finest moment of the day came when they all rode down to the beach – baases, horses, Kaffirs, and mules – and plunged into a sea turned gold by the setting sun. The astringent cold of it revived muscles that were tired beyond weariness; the aches and pains just floated away with the khaki-stained water.

Samson and his father dried off as they rode home. They loped in easy silence along the clifftop trail, well worn by now, beneath a huge yellow half-moon set in a cloudless sky. It was studded about with a myriad stars, grouped in constellations that had become as familiar as those they remembered from home.

When they dismounted and the grooms had led the horses away, the stillness was sudden and profound. Then it was punctured by the distant roar of a lion – an uncommon sound so close to civilization and the coast. It was answered by the familiar trumpeting of elephants.

"The risks we take every day – without even thinking about it, eh!" Finbar mused. He put his arm round his son's shoulder and said, "They'd never believe this in County Clare, would they?"

Samson did not like to be reminded of the oul' country –

of the days when Salome had been with them and the family was one. He made a noncommittal grunt.

"I'll bet you're tired," his father went on. "You did very well today. Don't you feel pleased?"

"I want to see it full," the boy replied.

"So do we all – and we will, soon enough now." They took a step toward the house, drawn by their supper, whose enticing aroma hung on the still air.

Samson felt a jet of saliva from his cheek hit the back of his front teeth. His father paused again. "D'you know," he said, "when you do a thing like that – making that dam – when you make a *mark* like that on the country – when you bend it to your will, is what I'm trying to say – then you make the place belong to you. And a part of you also belongs to it. Can't you feel it? I'd not go back to Ireland now – not for all the lakes in Killarney. Would you?"

Samson crossed his fingers in his pocket. "Never," he replied.

It was a flat lie, of course. One day he'd have to go back and find out whatever became of his sister. People couldn't possibly just vanish like that.

20

"Forgive me, Father, for I have sinned." The familiar words, usually so comforting to Miss Kinchy, now had an ominous quality. She was not even sure that the sin she had it in mind to confess was a real sin at all. And yet it filled her with guilt. Could there be guilt without sin? There certainly could be no sin without guilt – though when you saw Father Myers dead drunk on Saturday night and him standing at the altar for early Mass next morning, pale and pure as an egg on the dresser, it'd make you wonder. She ought to ask her brother, the priest of the family. He'd know. If he wasn't over three thousand miles away in America, she would. She'd written but he hadn't replied to that bit of her letter. His silence must mean something. "Leave well alone," she assumed. But she did not feel all was well, so she could not just leave it alone. And with Easter coming up she had to clear her conscience entirely. Thank God it was Father Hines taking confessions today.

She drew a deep breath and said, "Would it be a sin, Father, for a wee Catholic girl to be brought up a Protestant?"

The mouth behind the grille opened to speak but no words came. It closed again. A hand went to it, stroked the lips. Unkissed by woman those many years. His breath keened in and out of his nostrils, whistling in the hairs. "We are not *born* Catholic, my child," Father Hines said at last. "We become so by the sacrament of baptism, by the grace of God, by accepting the infallible . . ."

"I'm sure she was baptized into our faith, Father."

"She?" he echoed. "This is not *your* sin, then? It is someone's else? I cannot hear the confession of other people's sins in this . . ."

"No, Father. I understand that. What I mean is, if I know of a little Catholic girl, baptized a Catholic but being reared in the Protestant heresy, and I do nothing to prevent it, is that a sin? Should I confess it to you as a sin?"

There was a further lengthy pause before he said, "Why now? I think I can guess what you're referring to. Why have you waited three years?"

Relief flooded through her, for Father Hines would never speak to her like this if he thought there *was* a sin in it. Not in the confessional, where you were supposed to be anonymous and completely unknown to him.

"Sure, what can I do about it?" she asked laconically. It was like the sun coming out from behind a dark cloud; the whole day looked different.

He opened the door on his side and peered out into the church. "Wait outside," he told her. "I'll just hear these two and then we'll talk."

"I have other sins, Father," she reminded him.

She reeled them off her conscience, got absolution, and went down to the altar of Our Lady to repeat her penances.

"Well now!" Father Hines tapped his toes impatiently on the marble floor behind her.

She still had three beads to go. She separated them from the others, as far as the cord would allow, and put her rosary back in her bag. "Here?" she asked, looking at the nearest pew.

"Outside, I think. There are too many echoes in here." He turned on his heel and led the way down the side aisle. He genuflected and she curtseyed as they crossed the central aisle on their way out.

It had rained all morning but now a fitful sun shone through a ragged impasto of cloud, scudding across the sky before a strong westerly wind. Unlike the Protestant church, which dominated the main street, St Agnes had no graves around it, just broad lawns and maturing Irish yews. To Father Hines it always looked more like a place of learning than a simple working parish church; he hoped to make it so in reality, too – a place where theology was worked out, rather than simply dished out.

The grass was wet so they stuck to the gravel path between the side gate and the presbytery. "Now," he began. "What causes you to believe Salome Culham-Browne is – or was baptized – a Catholic? That is who you mean, I take it?"

"It is, Father. And I'm convinced she was a Catholic when she came to Cloonaghvogue. The prayers she knew then . . . you see, Father. She knew the Our Father but not the Protestant words at the end. And she's no Culham-Browne, either."

"Go on."

"She's a McKenna."

"From?"

"I don't know. And I don't think she does, either. Or not any more. If she does, she's never said it to me. We were in Tullamore one day after Christmas and she thought the Court House there looked familiar, so perhaps she's from there?"

"Hmm!" Father Hines's finger went to his lower lip and furled it a time or two. "I believe several were built in that same pattern, Miss Kinchy. The one at Ennis, for example, so she could equally well be thinking of that. You're quite sure she's not a Culham-Browne? I understood she was a by-blow of the Major's cousin, down in Clonakilty?"

"So we were all led to believe. But it doesn't tally with the way things were in that household . . ." She paused and turned to him in consternation. "This is still confidential, now, Father? Though we're not in the confessional."

"I shall treat it as if we were, Miss Kinchy, have no fear. You were saying? The way things were at Cloonaghvogue Castle when the colleen first came?"

"Yes, well, the first tale we heard was that Herself found the child wandering the streets of Cork, seemingly abandoned by her parents. I didn't believe a word of it, of course. The child was too well cared for – as grandly fleshed and bonny as anyone could wish. So then, when we heard she was really a Culham-Browne – though on the wrong side of the blanket, as they say – we were all the more ready to accept it."

"Her mother could have been a Roman Catholic, you realize?" he pointed out. "In fact, if it was the usual story – young master, young servant girl – well, you know yourself what the likelihood is."

"I know, Father. We both know – only too well!"

She was referring to Mary Horan, a servant at Cloonaghvogue who had 'broken her leg' with a young gentleman guest last Christmas – a problem that had only lately come to light and was still unresolved.

"So tell me what you *know*, Miss Kinchy," he said. "Leave aside, for the moment, what you suspect or believe, no matter how strongly. What are the facts you actually know?"

Miss Kinchy sighed. "There you have it, Father. What I *know* would hardly spoil a page. Her name is Salome McKenna. She's Irish. She's ten. She was born . . . somewhere, in nineteen hundred and six, on the third of July. Lord alone knows where but, by her speech, she's from Keelity or Clare . . ." A thought struck her. "So perhaps what you said about the Court House in Ennis is right! Anyway, that's all I know for sure – except that when I first heard her say her prayers she knew *our* version of the Our Father, not theirs."

"Very good!" He gave her an approving nod, for he always admired a mind that could sort out the wheat from the chaff.

They had reached the carriage sweep in front of the presbytery by now and he turned on his heel to saunter back to the gate. In passing he glanced up at his study window and was surprised to see young Father McDaid, his new curate, standing there. Of course, it was his study, too, but he thought the man was supposed to be over at Earlsfort, whose chapel was his particular responsibility. There was something disturbingly truculent in the man's stance – as if he were saying, 'I know what you're thinking, but just try and make something of it! I'll give you an answer will make you sorry you ever asked!' Father McDaid gave Father Hines the shivers.

He returned to Miss Kinchy and her problem with a sense of relief. "Let's leap to the other end," he said, "where everything is guesswork and supposition. And let's put the worst possible construction on it. At the age of six or seven, Salome McKenna . . ."

"She was just turned seven, Father."

"Very well. At the age of seven Salome McKenna is somehow separated from her parents – never mind how. The important thing is she's discovered by Mrs Culham-Browne, who had recently suffered a tragic bereavement of her own."

"Rachel would have turned seven on that very day, too," Mis Kinchy put in.

He stopped in his tracks and stared at her in amazement. "You didn't say that!" he exclaimed.

She shrugged. She hadn't told him the girl's shoe size, either – where did one start or stop? "Is it important?" she asked.

"It's a pattern," he replied. "God often chooses to speak to us through what *we* call patterns of coincidence. Was it coincidence that Fintan McNiece drowned in the bog last month, weighed down by the silver plate he stole from Earlsfort chapel?" He smiled at his memory of a most effective sermon on the topic. "Anyway, Mrs Culham-Browne finds Salome separated from her parents and . . . yes, let's suppose she discovers it's the little one's birthday. It would probably need a shock like that to make her do something so . . . so . . . I hesitate to call it outrageous. Let's settle for *uncharacteristic*. She decides that God has sent her this little waif as a replacement for her own departed daughter. Uncharacteristic of the lady, I grant, but not beyond the bounds of possibility. Who knows what burdens weighed upon her at that moment?" He turned to Miss Kinchy. "Do you – knowing the lady as you do – consider this so improbable as to be out of the question?"

Miss Kinchy shook her head slowly, reluctantly. She wished now with all her heart she had not started this hare.

"It is hard not to see the hand of God in all this," he went on.

"Would God put a baptized Catholic into a Protestant household to be brought up in error?" she asked in amazement.

"Would God send Satan to tempt His only Son? Yet He did. Would God – who could crush the entire world between two atoms of His fingers – allow the world to crush His only Son instead? Yet He did. Your question implies that God did not *know* that Mrs Culham-Browne is a Protestant when He allowed this fostering to occur." He laughed to show he was not censuring her for blasphemy, merely pointing out a transparent absurdity. "Of course He knew!"

"Is it sinful, then, to ask why He allowed it, nonetheless, Father?"

"It would be sinful to question the right or wrong of it. But not to examine the events themselves – in order to learn more of God's purposes. Indeed, that is our Christian *duty*."

After a pause Miss Kinchy said hopefully, "Well, I'm sure I can't imagine what purpose there might be in it, Father."

He marshalled his thoughts awhile before answering her. "Does it occur to you, Miss Kinchy," he said, "that a hundred years ago you and I could not have stood here, talking like this. That church was not yet built and my presbytery would have been a hidey-hole in someone else's house. I'd have given you the sacraments in the shelter of some hedgerow. And what did that do for our faith? Did it wipe us out – which was the clear intention of the English?"

"Indeed not, Father!" She chuckled grimly. "Didn't it make us all the stronger!"

"God's purpose, Miss Kinchy? Many at the time must have wondered why He allowed His faithful flock to be so persecuted. But we, their grandchildren, don't. Now look at that presbytery! And look at our church – especially the roof and the spire. Who built those for us, eh? Old Kelso Culham-Browne – as staunch a Protestant as ever breathed. But he was the one who did it for us!"

They stared at the two buildings; he noticed Father

McDaid was no longer at the window.

"Do you begin to see where reason and history are pushing my argument, Miss Kinchy?" he asked. "A century ago Protestant and Roman Catholic were at daggers drawn. But now we can all live together in some kind of harmony – cordial if not exactly hearty. We draw ever closer together, not farther apart. So, do you still imagine God may have *no* purpose in giving up a Catholic soul to be reared as a Protestant? Who knows what path in life He has not already marked out for your little charge!" He smiled benignly. "Like Saint Paul, we see though a glass darkly – but at least we are not entirely blind."

They had reached the gate by now. He touched her arm briefly, causing her to start. "Has that eased your mind, Miss Kinchy?"

She smiled gratefully, a gesture that was reinforced by her embarrassment that his touch had startled her. "Greatly, thank you, Father Hines," she replied.

As she made her way back to the Castle, more contented than she had felt for years, she met Father McDaid, walking toward the presbytery. She was so full of it that she burst out, "Oh Father – it's surely a wonderful thing to have the learning of a priest!"

And so Father McDaid came to hear of the Almighty's plans for the wee colleen. He did not, however, point out that, in telling *him* the tale – a priest with a lot more dedication to The Faith than the Jesuitical, face-all-ways Father Hines – a further strand was being woven into those same plans. Father Hines might be happy to leave things be, but McDaid would not rest until 'the wee colleen' was safe in Roman Catholic hands once more.

However, there was a strain of kindness in him. He saw, for instance, that there was no need to go confusing poor Miss Kinchy with yet another piece of advice; the poor woman had had enough theological buffeting for one day, or even one lifetime. He'd manage it on his own.

21

The statues in the lake had names by now – secret names, of course. Pan might be Pan to all the world but to Salome he was Dizzy, because she had made herself some pipes like that from the empty tubes of Japanese knotweed and tried to play them and that's what it made her: dizzy. Also he had a dizzy sort of light in his eyes; when you looked into them (which Salome had done last month when the lake froze and the ice would bear her weight), you'd imagine that if only you could hear his music, it would take you out of your senses. And the half-girl half-woman was called Pan, being short for Pandora, because Miss Kinchy said once that when a girl listened to the likes of *that* fella's music, she was opening Pandora's Box. Salome felt sure the box was somewhere down there under the water, by her feet, all covered over with leaves now, of course, but you'd find it there if only they drained the lake.

When she read that Pandora had opened her famous box years and years ago and let loose all the troubles of the world, she pointed out to Miss Kinchy that it didn't really matter now if anyone opened the box again because all the damage was done. But Miss Kinchy said it was like the lake itself. You could drain it all you wanted at one end, it only filled up again at the other. And everyone in the world – man, woman, and child – was born with their own personal Box of Troubles, which they could open at their peril, so she needn't think Pandora had done all the dirty work for her.

It didn't make sense, of course, or not completely. You could glimpse a kind of sense in it but the bits wouldn't join up. Salome didn't mind that. When she did the puzzles in

Girl's Treasure, she never started at the beginning and worked her way methodically to the end. The dots with numbers that you had to join up, for instance – she'd join 22 to 23 and 14 to 15 and 31 to 32 . . . and so on. And sometimes she'd only need to join half of them before she could see the whole picture clearly. She did her drawings the same way. Henny Bellingham started in the top-left corner and always ran out of space before she got to the bottom right; she said it didn't smudge, but she always ran out of space. Salome had to fix all the edges before she started to draw properly. And if you rested your hand on loose paper, it *didn't* smudge. So she didn't mind it when the things Miss Kinchy said and the things Aunt Marion said and the things Uncle C-B said didn't 'join up'. She knew they would one day and then she'd see the whole picture.

She used to visit the lake quite often. It had begun when the ice melted and she could no longer go close to Dizzy and peer into his disturbing eyes. She'd ride Hannibal, her pony, down to the low wall that surrounded the water and turn the pony loose to graze the clearing while she sat on the broad capstone and gazed at the two figures, trying to remember precisely what she had seen in those eyes.

One day she had been so absorbed in this pastime that she had failed to notice a young lad tickling for trout on the far side of the water. His cry of triumph had startled her, freezing an image of him in her mind for ever – half-risen on his left hand, the other flung wildly above and behind him, a glittering halo of lakewater drops all around him, and a silver-bellied trout, wriggling as it flew through the air to land somewhere in the undergrowth beyond.

"Oh!" She clapped her hands excitedly.

The lad gathered up the trout and ran.

After that she saw him a couple of times – or, rather, the colour of his heels as he ran away. So then she left Hannibal behind and hid in the bushes and watched him. He was not a ragged boy. Not a tinker or anything like that. He wore rough, country clothes but they were of good quality, and he looked clean and well fed. His patience was only amazing. He'd lie on the bank, trailing his right arm in the icy-cold water for hours and hours, until bits of Salome were *alive* with pins and needles. But he never went home without a fine fat trout.

Salome decided to let Miss Morrell in on the secret. Miss Morrell was her governess. Uncle C-B said she was weird but Aunt Marion said she had two university degrees and was the very best (although she, too, had enough reservations about the woman to say, "Live and let live," from time to time). Miss Morrell had taught Salome all her lessons except riding and sports for the past two years, ever since Aunt Marion had realized her own limitations – and Salome's brightness. Now all Aunt M taught her was sketching and needlework; and Uncle C-B took her for riding and sports. He said she'd be the first-ever lady master of foxhounds one day, the way the world was going.

Salome had long since realized that Miss Morrell, wonderful as she was at Facts and Knowledge and so on, was pretty useless at other things. When she'd told her what Miss Kinchy said about everyone having their own Pandora's Box, for instance, she was obviously trying to get a second opinion out of the woman. But Miss Morrell had said, "Don't look to me, Sal. I watched my father drive himself to the edge of his reason, trying to understand all the religions of the world. And he was a bishop, so he ought to have known better. You'd have to be Alice in Wonderland to believe ten impossible things before breakfast each day. But since you're not, then it's best to stick with just one. It doesn't matter what you believe as long as you only believe one thing and stick to it. So you might as well believe Miss Kinchy until you're old enough to have a mind of your own."

Aunt Marion said that was just inverted pride. Miss

Morrell's father was one of the foremost bishops in Ireland and his books on the world's different religions were very highly regarded.

The best thing about Miss Morrell was that she called Salome 'Sal' and never spoke to her in that special voice grown-ups use when speaking to children. And that was why Salome invited her down to watch the patient youth who tickled for trout.

They hid behind some rhododendrons. After about five minutes, during which nothing happened except that some midges discovered the few inches of bare skin that even the grandest lady cannot help revealing, Miss Morrell began studying the rhododendron, thinking she might as well turn their vigil into an impromptu natural history lesson. She noted a leaf that had obviously been sampled by some small grazing creature – who had equally obviously been discouraged from sampling it any further. She noted a small colony of aphids – but no attendant ants, alas, or it would have made an excellent lesson on cooperation. And she also saw that the buds were swollen and that one of them was opened a tiny crack, showing a streak of intense purple. She touched it. "I wonder if they feel pain just before they open?" she murmured. But she got no further for the young lad himself arrived at that moment.

"There!" Salome said proudly, as if she had made some special discovery of him.

Miss Morrell took one look and said, "Oh, but I know *him*. He's harmless."

It struck Salome as a very odd thing to say about anybody, especially when the question that they might be harm*ful* had not even arisen. Nevertheless, at the back of her mind there lurked a vague recollection that she had once, a long time ago – when she was with her first family – known someone else whom everyone had described as 'harmless'. But she hadn't understood it then, either.

Miss Morrell was going on: "His name's Harold . . .

something. Or Harvey? Begins with an aitch, anyway. They live in the cottage just beyond the church." She pulled a face. "He's heard us."

She stood up at once and shouted, "Little boy! Don't run away – we're not going to hurt you. We just want to talk." She lowered her voice and said to Salome, "He *is* a Simple Simon! I can't think of many twelve-year-old lads who'd believe me – can you?"

Salome couldn't think of any twelve-year-old lads at all. Except Hereward Bellingham, who lived at the other end of the county. And Quintin Buller, who burst into tears when he couldn't kiss her in *Queen of Sheba* at his eleventh birthday party and pulled her hair at his twelfth last month. She didn't know either of them well enough to help her answer Miss Morrell's question. But now she realized that 'harmless' meant 'simple-minded'.

Harold-or-Harvey whatsizname suddenly became extremely interesting to her. People often complimented her on being so clever, but when she asked Miss Morrell if it was true, she'd said, "Not really, Sal. You might be clever one day, but all you've got at the moment is an excellent memory. However, that's not to be sneezed at, so make the most of it while it lasts." So a simple-minded boy might not even have an excellent memory. Or he might, but just for a very limited number of things – like tickling for trout. In that case, he'd probably remember only the most importantest things of all – and that would make him interesting, of course.

Miss Morrell approached him with a smile. "Hallo, young man," she said brightly. "I believe I know you, though I can't think of your name for the moment. D'you know me? I'm Miss Morrell."

He grinned back, wiping his hands awkwardly on the sides of his trousers, uncertain whether or not to admit he recognized her, or even whether to give his correct name.

"And you are . . .?" she prompted.

"Ned Kelly, ma'am."

She laughed. "And last week it was Robin Hood, no doubt! It's Harold something, isn't it? Or Harvey?"

He gave a single crestfallen nod. "Harvey Kelly, ma'am."

"You've met Miss Salome, no doubt?" She shook hands with him and then put his hand into Salome's, who said, "You ran away once when I came down here on my pony."

He gave no sign of recalling the incident. She thought he looked very handsome, and yet there was an eerie sort of vacancy behind his eyes.

She remembered a foal that had been born dead recently, and how puzzling it had seemed – nothing wrong with it, everything there, and all looking so perfect. It was even as warm as a living foal. It made her wonder what was missing. In a way, Harvey Kelly was even more puzzling. He could walk and talk and wear clothes – and even do complicated things like tickling trout – and yet anyone with twenty eyes would only need one of them to see there was something missing there.

"And are these the magical hands that can scoop the trout out of clear water?"

"No, ma'am!" he replied in alarm, for he knew very well what a roasting he'd get from Willy Mangan, the head gamekeeper, if he was ever caught. Then, seeing he was not believed, he said, "What's trout, ma'am?"

Miss Morrell stared at him solemnly and then, pointing to the ground beneath his feet, said, "What are *trout?* Surely everyone knows what trout are? Why you might be treading on them at this very minute. They live underneath the leaves there and down in the clay. They look like little baby snakes, except they're all pink or brown – and the fishermen do be digging them up to use as bait to catch the worms swimming in the lake. Didn't your Mammy ever tell you that?"

Harvey Kelly, who had listened to the first half of her

'explanation' in utter bewilderment, suddenly realized it was all a cod. He burst out laughing and clapped his hands.

Miss Morrell persisted a while longer. "But you're cleverer than that, aren't you, young fellow. You don't need to go digging up a pailful of trout to bait your hook – not you! You haven't even a hook, let alone a line. You catch the worms with your bare hands, eh!"

"Trout, ma'am," he replied with a forced weariness, implying the joke was funnier the first time.

Miss Morrell, who was inclined to gauge a child's intelligence by the number of times it could laugh at the same basic joke, began to suspect that Harvey Kelly was not as simple as people made out. "You catch *trout* with your bare fingers?" she asked.

He nodded and pressed his lips tight together, implying: 'As if you didn't know!'

"And out of the *water?*' Her incredulous tone implied he was opening up a wonderful new discovery for her.

"Will I show you?" he volunteered eagerly.

"I think we simply have to see this for ourselves, don't you, Miss Salome?" She began edging him toward the bank. "Do we have to keep deathly quiet?"

"Ah no, you're all right, ma'am," he assured her. "If ye stand back from the bank – or a fair few paces upstream or down. There's a point where you may see in but the fish can't see out."

"That's because of the refractive index of the water with respect to air," she explained to Salome. "Have we studied that yet?"

Salome shook her head. It didn't sound at all interesting so she didn't wish to appear too keen.

The governess understood well enough, though. "We'll do it tomorrow," she said. "It's BBU." That was her shorthand for Boring But Useful.

Miss Morrell did not believe that learning should follow a set curriculum; the very idea of a steady and logical progression from ignorance to knowledge was anathema to her. She thought the best way to educate any child would be to lock it away in a big library for twenty years and let boredom and inquisitiveness do the rest. If you wanted to teach a little girl about gravity, you waited until she fell off her pony; then she'd listen. Salome hadn't even heard the name of Oliver Cromwell before she saw an old woman spit at its very mention; now she could tell you as much about him as anyone needed in order to get through life. She could certainly tell you why he made the common people of Ireland spit, though he was revered by their counterparts in England. So, thought Miss Morrell, refractive index would come in very handy after a practical lesson like this.

Harvey Kelly rolled up his sleeve, almost to the shoulder, and then lay flat on the ground, about a yard from the water's edge. He rolled himself slowly toward it. The way he slid his hand into the water was the nearest thing to a water snake, Salome thought – not that she had ever seen such a creature, but she had seen the snakes at Dublin zoo and the Kelly boy's arm moved just like them.

To his chagrin, a fine trout almost volunteered to be tickled to its death. Thoughts of his mother's praises when he brought home such a fat specimen vied with his desire to make the business seem about as difficult as possible – else they would hardly admire his skill. The maternal praises won. The governess and her young pupil were still wondering if that vaguely shimmering thing at the bottom of that wavy pink line joined to the lad's shoulder could possibly be a trout when they saw it arcing through the air in a whole convoy of shining beads. It fell among the dead fronds of last year's ferns and lay wriggling like a dervish.

Harvey sprang to his feet and stood over it proudly. "Jayce what a whopper!" he crowed, several times.

The other two approached it guardedly – not for fear it might harm them but out of respect for the act of dying.

"It's drowning in air, just as we would drown in water,"

Miss Morrell said as they watched its struggles grow weaker. "You should put it out of its misery. You know the way fishermen do that?"

"Me Mammy does be telling me not to, ma'am," he replied.

Miss Morrell was about to argue when she realized why. She said no more about it for the moment.

They thanked him for his little demonstration and turned to go.

"You'll not tell the quare fella, ma'am?" he called after them.

Miss Morrell eyed him severely. "As long as you don't take too many," she said. "And don't be telling the whole of Cloonaghvogue what you're after doing."

They went another few paces before he called again: "Would I see Miss Salome down here again?"

To Salome's surprise (except that Miss Morrell was always surprising her) it was left to her to answer. "Sure I'm often down here," she said casually.

Her governess rewarded her with an approving smile. "That was a good answer, dear," she said as they crossed the footbridge and regained the driveway back to the house. "Now, d'you know the way a proper fisherman kills a struggling fish?"

"The poor thing!" Salome's voice was not overburdened with sincerity.

"They stun it – quick as lightning. It feels no suffering at all."

"How?"

"They pick it up by the tail and dash its brains out on the toe of their boot."

"Yeeurgh!" Salome was appalled; this imagined fate, in her mind's eye, seemed far worse than the gradual expiration she had just seen in reality. Anyway, she could just see herself being picked up by some giant, holding her round the ankles while he dashed her brains out against his castle wall. She thought she'd far rather sink beneath the water and drown than have that happen to her. However, she kept these opinions to herself.

Miss Morrell was saying, "Why d'you suppose his mother forbids him to do that?"

"Perhaps she doesn't want him to get his boots all covered in gore?" Salome suggested.

"Think again. I said a *proper* fisherman just now. Perhaps I should have said a *lawful* fisherman!"

"Ah!" Salome laughed. Miss Morrell sometimes knew just the right word to use so as to tip your thoughts in the required direction. As soon as Salome heard that word *lawful*, she knew the entire answer, complete and all at one go – not assembled painstakingly, word by word. But, for that very reason, she had a struggle to express it – the words kept tripping over each other: "Because Mister Mangan, you see, if he caught Harvey Kelly, the fish, he'd know, I mean he'd only have to look at it and he'd see – because there wouldn't be all that – because its head wouldn't be all gory, he could say he just found it. But if it *was* – all smashed in, I mean – then he'd know, wouldn't he?"

"Know what?"

"That it was alive when he found it. Because who'd be the fool to go knocking the brains out of a *dead* fish?"

Miss Morrell drew a deep breath of satisfaction; but she said – in the same severe tone she had lately turned upon the young trout-tickler – "What a ragbag of verbosity, Miss! Close your eyes, count slowly to ten, and then say it properly."

Salome closed her eyes, counted to ten . . . but what she said was, "*Could* I go down there and play with him sometimes?"

"Why?" the other asked sharply.

"Because I don't ever play with anybody and it's not fair."

"Nonsense, girl! Only last week you were driven over to

Castle Moore to play with Henny. And Hereward. And when summer comes you'll swim in their lake. And two weeks ago I myself took you in to Parsonstown to play with . . ."

"Yes, but I'm always *taken* somewhere. I always have to wrap up and wear gloves and stuff. I never play with any of the children in Cloonaghvogue. I don't even know their names, most of them. You knew Harvey Kelly's name. I didn't."

"Ah," was all Miss Morrell could say to that – for the prohibition against playing with 'the village ragamuffins' came, of course, from Mrs Culham-Browne, who feared that Salome's plebeian origins might burst out, like some long-suppressed sickness, if given half a chance.

"So can I?" Salome asked anxiously.

The governess peered at her for a moment before saying, "Why? D'you think he's handsome? I suppose he is in a vacant sort of way."

Salome's ears turned bright red but she made no reply – except, eventually, to repeat her request.

Miss Morrell sighed. "I don't think you should ask me that sort of thing, dear."

"Why not?"

"Don't whine! I'll tell you why not. Once upon a time, there were two monks – a Franciscan and a Jesuit – both of them slaves to tobacco. Franciscans, as you may know, are terribly good-hearted but if they get a midge in one ear, there isn't a great deal to prevent it flying out by the other, if you see what I mean. So the Franciscan asked his superior if he might smoke during meditation – and his superior, quite naturally, sent him off with a flea in his ear. But . . ."

"And it jumped right out by the other!" Salome giggled.

Miss Morrell put a hand to her brow and said, "Oh dear! I'm sorry – that was quite unintentional. *Not* the point of the tale. Forget I said it. His superior ate him a mile off – is that better? Told him he was no true monk if he couldn't defeat the cravings of his weak and fallible flesh, snish-snish, and all that. But the Jesuit! Oh, those fellows have more up top than is good for them. The Jesuit priest went to *his* superior and began their conversation by saying that every now and then he'd pause from his busy round and enjoy a quiet cigarette. It only took him ten minutes or so but it had often struck him that ten minutes was ten minutes and if you added them all up, it could soon come to quite an interval. So what he'd been thinking was this. Would it be *sinful* to employ himself in quiet *meditation* at the same time as he puffed his cigarette? And of course his superior commended him as a pious and dedicated member of his order. D'you understand the point of that little story, Salome?"

"Yes, Miss Morrell." She grinned.

The woman looked at her in surprise – tinged with something like admiration. "I say!" she murmured. "Do you really?"

22

The chauffeur, Alf Gorman, had at last twigged that when it came to tying a hot exhaust tube to the chassis of his employers' Straker-Squire ('The World's Best Medium-Priced Motor'), wire had the edge over string; so, apart from three punctures, the journey to Castle Moore was uneventful. It was a soft day; bouts of fine, soaking drizzle alternated with brilliant sunshine, which fetched steam off the roads and meadows and made the car appear to be floating through a dream landscape. At times Salome found herself wondering whether all the people in the fields were real. When it drizzled she was glad to be all snug and warm inside the car; but when the sun shone she wanted to stop and join them and do whatever they were doing.

"What *are* they doing?" she asked Miss Morrell at last.

"Planting potatoes, dear," she replied. "The Shannon has subsided earlier than usual this year, so the land must be dry enough." It was Easter Monday, which most people took as a bank holiday; but if you had seed potatoes to plant and conacre to plant it in, holidays were not for you.

Salome felt briefly ashamed. Of course they were planting potatoes! Hadn't she done it herself, in her other life! In her mind's eye she saw the ass-drawn spreader open up the rich black clay, and the men and women bent low, hobbling backwards as they dropped the seed from the pails. She could see the neatly spaced blobs, pale against the clay, stretching down the field. "I used to cut the seed," she said. "The first time I was let use a knife." She sat up straighter, remembering her pride in herself that day.

"*Allowed to* use a knife," Miss Morrell corrected her. "Why did you have to cut the seed at all?" It fascinated her that Salome would revert without thinking to her old dialect whenever she spoke of the days before she came to Cloonaghvogue. The child knew perfectly well that 'allowed to' was better than 'let' . . . and there the thought dried up, overtaken by something much more vague: a suspicion that there were always two Salomes inside the one body.

She pursued it no further, for the child was prattling on: "Because it might have three eyes. So you'd cut it in three seeds that had one eye each. They'd grow just as well and you'd waste nothing."

"There was a time, about fifty years ago, when they failed to grow at all, you know. It happened three years in a row. They sprouted. They got up a lovely head of green. And then, between one day and the next, they'd wither, turn black, and rot. Did you ever hear people talk of the Famine?"

Salome nodded. "My Nan told me. She said the English saved us."

"That's one way of putting it, I suppose."

"They saved her, anyway."

"They saved enough of us to go on being useful to them afterwards. And they let enough of us die to allow the land to fall back into their ownership. And that's the truth of it. Before the Famine there were seven or eight million of us. After it there were only three. I mean three million, of course."

The girl's jaw dropped. "And the rest died?"

"Millions died. Millions emigrated."

"And millions turned Protestant for the soup, ma'am," Gorman put in. It disturbed him to hear Protestants take the anti-English line. There was a lot of it about these days. Everyone knew Home Rule was coming – indeed, they'd already have it but for the Great War. The Protestants could see it as clearly as anyone – more clearly, perhaps, for weren't they closer to the reins of power! And they wanted to hold on to those reins, of course. They'd take the independence, let alone the bread, out of *real* Irish mouths. If they were let. Or 'allowed to' – he smiled primly.

Miss Morrell, goaded by that grin, said, "Those turncoats showed their true colours, though, when better times returned. Little honour they brought to those who accepted them back."

"There is more rejoicing in heaven, ma'am . . ." the chauffeur replied. But he left the quotation hanging because he couldn't remember whether it was about a stray lamb or a prodigal son or a steward who was given ten talents to multiply.

Miss Morrell smiled at Salome but the girl could see she had lost. The battle was obscure and she didn't understand even half of it, but the losing was plain enough. Anxious to help her governess in some way, she said, "Will we go on the steam yacht today, I wonder?" She knew it was most improbable, not on the first day of a week-long visit, but the topic would effectively exclude Gorman.

And so it proved; there wasn't another squeak out of the man for the rest of the way. As the miles flew by, Salome forgot her previous scorn for the Bellinghams, forgot the inconvenience of their living at the far end of the county, even forgot her new, clandestine friendship with Harvey Kelly, and instead prattled gaily about the rare oul' times she'd enjoyed at Castle Moore.

To Miss Morrell it had always seemed a wonder that Marion Culham-Browne allowed her precious darling within ten miles of the Bellinghams, for the arrangement at Castle Moore was a notorious ménage-à-trois. True, it had been established for almost thirty years by now. The scandal was over and done with before Miss Morrell was even born – or it had been waning, at least, for no scandal ever quite dies in Ireland. She wasn't absolutely sure of the details – indeed, she hoped to discover most of them during this week-long visit – but she knew what was public knowledge.

The owner of Castle Moore was Richard Bellingham, of course – *the* Richard Bellingham, author of *Héloïse of the Sorrows*, *The Dastard*, *When the Wind Blows* and so many others; she'd forgotten how many. His family had been murdered in their beds by Land Leaguers or something when he was a baby. They must have been an odd family even then, because most people would have sold up and got out; but they decided to go on flying the Bellingham flag from the Castle Moore battlements and so they left the baby there to be brought up by visiting relations and the servants. It must have given young Richard a strange outlook on life, so you couldn't honestly blame him. Anyway, he'd married one of the notorious Dalton girls, the Hon. Guinevere and the Hon. Laetitia – sisters of Lord Vigo, the State Steward at the time. As a matter of courtesy they were both called 'the Honourable Mrs Bellingham', but was it Gwinny or Letty who actually married Richard? That was one of the things to find out. Anyway, it hardly mattered, because they all three slept in the same bed and he had children by both of them.

The sisters were notorious bluestockings – which was only to be expected if you gave them names like Guinevere and Laetitia. Miss Morrell remembered her mother saying that Vigo had been lucky to get them off his hands in any way he could. Of course, when the scandal first became known, he'd had to resign as State Steward; but he'd only taken the position for the sake of its highly prestigious address – Dublin Castle – which would more than double his chances of marrying them off during the Dublin Season. So that was no great sacrifice.

When one looked at it all round, Miss Morrell thought, one could see why society had come to accept the situation – and the people involved in it. Bellingham was a rich landowner who wielded a great deal of patronage in County Keelity; half the county wouldn't dare cross him, even if he turned out to be Bluebeard reincarnate. And everyone admired him for staying on after that ghastly tragedy and 'showing the flag' to the Fenians – even though the decision had hardly been his at the time. Also he was an artist . . . artistic licence and all that sort of thing.

So, what with one thing and another, Miss Morrell had been looking forward to her brief visit to this centre of infamy far more than had Salome, who only began to get excited as they approached the castle gates. She knew the place well, of course, for she had often brought Salome here for parties and picnics in the steam yacht. But she had never stayed here and never had a chance to talk to people and learn the real truth about the household.

As a final annoyance to the chauffeur she waited until they were within hailing distance of the entrance and said, "It's just around this next corner, Gorman."

The man, who prided himself on never getting lost,

clamped his jaws tight together and said nothing. Near the top of the drive he nearly died of fright, though, when a Red Indian brave and his squaw leaped at them from the ambush of a clump of pheasant bower. They stood on the running board, clinging precariously to the doorhandles, and the brave, pointing to the carriage sweep in front of the castle, said, "We headum off at pass!"

Salome wound the window down and punched the brave on the arm. "Hereward!" she cried. "What *have* you got on your face?"

The question floored him. His knowledge of genuine Indian folklore was – like the stage makeup he had used – only skin deep. "Head woad," he said, blending cultures shamelessly.

"Me born brown as berry," Henny said, giving her elder brother a reproachful glance.

"You see, dear!" Miss Morrell told Salome. "Women make far more natural deceivers."

This little intervention had the effect of making each Bellingham feel superior to the other. Hereward gave a war whoop as Gorman turned the car and drew up before the main door. Guinevere Bellingham, a tall, dark-haired, graceful woman with an aquiline nose, stood in welcome – another sign that this was not a conventional household. She peeled the children off the running board as if they were something distasteful that had stuck to the car during the journey. She smiled apologetically at Miss Morrell. "The doctor's children get the worst medicine – and the writer's children read the worst books, I'm afraid. Everything has gone Red Indian around here. Welcome to our totem or whatever the right word is."

"Teepee!" the two youngsters chorused wearily.

"Come on, Sal!" Hereward grabbed her by the elbow. "We'll get you made up."

"Initiated!" his sister said severely.

They ran up the front steps to the massive front door but

before they reached it Guinevere called out, "Passing Cloud!"

He stopped and turned impatiently. "Yes, Gwinnie?"

The familiarity startled Miss Morrell, who had never heard the children call their dual mothers anything, except a very occasional ma'am. So it probably meant that Guinevere was not Hereward's mother.

"Luncheon . . . or pemmican . . . or whatever you people call it – in the nursery teepee in fifteen minutes. And in your dressing gowns, please. I won't have you sitting around half-naked, catching colds. You, too, Running Deer."

"Yes, Gwinnie," both children said.

So, Miss Morrell decided reluctantly, it probably *didn't* mean she was not Hereward's mother. The English teacher within her realized she had just discovered a double-negative that did not imply its contrary. A grammatical gem. It must be something in the air, she decided – stray thoughts from the great writer that just drifted around the place. "Is Mister Bellingham at home?" she asked.

Guinevere looked at her with some amusement. "As a matter of fact, he is." Her smile broadened. "Can you wait fifteen minutes or shall I take you to him at once?"

Miss Morrell blushed. "No . . ." she faltered. "I don't know why I asked. I mean, I *do*. I was miles away – thinking of some obscure point in grammar. It just popped out."

"As *it* is wont to do," was the questionable reply. "Well!" she rubbed her hands briskly. "Time for a small snorter before luncheon?" She took Miss Morrell's arm and propelled her up the steps. "Come and meet Letty."

"I don't usually, you know," Miss Morrell pointed out. "Drink before luncheon, I mean. In fact, I don't usually drink at all."

"Give it a week's trial," Guinevere suggested.

Letty poked her head out of the doorway to the drawing

room; she was shorter and even darker and more curvaceous than her sister. Variety was certainly the spice of Richard Bellingham's life, Miss Morrell decided. "I thought as much," Letty said. "I heard a war whoop. Does Miss Morrell want a drinky?"

"Try her on a cream sherry," Gwinnie replied. "She's still running-in." She maintained her hold on Miss Morrell's arm as she led her into the room. "We simply can't go on calling you Miss Morrell all week," she said. "Especially as we've all gone over to Christian names in this household. You know we're called Letty and Gwinnie. Were you, in fact, given a first name at all?"

Miss Morrell laughed – and then blushed as she admitted to, "Maisie, I'm afraid."

"Miss Maisie Morrell," Letty said as she handed her a sherry, carefully not too generous. "It's a darling name. Good title for a book, too: *The Ordeal of Maisie Morrell.*" She smiled sweetly and sat down.

Miss Morrell was not the first visitor to feel the sweet-and-sour hospitality of the Bellingham ladies. Some imp told her that, if only she set aside her own social inhibitions, she could give as good as she got, and for a brief moment she was tempted to try it at once. But a caution born of her socially ambiguous status as a mere governess warned her to hold back until she knew more about the local terrain – even if that meant taking a few small flesh wounds in the meantime. "It sounds exciting," she said. "Is it a physical or a mental ordeal, I wonder?"

"We could make it either," Gwinnie said lightly, as if they really were talking about a book that was yet to be written. "Which would you prefer?"

"Mental, I think." She took a sip. "When it comes to physical ordeals I'm a bit of a coward."

Gwinnie and Letty exchanged glances. It was clear to Miss Morrell that they had planned some gentle fun at her expense – and that she was proving something of a surprise to them both. She did not grudge them their fun. After all, she knew better than most the crushing tedium of life in a large country house with little but the next clodhoppers' ball to look forward to; all she wanted to do was broaden the scope of their enterprise to include herself as well.

A bell rang outside in the hall, long and urgent. "Telephone," Letty explained. Gwinnie half-rose but the ringing stopped abruptly. "Good man," she murmured and seated herself again. "Well, Maisie, I don't know if you've planned much for this week? We rather thought the children might like to run wild for a bit. They're keen to sleep on the island and catch fish and . . . look for buffalo droppings, and so forth. We can rescue them before they starve to death. D'you think the Culham-Brownes would object to that?"

"Mrs Culham-Browne thinks Salome has a weak chest," Miss Morrell responded.

"And you don't?"

She sidestepped the invitation to disloyalty. "As long as she wraps up well, I'm sure there can be no . . . no . . ."

"Consequence?"

"Objection, I was going to say."

"I wonder who's ringing Richard?" Letty said suddenly.

"The stockbrokers," Gwinnie replied; her tone implied it happened daily at this hour.

"On Easter Monday?" Letty replied.

Gwinnie bit her lip. "Yes, of course. I wonder who it is, then?"

The conversation drifted toward the generalities with which it ought to have begun – what sort of journey it had been . . . how were the Culham-Brownes? . . . what dreadful news from the Dardanelles . . . and so forth.

It petered out as the door slowly opened and framed a tall, strikingly handsome man in his late forties.

"Richard!" Gwinnie cooed. "Come and meet Maisie. She's absolutely dying to . . ." Her voice trailed off when she saw how pale and shaken he was – something that had been obvious to Miss Morrell from the start. "What ever is the matter?" she concluded.

Bellingham came in then and went straight to Miss Morrell. "Do forgive me," he said, taking her hand. "Miss Morrell, isn't it. I remember you well. Welcome to Castle Moore." He swallowed heavily; his voice was shivery. "Is there a brandy?"

"Brandy!" Letty rose in alarm.

"Yes – I've just had rather a shock."

"The phone!" Gwinnie said as her sister went to pour the unaccustomed tipple. "Who was it?"

"Your bro, actually. He says there's been a rebellion in Dublin – an armed rebellion. The Republican Brotherhood or something like that has seized the General Post Office. There's been some bloodshed."

"The GPO!" Letty was aghast.

They all turned to her in surprise, for she spoke as if she owned the property.

"I've just posted a parcel containing *all* Henny's and Hereward's grown-out-of clothes to Cousin Margaret for Sarah and Tony! Oh, this *bloody* country!"

23

It was a storm in a teacup, everyone agreed. A bunch of romantic hotheads had got drunk on their own verbiage: 'In the name of God and of the dead generations from which she receives her old traditions of nationhood, Ireland, through us, summons her children to her flag and strikes for her freedom . . . !' Dublin groaned and wished Ireland would just leave it alone for a change. And as for Ireland itself, well, Ireland had heard it all before, to the point of weariness. Genuine patriots were outraged; they were as keen as the next Celt to see the back of Perfidious Albion – but not as a target for their daggers. The mere sight of them on the ferry gangways at Kingstown would do very nicely. The Sons of the Fianna didn't stab an enemy in the back. And that was just what these hotheads in the GPO were doing, stabbing away while England had her back turned, fighting the Hun. It wasn't an honourable way to win.

Anyway, they clearly weren't going to win. Nationwide investigations (the same investigations Martin Woods had used to cloak his inquiries on Georgina's behalf) had clearly repaid all the effort. So that when the Germans tried to land guns and ammunition on the Kerry shore – the weapons that would have supported a national rising – they sailed straight into a trap. The rebellion was over before it started – which left Dublin to go it alone, pitting a ragtag army, less than two thousand strong, against the imperial might of England. A *flurry* in a teacup, indeed; you wouldn't dignify it with the name of storm.

All the same, Richard Bellingham and his ménage felt they could hardly behave as if *nothing* were happening that Easter Monday; some sort of gesture was called for. His very life, his continuous presence at Castle Moore ever since the Fenians (or Land Leaguers or some such brotherhood) had murdered his parents and three elder siblings back in 1881, was a gesture of sorts. Unfortunately, the English had hanged four innocent men for the crime, which had turned Richard from a flag-showing Anglo-Irish gentleman into 'a plague on both your houses' artist, a man of the world, far above the demands of *anybody's* petty nationalism. So it was not easy to hit upon a gesture to match this so-called Easter Rising. In the end they decided to dress formally, as if for a garden party at the Viceregal Lodge, and take tea in the marble pavilion across the lake – the site of the Castle Moore Murders, thirty-five years ago.

Of the five older Bellingham offspring, Ricardo and

Prosper were in the trenches, while Lavinia was filling a nursery in London; Dorinda and Camilla were only a few miles away, but still out of immediate reach, preparing a dramatic presentation with the Simonstown Players. Thus only the two Apaches – Hereward and Henny, augmented for the present by Salome – were available. They were washed and restored to civilization in the nick of time. At a quarter to four a procession set off for the pavilion. It was more reminiscent of the Castle Moore of forty years ago than anything the ancient stones had witnessed recently: four adults, three children, two footmen, and four parlourmaids.

They crossed the carriage sweep and paused a moment to take in the view; the servants, carrying the hamper, the cushions, the parasols, and the rugs, continued on their way.

The castle, standing as it did two-thirds of the way up Mount Argus, commanded one of the finest views in the county. Richard pointed out its features to Miss Morrell, who felt rather flattered at the interest the great man was taking in her.

"My grandfather dug this lake during the Famine," he said, "to provide relief for the poor." His finger led her eyes down over five terraced lawns to a long, roughly oval stretch of water where half-wild swans were busy guarding their nests or sitting on their eggs. On the farther shore, dominating a slope of wildflower meadow, the pavilion shimmered white in the thin Easter sunshine.

"How do we get across?" she asked.

He alarmed her by leaning even closer but it was only to point to a boathouse at the head of the water. From it one of the gardeners was rowing out in a large boat. "And that's Lough Cool beyond," he added, "as if you didn't know!"

"Yes, we can just see the southern end of it from the battlements at Cloonaghvogue. We can also see Coolderg Castle, but we can't see you."

"Of course not. That's why you have to come here in person."

His engaging smile filled her with panic. How *could* a man be so flirtatious with his wife and . . . er, the other one . . . standing almost at his side!

"And over there – see that blue-green smudge?" he went on.

"The shore of County Clare," she said, surprised he should ask.

Salome started in surprise at the words. True, from her bedroom at home you could see what people *said* was County Clare, but it was just an imaginary line in a band of green. From here it had an edge, a definite beginning.

My old home, she thought, but the words had lost their power to stir her. She could still weep if she tried very hard and thought of Maggoty Meg all alone in the Cape; memories of her mother and father could raise an occasional lump in her throat; she sometimes tried to imagine Samson and Martha, who would now be eleven and seven, and baby David, who would now be four, but it grew more difficult with each month that passed. By now, in fact, they were almost wholly imaginary people. In her mind's eye she saw them playing beneath the cactuses (borrowed from Uncle C-B's *Travels in Many Lands*) with the dear little piccaninnies (borrowed from *Uncle Tom's Cabin*), and felt a stab of jealousy; but all her deeper feelings about her loss seemed to have evaporated long ago.

She looked up and found Miss Morrell staring at her. She smiled and shook her head, as if her governess had asked an actual question. Miss Morrell smiled back, a rather preoccupied smile, and darted a nervous glance at the other two grown-up ladies.

"Have you ever been to Linford in Clare?" Richard asked. "D'you know the little group of whitewashed cottages at the northern end of the village?" He pointed to some pale specks at the extreme limit of the visible farther shore and moved half behind her so that she could sight along his arm; now they were almost cheek-to-cheek. "There – see? We must go over there one day. Lovely crayfish teas they do at the inn."

His use of 'we' was ambiguous enough to fluster Miss Morrell still further. "Is that Turk Island?" she asked hastily, pointing to a dot on the limpid waters to the south of them. She took the chance to move a little away from him – though, if they had been alone, she realized, she would not have done so, for she found she enjoyed his nearness and found his dark voice quite thrilling.

"Yes. The strange thing about Turk is that it's almost an exact replica of our island here." He indicated a much closer island, about a third of the way across the lake from Castle Moore.

"Is it really *your* island?"

He assumed a mournful, apologetic expression. "I'm afraid everything you see, from here down to Turk Island, is ours, Maisie – this side of the lough, of course. Isn't it absurdly feudal! I feel quite ashamed at times."

"But how grand to own an entire island!" Maisie responded. "Is Turk Island yours, too?"

He chuckled. "No – but there'd be little point in owning both. As I was saying – they're Tweedledum and Tweedledee." He grinned at his wife and sister-in-law. "Land on either of them in the dark and I'll swear you couldn't tell t'other from which."

Gwinnie cleared her throat heavily and said, "Are we going to stand here all day?"

"Plenty of time," he replied mildly. "I thought we'd let the servants cross the water first and get everything set up for us. You and Letty stroll on if you wish. All this is quite new to Maisie."

"You think so, do you?" Gwinnie asked sweetly as she grasped her sister's arm and propelled her toward the path that led down to the boating lake. "Come on, children!"

"What did you mean by that?" Letty asked before the children caught up with them. "D'you think Maisie Morrell has *experience?*"

"Not by what I've *heard* of her," Gwinnie replied. "And yet almost her first question to me was to wonder whether Rick was here – the moment she stepped out of the car!"

"The hussy!" Letty laughed with delight. "Perhaps Rick has met his match. The spider weaves his web to catch a little *mouche*, and suddenly finds a predatory female advancing toward him along the silken strands!"

"And we all know what female spiders do to the male of the species."

"*Afterwards!*"

The children caught up and they dropped the subject for the moment.

"What did she mean by that?" Miss Morrell wondered aloud as the sisters moved out of earshot.

"*May* I call you Maisie?" he asked. "We're not a terribly conventional household here at Castle Moore – as you may already have observed. What did she mean by what?"

"Wondering whether I'd seen this view before."

He chuckled, as if he thought her question merely perverse – which, in turn, helped her grasp the real import of Gwinnie's question. She felt herself blush. He saw it at once and realized how undeserved his wife's sneer had been. Miss Maisie Morrell was utterly, captivatingly green! "You're shocked now," he said.

"No, no!" She swallowed heavily. "Please do call me Maisie – though I shall find it very hard to call you Richard."

"You needn't," he offered magnanimously. "It's Liberty Hall here. You may continue with 'Mister Bellingham', if you prefer."

The joke relaxed her – to such an extent that she was able to dig him in the ribs with her elbow and say, "You!"

"First advance rejected," Gwinnie said. She, having the

better distance vision, had placed herself beyond Letty so that, while ostensibly talking to her, she could keep a sharp eye on their man and his quarry. "But very playfully, I must say. She'll give in before the week's over."

A dozen or so yards ahead of them Salome, realizing that the Clare shore would soon be hidden behind the plantation of evergreens that formed a dark backdrop to the white of the marble, pointed across the lough and said, "That's where I come from, you know. Somewhere over there."

"Cloonaghvogue?" Hereward asked in disbelief. But his question was not as naïve as it might seem. When Salome had first entered their circle, he twigged there was something a little odd because she wasn't called Culham-Browne straight away; but he'd simply assumed she was a distant relation of the family. This past week or two, however, since her visit had been arranged, he'd heard one or two things that had made him aware of a deeper mystery – which he was now minded to probe. He rather prided himself on worming things out of people when they didn't even know he was doing it.

"No. County Clare. The place where I was born. Before I ever came to Cloonaghvogue."

Henny then spoiled it by asking, "Did you lose your parents, Sal? I often wondered why you're living with the Culham-Brownes."

"It's *her* business," Hereward said, startling them both with his anger. "Don't answer," he commanded Salome.

"But it's no great secret," the girl protested. "You mean neither of you *know* about me? You haven't heard how I came to be with the Culham-Brownes?"

They both stared at her so agog with interest that she suddenly panicked, thinking that the rather humdrum truth would come as a bit of a let-down. Besides, they had this fabulous castle and its gardens and boating lake and everything – glory in which to bask; she had nothing. So she heard herself saying, "Aunt Marion bought me off a taxi-driver in Cork one day."

"*Bought* you?" Henny's jaw dropped.

"For five pounds." Salome, committed now, nodded solemnly in an attempt to suppress her elation.

"Were you a . . . slave?" Henny was still incredulous.

"Something like that," Salome admitted. She kept walking briskly to mask any little hesitations.

"Why from a taxi-driver?" Hereward asked.

The Water-Babies came to her rescue. "He was taking me to a chimney sweep. I was to be put up chimneys to rake down the soot."

The boy frowned. It wasn't that he disbelieved her – in fact, he found her tale all too convincing. But it distressed him to be so swiftly relegated to the status of *second*-most-interesting person at Castle Moore. "How old were you?" he asked suspiciously.

Salome thought swiftly. If she told the truth and said seven, they'd reasonably expect her to remember something of her childhood. "Four," she replied firmly. "I don't remember much about before coming to Cloonaghvogue."

Hereward bit his lip in frustration. "I can remember when I was *two*," he boasted. "I was being wheeled up Grafton Street in Dublin and Nanny Walker held me up to watch the Lord Lieutenant go by in his plumed hat. I can remember that – the plumes and the sunlight on his medals." He stared challengingly at Salome.

They had reached the little stone jetty by now; the servants had disembarked on the far side and the gardener-boatman was rowing back to collect the main party. Salome realized there was no competing in grandeur for her; she had to go as far in the other direction as possible to retain the advantage she had accidentally stumbled upon.

"Was the taxi-driver your father?" Henny asked.

Salome sighed. "I remember nothing – except a vague

picture of cows. I seem to remember driving cows in from the fields. Aunt Marion says it was in County Clare. And I also remember the bitter cold in winter – and me just in rags." She shivered dramatically. "That's the sort of thing I remember – feelings and impressions, you know."

"Were you *barefoot?*" Henny asked. Poverty and deprivation fascinated her; when she grew up she was going to help the world put an end to it.

"All the time," Salome assured her. "But the reason I remember so little is they kept me pretty stupefied with gin most of those years."

Hereward gave up a struggle to which he was obviously unequal. Every question they asked merely allowed Salome to increase her advantage. "I wish you could remember more," he said sympathetically. "It would be jolly interesting if you could." He turned to his sister. "But as she can't, it would be uncivil to press her, so let's change the subject, eh?"

"Bits of it come back now and then," Salome assured them eagerly. "Sometimes I think it's all a dream and then other times I just know it really happened. I'll tell you if any bits come back to me."

The boatman drew alongside the jetty; they admired the skill with which he merely nudged the stone as he halted. Hereward got in first, ostensibly to stand in the bows and hold the iron ring, but really because he just wanted to stand in the bows and brood. He reminded Salome of *Napoleon Bound for Elba*, an oleochromolithograph in Uncle C-B's business room. She realized how unhappy Hereward was to be upstaged by her tales of her poverty-stricken childhood.

They crossed the narrow stretch of water in silence. As they stepped off, she took him by the arm and pulled his reluctant ear close to her lips, "Is it true," she asked in a whisper, "that your grandparents were shot by republicans on this very spot?"

It was like watching a flower unfurl at the touch of the sun – except that it happened in seconds rather than minutes. He turned triumphantly to his father. "Rick?" he said. "Sal wants to hear about the Castle Moore Murders."

"Salome!" Maisie exclaimed in scandalized tones. "How could you!"

But Rick put her on the spot. "Why shouldn't she want to know?" he asked. "What could be more natural? Or d'you think we shouldn't ever mention it? Bad form, eh?"

Maisie was gripped by anger, though whether more at herself for her thoughtless intervention than at him for making her feel so petty she could not say. Fortunately no one was taking any notice of her; all eyes were on Rick, who had already gone to Salome's side and, taking her by the hand, began to lead her up across the meadow.

"I'll tell you a secret that's stood me in good stead all my life, young lady," he said. "I can't deny that having to watch helplessly while a gang of desperadoes shoot one's parents, one's eldest sister, and one's two eldest brothers to death is a pretty harrowing experience. And you're quite right – it happened to me, here, on this very spot, the best part of thirty-five years ago. It was my sister Henrietta's sixteenth birthday. I was twelve – the same age as Hereward, now." He smiled at his son. "Of course, I was much better-looking."

Hereward laughed and hit him playfully, making Salome wish she had such a father – or had *ever* had such a father.

Rick continued: "A neighbour's daughter turned fifteen on the very same day." His eyes raked the heavens. "What *was* her name?"

"Judith," Gwinnie said wearily.

"Judith Carty," her sister added.

Maisie understood that he was teasing them; there had probably been something between Rick and this Judith girl at some time.

"Judith – of course!" he exclaimed, tapping his brow. "So we had a joint sort of birthday dinner down here in the pavilion."

They had reached the apron of the circular building, the front three-quarters of which consisted of a ring of seven marble pillars in the Ionic style; two of them were actually half-pillars, or pilasters, set like book-ends into the curved marble wall at the back, which made up the remaining quarter-circle. Most of the interior was occupied by a simple, elegantly proportioned marble table and benches, with wrought-iron thrones at each end. The footmen and maids were now busily arranging the sandwiches and scones, cakes and biscuits, and jam, clotted cream, and butter upon it.

"So picture us all here" – Rick wafted a showman's hand toward the table – "with the setting sun casting a long shadow of the pavilion down the slope and onto the water . . ."

Maisie did more. She imagined herself sitting there – and understood why the Bellinghams had built their little summerhouse facing east, when all her instincts would have been to face it west, looking across the lough toward the sunset. If Rick had not so recently pointed out that he owned everything in sight on this side of the lough, she might not have tumbled to it so quickly. But from that table you could feast your tongue on the delicacies the servants had carried before you, and your eyes on your mountain, your castle, your boating lake, your lawns, and your gardeners – busily tending your little paradise.

It was as if Rick read her thoughts for he sprang back, crying: " . . .when suddenly!" – he adopted a semi-crouching position, as if aiming a gun – "Bang! Half a dozen gunmen between you and the most pleasing prospect on earth!"

Salome ran a hand over the polished marble of the table. "Were you sitting here, Uncle Rick?" she asked.

"It's plain Rick nowadays, if you don't mind, Miss Culham-Browne. But, to answer your question – no, I wasn't. Henrietta and I had strolled over to the boathouse, to see if we'd got enough steam up in the launch. So we had to watch it from down there. The murderers all standing round here, firing volley after volley. You can see the marks of the bullets on the pillars still, where the marble spalled away."

Salome, who had taken the blemishes for mere marks of age, touched one in a kind of wonder.

Gwinnie stepped forward then. "What Rick is too modest to add," she said, "is that he struggled to get up and attack the murderers while the boatman restrained him – and that he eventually struggled free and ran at those men with his fists. And one of the murderers turned, and aimed his gun at Rick, and pulled the trigger!"

"Oh!" Salome gave a little start and stared at Rick, who laughed and assured her he wasn't a ghost. "The cartridge didn't fire," he explained. "Otherwise I shouldn't be here to tell the tale." He took her hand again. "But actually, Sal, this isn't what I really started out to tell you. All you've heard so far is just the background. The thing I really want to tell you about happened the following week, when all the family turned up for the funeral. The first to arrive was my Aunt Bill – Wilhelmina was her proper name. And I brought her down here and d'you know what I did? I *acted* everything that had happened! I didn't just tell her – the way I've told you, now. I acted every part – my parents . . . the murderers . . . me and Henrietta over there . . . me running up the hill, fists flailing! D'you understand? I *became* those people for a moment or two. And that's the important thing to tell you." He squatted on his heels to bring his head level with hers; he grinned and tapped his breastbone. "Don't bottle things up inside. They'll only fester and turn sour. Get them out into the open! Act them. Write them down. Speak out about them. It matters not how – just as long as you don't bottle them up. D'you understand?"

Somewhat to his surprise, Salome flung her arms around his neck and cried, "Yes, yes, yes!"

24

It had been a mixed day with the Cloonaghvogue hounds. They had drawn the first three coverts blank; they had found at the fourth but lost the line soon after; then, on the point of calling it a day, they had found a new line in the middle of nowhere and owned it for miles – giving a splendid chase on which to end the outing. True, there was no kill, but it had been a magnificent pursuit over good terrain behind a well-behaved pack. People went home happy enough; Charley Fox might have had his day today, but they'd get theirs tomorrow – or the day after.

The least happy man on the field was the master himself, Culham-Browne of Cloonaghvogue. Several people noticed it but only Eddie Lodge, who'd lost a foot in the first week of the war, was brash enough to raise the topic. On the ride home he fell in beside C-B and said, "What's up, old boy – lost a tanner and found a tickey, eh?"

C-B merely grunted.

Lesser men would have shrugged off the rebuff and left the curmudgeon to his own devices. Lodge pressed on: "Surely you're not worried by these republican oafs in Dublin? We're pounding them to smithereens, I hear. There'll be nothing left for the firing squads to shoot by the time it's all over."

"It is going bloody well," C-B agreed.

After a brief silence Lodge tried a new tack: "The memsahib's away, I hear. Not in Dublin, I hope?"

"No, she's down in Castlemartyr, consoling her cousin, who's just discovered she's a widow."

"Ah . . . really? Poor woman." The language of condolence was running thin by 1916. Lodge hardly knew what to say. "Young or old?" he tried.

"I don't know. I've never actually met the creature. Young, I think. Name of Edith Summers – maiden name. She was only married four months. Quiet wedding in Hampshire."

"To anyone we know?"

"You may know him. I don't – or didn't. A very decent chap by all accounts – called Martin Woods. He was an RIC inspector before the war. Bought a little estate outside Castlemartyr, mainly for the fishing. Damfool could have stayed in the force but he insisted on volunteering for the gunners. Cousin Edith was all set to spend his next leave with us – show off her new husband and all that sort of thing. It was all arranged. And now he's been killed on the Somme."

"I didn't know there was a push going on. Of course, we only hear about these things long after . . ."

"No, no. He trod on a mine." C-B sighed. "One of our own, too."

"God! Rotten luck, eh! Only four months married, you say?"

"Mmm. Probably left a bun in the oven. If he did . . ." The sentence trailed off.

Lodge glanced around to see what might have distracted the master; finding nothing he prompted the man: "Say?"

C-B sighed again. "Well, my dear lady's propensity for gathering up lame ducks is no great secret, is it!"

"Ah, you fear she may bring the pinion'd dove back home. Well . . . they are cousins."

C-B nodded morosely. "A grieving young widow in an interesting condition is not the sort of guest *I* particularly welcome at Cloonaghvogue. Family or no family."

They reached the point where their ways home separated from each other's. C-B suddenly turned and said, "Are you doing anything in particular tonight, Lodge? Wouldn't care to take pot luck at Cloonaghvogue, I suppose?"

The other licked his lips uncertainly.

"I've a superb Croft's 'Eighty-six. We could crack a couple of bottles." C-B grinned. "You'd have to stay the night, though – there'd be no riding home after *that!*"

Lodge grinned. "You said the right words, old boy!"

But it took a good, belly-filling dinner, a roaring fire, and most of the first bottle of the Croft's 'Eighty-six – which was, indeed, superb – before C-B unburdened himself of what was really on his mind. Once again it was Lodge who prompted him, when he said, "Talking of the lame ducks and pinion'd doves your memsahib collects, I haven't heard the trill of girlish laughter this evening. Have you brought the little filly to heel at last?"

His host now had too much port in his veins to fall back into his former, rather morose defeatism. Instead he let out a single, explosive *Ha!* and said, "That's something that can't be allowed to continue."

He startled even himself with this sentiment for it was the first time he had dared frame it so starkly – and certainly the first time he had expressed it aloud.

"Bit late, what?" Lodge ventured – blessing that imp of adventure which had prompted him to accept this evening's invitation. He reached for the decanter, symbolically lifted and replaced the stopper, and nudged it back toward his host.

C-B helped himself to another consoling tot. "Never too late to mend," he replied.

"You surprise me, old boy. I thought she fitted in rather well by now. Mrs C-B told me you have her down for Harrogate Ladies' College next year?"

"*If* the good Father McDaid will *permit* it!" C-B replied with heavy sarcasm.

"That Fenian papist!" Lodge was outraged. "Show him

the toe of your boot. The nerve of the man – after all the Culham-Brownes have done for his crowd! Why might *he* not permit it, anyway? He's only the curate, surely?"

C-B nodded. "I was half-joking. McDaid's a firebrand but Father Hines will keep him in order – the very *best* kind of RC padre, don't you know." He frowned. "What was I saying? I've lost the . . ."

"About the cuckoo going off to school. Why should McDaid object, anyway?"

"Oh, he's got some bee in his bonnet that she was born a Roman Catholic and should be brought up one."

"Ye godfathers! The man should be horsewhipped!"

C-B smiled and said. "I offered him the chance, actually – just to draw his fangs. 'Have her a couple of afternoons a week,' I said. 'Teach her anything you like.' Let her decide for herself when she's old enough."

Lodge was too astonished to say anything.

C-B's grin grew broader. "Of course, I knew I was on safe ground. He wouldn't hear of it. An all-or-nothing man is our Father McDaid. So – as my good lady has obviously told you – our cuckoo is off to school next year."

Lodge found his tongue at last. "She didn't exactly tell me that," he said.

C-B frowned. "I thought you said . . ."

"From what your memsahib said, I rather gathered it would be over her dead body."

C-B's face went blank. He sipped his port and said nothing.

"You're having second thoughts, eh?" Lodge guessed. "About keeping the cuckoo here at Cloonaghvogue?"

"First!" C-B barked.

"Say?"

C-B, so fluent in speaking of his clash with McDaid, became barely coherent now that the subject was once again Salome. "First thoughts. Soon as I clapped eyes on her. Little seven-year-old waif in the car. *She can't stay!*

That was my very first thought – I tell you. *Got to go!*"

"Me, too." Lodge rose to his feet, the one of flesh, the other of steel. After a few more glasses he'd start challenging his host to guess which was which. "Under the stairs, isn't it?" he asked.

After a moment's incomprehension C-B laughed and rose unsteadily to his feet, too. "Yes," he said. "You go there. I'll use the bushes. It does them good."

The chill night air soothed him. He was a lot less fuddled when he returned to the fireside, where his guest had already reseated himself. Fresh logs were crackling in the gigantic hearth. C-B dimmed the lamps before he resumed his seat, saying, "Ah! That's better. Now we can get down to some serious appreciation of one of the noblest ports that ever left Iberia's shore."

"Quoth he!" Lodge was impressed at his friend's poetic turn of phrase.

They recharged their glasses and Lodge proposed, "Absent friends."

C-B took a sip and added in a murmur, "Don't hurry back!"

They settled into a long, silent, comfortable reverie, enjoying the play of the flames and the hissing of the steam from the damp logs. Then Lodge said, "D'you know that poem about logs burning – comparing them to virgins and ladies of experience?" Without waiting for a reply he recited the verse:

"In chimneypiece you've often seen
A sullen faggot, wet and green,
How coyly it receives its heat
And at both ends doth fume and sweat!
'Tis thus with th'inexperienced maid
When first upon her back she's layed.
But the kind, experienced dame
Cracks and rejoices in the flame!

– or something like that," he added modestly as his host dissolved in laughter.

When silence returned, C-B heaved another sigh and said, "Many a true word spoken in jest, though, old chap. The 'kind, experienced dame' may give one a better . . . well, I was going to say a better run for one's money – but I'm not talking about *them*, you understand – the females you pay."

"Better *sport*," Lodge suggested.

"Precisely! The 'kind, experienced dame' may give one better sport . . ."

"A more exciting hunt and a cleaner kill, what? What?"

"Listen, or I'll lose my fox. But 'th'inexperienced maid' is the one who . . . I mean, she's the one we all . . . you know what I mean?"

"She's the one who *pricks* our interest, what? Eh? What?" Lodge laughed heartily.

"Precisely!" C-B merely smiled, meaning to show that, while he appreciated the joke, he was not to be deflected yet again. "That's the thing I was saying about . . . you know – the little girly-cuckoo in our nest. My first thoughts and all that. I was right." He tapped his forehead. "Something in here must have warned me, even then. Little seven-year-old cuckoo – sweet and charming. Gladden the cockles of your heart. D'you follow?"

"Absolutely, old man." Lodge sipped his port and nodded sagely at the fire, where the 'sullen faggots' were no longer hissing quite so fiercely. "They can twist one round their little fingers at that age."

"And now she's ten," C-B continued. "Three years gone by – *pfft!* Like that! Soon be another three. *Pfft!* And another. Flash by. And hey-presto, she's sixteen all of a sudden! Nine years at Cloonaghvogue. Be a hard job to turf her out then."

Lodge sat up with the shock. "Turf her out?" he echoed incredulously. "I say . . . what?"

C-B drew a sharp breath, intending to make a defiant answer. But before he could vent it his spirit died. His whole body slumped. "You're right," he said despondently. "Can't do it, even now. Even three years is too long. Should have done it at once."

"Why didn't you?" his guest asked rather brutally.

C-B smiled wanly. "If you'd seen the happiness in her eyes . . ."

"Whose? The cuckoo's or the memsahib's?"

"Both, actually. Couldn't do it, you see. Soft as a sucking duck, as they say in Yorkshire." He forgave himself with a magnanimous groan before adding, "However, this widow-cousin Edith is another matter altogether. I shan't let them turn Cloonaghvogue into a lying-in hospital. She can go back to Hampshire to farrow the brat. There's no bombing there. Safer there than here, in fact." After a pause he added, "In a way, you know, it's a pity they intercepted the German arms in Kerry."

Lodge stared at him admiringly. "Gad, I thought so too – not that one dares say such things too loudly. But if we'd let all the republicans in the country get those things into their hands, they'd have risen along with Dublin and we could have biffed the lot in one fell swoop. Now they'll just sit tight and wait their next chance. We've got to face it sooner or later. We could have sanitized the whole country. Missed opportunity, in my view." His eyebrows canvassed C-B's agreement.

"You could be right," his host conceded. "Though, actually, all I meant was that if there were a general rising all over Ireland, we'd have a jolly good reason for packing Cousin Edith off to Hampshire."

The note of determination in his words pleased him. He relished their echoes in silence awhile before Lodge took another sip of port and said, "Talking of getting a good run for your money . . . you know – what you mentioned just now. The females one pays?"

"Ah yes!" C-B looked up with interest, a vacant grin parting his lips.

"I don't know if you're a collector of such establishments but I found a little corker in Dublin last month."

C-B chuckled. "I can tell you of a little Dubliner in Cork, too."

Lodge held his nose in playful rejection of the pun – a boyhood gesture that both men recalled. "It's only a small place," he went on. "Very discreet. Very select – all tradesmen's daughters. No riffraff. Young and jolly – and full of bounce." He mimed the idea of buxom fleshiness. "If you prefer 'em pneumatic, you won't find better in the whole kingdom. Would you like the directions?"

C-B answered with a nonchalant nod. "One never knows," he drawled. "If my good lady insists on filling the place with nubile young widows and growing girls . . . one may need a place like that, to open up the old safety-valve, what?"

"Just so. Remind me before I leave tomorrow morning." Lodge stretched his legs toward the fire and emptied his glass. "See those two feet of mine?" he begun.

25

The children were equipped for an entire week, so a twenty-four-hour stint as castaways on the island promised adventure without hardship. They had two tents, two sets of clothing, two boxes of matches – *each* – and enough kindling to set half Keelity ablaze; and everything was wrapped in flood-defying, rain-denying oilcloth. They also had a flagpole on which they were to fly in an emergency a red flannel petticoat borrowed from one of the housemaids. The idea of leaving them a rowing boat had been canvassed and dropped; long and relatively narrow stretches of water like Lough Cool are notoriously treacherous. They give the wind a mighty fetch across open water and then confine the resulting waves between narrow shores. The children would be safer flying their emergency flag and waiting for a larger rescue boat to put out from Castle Moore with a grown-up at the helm. Besides – what could go wrong? A broken leg at worst.

Rick and Miss Morrell made one final check of everything – especially the guy ropes to the flagpole – while the impatient children bantered with them to be gone and they'd be all right and honestly you'd think they were going to the North Pole for a year the way people were fussing. Then Hereward ran ahead of them, down to the little ramshackle jetty, eager to help them on their way so that he could become lord and master of the little kingdom. He held the prow of the rowing boat while his father steadied the stern for Maisie to climb aboard. To a man of Rick's generation the new ankle-revealing dress lengths set the pulse racing and brought out the gallànt in him. He pulled away from the shore with all the zest of a man half his age – which, he reflected wryly, would make him Maisie's age almost exactly. Why did he not *feel* twice her age, now?

They were still in earshot when Hereward called out, "Now see here, you two – the first thing is to make sure this island's free of savages. If we find any, we'll convert them and they can be our servants. You take the west shore, I'll take the east, and sing-out-me-hearties if you spy any of the varmints!"

Rick raised an amused eyebrow at his young companion. "Long John Silver visits the Wild West!"

Maisie laughed. She had laughed rather a lot since coming here to Castle Moore, the day before yesterday, although, curiously enough, she had not been aware of any great lack of laughter in her life at Cloonaghvogue. But everything here was so intense – not in a solemn, earnest way, mind you – quite the opposite. They did everything with such panache, such style, such confidence. She could understand how they had induced society-at-large to accept their unconventional domestic arrangements; they simply made one feel so petty-minded if one took offence at it. People would trundle out the big guns of moral outrage, load them, prime the fuses, raise the hand to give the order to fire – and suddenly, to their great consternation, they'd find themselves staring straight into the mouths of their own cannon – or canons. It was a lesson she was still young enough to assimilate almost without effort: Do anything you like, but do it with flair and you'll carry the world with you.

"Hereward was right, of course," Rick was saying. "I fuss too much. I can't help it, though. That island has associations for me that he will never understand – at least, I hope he won't."

"Associations with danger?" Maisie asked.

He nodded. "Keep this from the children, but seven years after the Castle Moore Murders – seven years to the very day, in fact – you know how important precise anniversaries are to all Celts! – one of the murderers (one of the real ones, obviously) came back to finish me and my sister off. Mick O'Leary was his name. He was the one whose gun had jammed when he tried to shoot me on the evening itself. And he laid an ambush for us on that island. We were the only people left who could identify him, you see."

Maisie turned and stared at the peaceful little scene. A shiver passed through her. "I suppose every bend in every lane in Ireland has some sort of blood on its stones – if you go back far enough. Have the Dublin rebels been defeated yet, by the way? How easy it is to forget anything's happening up there, when it's all so peaceful here!"

"They're holding out rather longer than expected," he told her. "There was quite a pitched battle in Saint

Stephen's Green. The army took over the Shelbourne Hotel and drove the rebels back to the Royal College of Surgeons. The reinforcements are pouring in. It can't last long now – poor devils."

She stared at the island once again. Rick wondered how often he could induce her to turn her body like that, bringing her shapely bosom into loin-stirring profile.

"How innocent it all looks now," she said. "Was he caught – the murderer you could identify?"

"No. It was the strangest affair. He lay there in ambush, fully expecting to kill us and then be killed in turn. The countryside was crawling with police and secret agents. There's nowhere to hide on the island and little chance of escape even in pitch darkness. He *knew*, you see."

She gazed back toward the land. "Aren't we going home?" She tried not to make it sound as if she actually wanted to go back to the castle at once; she injected just enough inquiry into her tone to show that she knew the conventions – and thought them of little importance. Mind you, if this had been the steam launch, with its snug cabin and wide padded seats, it would have been a different matter. She'd have felt obliged to be more insistent then. But on an open rowing boat in the middle of an almost glass-smooth lough . . . I ask you! What could the most conventional soul object to?

"Call me a fusspot," he replied mildly, "but I thought it prudent to hang about for an hour or so. In case of mishap, don't you know? I've brought a rod, if you're interested?"

"Me – fish?" she asked with a laugh.

"Why not? I brought it for you."

It was an obvious lie but it pleased her. "No, really," she assured him, "you cast it or whatever the word is."

He chuckled. "I can't fish and row."

"I'll row, then. That's something I *can* do."

He tugged dubiously at his lower lip. "Changing places in a little boat like this can be tricky." He half-rose, gripping the gunwales in his outstretched hands, inviting her with his eyebrows to do the same. "Feet squarely each side of the keel," he added.

She realized that he, too, was not above playing to the conventions when it suited his purpose. He must have grasped by now the fact that she was as familiar with small boats and how to behave in them as he was. She needed no directions in order to complete this elementary manoeuvre. Nonetheless, she permitted him to dictate the business.

"Now," he went on, "move both your feet to starboard while I go to port."

With an amused smile she obeyed. The boat hardly rocked.

"Anyone would think you've done this before," he remarked. "Now for the tricky bit: You shuffle forr'ard while I shuffle aft. Six inches at a time – ready? One. Two. Three . . ."

At the fifth small step they were face to face, touching each other. The fact that she *knew* it was going to happen made it easier to permit. He pretended to lose his footing, the boat rocked – never dangerously, but enough to justify his grasping her by the hips and pulling her tight to him. She closed her eyes and raised her lips to his . . .

"Oops!" he exclaimed, moving her firmly on past him and ignoring her invitation. "For those in peril on the seas, eh!"

Relief and disappointment were equally mingled in her. But all the tension – the delicious, exciting tension between them – returned when the exchange was complete and they were facing each other once more, he at the tiller, she at the oars. For then she could see his smile – and see, also, that it was impish enough to assure her that what she had taken for an unfeeling rebuff was, in fact, a mere postponement, and of the most piquant kind. They were sophisticates, she and he, not amateur fumblers who must grab in desperation at every little opportunity.

"He probably wanted martyrdom," she said as she took up the oars and tested their balance in the rowlocks.

"Eh?"

"The last of your real murderers – Mick O'Leary, did you say? A life in hiding must be very . . ."

"Oh, him! Funnily enough, he wasn't in hiding. In disguise, perhaps – I mean, he'd dyed his red hair black and shaved his face clean, but he was living quite openly in Parsonstown."

"Doing what?"

Rick gave a single, baffled laugh. "The ironies of life! He was living with Violet Darcy, who owns Darcy's the printers. They printed our *New Hibernian Quarterly* until it died. But listen to this – Violet was the sister of Ciaran Darcy, who was one of the four men the English hanged in error for the Castle Moore Murders. How's that!"

"Good heavens!" Maisie let go an oar and put a hand to her mouth. "Did she *know?*"

"Of course she did! She hadn't a political thought in her head until the English hanged her brother. Then she became more Fenian than the Fenians. The military mind never learns, does it." As he spoke he began to bait the hook with a live worm. "But to go back to your point – O'Leary was hardly living a life on the run. If he had been, he'd probably be alive today."

She frowned in bewilderment.

"There'd be some excitement in it for him. But to spend your life sorting little bits of metal type in and out of cases in order to record such facts as that Mesdames Quinlan, O'Rourke, Hennessy, and Flannery had raised a record sum of five mounds, seventeen shillings, and threepence farthing on the cake stall at . . ."

"Five *mounds?*" Maisie queried.

He smiled as he hefted the rod, ready for his first cast. "It's the sort of thing that happened more and more frequently as the boredom of it all seeped into his very soul, poor fellow. He came to believe that the only moment in his long, tedious existence when he'd really and truly felt *alive* was when he stood in front of our summer pavilion and exterminated the oppressor . . . the usurper. He'd rather die doing that again than slave in the galleys forever."

A further thought appalled her. "You said the country-side was alive with police – does that mean you *knew* he was coming? Were *you* the bait in the trap?"

He saw her eyes prepare for a spell of hero-worship, but, with some reluctance, he stuck to the truth. "Not me," he replied, letting the rod rest again. "I wish I could claim to be so brave. No, the bait in the trap was the neighbour's daughter I mentioned – the one with the same birthday as my sister Henrietta. She also escaped being killed, of course."

"Judith Carty," Maisie said. She remembered how he had teased Gwinnie and Letty with the name – pretending to forget it and forcing them to remind him; she had drawn certain rather obvious conclusions from that little bit of byplay.

He raised an admiring eyebrow, but his tone was more peeved than complimentary. "What a memory you are blessed with, Maisie!"

"Actually, Richard," she was stung into saying, "I have a very poor memory for mere facts – bald facts."

"But . . .?" He prompted her to complete the thought.

"But the moment I sense that a fact carries an emotional significance for someone, I find it lodges in my head quite easily." She was glad he had unwittingly provoked her into emerging a little farther out of her shell; she wanted him to understand she was no mere cork in a millrace here. His expression told her he was beginning to grasp the fact.

"Yes." He regarded her with a new respect as he continued his tale. "Judith Carty was the one who tracked O'Leary down. And *she* provoked him into casting aside his assumed character. She was the bait, not I. In fact, I'm ashamed to say I was drunk at the time." He turned around and stared back at the island, which was now almost half a mile distant. "We were all out for a jaunt in the steamer – half a dozen young folk. We had no idea O'Leary was hiding on the island – only Judith knew that. She asked to be put ashore – call of nature, she said. And she just . . ." His voice trailed off.

"Let him shoot her?" Maisie guessed in an appalled tone.

"No. Incredibly – especially if I know anything about Celts and their blood feuds – she talked him out of it."

Maisie stopped rowing and gave a silent whistle of amazement.

"Hard to believe, eh! You'd have had to know Judith to realize it was even possible. She had a pistol – given her by a captain in the Secret Service who had rather a soft spot for her. She drew it, aimed it at O'Leary's heart – made it quite clear she could polish him off – and then handed it to him, as if to say, 'Now it's your turn!' But what she actually said was, 'It's got to stop somewhere.' A simple gesture and half a dozen words that somehow penetrated all his blindness, all his rage . . ." Again his words petered out into silence and a faraway look crept into his eyes.

She risked saying, "The captain who gave her the pistol wasn't the only one with a soft spot for her, I somehow feel?"

"She was the finest woman I ever knew," he murmured. Then, in a more lively tone and with a provocative grin for Maisie, he added, "Much too good for the likes of me! I've got what I deserve instead!"

She was too nonplussed to reply – or too caught between frivolity and seriousness.

"Now I've shocked you," he said.

"Not at all, Richard. I'm sure it's no business of mine – except insofar as it explains your feelings about that island,

and your reluctance to leave the children alone there, all at once, anyway. Aren't you going to cast that line? That poor worm! I hope it's true they have no feelings."

He hefted the rod again and this time cast the hook and sinker a fair way off to port. "Now, if you'd be so good as to row slowly westward . . .?" he suggested.

"It's warm work," she said, resting the oars a moment while she unbuttoned her jacket and fanned herself a time or two with the loose lapels – enough to satisfy herself that his eyes were agog at the minor revelations this action permitted. As she settled back to her rowing she pondered her own behaviour quite dispassionately, as if she were a bodiless observer hovering in the air a few yards away. It surprised her that she felt so little emotion of any kind – not shame, not excitement, not alarm . . . in an odd way, not even curiosity.

She was self-aware enough to realize she was behaving like some of the women Richard wrote about in his novels. In *The Mountainy Road*, for instance, Hester Rivers, the heroine, sets out quite blatantly to seduce a young man she meets at a house party. But Richard didn't make it easy for his lady readers. All the conventional excuses one might advance for Hester's disgraceful actions were . . .

"Penny for your thoughts?" Rick, aware (not entirely consciously, perhaps) that the initiative was slipping from him, cut across her reverie.

She smiled. "I was thinking of Hester Rivers."

He frowned. "I'm not acquainted with anyone of that name."

For a moment she thought he was joking, but he persisted beyond the point where the joke would be still funny. "*The Mountainy Road!*" she said sarcastically.

"Oh God – I'm sorry!" He thumped his free fist against his forehead. "That must sound like the most dreadful pose but the truth is, the moment I return the galleys, I forget them entirely, I'm afraid. Of course, I remember

Hester Rivers now. What about her?"

"I was just thinking of the way you make the reader accept her behaviour, even though it's quite outrageous."

"D'you *really* think it outrageous?" he asked, suddenly quite serious. He pinned the rod between the gunwale and his knee so that he could lean forward and peer earnestly into her eyes. "Really and truly?"

"No," she murmured. Her heart dropped a beat and then caught up in a flurry. "At least," she added, "I didn't think so when I finished the story. I kept veering toward that judgment while I was reading it – but you were always there like some . . . I don't know – like some supernatural sheepdog. I mean omniscient. You always seemed to know the way my mind was going. You were always there ahead of me, herding me back toward the line you wanted us to follow."

"Us?"

"Your readers. I mean, all my friends – everyone I discussed it with – we all said, 'Isn't it shocking!' And the most shocking thing of all, we agreed, was that we weren't actually shocked. You'd made Hester so understandable."

"These friends – they were all female, I presume?"

Maisie laughed at the very thought that she might have discussed the tale in those terms with a man.

Rick persisted: "So when you say I *herded* you – collectively – you're passing some kind of judgment on yourself and your friends? Perhaps on womankind in general?"

She smiled ruefully. "Perhaps I am. Yes, of course I am. We *are* the herd, aren't we? Or the flock. We're the ones who constantly look around for the approval of other women." She imitated the baaing of sheep.

"Don't you think men do, too?"

"Yes, but not as much as women. There are a lot more men who're quite happy to be considered *different* – even downright odd – than there are women. Call a man 'different,' and he sounds quite interesting. But say the same of a woman and she immediately sounds a bit suspect." When he made no reply to this she prompted him, "Don't you agree?"

"Absolutely. But the really important question is *why?* Take the interesting ménage we have here at Castle Moore. Do I embarrass you?"

"Er . . . no! Not at all! Honestly!"

"Good. When the situation between Gwinnie and Letty and me first dawned on people, they got pretty hot under the collar. But the curious thing is, most of the heat was directed against poor Gwinnie and Letty. I was still quite readily accepted in places where they were *personae non grata*. And that made *me* hot under the collar, I can tell you! I wrote a score of worthy pamphlets attacking society for its hypocrisy and double standards, but my two dear ladies – wiser than me in every way – refused to let me publish them." He grasped the rod, gripped it tight for a moment, and then relaxed, saying, "False alarm."

"Why were they the wiser?"

"Because at the age of twenty-aught they understood a fundamental truth about women that has taken me all these years to grasp. We're all prisoners of our own particular society – that goes without saying. Even if we rebel against it, we rebel against *it*. The Christian atheist is quite a different person from the Mohammedan atheist. Nonetheless, there are certain fundamental truths that are quite independent of this society or that society. And one of them is to do with the nature of women, as distinct from men. We find it a particularly difficult truth to grasp because our society has spent two or three centuries trying to deny it. But go back four centuries – even here in Christian Europe – and you would meet people who'd think it too obvious to need stating."

"What? I can't imagine!" She rested her oars and leaned forward, anxious not to miss a syllable.

"Put quite simply: We've attempted to stand truth on its

head. We teach our young that little boys are made of slugs and snails . . ."

" . . . and puppy-dogs' tails!" she put in.

"And little girls?"

She preened herself. "Sugar and spice and all things nice!"

"And d'you believe it?"

Her eyes gleamed pugnaciously and she shouted the word: "No!" Then her own vehemence embarrassed her and she blushed to the roots of her hair.

"See!" He pounced. "I rest my case. You already *know* the truth about women. And in a playful situation like that you can be induced to roar it aloud. But then – oh dear! – you recall every myth you've ever been taught on the subject, all of which run absolutely counter to the fundamental truth, and you get thoroughly embarrassed." His smile was kindly. "Do I need to put it into actual words?"

She shook her head. After a brief silence she said, "Funny! It's one of those things you know – and yet thrust aside all the time. I mean – all those thoughts you put into Hester Rivers's mind – the scandalous things she was thinking even while her mouth was spouting all the usual platitudes – one read them in mounting horror. But it wasn't the sort of horror that said, 'The hussy! The shameless, abandoned creature that she is!' It was . . ."

"Plenty of critics said as much," he pointed out.

"Yes, but they more or less had to. They were on public display. But the horror I felt was the horror that someone had taken the top off my brain and peeped inside! And all my friends – I mean, any woman I discussed it with – said the same." She laughed feebly. "Why do we do it? Why do we all subscribe so ardently to what we all know is an outright lie about ourselves? The misery it causes!"

He made no immediate reply but there was enough doubt in his expression to show her he did not wholeheartedly agree. "It may have a useful purpose after all," he said at length. "It's becoming fashionable nowadays to say we're only animals – and when you read the news from France and the Dardanelles, it's tempting to agree. But we're not *only* animals. We're animals who have created high civilizations *only* by turning our backs on certain animal . . . what can I call them? Animal qualities? We know they're there but we have to ignore them. Or else!"

He saw a certain disappointment in her eyes and was delighted to realize that she had been looking forward to some high-minded justifications for certain low-minded activities. It was all the encouragement he needed from her. "Paradoxically," he said, "it poses the most acute difficulty not – as you might expect – to those of the lowest character and mentality, that is, to those with the largest share of humanity's base, animal inheritance, but to those with the highest character and most civilized mentality. People like you and me!"

"Yes!" Her eyes shone and she had to row with some exertion to mask her sudden shortness of breath.

He went on: "If I have a printing press that prints perfect forgeries of five-pound notes, it's useless to me if everyone else has one, too, and is determined to use it. But if I know that everyone else is either too moral or too afraid of the consequences to use *their* presses, I can print my own forgeries (that is, behave immorally) to my heart's content – knowing I shall inflict scarcely measurable harm on society at large."

She laughed with delight and felt emboldened to ask: "Is that the principle on which your ménage, as you call it, is based, Richard? You can risk it because you know it won't catch on and become general, eh?"

Looking her straight in the eye he replied, "It's the principle upon which *all* my actions are based, Maisie. I'm sure you understand?"

He picked up his rod and wound in the line. The worm had gone; the hook gleamed in the watery sunlight. "I don't think I'll catch anything today," he sighed.

"Not on *that* hook," she told him.

26

Henny grew tired of making shadow-rabbits and butterflies on the tent wall. She lay back, turned the lantern wick low, and stretched luxuriously in her sleeping bag. Her sister Camilla had told her how important it was to scoop out a proper hole for one's hip, and now she blessed the advice; poor Salome, who was trying to make a virtue of discomfort and spartan living, must be in agonies, she thought. "Poverty," she sighed. "Tell me more about it, Sal. Is it really . . . you know . . . really detestable?"

Salome sighed, too, wishing she had never begun this living lie, for Henny had camped in her ear ever since. And now she was running out of ideas. She'd borrowed everything she could remember from *Oliver Twist*, *Uncle Tom's Cabin*, *Silas Marner* . . . and so forth. Sooner or later she was going to hit upon a book Henny had actually read; then she'd be exploded. "One remembers so little . . . really," she said, hedging her position more carefully now that the first careless rapture of storytelling was behind her. "A veil of discretion is lowered over all that unpleasantness."

"What's a veil of discretion?" Henny asked. "I thought that was after people kissed."

"Go to sleep!" Hereward grumbled from his tent next door. "Yap all day and yap all night! You're like little puppy-dogs."

"Slugs and snails and puppy-dogs' tails!" Henny sneered in reply.

"I'll come in there at first light and pour cold water over you," he threatened. "See how you like that!"

"Boring! Boring!" his sister chanted, but with little conviction.

"He wouldn't dare – would he?" Salome whispered.

"He would," she admitted glumly. Raising her voice she added, "Tomorrow I'm going to move our tent to the other end of the island."

"Capital idea!" was the enthusiastic reply.

Salome, who had taken a rather intense liking to Hereward, was disappointed at the plan but she said nothing.

"Were you barefoot all the time?" Henny whispered. "Even in the cruellest winter blast?"

"No," Salome told her. "It was worse than that. My Mammy would get given old boots and shoes by kindly folk of the quality. I'm sure they *meant* well, but, of course, the boots hardly ever fitted us. They rubbed our feet raw."

"Blisters?" Henny asked excitedly – encouraging her friend to excesses she would not otherwise have dared.

"Worse yet!" she said in sepulchral tones. "Sometimes my feet would be squelching in pools of blood."

"Aaah!" Hereward shouted. "I couldn't hear. Did you say blood? D'you need the first-aid box?"

"I thought you didn't want to listen," his sister said coldly.

"I don't. But if I'm forced to, at least I want to *hear* what I'm listening to."

Salome, greatly daring, said, "Why don't you lift the side of your tent and I'll lift the side of ours and then you can hear properly?"

The two sides were actually touching, so the idea was quite feasible. But Hereward, who was manfully resisting a fateful attraction for Salome, quashed his delight and said, "What? And have to share your foul breath?"

"Hereward!" his shocked sister exclaimed. "That's not civil!"

"And anyway my breath *isn't* foul," Salome pointed out. "I've been sucking cachous."

"Not your breath, perhaps," Hereward grumbled. "I meant *hers*, really."

"Nor is hers foul, either. And in any case, she's on the far side of the tent. So you'll have my sweetly perfumed breath in between to spare you!"

After a thoughtful pause he said, "Cashews? The nuts?"

"No! The other kind."

"He doesn't know *anything*," Henny said.

"Got any left?"

"Heaps. Miss Morrell gave me a whole box."

"Giss one?" Henny begged.

On an impulse Salome leaned over her and kissed her on the lips, pushing the cachou she was then enjoying into Henny's mouth with her tongue – which the girl was too surprised to resist.

When she recovered her wits she spat it out with an exclamation of disgust – but then all sorts of possibilities occurred to her and, with an impish smile, she picked it up off the groundsheet, popped it back in her mouth, and – with the sparkle of an obvious challenge in her eyes – said, "Yes!"

Salome looked at her in consternation.

"Go on, then!" Henny reached over her and furled up the wall of the tent to match the portion her brother had raised on his side.

Despondently Salome took one tiny pastille between finger and thumb and popped it in between Hereward's open lips. They were rather lovely lips, too.

"Nye-eh!" Henny cackled triumphantly on two notes. "Cowardy cowardy custard! I knew you wouldn't dare."

"I would if I wanted to." Salome tried a withering tone.

"What?" Hereward asked.

"Salome has a special way of giving people cachous," his sister told him.

"I have not."

"She has, so. But only for people she really and truly

likes. Otherwise, to people she can't stand the sight of, she just hands them out the way she did to you."

"How?" he asked scornfully. "What special way? You're just trying to cod me – not very successfully, I must say."

"Like so!" Henny sprawled across Salome as if she were no more than a log of wood in her way – and she took her brother by as much surprise as Salome had taken her.

And with the same result – except that his cry of disgust was a roar, and he spat out both cachous beyond recovery. Then, just as it had with Henny, a new world of possibilities opened up for him. He grinned at Salome and said, "Is that true?"

"No," she said in a panic as, unthinkingly, she popped another one into her own mouth.

"She's getting ready to show you," Henny said excitedly.

"I am not!" Salome responded angrily.

"See!" She turned her triumph on her brother. "She *doesn't* like you enough."

"I do!" Salome protested. "Oh – I mean . . . it's not the point."

"What's not the point?" Henny's great searching eyes stared merrily into hers.

"It's not what *I* like or don't like. Hereward doesn't want it that way, so there's an end to it."

Henny looked at her brother and aped her friend's words sarcastically. "You don't want it that way – so there's an end to it, eh?" To Salome she added with a sigh, "He doesn't like you, either."

He licked his lips nervously, racked by doubts. If he had the slightest cause to believe the two she-devils had hatched this all up between them, he'd drop his tent wall again and weigh it down with the heaviest stones he could carry. And he'd pass the rest of their exile in a dignified and utterly crushing silence. He'd have them in tears. They'd go down on bended knee, begging him . . .

On the other hand, he told himself (before he began to

enjoy that pleasing fantasy too much), if Salome was really as reluctant as she seemed to be . . . well, it stirred quite a different set of emotions. Then he became Hereward the Hunter in pursuit of the shy and comely maiden, overcoming her proper modesty, and treating her with chivalry . . .

"How do you know what I like and don't like?" he sneered. "You don't know the first thing about me."

Henny smiled at Salome. "I think he's trying desperately to say he *does* like you!"

Salome, realizing that she need do absolutely nothing to hurry things along, did absolutely nothing to hurry things along; but she was careful not to smile. Some canny instinct warned her that any hint of open collusion between her and Henny would grease the rails under Hereward and she'd get to kiss no more than the dust of his departure. She merely lay back on her elbows, staring from one to the other, hoping her eyes were large, dark pools of mystery, praying that she looked like a frightened gazelle. In everything she'd read, that sort of look was most efficacious.

"I didn't say that, either," Hereward responded awkwardly.

Henny sighed and patted Salome comfortingly. "He doesn't know what he likes or doesn't like. Poor boy – the strain of having to outshine you and me all the time is proving too much for his poor feeble brain."

"Oh, you're so clever," he said wearily.

"Well do you or don't you?" she challenged him. "I'd have thought it simple enough to say. You're shivering like a leaf!"

"I'm not."

"You are. Hold out your hand."

"Shan't! I'm not your slave."

Salome yawned ostentatiously – which happened to show the little pink pastille on the tip of her tongue. A shiver passed down him and he almost fainted from his longing to kiss her – no, to be given a sweet in that naughty way.

"Well, if it's *got* to be that way," he said, struggling hard to keep his tone nonchalant, "I'd a million-million times rather it was from Salome than from *you!*" He pulled a face at her and turned expectantly to Salome.

Hesitantly she moved her mouth nearer his.

"No!" Henny plucked angrily at her arm. "Make him ask properly: 'Please, Salome . . .' like that. Don't just give in."

But Salome had a better grasp on reality – that is, on what was possible and what was not – than Henny. She realized that the time for neutrality was past. She prepared a withering glance for her friend (but softened it with a wink when her face was fully turned from Hereward) and then, as if the intervention had compelled her to be more brusque than her natural maidenly modesty would like, she pressed her lips to his and jiggled the cachou forward in readiness to transfer it.

Sufficient maidenly modesty remained, however, to restrain her from taking any further lead in the matter. And in any case she was exploring the novelty of the kiss, the action of kissing, the sensation of alien lips in prolonged contact with hers.

Actually, it was rather a let-down after all the thrilling things she'd read about it. There were no tintinnabulations of faerie bells as 'twere from afar, no distant susurrus of angelic choristers . . . just a rather solid, dead-meaty obstruction against her mouth. In fact, it was so exactly like kissing the backs of her own fingers, which she had done for practice after reading about kissing in general, that it didn't even have the virtue of novelty. She was just wondering whether or not to switch to the Eskimo mode of greeting, which she had also read about and never had anyone to try it with, when Hereward relaxed his muscles and his lips went all soft.

Suddenly, anything *less* like kissing her knuckles would have been hard to imagine. It was a revelation. His lips trembled involuntarily – or was it hers? She couldn't tell. But there was no doubting that another person was there behind them . . . different . . . excitingly different. Not exactly foreign but decidedly . . . *other*. His lips were quite unlike hers in every way. Hers were full and soft. They stayed where they were against his when she moved her head a little this way and that. His were soft, too, now he'd relaxed, but they were finely drawn – the softness of a peach rather than of a marshmallow.

"All right, that's enough," Henny barked from about a thousand miles behind her.

Neither of them paid the slightest attention; she shouldn't have started it if she was going to flag halfway.

Alexander the Great must have had lips rather like Hereward's, she thought. Or Brutus. Yes – Brutus in the print on the half-landing at Cloonaghvogue, *Photogravure by Kunz of Zürich*. The lips of a nobleman.

They had been in contact so long she was beginning to lose the sensation. Also her elbows hurt. And her shoulder sockets. She fell away from him, not enough to lose contact – just to show she was intending to move. His lips darted after her. She withdrew a little farther . . . farther . . . until at last she was lying down and her aching joints could sing hosannas of relief.

"All right!" Henny shouted furiously. "You've proved your point – whatever it was."

Salome, still with the half-dissolved cachou on the tip of her tongue, pushed it hard against her lower lip, making it bulge. He remembered then the original – or ostensible – purpose of this osculatory adventure and, with hesitant daring, parted his lips the merest fraction of an inch – barely enough to extrude the tip of his tongue toward her.

As if she had been waiting for it (though she would have denied as much), Salome allowed her own lips to part to the same minuscule degree. His tongue fell into the gap. She opposed him with her own tongue, pushing the remnant of the sweet at him. It was the nicest feeling of all. She wondered that no one had ever described it in novels. People in novels merely 'kissed' – passionately, tenderly, lovingly, hastily . . . *something*-ly – but you never got anything in the way of detailed description, nothing that told you it would feel like this. Perhaps this was real kissing and she'd discovered it all by herself? With Hereward's help, of course.

His tongue detected the little pearl of cachou and neatly scooped it up. The friction of his tongue on hers sent the oddest *frisson* of pleasure through her, like the shock from Aunt Gwinnie's galvanic nerve restorer, which they'd played with yesterday evening, only not so harsh.

Now he had possession of the sweet, his excuse for this soppy behaviour no longer permitted it to continue. Anyway, he could feel the saliva pouring out at the sweetness of its taste.

"About time!" Henny said huffily when at last he lifted his lips from hers.

"Now you're my squire," Salome told him.

Words like that made a fellow think. "I suppose I am," he replied solemnly. He was already a little worried at the thought of what new responsibilities he had unwittingly assumed. "Tomorrow we can cut our arms and mix our blood," he told her. "I suppose that's the best way to begin."

His Daddy – Richard – had explained about all that. It was all the rage when he was a boy. Blood-brothers, they called it. Richard and his best friend . . . something or other, he'd forgotten the name. Anyway, they had mingled blood and sworn lifelong loyalty, and then this so-called 'best friend' had gone and married . . . he'd forgotten her name, too. Richard's best lady friend. So it wasn't the total answer to treachery and betrayal. But Richard said it was no good looking for total answers to *anything*.

"And Henny, too." Salome began to rebuild a few bridges.

His beautiful lips curled in distaste. "I'm not mingling my blood with hers."

"It's the same blood, anyway, you howling ass," she replied in an exhausted tone.

He wanted to protest that it wasn't – that he was Gwinnie's and she was Letty's – but they had been strictly brought up never to discuss lineage with strangers. Of course, if he was Salome's squire and she was his . . . what?

He lost the thread of his thought in seeking the appropriate word for her new relationship to him.

"Well, Henny can mingle with mine and I'll mingle with yours – so you won't have to do it directly," Salome said firmly.

"If I'm your squire, what can I call you?"

"You may call me Salome," she replied grandly.

"No! If people ask me who you are, what can I say? That's Salome Culham-Browne – she's my . . . what?"

"Mistress, of course," Salome replied. "If you catch me out wandering, you can say, 'Oh Mistress mine, where are you roaming? Oh stay and hear, your true love's coming.' I'll be your mistress for ever and ever – that's what we'll pledge when we mingle blood tomorrow."

"If this mistress should chance to roam, box its ears and send it home!" Henny giggled.

Neither of the others joined in.

"It doesn't scan," her brother said disdainfully.

"It doesn't even make sense," Salome added.

"Doesn't make sense!" Henny echoed. "I suppose you think *you* make sense! Where's Bridey Murphy's red petticoat! I'm sending for help!"

Shortly after that they settled to sleep.

Outside, on the little patch of sand where the children had decided to pitch the tents, young Father McDaid stretched his right leg to fight off an attack of the cramp.

The cool night had sobered down his earlier spiritual drunkenness. That's what it must have been. But it was hard not to see the hand of God in every little apparent coincidence – like this afternoon, when he'd come to visit Father O'Shea at Coolnahinch and they'd gone fishing on Lough Cool and who should he see but the McKenna girl, and her camping with the planter's children and not one adult within a mile of them! It was like the Almighty saying to him, 'I've brought you this far, d'you want me to write it all down for you?'

But now, after a few cold hours in which to think it over, the grand certainties had gone. Where would he keep the colleen till the hue and cry died down? Where would he send her then? How would he stop her telling her story?

Wasn't God telling him another tale altogether – putting all those sensible questions into his mind, making him see that he must have answers to them before he made any move at all. He'd get only one crack of the whip, so it would have to be the right one.

The ground had to be prepared back home in Cloonaghvogue. Maybe the first thing to do was to stir things up at the Castle.

And, what with the rising in Dublin, hadn't he the perfect means to hand!

27

There are moments in the life of every priest when he thinks, 'Why was I not born a slave . . . a dog . . . a worm? Why was I born at all? Why *this*, O Lord!' For Father O'Halloran, late of St Francis Xavier, Cape Town, now transferred to the Church of the Sacred Heart, Port Elizabeth, such a moment came when, in the confessional one morning, shortly after the Easter of 1916, he heard the ritual 'Bless me, Father, for I have sinned' in the tones of Mrs Deborah McKenna.

"I'm going to stop you there, my child," he said when she came to the end of her rollcall of venial sins; and he went on to hand out the usual penances.

"But I didn't finish yet, Father," she protested.

"Is it about Salome?" he asked.

"Sure you know it is."

"Then you know what I'm going to say, Mrs McKenna. I'll come out of this confessional and talk with you about it." He gritted his teeth and added, "Gladly. But . . ."

"It isn't talk I'm wanting," she replied. "It's absolution, Father."

"But I've already given you that, woman. Much against my own conscience, I may say, for in my view you've committed no sin that calls for it. But I gave it you nonetheless."

"Then why can I not cast off my guilt? Why does it *heap* me so, day and night?"

She would have said more, much more, but he rose abruptly and, after a glance at the nearby pews to make sure there were no more penitents waiting to be confessed, drew back the curtain on her side. "Come on out of there," he said. "It's no fit place to be holding such a conversation at all."

He took off his stole, kissed the cross, and laid it over a pew. Even in the depths of her misery Debbie appreciated the gesture; for no one who saw them in conversation would connect it with the confessional.

Blinking, even in the gloomy autumnal light of the church interior, Debbie emerged from the one place in all the world where she could feel the safety of hope for a few blessed moments each week – back into the pitiless world, where 'hope' was a word without meaning.

"I don't know what more I can tell you," Father

O'Halloran said despondently. "I thought I said everything there was to say when you brought your troubles to me in Cape Town . . . when was that? Almost three years ago?"

"Three years come July," she confirmed as they began a slow, aimless stroll around the aisles.

"Three *years*, Mrs McKenna. Surely it should have resolved itself by now? I tell you with all the authority vested in me – but, even more important, with all my experience of God and the ways of man – I tell you: There was no sin in what happened at Queenstown that day you left your little girl behind."

"She'll be ten in July," Debbie said.

"A little girl no more."

"And I missing all those lovely years!" Her voice broke but she persisted. "Why, Father? Why is He so hard on me? For one moment's lapse of attention! The suffering it is. The pain it is. The nights I've spent on my knees offering Him anything He wants . . ."

Their wandering had brought them to the main aisle. Instead of bobbing a curtsey to the altar she pointed an accusing finger toward it and shouted, "*Anything!* Don't you *hear* me? Take anything – only give me back my little girl! Why do you not answer? Why have you forsaken me?"

Shocked, Father O'Halloran grabbed her wrist and pulled her arm down. Two nuns who were sweeping the floor near the sacristy stopped their labours and stared. "What blasphemy is this, child!" he said severely.

One of the nuns caught sight of his stole, hanging over the pew, and trotted officiously to retrieve it.

" 'Tis the words of my heart," Debbie replied tonelessly. The silence in that church was the absence of God from her – not from the world, just from her.

The priest's shock was, he suddenly realized, quite superficial. Beneath it he was vaguely aware that he had somehow stumbled into one of the most profoundly religious moments of his entire life. His blood began to race with the excitement. God was very near; he could hear the roar of His breath, the beating of His angels' wings.

"Those words you just used," he said, struggling to maintain his exterior calm, "*Why hast Thou forsaken me?* You know whose words they are?"

She appeared not to hear him. "The times I've stood on the cliffs at Suidhoek," she said, "when the tide was in and the waves dashing the rock below me! The times I've said, 'I'll cast myself down, so I will – in the sure and certain faith that Thou wilt bear me up again!' "

The hair prickled on Father O'Halloran's neck. "But why?" He watched her in fascination, being certain now that God himself was speaking to him through her. It could not be coincidence. First Our Lord's despairing cry from the Cross, and now His temptation by Satan in the wilderness.

She turned her big, dead eyes towards him. "Sure if faith can move mountains, can it not bring one wee mite of a colleen back to me over the waters?"

All at once the priest knew what God now required of him – why this woman had been sent to him with these two signs, and what he was to do with her. Faith! It was so simple – *so* simple, indeed, that the Church, with all its rituals and hierarchies and canons and theologies, was in danger of forgetting it: the simple power of faith!

"You fill me with shame," he said gently, knowing that only some shocking notion like that would capture her attention.

And so it did, of course. She stopped dead and stared at him.

"You do," he assured her. "You walk so close to God. He speaks through you – and you are not even aware of it!" He shook his head as people do at amazements too great to grasp.

"I . . . ?" she faltered. "I don't understand."

"But you *do*," he insisted. "In the first place you

understand enough to come here and tell me about it. But far more important than any of that – more important than anything I can tell you or anything you could read – is what you already understand here!" He tapped his breastbone and pointed at her.

She continued to stare at him, shaking her head.

"Those words you have just spoken," he reminded her. "About standing on a high place and casting yourself off as a proof of your faith. Tempting God! You surely know the same thing happened to Our Lord in the wilderness. But He saw through Satan's wiles." His finger drilled through the space between them, aiming straight at her heart. "Like you, He saw that faith is not given us in order to perform conjuring tricks with nature . . . floating on air . . . wafting a missing child over the oceans!" He fixed her with an ambiguous stare, part-accusing, part-admiring.

"I don't see that at all," she said, but with little certainty in her voice; the truth was, she no longer knew what she saw and didn't see in anything – except the pain of her loss. And she didn't exactly *see* that, either.

"Of course you do," he insisted. "Otherwise you'd have completed your intention – your demonstration of the power of faith. Your understanding may not have trickled through up *here* yet." He reached out and tapped her forehead. "That's often the very last bit of us to catch hold of the truth. But the very fact that no one has fished your body out of the waters yet is proof that you know – somewhere deep inside you – *the* most important truth about faith. The only important truth about it, when all's said and done."

Her eyebrows asked for more.

He offered up a silent prayer of thankfulness that she had come to this moment at last; he knew how Blondin must have felt when crossing his tightrope over Niagara – that moment when the last five yards stretched between him and the safety of terra firma. Surely he must also have prayed, *Don't let me slip now!*

"D'you wish me to put it in so many words?" he asked.

She nodded and held her breath.

"Somewhere deep inside you, Mrs McKenna, you know a truth that the saints and martyrs struggled most of their lives to grasp. Our Lord Himself did not grasp it fully until the week before His death – and the understanding almost deserted Him again when He uttered that bleak and fearful cry: '*Eloi, Eloi, lama sabachtani!* – My God! My God! Why hast Thou forsaken me!' " He glanced toward the altar, saw that the nuns had gone, and then turned his gaze back to her. "Yes, Mrs McKenna," he said softly. "Can you doubt any longer Who spoke those words just now – through your lips? Can you doubt that He is suddenly very close to you in this trial you are undergoing? This is the moment when He is about to change your life forever. Let Him in! Don't turn from Him now!"

Debbie felt the blood drain from her face; there was a roaring in her ears and the world became insubstantial all about her.

Father O'Halloran continued: "You have been given this ineffable privilege – this profound understanding of faith – because He requires something correspondingly great of you. There can be no doubt of that."

"What?" She barely managed the word.

"Ah – if only we knew! But His promise is this: You *shall* know when it is His will that you know."

"And meanwhile?" She could only whisper the question.

"Be ready! Be ever ready for His call. Step out of that darkness in which you have dwelled those three years past. You believed it was a darkness over your soul, but it was not. It was the dark of simple ignorance – a childish lack of understanding. Now, by His grace, you have replaced it with the light of faith – that child*like* faith we all find it so hard to cultivate. He has given it to you. Do not cast it back in His face."

As the priest spoke these words Debbie felt a surge of confidence pass through her. Her former weakness fled before it. Her palpitating heart was calmed, its beat became slow and strong. Every fibre of her being seemed to glow with strength and resolution. The grieving woman who had entered this place not twenty minutes earlier, burdened with cares she could never cast off, now seemed as remote from her as her own childhood self – a creature lost in ignorance and inexperience, to be smiled at with a sort of pitying tolerance.

"Thank you, Father!" She drew herself up to her full height and inhaled deeply. This incense-laden air had never tasted so invigorating as now.

"Not me! Not me!" he responded in what sounded almost like a panic. He wafted a hand toward the altar. "You know Who you must thank for this great blessing."

She curtseyed and began a dignified, confident walk toward the rail. And Father O'Halloran, as he watched her figure diminish, no longer wondered why he had not, instead, been born a slave . . . a dog . . . a worm.

28

Samson had swum barely halfway across the dam when Martha panicked. The arm that had clasped him loosely round the neck tightened suddenly and she screamed. And he had not enough breath to shout, to frighten her into letting go. In fact, he had no breath at all, and when he clutched at her arm with both his hands he naturally sank.

He could, in fact, have stood up at that point. It would have needed only the tiniest jumps to keep his head above water. He could have kept that up until his sister's panic had run its course; but, instead, that same panic had now seized him. He gasped, breathed in water, coughed the last air from his lungs, breathed in water again.

His last conscious thought, just before he drowned, was, *Now she'll be sorry!* His life flickered out in images, increasingly random and disjointed, of his mother grieving for him as she had never grieved before for anyone, not even for her dear little Salome. It was the greatest happiness of his life, for it was both atonement and reward. Nobody understood why he was smiling when Shadrak, one of the Kaffirs, pulled his lifeless body from the dam – Samson's Dam as it was (and would now forever be) known.

Martha, who was actually the cause of his death, would have died with him if Shadrak had not hauled her from the water in time. He drew out both children, who were naked, and held them up by their ankles, shaking them like a terrier with two rats, risking dislocations to every joint in their limbs, until the water ceased to fall from their gaping mouths. When he saw Martha was breathing he dropped her on the bank like a newborn calf, all jelly and bones, and concentrated on the lifeless young boy.

But when he realized that all his efforts were to no avail, he turned once again to the little girl, who was now sitting up in the sand, staring blankly before her, shivering all over, despite the fierce sun. He found her clothes – and Samson's – and helped her to dress. He put Samson's trousers back on but then recognized that attending to Martha was more important. He carried Samson into the sparse shade of a thorn bush and covered him with undergrowth to keep off the flies. Then he hoisted the girl upon his shoulder and set off on a tireless jog for the farmhouse.

She made no sound, not even a sigh, all that way. Only when they drew near and she saw her father among the ostriches did she let out a great wailing, so terrible that he knew something was wrong – and very badly wrong – before a word was spoken. He dropped his clipboard and pencil and came running to them.

"Samson?" he called as the gap between them narrowed. "Where's the boy?"

Shadrak lowered his eyes as he passed Martha over to her father. The little girl, slight for her seven years, flung her arms around his neck and howled, "He's dead! It was me! It was my fault!"

He soothed her as best he could and continued to question the Kaffir with his eyes.

The man waved a hand toward the bush. "I tried, baas," he said in Afrikaans. "I was too late."

Finbar was suddenly aware how wet his daughter's hair was. "Drowned?" he asked.

The other nodded.

"Is he in the water still? Did you fish him out?" His mind was reeling with possibilities, each of which kindled a forlorn hope.

Shadrak shook his head and turned back toward the bush. "I'll go fetch him," he said.

"No!" Finbar called after he had gone no more than a pace or two. "I will. I'll come with." He set Martha down and crouched to bring his eyes level with hers. "Now you've got to be a brave little girl," he said. "Go to Aunt Georgina . . ." His voice petered out as he remembered: Georgina and Debbie had driven in to Port Elizabeth that morning. They'd be away all day. "Go and find Aunt Queenie," he went on. "Tell her what happened. Tell her I've gone to get Samson." There was a wrenching in his guts at the inappropriate usage but he could not say 'Samson's body'. He gave her one further hug before releasing her. "Off you go then," he said as he rose to full height once more.

He watched her run a dozen paces before the urgency of his errand tore him from the scene. He and Shadrak ran side by side in the same all-day jog. "I *told* him!" Finbar said despairingly, several times, before they arrived at the spot where the Kaffir had left the body.

His clothes were still there – at least, his shirt and one shoe remained – but of the rest, and of the body itself, there was no sign. Or, one might say, there were all too many signs – for a herd of baboons had passed this way in the last ten minutes, about forty, Finbar reckoned, young and old.

Shadrak pointed to the spoor where they had dragged the boy's body with them. They had travelled downwind.

Finbar nodded and cocked an ear in that direction, though with little hope of hearing anything. There was a faint sound, a sort of whooping-cheering gabble, but it could have been anything. It could have been children splashing about in the dam!

Finbar shook a great fist in their direction and shouted, "I *told* you! Oh Samson, I told you!"

He unholstered his pistol and nodded at Shadrak, who stooped and gathered stones until his pockets were full. They set off in pursuit, walking now, not running.

The baboons wouldn't eat the body, of course – not when there was such a lovely field of ripe mealies waiting for them down by the farmhouse! They'd have carried it off out of curiosity, like a plaything. They could drop it at any point on their aimless wandering. They probably would if they felt themselves under pressure from their pursuers.

The men lost the trail several times, usually where it crossed stretches of bare rock. By some strange instinct the pack never departed from such an outcrop in a direct line with their point of entry. Always at an angle. They might later veer back toward their original line, but there was no certainty in it. So the men had to search the perimeter, each taking one side, to discover their point of exit. It was during one such search that Shadrak called Finbar over to join him.

At first he thought the Kaffir had found the body, but as

he drew closer he saw it was a different spoor that had attracted the man's notice – something like the tracks of a dog. Whatever it was it had relieved the baboons of Samson's body, for the drag marks were plain to see as well.

A hyena? he wondered as he stooped to examine it. Hardly. The species had been extinct in these parts for decades. So had lions. On the other hand, people claimed to have spotted them at Uitenhage, only thirty-odd miles away – both lions and hyenas. It was not impossible that one had strayed right down to the coast.

"Wild dog, d'you think?" he asked Shadrak.

His nod conceded it was possible. "Or tame dog gone to the wild, baas," he said.

That was most likely of all, of course – a feral dog. There'd be no hope of recovering his son's body now. They'd be lucky to find his bones. Still, one must do all one can. He unclipped his pistol from its lanyard and passed it to Kaffir. "Follow it, Shadrak," he said. "Shoot it if you can. But come back before sunset, with or without the body. Understand?"

The man began to empty his pockets of stones, mumbling his apologies for leaving the corpse behind at all. But Finbar cut him short. "It was a million-to-one chance those baboons would come along, man," he told him. "You looked after Martha. You did absolutely the right thing."

On his way back to the farmhouse he visited the dam – Samson's Dam. The marks around the edge showed only where Shadrak had skidded in his frantic attempts to pull them out. Of the tragedy itself there was no sign. In his mind's eye Finbar saw the little boy as he had been on that day they built the dam – only seven weeks ago! There he stood, full of importance, clutching his clipboard and pencil, noting down each scoop the mule teams scraped up onto the wall. A desperate lump in his throat almost choked him and the world swam beyond his tears. And then he gave way to his grief and let it have scope.

When it had run its immediate course he stooped to wash his face clean at the water's edge – and then, on a sudden impulse, stepped into it and waded to its deepest part.

It barely came up to his waist! Samson could have stood with his head clear of the water at any point in the dam, which was, as yet, barely one-third full. How *could* he have drowned in it? Then he remembered Martha's saying it was all her fault. What could she have meant by that? How could she have drowned her brother – or caused him to drown? His heart sank at the thought of the inquisition that would have to follow – not the one in the coroner's court, though that would be bad enough – but the one within the family.

All at once he doubted he could go through with it. The three-year-long inquisition Debbie had conducted into her own neglect (as she insisted on seeing it) had left him with no stomach for anything of that kind with his daughter, never mind her tender years.

He was dry again by the time he returned to the ostriches.

All that afternoon he kept his ears peeled for the sound of a revolver shot. It came just before five, when the sun was well down in the sky. It was hovering on the horizon by the time Shadrak returned – empty-handed. All he carried was the pistol, which he returned at once to Finbar.

"You saw the brute?" Finbar asked.

"Just a little bit, baas. A wild dog, too far off. I shoot once but no luck."

Finbar knew it was a lie. The dog had got well away. The man had fired in rage and frustration, that was all. He'd have done the same. He held out his hand – a rare gesture, which Shadrak was reluctant to reciprocate. "Thank you for all you've done today, man," he said.

The Kaffir lowered his eyes and murmured, "Baas."

The women returned shortly after, just in time, for

twilight had only minutes to go. Debbie leaped from the gig and came running to him. She flung her arms around him and hugged him tight. "Oh God!" she moaned. "It's awful!"

"You know!" he said in surprise.

She drew back sharply and stared at him in amazement. "Of course I know. But how do *you* know?"

"Because . . ." he began and then broke off. "What is it?"

"Paul, of course. There was a Sinn Fein rising in Dublin and Paul's been killed. His first day back with his regiment and he gets killed! Not even fighting the Germans, but . . ." She fell silent and stared at him in horror.

Aunt Queenie had come out of the house with a face as long as could be – and the wan, pale creature who clung to her skirts was barely recognizable as little Martha. "What did *you* mean?" she asked in a whisper. "When you were surprised *I* knew – what?"

Words deserted him. He stared over her shoulder at poor Georgina, who was still standing by the trap, resting her forehead against the cold iron of the brake lever, staring at the emptiness that was now her life, too. *I must go to her*, he thought. And then, *How can I!*

Detached from himself he heard his own voice recounting the horrors of the day at Fountains – while he looked into his wife's eyes and wondered why his words seemed to rouse no emotion there.

"Yes," was all she said – and in a tone quite void of expression.

Martha left the safety of Aunt Queenie's voluminous skirts and ran wailing to her mother. Yet again she was shouting that it was all her fault. Then at last Debbie was galvanized to some action. She squatted on her heels and, gripping her daughter fiercely and staring deep into her eyes, shrieked, "No! You are *not* to blame – d'you hear me? I *know* why this has happened and I *know* it has nothing to do with you. So don't you ever, ever, *ever* let me hear you say that again!" She flung her arms around her daughter and hugged her out of breath.

Martha was too frightened by her mother's vehemence even to cry.

Georgina had by now taken in this second awful bit of news. She shuffled forward to where Debbie was squatting still, with the girl half-smothered in her arms, and touched her on the shoulder. "Debbie?" she said softly. "I'm so sorry, my dear."

Debbie rose to her feet, clutching Martha to her. "It is God's will," she said simply; there was almost a hint of satisfaction in it.

"For God's sake!" Finbar shouted at her, before rage made him incoherent. He knew she had found it hard to love their son – ever since that fatal day in Queenstown, three years ago. But to be so complaisant about his death within a minute of first hearing of it – that he could not suffer. He turned on his heel and strode off into the bush.

They all called after him but he paid no heed. Far off he heard the barking of baboons, and then he knew what he had to do.

For weeks now the creatures had been raiding the mealie field by night. Paul had started putting an electrified fence around it, using the necks of broken bottles as insulators. He had stopped, only because they had run out of bottles. And then he had left to rejoin his regiment in Ireland. Last week, however, large numbers of unbroken bottles were deposited on the sands at Suidhoek; a passing vessel must have disposed of its 'gash' quite close inshore. And Finbar had completed Paul's handiwork only yesterday; he must, he thought, have had an intuition.

He sat in the battery room smoking cigarette after cigarette, waiting for them to arrive. They'd have no fear of the electrified wire, of course, because it had never carried current before today. The moon was well up in the sky by the time he saw them, skittering down over the rocks, vanishing in the bush, reappearing briefly in the open spaces. The ones in the middle kept low and scurried along on bended legs and knuckles. Here and there on their flanks the young male sentries stood tall, crooning their simian equivalent of the watchman's 'Eight o'clock and all's well!'

Finbar dropped his cigarette in the sand and squashed it dead. His hand stole forward to the switch that would put the voltage on the line. He clutched it, trembling with an excitement whose savagery matched that of the advancing horde. Two cheeky youngsters leaped to the wire before the huge male leader of the tribe. Finbar let them go. It was the leader he wanted. All the rest held back.

At the foot of the fence the great brute halted. It was as if he knew what hunger his underlings felt; he, as always, had enjoyed the best of that day's foraging, but many of the others would be empty-bellied until they got into that field. But he stood his ground, lazily scratching his arse, daring them to follow the two youngsters into the mealie-paradise beyond the wire.

"Come on! Come on!" Finbar whispered. His hand was trembling on the lever and he feared he might throw it too soon.

When the leader made his move at last he almost caught Finbar off guard. A fraction of a second later and he'd have been in contact with only one of the wires, and would no more have felt the shock than does a bird on an overhead cable. But the juice caught him just in time.

He let out an eldritch scream, quite unlike anything you'd expect to emerge from such a fearsome bundle of muscle and fang.

Finbar watched him twitching there for several seconds, to be sure he was well and truly trapped, before he picked up his rhino-hide sjambok and started down the line of the fence. The creature screamed and twitched, and snarled at his approach, but it was quite unable to let go, even when the first cruel lash bit into its hide.

Finbar saw little of the actual scene before him. Deep in the red, hate-filled cavern of his mind he saw this creature and its obscene pack of followers dragging the limp, helpless body of his drowned son off into the bush. He revenged himself lash by lash while the blood flowed and the screams faded to piteous whimpers. The rest of the pack, having watched in appalled silence for the first few strokes, turned and fled in loquacious panic.

Finbar did not stop. In fact, he was stopped. A hand touched him from nowhere, from a world he had quite forgotten by then. But for that he would have flayed the creature to death.

"Enough," Georgina said quietly. "It is enough."

She took him loosely by the hand and led him back to the safety of the battery hut. "I knew I'd find you here," she said as she slipped the bolt behind them.

But she need not have bothered. The huge baboon had not an ounce of fight left in him. When Finbar pulled the lever and the current ceased to flow, he fell to the ground and, moments later, they saw him dragging himself wearily after the family that had deserted him. The silence of the veldt was profound – as if the whole of nature was in shock at the outrage it had witnessed.

"I doubt if they'll be back this side of Christmas," Finbar said.

The idea of 'coming back for Christmas' was too poignant for her. And, when she burst into tears, it proved too much for him as well.

They wept alone for a moment, standing side by side in their own isolate grief. Then, as if some cosmic sympathy moved them, they drew closer, touched, leaned together, and finally embraced. They clung tight, as if their grief were a flood from which only their closeness could save them.

"What am I going to *do*, Finbar?" she pleaded in a

whisper. Her lips grazed his ear.

"And me?" he whispered back. His lips touched her ear and he turned it into a kiss.

She shivered and fell against him. She was wearing very little. No petticoats. He could feel every curve . . . her mound. She pressed her mound against him, hard, in case he should doubt her need.

He hardened and had to withdraw a moment to ease himself.

"Finbar!" she shouted angrily, as if everything were now his fault – Paul's death, Samson's death, the overwhelming forces that had drawn her to him there.

He tugged at her blouse, drawing it out of the confinement of her waistband. "No!" she cried out, even as her fingers winkled the buttons from their holes.

When they were as naked as need be she stood on tiptoe and pressed tight against him, while he bent at the knees and scooped her onto him. They both came almost at once, shouting, laughing, shivering – and then pressed on as if nothing had happened yet, hungering for more, more, more . . .

Later, on their way back to the farmhouse, she said, "I don't understand Debbie at all."

He answered with a single, despairing grunt.

"When we saw Paul's name in the lists outside the post office," she went on, "I mean – she was almost more distressed than me. You know? I was the one who ended up comforting her. I was just numb. I still am, come to that. I'll never be able to accept it."

He squeezed her hand but said no word.

"D'you mind if I talk?" she asked. "D'you think I talk too much? I envy you your silence. Your strength."

"Go on," he said.

After a pause she said in amazement, "All those stars!" Then, in quite a different tone, more like disgust: "They don't give a damn, do they! What were we talking about?

Oh yes – Debbie. All that anguish at Paul's death, and nothing left over for poor little Samson! Perhaps that's it. She'd used it all up. You ought to be with her, Finbar. Her reservoirs of grief will refill and she'll need you."

"She hasn't needed me for . . ." He specified no time but she knew at once what he meant.

"Did I steal anything of hers back there?" she asked.

He shook his head. She felt it rather than saw it for they were in the silver-black shadow of a little kloof at that moment. It led up to a rise overlooking the house. In the distance, on a night like this, you could just see the lights of Port Elizabeth. When they reached it they paused. He slipped an arm around her. A moment later she slipped both hers around him.

"What a bloody beautiful country it is!" she exclaimed.

"Yes," he said.

"Could you ever go back to Ireland? To live, I mean."

"Not now," he replied.

29

Marion lugged the heavy box to the table by the window, where the light was better. A rustle of clothing caused her to turn toward the door. Its black gape now framed the spare, slender figure of her cousin Edith. She smiled sympathetically and asked if she was feeling any better.

"If only I could actually *be* sick," Edith said in a flat voice. She leaned against the jamb and pressed her forehead hard against its scarred pine surface.

"I can remember that feeling," Marion said cautiously. "When Rachel was first on the way."

"Marvellous!" Edith's tone was still quite flat.

"Well, it is marvellous in a way, isn't it?" her cousin

cajoled. "Something of Martin will live on. Or don't you see it like that?"

Edith did not open her eyes; keeping her forehead firmly against the wood, she nodded slightly. "But I'd sooner have five minutes of a dentist's drill on an open nerve than . . . this," she said. "Day after day."

"It'll go away after lunch, dear. At least, that's been the pattern up until now. D'you want to lie down?"

For the first time Edith showed some animation. "God no!" She almost laughed at the thought.

"D'you want to go through these papers, then? You need *something* to take your mind off it." Marion opened the lid of the box invitingly.

The quantity and variety of papers inside was depressing to see. Edith crossed the room, glanced at it, and shook her head. "Why don't we just drop it and go out for a bit?" she said.

The idea of a walk was seductive to Marion. The overnight rain had passed and the sun was splitting the trees. Veils of steam hung like wraiths in the still air. But she took one look at the boxes that were yet to be sorted and sighed regretfully. "We really must get through it all by the weekend, darling," she said. "If I abandon C-B to his own devices too long . . ." She left the rest hanging airily.

"What?" Edith asked with an amused grin.

"He gets . . . cranky. Cranky ideas. You won't believe me when you meet him, because outwardly he's a perfectly ordinary huntin'-shootin'-fishin' squire. But inside . . ." She waved a hand vaguely. "Indescribable. Why did you smile just now?"

Edith hung her head in pretend shame. "I thought you were going to say he'd start turning to other women."

"Hah!" Marion gave a single, scornful laugh. "There's little hope of that!"

Edith blushed – which led her cousin to realize what an ambiguous response she had just made; the girl must now be wondering if C-B was impotent . . . or still besotted with his wife after all these years . . . or too mean to turn to fancy women. She felt disinclined to add any correction, however. "Why don't you go out and fill your lungs?" she suggested. "And leave me to . . . well, break the back of this heap of papers, anyway. I'll put aside anything that's still relevant. Most of it is probably . . . you know . . ."

"Napoo!" Edith supplied the soldiers' word drily. Then, with something approaching warmth, she added, "Okey-dokey! Shan't be long."

Her good humour was not reassuring. As Marion watched her go down the path to the front gate she could sense the weariness, the trapped desperation that bore her cousin down. Sympathy vied with envy. Would her own life have been any better if she had ever loved a man with the intensity of Edith's love for Martin Woods?

Better? How could you measure *better?* In what scales could you weigh a war-widow's pension against the memory of such passion? By what units would you balance her own tolerably comfortable, albeit loveless, marriage to a wealthy landowner like C-B against a love that had burned – and now hurt – like Edith's? Would Edith have indulged in such a love even had she known it meant losing him so soon? Probably. There was a strength in that slender frame.

And she herself – would she have been as strong if such a passion had ever come her way? Or had she unwittingly taken the wiser course? After all, if some act of violence (or even a simple hunting mishap, come to that) were to carry off C-B . . .

No – one simply must not start thinking along such lines.

She turned to the box of papers.

She'd still have Salome; she was all that really mattered.

She grasped a sheaf of documents and lifted it, intending to spread them out on the desk. But her eye was caught by the writing on the sheet that was now uppermost in the box.

SALOME MCKENNA.

The name was written in Martin's neat policeman's hand. At first Marion thought it must be some trick of her imagination – because thoughts of Salome had been uppermost in her mind when she exposed that particular sheet. She peered at it closely, fully expecting the words to resolve to SALLY MCMENAMAN or something similar. For a moment – such is the power of human expectations – the marks on the page did, indeed, hover uncertainly in a sort of no-man's-land between a variety of alternatives. But only for a moment. There was a sort of cymbal clash in her mind as they once more resolved into the name – the *original* name – of her own dearest little girl: SALOME MCKENNA.

Her hand trembled as she lifted the sheet and turned it toward the light.

A minute later she crumpled it in her fist and held it tight against her chest, as if to still her wildly beating heart. God, how close they had come! And so soon after it had happened, too. They had uncovered almost everything: the date, the place, the time . . . her description, Salome's description . . . the cab driver – he had even interviewed the cab driver! And that bit about his putting them down in the vicinity of the Royal George! Eamonn Corcoran – she must commit his name to memory before she destroyed this paper.

Her thoughts raced on to embrace the further implications of this awful discovery. Since this was a copy of a letter to the McKennas, via their employers in the Cape, Salome's *first* mother (Marion still could not accord her the solo title) was now in possession of all these facts. Thank heavens the club servants had said nothing!

But would they continue in their loyal silence? Of course, they would never breathe a word to the police. But what Carmel Flahertie might say to Mrs Deborah McKenna if the pair of them were ever brought face-to-face would make quite a different tale.

Marion felt as sick as cousin Edith had looked.

In fact, it wouldn't need anything so dramatic as a direct confrontation between the two women. There were the world-wide tentacles of their church. Mrs McKenna might prevail upon her priest in the Cape to get in touch with the priest of the parish in which the Royal George lay . . . Then, one day at Mass he'd give out: "If any of yeez saw a little orphan girl in a blue check dress in the company of a grand lady at Queenstown or near the Royal George on the third of July in the year before the war, yeez are to call on me in confidence." It could happen any Sunday. Would the club still hold records of who stayed the night so long ago? Three years – all but a few months? Not so long ago. Yes, of course they'd still have records.

Oh God – where did it stop? Had Martin Woods followed up this suspicion and looked into the club's records? She glanced at the box again, and at the pile of papers on the table. Was there somewhere among them – or *anywhere* in this house – a list of guests who stayed the night of the third of July, 1913, her name among them . . . the missing link in the chain that would lead inexorably to her unmasking.

Her terror was complete when she suddenly realized *it could already have started!* Even now, messages might be making their measured progress to and from the Cape – priest speaking unto priest, then bishop unto bishop. How far had it gone? Perhaps this very week the Papal Nuncio would call upon the Lord Lieutenant in Dublin and hand him a slim folder containing . . . all the facts!

No – of course, not *this* week! This week of all weeks. Praise be to God for the rebellion! Long live Sinn Fein!

The first thing to do was to go through the box – and all those other *bloody* boxes – and extract every scrap of paper that mentioned Salome, the *Knysna*, the Royal George, and anything else touching on Martin's inquiries into the little girl's disappearance.

Only then did it strike her that, in her panic, she had

overlooked the greatest surprise of all: that the McKennas' new employers in the Cape – or one of them – should be related to the police officer who had conducted the inquiry. Further thought, however, made her see that it was probably the other way about: Georgina Delaroux must have been on the *Knysna*; she was the one who started the process. First she must have befriended Mrs McKenna in her distress. Then she'd have remembered her cousin in the RIC – and him living a mere stone's-throw from Queenstown, and . . . well, the rest simply followed.

In fact, the *real* coincidence in all this was that Martin should have married cousin Edith.

She sat down abruptly and held her stomach tight against the sudden hollowness there. Suppose he had lived! Edith would surely have brought him to Cloonaghvogue – where Salome's name would surely have triggered his professional suspicions. The game would have been up in five minutes.

She suppressed the incipient thought that his death had been most timely and forced herself to think back over what Edith had told her about meeting Martin and the courtship that had led to their rather hasty marriage before he enlisted. *Was* it such a coincidence after all?

Why this obsession with coincidence? she wondered.

Because the other name for coincidence was The Hand of God!

Despair gripped her. She was mad to have supposed she could ever get away with it. The fact that nothing had happened over the past three years had more to do with the war, and the local preoccupation of the police and army with Irish rebellion, than with her own cleverness at covering her tracks. If the wheels of justice and retribution had not yet started to roll, they surely would the moment the war ended and normal communication became possible once more.

The best she could hope for, probably, was to postpone the evil day. If she could keep Salome until she were, say, fourteen or fifteen, her parents might then agree to let her stay on at Cloonaghvogue as a sort of courtesy niece.

Actually, her best course might be to beard the lion in its den. Write at once to the McKennas, explaining how she came to be here in Castlemartyr, sifting through Martin's papers, when . . . to her delighted surprise . . . et cetera.

It might work. It might be best.

Plus a letter from Salome saying how happy she was and what spiffing friends she had . . .

Yes, a few words like 'spiffing' and 'top hole' would speak volumes as to what sort of daughter they'd be getting back if they insisted on her return.

Perhaps she ought to offer to send Salome to the Cape every summer once the war was over? Spike their guns.

And she could also write a private letter under separate cover to Mrs Delaroux, describing the present circumstances of Salome's life, her prospects if she remained at Cloonaghvogue for nine months of the year . . . snish-snish. Make an ally of her. She'd surely be able to read between the lines and offer gentle advice to leave things as they were?

It was so difficult to know what to do for the best. If only there were someone she could talk it over with.

Cousin Edith?

Why not?

The more she thought about it, the better it seemed – to her reasoning mind, anyway. Her instinctive mind was seething with thoughts of a quite different kind; but she recognized them as the response of a trapped animal. They urged her to destroy every scrap of paper here that could lead anyone to unravel her secret – to maintain her silence, to deny everything.

But, though the simplicity of that course attracted her, she realized it would achieve nothing. These papers were mere copies; the originals had already done their damage out there in the world, actually in the hands of those who could use them to the most devastating effect in years to come. And if the war ended soon, as everyone said it must, those years would come soon enough.

Her best course, therefore, must be to prepare for the worst. And to do that, she must now discover how much of the mystery Martin Woods had unravelled in the course of his inquiries.

She worked at it like a beaver. Fortunately, the man had been methodical to a fault and it soon became clear that the papers on any given topic were filed in perfect order. For instance, all his letters to his parents followed all his letters to his grandparents . . . to his cousins . . . to those school chums with whom he'd kept in touch . . . and so on. And within each group they were all ordered by date, the oldest at the bottom. She checked among several of these other categories for letters dated around September–November, 1913; to her relief none mentioned his inquiries on behalf of his cousin Georgina.

She did, however, unearth one further document – which answered a question she had posed earlier. The bottom-most page of the sheaf she had first lifted out of the box contained a list, in Woods's hand, headed: 'Royal George Club, Tivoli: members who stayed overnight on 2nd and 3rd July, 1913.' Her own name and Maude's were there, with 'Room 8' bracketed against them, in the first column. In the second column, for the third of July in the same room, her name stood alone. There was no addition such as 'child' or 'guest.'

But there was an asterisk – the only one on the page.

This was almost more infuriating than if it had simply read 'and female waif' or some such positive statement. Had Martin copied it directly from the club's ledgers? She doubted it; he would never have been granted access. Was it a neat version of notes he had made after talking to one of the servants? That was more likely. Or a copy of something a servant had smuggled out to him? And why did that asterisk stand beside her name? And why on the second day but not on the first?

The paper was undated, but the fact that it had lain on top of his copy of the letter to his cousin in Port Elizabeth suggested that it related to some follow-up investigation, carried out *after* he had posted that letter. Had he, then, written a subsequent one setting out these additional facts?

She sighed. There were too many questions to which she could not even guess the answers.

The front door slammed and a much more cheerful Edith came prancing into the room. "You simply *must* come for a walk after lunch," she enthused. "You missed one of the most gorgeous spring mornings I've ever . . . Marion! What's up? You look as if you've seen a . . ."

"Nothing!" Marion took a grip of herself. "Actually, I think I'll take you up, if that's a firm invitation. There's something I'd rather like to tell you. I need your advice."

30

Hereward and Salome did not become blood-brother and sister until the Friday of that Easter week, when they were due to be rescued from their coral island and returned to civilization. "In case gangrene sets in," Hereward had explained laconically. To get the blood for the ceremony they didn't open a vein. Instead, Hereward put a good edge on the tip of his Indian-scout knife and, after purifying it in the flames, lightly scratched the words TE AMO on his forearm – in swift, spidery lines laced with droplets of bright red. Then he pressed his arm to Salome's so that the trace of the words was printed in mirror writing on her forearm: OMA ƎT.

"The mirror image," he said with an almost priestly

intonation. "As left hand is to right." He placed both hands together in case they should doubt it.

"Shakespeare!" Henny guessed scornfully.

"It's not," he protested. "I made it up on my own."

He passed the knife to Salome so that she could cut the corresponding traces in her own skin; she was surprised to feel almost no pain at all – no more than you'd get walking bare-legged through furze.

"Mine's all clotted again," he said when she had done. And then, with nonchalant bravery, he scraped the blade over his self-inflicted wounds, bringing out tiny red pearls of fresh blood. "Quick – before yours dries off," he urged.

And they pressed the two legends together and mingled blood into blood. It was like a new sort of kiss, Salome thought. Skin did not actually move on skin but you could feel the living muscle underneath. She was all set to giggle but her eyes met Hereward's and a solemnity overcame them both – a solemnity for which neither was prepared.

It was one of those moments when the heedless rush of childhood is suspended and the first notions of pure thought intrude – the sort of moment that makes one say, in later years, 'I'll never forget it.' By then, too, words have replaced the mere hints, the fleeting intimations that the child experienced at the time.

Hereward was filled with a strong passion for which he had no words. All at once Salome seemed different from every other person he had ever met. Other people were just . . . well, other people. They just existed. Like trees or furniture. You had to take notice of them but they didn't really affect you. And you didn't really want to affect them if you could help it. You stood off and they stood off, and that was best all round. It left you free to get on with things.

But – quite suddenly – Salome was not at all like that. Not just a slightly different bit of furniture. She was actually a *person*. As real as himself. He had never experienced such a thing before.

He did not think with such clarity at the time, of course. His mind whirred with mere glimpses of strange ideas and new feelings, which he knew were big; but they were the seeds around which his understanding would later crystallize and grow.

When Letty had read him that bit in *Alice* about the whole world being a dream in the Red King's mind it had given him night-terrors for weeks because it confirmed certain vague ideas that had already flitted through his mind – that his whole life was really nothing but a dream. It was all in his imagination and one day he'd wake up and it would vanish. And that was because no one else was real – not *really* real.

And now someone was. Peering into Salome's eyes, feeling her warm, lithe arm trembling with excitement against his, he suddenly became aware that she was in every way as *absolutely* real as himself.

And then he wanted to know what it felt like to be *another* real person. What was she thinking? What was going on behind those misty grey-green eyes?

He leaned his forehead against hers. Perhaps it would be like telegraph poles, where you could put your ear to them and hear the conversations singing and buzzing like insects, and Mick Hannon, who repaired the lines, said he'd learned to understand the noises and he'd tell you all the scandals of the village. But all Hereward could hear was the breath in his own nostrils and the breath in Salome's. Both were a bit shivery.

Salome's emotions at that moment, though just as powerful as Hereward's, could hardly have been more different. Being younger than he was, she was even farther from being able to boil it all down into actual words, though her life as an only child who spent most of her waking hours in the company of an intellectually challenging woman like Miss Morrell had given her a verbal maturity beyond her years. Nonetheless, the turmoil she now experienced was more of feeling than of thought.

And the one feeling that seemed to have dominated her life until now was a nagging fear that she herself might not actually exist – or not in the same way as other people existed. It seemed almost painfully obvious to her that everyone else was real. They all had their places, their duties, their rewards. Even Harvey Kelly, the harmless boy poacher, had his place in the sun – and the rain. But she had never felt more than a guest of reality – a surprise visitor who had knocked at the wrong door one evening and had been invited in by an hospitable world; she was no more than a tourist among its many wonders. One day someone was going to remind her, in the kindest, gentlest, nicest way, of course, that she really ought to be moving on to . . . well, wherever she was originally intending to go.

And now, suddenly, with a few strokes of his knife, Hereward had changed all that. TE AMO he wrote – in his own blood in his own flesh: *I love you*. And OMA ƎT she had carved to his imprint. The mirror image, as left is to right. What would be the mirror image of 'I love you'?

'I am loved by you' – surely?

I am loved!

It was a wonderful feeling in every way but the most wonderfullest thing of all was that it meant you were *real*. You had to be real before you could be loved like that – blood mingling with blood and so on.

How warm his arm felt – how gentle and yet how firm! There was no doubting *his* reality – which, therefore, became guarantor of hers. Now no one could ever tap her on the shoulder and tell her it was time to move on to some other destination. She was there already.

"I'm hungry," Henny grumbled, giving them a shove and breaking the spell.

Salome, feeling guilty at her neglect, turned to Henny and asked brightly, "Would you like to be blood-sisters with me?"

"No *thank* you!" Her lips curled in scorn. Then, realizing how churlish it had sounded, she added the explanation, "Not until *his* blood has all gone away." She showed her brother the tip of her tongue.

He grinned and raised his knife to mime cutting it off, a mere inch or two from the tongue itself. Truculently she stared him out.

Salome, remembering the tricks she had learned from the Kelly boy, said airily, "I'll get us some fish for our final lunch if you like."

Hereward, eager to share her every moment now, said, "The rod's behind the back of my tent. I'll dig some bait."

But Salome rolled up her other sleeve and flexed her fingers with a magician's *savoir-faire*, saying, "Don't trouble yourself, my dear fellow. I know a much better way than all that!"

She knew the place, too. While playing one-two-three-block the previous day she had hidden behind a boulder on the eastern edge of the island, where she had spotted a magnificent rainbow trout idling close inshore. She had been about to tickle him out when Henny had discovered her and she'd had to make a run for the pine tree that was their block for that game.

Now she put a finger to her lips and led them over the ridge to that same place. She approached it with all the dimwitted patience Harvey Kelly had taught her; the two Bellinghams watched in fascination – of a slightly cynical kind, for they were unwilling to believe that fish could be caught in such an obviously primitive manner. In their world it required ghillies, boatmen, hampers, groundbait, flies of incredible complexity, and equipment costing pounds and pounds.

Salome thanked her stars that the fish was there again today – two of them, in fact, almost nose to nose.

"Stay back!" she whispered urgently to her companions.

"If you creep down where that purpley flower is, you can watch from there."

She dipped her fingertips beneath the surface as far from the trout as she could reach and began the long, boring business of drifting closer, closer, closer . . . in barely perceptible stages. By contrast, the stages through which her feelings passed were as forceful as her movements were slight: the chill of the lake water, the icy numbness of her skin, the discomfort in every joint, the pins and needles, and the silently screaming urge to make a sudden dart to try and grab up the fish at once.

"You'll never do it," Hereward whispered.

"Shhh!" his sister replied sharply.

He bit his lip against an equally sharp response and watched, hardly troubling to breathe. All at once he noticed his breath forming steam – which it must have been doing all morning without his seeing it. The air *was* chill, too, especially when one had to stay absolutely still like this. How much worse it must be for Salome, his new blood-sister, lying there on the stones and dewy grass. He wanted to join her, to take off his jacket and cover her up, to shiver manfully while she relished the gift of warmth.

From their vantage they could just about make out something speckly that might be a trout, or a couple of trout, though their complacent stillness while that alien arm drew ever nearer seemed to deny the possibility.

By now Salome's arm was so numb with the cold that it no longer seemed part of her. She watched it quite impersonally, admiring its stealth and wondering that it moved its fingers almost as she willed it to. It helped, of course, that the arm in the water was about a third shorter than the one she knew and loved.

By now the tips of those alien fingers were directly beneath the smaller fish's tail – which she carelessly brushed in trying to move forward to the proper tickling position. It darted off at once – only eighteen inches or so, but out of reach for all that.

"See!" Hereward said triumphantly.

"Shut up!" Henny rounded on him.

"Both of you!" Salome whispered fiercely – and with a renewed excitement in her tone, as well. For the larger trout gave a lazy flip of his tail and edged forward until his belly was perfectly poised over Salome's fingers; it was almost as if he had been waiting in line for his smaller companion to go.

"God be good to me!" Salome borrowed Miss Kinchy's phrase and willed her hand to move slowly, slowly . . . slowly up until she made contact with the fish at last.

This was the moment when Harvey Kelly liked to show off. He'd tickle the trout for ages, just to show his mastery of the technique. But Salome was in no mood to take chances. As soon as she'd got her hand well round the creature she jerked him from the water with an action that almost dislocated her shoulder. She had a brief, snapshot glimpse of the trout wriggling against the sky – all silver and iridescent colours in the anaemic sun. And then came the cries of astonished admiration from her two companions.

Hereward pounced on the fish and clubbed it to death on a stone; no gamekeeper was going to ask *him* an awkward question, Salome thought wryly. With a gambler's reckless spirit she said, "You go and gut that lad and start cooking him. I'll bring the other in a jiff."

She managed it, too, but it took longer than a jiff. In fact, it took almost the identical time that Rick and Maisie Morrell took in rowing out to the island – or, rather, up to the moment at which Maisie passed from serenity to a state of terror and let out a scream they must have heard in County Clare.

The serenity in which her brief voyage began was all thanks to her escort, one of the most interesting, chivalrous, pleasant, attentive . . . and, oh, in every way admirable gentlemen she had ever met. It was quite clear to her that neither of the women in Rick's life – neither his wife nor . . . the other one – appreciated him properly. He was being noble about it, of course, bearing his cross stoically, with never a hint of criticism; but a sensitive soul like hers could just *feel* how he must be suffering beneath that façade of carefully cultivated indifference.

She was still pondering ways to let him know how kindred – how very, *very* kindred – her spirit was to his when her eye fell on a little blob of colour lying quite still at the water's edge on the eastern shore of the island.

Salome!

Beyond all doubt it was Salome – drowned, washed up on the lake shore, lying there, cold and dead, while the two Bellingham monsters horsed around near the tents.

"Aaaargh!" She keened a long, formless wail – a wordless prayer to every god of time and space, begging them to reverse the course of the universe and bring her darling back.

Her darling leaped up in surprise at the eldritch cry – to which she joined an equally loud whoop of triumph as the smaller trout landed among the pine needles and rock roses, almost halfway across the tiny island.

Rick stared at Maisie in amused surprise; she gazed at the resurrected Salome in an angry astonishment that would have been ungrateful if the gods had truly heeded her inarticulate cry. And Hereward and his sister ran to where the creature lay. They picked it up and crowed in savage triumph, doing a little dance that culminated with Henny leaping upon a rock and calling out, "Salome's ever so clever, Rick! She can catch trout just by tickling them with her fingers."

Maisie beat her fist to her forehead. "I should have realized! I should have realized!" She bit her lip like a naughty schoolgirl and begged Rick's forgiveness with supplicant eyes.

To him, of course, they were come-to-bed eyes. For his part he wondered how much longer he could postpone that obvious consummation of their *petit amour*. This Dublin rebellion had made things rather awkward. It might turn the planned nine-day visit into one lasting a fortnight or even longer – and he didn't want to start something that might turn rather steamy if prolonged that far.

Still – those eyes were . . . heart-stopping. Something would have to happen soon.

"Did you suppose she was dead?" he asked.

She nodded on an inward-breathing sigh and tilted her head to an even more contrite angle. "I feel such a giddy ass," she confessed.

He rested the oars and leaned forward to pat the only part of her within reach – her ankle. "Your response was instinctive, my dear," he assured her, changing from a pat to a tender caress – seemingly without being aware of it. "Instinctive and commendable. Your devotion to that child fills me with envy."

He laid just enough stress on that 'me' for her to take his meaning. She drew breath to assure him that there was more devotion – much more – where it came from, and he only needed to give the sign . . . But prudence stopped her after a stammered word or two.

He saw her indecision and came to the rescue. Letting go her ankle he sat upright again and asked, "Why did you say you should have realized? What should you have realized?"

"That!" She pointed over his shoulder to where Hereward was still brandishing the no-longer-twitching trout. "There's a little poacher boy, the village simpleton – or one of several – whom we caught tickling trout in the Pipes of Pan lake, as I call it – at Cloonaghvogue. He has taught Salome how it's done."

Rick, gazing at his son, said, "The Pipes of Pan, eh? Those two statues have always fascinated me. How perfectly they are in their arrangement – the goat-foot god and the bashful maiden – hiding her charms from him yet glancing coyly over her shoulder. Did you ever try to imagine them in some different position, closer together . . . farther apart, or . . ." He paused before adding in a more significant tone: ". . . facing each other?"

"Yes!" Maisie was delighted. She had often juggled the two statues around in her imagination but had never mentioned the fact to anyone. How uncannily perceptive he was! Almost as if he could read her mind.

"Facing each other?" he repeated with interest.

She frowned in concentration. No, that was one variation she had never thought of. She shook her head.

"Why not?"

They were approaching the little jetty now. He rested on the oars and leaned toward her again, staring as if her reply were the only thing that might release him from such an uncomfortable position.

She tried to imagine it – the coy maiden in all her nakedness – facing the grinning god as she glanced back over her shoulder. And she saw how completely it would transform the relationship between the two figures. The girl would no longer be shy of Pan but merely of being observed by outsiders as she flaunted her *charms*, as Rick called them, for the goat-god's delectation.

"Why not?" he repeated. He was smiling now, for he could see she had the tableau clearly in her mind's eye.

"It never occurred to me," she replied. "Until now."

"And now it does?" He gave the oars the last few touches that brought them to the jetty.

"Very much so," she assured him.

31

By the time Marion had finished telling her story to Edith their walk was over and the two women were back at Martin's cottage. Then, of course, Edith wanted to see the papers for herself. She read them carefully while Marion busied herself making the tea and buttering the scones; they had decided not to employ servants while staying at the cottage – not with the country in such a turmoil and with so many papers of unknown content lying around. Major Haston had told them to bring anything of an official nature to the police barracks immediately, not even to keep it overnight.

"Tea's ready!" Marion, brightly nervous, called from the parlour. When Edith came through empty-handed she added, "Didn't you bring the documents?"

The other shook her head. "They're not really the point," she said.

Marion seated herself and lifted the teapot. "I'll be mother."

Edith looked up at her rather sharply, as if she thought Marion were making a joke. Then she said, "That *is* rather the point, isn't it!"

Her cousin frowned. "Is that too much milk?"

Edith shook her head. "As it comes. D'you mind if I say something rather brutal? Or it may *sound* rather brutal."

"Good heavens!" Marion gave a nervous laugh. "What can you mean?"

"Just this: You're a mother yourself – or were. You lost your own little girl at the age of seven . . ."

"Not quite." Marion passed the cup with trembling fingers.

"All right – at around the age Salome was when you found her. Don't quibble. What I mean is you know what it's like to lose a daughter – and yet, in everything you told me during our walk – I mean, all the while you were talking I kept waiting to hear one word, one single word, of sympathy for Mrs McKenna. And I waited and waited."

Marion shook her head defiantly. "*She's* the one who left Salome behind. Don't forget that. It was nothing to do with me. And I've done everything . . . *everything* . . ."

Edith interrupted her. "Marion! Darling! You might have been able to make that excuse to yourself until this morning. *She* abandoned her child! *I* rescued her. But now you *know* that wasn't the case. The poor woman was out of her mind with grief and worry. And yet you . . ."

"Well, aren't I suggesting we write to her? Isn't that what I said? We'll write to her, explaining what happened, and . . . I mean, showing her I didn't deliberately . . . you know."

Edith shook her head sadly. "I don't enjoy doing this, darling. But it's no good asking *my* advice if you then expect me to behave like the shallowest of fair-weather friends and tell you only what you hope to hear."

Marion nodded, accepting the justice of her cousin's words. "But I am proposing to write," she pointed out. "It's not as if I'm running away or burying my head in the sand."

"You're proposing to write the sort of letter that will make Mrs McKenna feel a double-traitor if she claims Salome back." Edith smiled and tilted her head so as to temper the accusation.

"But I have to point out all I've done for Salome – surely?"

Edith shook her head. "Suppose a man walks into the National Gallery and steals a Raphael . . ."

"But I didn't *steal* Salome. There was no kidnap. That's my whole point, don't you see? I *found* her . . ."

"All right. Suppose a man *finds* a Raphael – never mind how improbable the circumstances. He just *finds* it – all right. It's pretty obvious it belongs to some important collector, public or private – just as it was pretty obvious Salome was a well-fed, well-cared-for little girl, not some barefoot ragamuffin. Objections?" She smiled and quizzed Marion with raised eyebrows.

Marion reluctantly shook her head.

"Very well. Now suppose this man keeps the Raphael for

two or three years in absolutely *perfect* conditions. Never lets the sun shine on it. Even temperature. Never damp, never too dry . . . snish-snish. You understand, I'm sure. Then along comes someone who recognizes it at once and says, 'Oh, I know where that painting *really* belongs. It belongs to the Louvre in Paris.' And they prove it every way to Christmas, so no one can have any doubt. D'you still think that man could claim any rights in the painting – just because he took such care . . ."

"But that's not fair, Edith! That's like saying Salome is really the daughter of . . . I don't know – the king. Or some royal duke. If Salome proved to be the daughter of the Duke of York, say, I'd have absolutely no qualms about handing her over. Don't talk to me about the Louvre – what if this Raphael painting belonged to someone who lived in a turf shed? I mean, one has a duty to the painting as well as to the person who accidentally owns it, don't you think?" She squared herself triumphantly and sat tall.

"And which of you accidentally owns Salome?"

Marion stared frostily at her cousin but all she said was, "Pass the strawberry jam, please."

Edith placed it in front of her, smiling as if she were about to say, 'Checkmate!' What she actually said was, "Being a farm manager in the Cape with a hundred Hottentots or coolies under your command is *not* the equivalent of a turf shed!" Then, however, she brushed her own words aside. "But that isn't the point – and you know it. The point is: How d'you think Mister and Missus McKenna feel about their daughter's loss? And how d'you think they're going to feel when they get a letter from the oul' country telling them she's been found again? You – as a mother who has been through that same valley of despair – are far better qualified to answer such questions than I am."

Marion drew breath to fire back an immediate answer . . . and then fell silent. After a long pause she let out her breath and, almost in a dying gasp, said, "You're right, of course. I'm a bitch."

"Don't go to such extremes," Edith said evenly.

"But I am. I've known from the very beginning that it was wrong – the way I've behaved. I should have put announcements in the papers. I should have written to the Algoa Line. On the day itself I should have told the harbour police." There was a catch in her voice as she added, "D'you think I didn't know such things?"

"Of course you did."

Marion stared helplessly at her cousin. Why didn't she say more? Make it a real conversation. She just responded with some empty little phrase – the absolute minimum – and then sat back and waited to hear more. Well, she wasn't going to get any more.

But the resolve lasted less than a minute. At length, Marion could endure the silence no more. "Wait until you see Salome," she said. "You'll realize it's not all cut and dried."

"It never is."

After another pause Marion said, "It was so easy for our parents – this business of right and wrong. Everyone *knew* the difference. It was black and white – with no shades of gray in between. But now it's *all* gray. The Bible says, 'Thou shalt not kill' – and we're killing tens of thousands every day. And the bishops on both sides are cheering them on – forget the Bible, they tell us – *this* is God's will!"

"We're straying from the point, dear."

"No, we're not! Don't you see, Edith? There's no absolute right and wrong any more."

"How convenient!"

"But there isn't! There's *more*-wrong and *less*-wrong, but everything's relative. Salome herself said she didn't want to go back to her parents – very soon after she came to Cloonaghvogue. It only took her a couple of months to reach that decision."

Edith frowned and looked at her cousin with open suspicion.

"Nobody prompted her," Marion asserted. "She just said it, out of the blue."

The other's expression did not change.

"Her first Christmas," Marion added.

Edith smiled knowingly at that. "Let me guess – when she got her first pet kitten? Puppy dog?"

Marion sipped her tea and replied, "There's obviously no talking to you."

"Not if you're just seeking *carte blanche*," Edith agreed amiably.

"Well, who appointed *you* keeper of my conscience, anyway?"

"I rather supposed *you* did – when you asked me what I thought you should do for the best."

"Yes . . . well . . . I didn't imagine you'd take this line at all."

Edith merely chuckled.

Marion swallowed heavily and tried to blink away the tears that suddenly flushed her eyes. "I don't want to lose her," she said in a strangulated whisper.

Edith's attitude changed at once – from impartial moralist to caring friend. She set down her plate, rose to her feet, and walked round the parlour table to stand at her cousin's side. She laid her hand on her neck and, massaging gently, said, "Of course you don't, darling. But you have to think ahead, too. You have to think of every possibility – or someone has to."

The suggestion that there was some unforeseen menace waiting out there in the future did more to dispel Marion's tears than her cousin's sudden tenderness. "What possibility?" she asked.

Edith sat in the chair next to her and said, "You might keep her now only to lose her later – have you thought of that?"

Marion shook her head. No likely circumstances suggested themselves. "How?"

"Well, when she's grown up she's bound to wonder what efforts you made to trace her parents. *Did* you write to the shipping line? *Did* you put announcements in the papers? *Did* you tell the harbour police? Suppose she meets her mother again sometime, ten years from now, say – and discovers that the poor woman's life was ruined. You can picture it for yourself, surely? Salome – the heiress to *your* money if not to C-B's, the belle of every ball with a string of eligible bachelors at her heels . . . and don't try telling me that isn't the future you have in mind for her! And then our golden girl meets this defeated, downtrodden woman who never ceased grieving for her loss and praying for her return. How d'you think she's going to feel? The guilt, Marion! The guilt! You know how idealistic girls can be in their early twenties!"

Edith spoke these concluding words with some irony since she herself was only twenty-four.

"I know how *ruthless* they can be," Marion responded with some feeling.

"That, too. Idealism and ruthlessness – a dreadful pair if they get turned against you. Joking apart, that's what could happen. That *sort* of thing."

Marion picked up the last of her scone, looked at it, and put it down again. She pushed the plate from her and slumped between her shoulders. "I honestly don't know *what* to do any more. Just tell me. I wish I'd never laid eyes on those papers."

"The papers are a red herring. Or, actually, they may be a blessing in disguise. But the mistakes you've made were there before – even if Martin had never written a word, they were still there, waiting to explode in your face one day, maybe."

Clutching at any straw, Marion said, "Why d'you say they may be a blessing in disguise?"

"Because their discovery now, today, has made you realize you have to *do* something. You wouldn't even have considered writing to the McKennas otherwise, would you! Also – if you think about it calmly – it isn't too late to undo some of the wrong that you yourself admit you did."

"You should be a priest," Marion commented with lacklustre sarcasm. "Or a mother superior."

"An expectant mother superior – that would be a most intriguing novelty!"

The absurdity, and irrelevance, of this last exchange struck both women as so funny that they dissolved in helpless mirth – which was the state in which a somewhat shocked Liam Murphy, the local postman, discovered them when they finally heard his knocking.

"Telegram for yourself, ma'am," he said, holding the envelope out to Marion.

This sobering intrusion from the outside world made both women realize how out of touch they were with the stirring events of that particular week.

"What's the latest from Dublin?" Marion asked while Edith went inside to fetch a threepenny tip for the man.

"They have the rebels surrounded in the GPO, ma'am. 'Twill be ours again by tomorrow, they say. There was shelling at the Four Courts and little left standing in Sackville Street. Boland's Mills is attacked."

She wondered what he meant when he said the GPO would be 'ours' again. Was he a Loyalist or just a loyal Post Office servant? "Terrible times," she said.

He darted a nervous glance at the envelope in her hand and said, "Aye!" in such a dire tone that she knew it contained bad news.

Edith returned with his tip; he was clearly disappointed at having to leave without seeing them read the telegram.

Marion carried it into the kitchen and slit it neatly open with a sharp potato knife. But then her courage deserted her and she handed it to Edith to read. "As long as it's nothing to do with Salome," she murmured. "I don't care what else has happened."

Edith unfolded the paper, scanned it quickly, and gave her a wan smile. "No harm to Salome," she said. "But . . ."

"Yes?"

"It's not good." She quoted: " 'Cloonaghvogue attacked last night stop we saw them off but damage considerable stop thank heaven you weren't here stop come home soonest possible stop Salome remaining at Castle Moore stop C-B.' See for yourself." She passed the paper across to her cousin.

Marion read the words in a daze. She understood them and yet somehow failed to take them in. "Damage considerable," she repeated. "That could mean anything."

"Why not go down and telephone him right away?" Edith suggested.

"Then it'll be all over the village."

"It'll be all over the village anyway. Phone him from the police barracks. They must have lines that people don't eavesdrop into."

"I could phone Rick Bellingham and see if they've been attacked, too."

"Surely C-B would have said?"

Marion waved the telegram. "All this tells us is that Salome was safe" – she checked the transmission time – "two hours ago. As far as C-B knew."

They drifted back into what had been Martin's study, where all the papers were stored. Marion looked about her as if she had never been there before. "I think I'd better just go straight home, dear," she said. "D'you mind if I abandon you?"

"Good lord, no! Not in the circs. Or d'you want me to come with you? We can lock up here and come back any time." She picked up the papers relating to Salome. "It rather puts all this 'on the long finger' – as Martin used to say."

32

Rick replaced the receiver and stared at the instrument a long while. The darkest day in his life was when he realized he'd finally lost Judith Carty – that she was going to marry Fergal McIver, his best friend. Even then, when he thought he might as well end his own life on the spot, for the sun would surely never rise again . . . even then a cool little voice inside him had said, 'Make a careful note of all these stray feelings, my boy. You'll get a good novel out of them one day!'

That particular novel had yet to be written but the cold, dispassionate voice had never been silent for long. This news from Cloonaghvogue Castle was dreadful. True, Culham-Browne was a pretty awful fellow. (Poor Marion!) And one did sympathize, at heart, with the rebels. But still, this was no way for them to go about winning their cause – burning historic buildings and destroying beautiful furniture and works of art.

But even as he commiserated with C-B and told him that, of course, little Salome could stay as long as they liked, another part of his mind was racing ahead, thinking of all the ramifications . . . Maisie Morrell, ready, willing, and able . . . the possible rebel threat to Castle Moore and every other landlord house in Ireland . . . perhaps he should begin moving his papers into the old castle tower, the only really noncombustible part of the house . . . tomorrow could be too late . . . and tonight could be too early to seduce Maisie if she were going to stay another two weeks or more . . .

And while this jumble of thoughts churned over in his mind that voice was there, too, telling him to make a note of this and that, because 'there might be a good novel in it one day.'

"Who was that?"

He turned and saw Maisie standing in the doorway, one hesitant foot over its threshold. *Funny*, he thought. *She knows what she wants. And I know what she wants. And we each know the other knows, too. And yet we'll neither of us say a word. We'll simply let it happen!* "Come in, my dear!" He beamed at her and held his hands wide in a priestly sort of blessing. "No. Actually, I've a better idea. Fancy a walk before dinner? Work up an appetite, eh?"

"Dinner? We haven't had tea yet."

"Skip tea," he said. "A good long trudge through the rain-soaked woods. Forget the war. Forget the rebellion. It'll do us the world of good. Do say yes?"

There was a subtle change of tension in her stance, a new glint in her eye.

She knows, he thought. *This is it*.

He could also tell she was teetering on the verge of turning down the suggestion – not turning *him* down, merely the idea of a walk in the rain. Sheer coquetry, really. He nodded toward the telephone. "That was old Culham-Browne," he said. "Some unpleasant news, I'm afraid."

Her face fell. "Not . . . nothing to do with Marion?"

"No, no. Nobody's hurt." He rubbed his hands briskly. "I'll tell you during our walk."

That put the kybosh on any idea of a coquettish refusal.

The rain had been no more than a prolonged shower. The sun was out in a cloud-mottled sky by the time they emerged, she in a soft, navy-blue macintosh, he in a fawn trenchcoat. He had a gnarled old walking stick made of contorted hazel; he pointed it down the drive, saying, "Let's start off on firm ground at least, eh?"

"Tell me about Cloonaghvogue," she said as soon as they were away.

After a pause he said, "I'm afraid they were attacked last night."

"Attacked! by whom?"

"These rebels. The papers have concentrated on the rising in Dublin. I don't think we're being told the full story – in fact, I'm damn sure we're not. There have been numerous risings, or *incidents*, anyway, all over the country. And one of them was at Cloonaghvogue Castle last night. A bit stupid of them, really, when you consider that there's no other house in the country better furnished with the means of sudden death. Nor one with such loyal servants, as it now appears."

"They fought them off?"

"Of course. But it's hardly a victory. Half a dozen new widows or grieving mothers – and a half-gutted castle. Nobody wins."

Maisie stopped in her tracks. "I don't know how you can take such a lofty tone," she complained. "All my worldly goods are there. All my books . . ." She bit her lip. "My God! All my books!"

He slipped his arm through hers and forced her to walk again. "Nothing in the Georgian part of the house was touched," he assured her. "It all began when they threw fire-bombs into the ground floor of the *old* castle. Two floors have been burned out and the third one is . . . they don't think it can be saved."

"And all the paintings?"

He nodded. "All the paintings. That wonderful tapestry. The carpets. The furniture – all gone. It's senseless."

They walked a few dozen yards in silence, into the wooded part of the drive. He released her arm but she responded immediately by taking his. "Poor C-B," she said. "He must be beside himself."

"He sounded on top of the world to me. He wants to persuade the local army commander to give him cover tonight while he lobs fire-bombs into every known republican house in the village. He's always resented being turned down by the army for this war. He sees this as his big chance to do something."

She laughed.

He did not join in. "The whole thing is such a tragedy," he said. "If only they'd waited! But they were so dead set on martyrdom. And by God, the English will give it to them. And that'll be the end of this poor country."

"I don't understand."

He laughed suddenly. "This, I may say, is the last sort of conversation I expected us to have."

"Me, too," she replied with some feeling.

"All right, let's be done with it," he said. "You know what the English *ought* to do? It's pretty obvious the rebellion's going to collapse by the weekend and they'll all be rounded up – those who survive. You know what the English ought to do then?"

She shook her head.

"They should announce to all the world that they've smacked them all soundly and sent them to bed without any supper. And then the next day they should let them all go free. That'd be the end of rebellion in Ireland for all time. It would turn the very *idea* of rebellion into a music-hall joke. But since the military mind has less imagination than a flea, they'll never do it. They'll do the worst possible thing, instead."

"What?"

"Shoot the lot."

The idea was so preposterous she laughed.

"They will," he assured her earnestly. "You'll see. And then it'll be civil war, not just in Dublin but everywhere."

For a moment his prophecy seemed so real that she could do nothing but cling even tighter to his arm. "Isn't there *anything* we can do?" she asked.

He slipped his hand over hers and grinned. "We can eat, drink, and be merry," he said. "For tomorrow we die."

She leaned her head against his arm and closed her eyes. "All right," she said quietly.

He turned them toward a dense patch of undergrowth, beneath an ancient cryptomeria whose dense foliage would have kept it perfectly dry – and whose tiny fallen leaves would provide a bed as soft as goosedown.

She let him lead her there without demur.

And Hereward and Salome were such skilled braves by then that Rick's final, lord-of-all-he-surveyed glance around the woodland failed to pick them out.

33

It was not enough for Debbie to suspect that something was going on between Finbar and Georgina; she felt she had to know. Suspicion carried its own torments, of course – torments she welcomed joyously – and she did not want to risk alleviating them by discovering that her fears were unfounded. Now that she had realized that God had a purpose in heaping torment after torment on her spirit – which was to test her devotion to Him – she was ever on the look-out for new signs of His especial favour. If Finbar were deceiving her, that might be the next one.

The corrosive pain of it would enable her to make another great advance in her own spiritual odyssey. If, on the other hand, he proved innocent . . . well, perhaps she could learn to see it as a reward for the devotion she had shown so far. But it would be like marking time instead of pressing forward.

She wanted Him to know that, like Job, she was ready for any scourge He might visit upon her. And yet, of course, He did already know. He knew everything that was going to happen in the world, to the very end of time – and He had known it before time itself was even created. So, the more she thought about it, the more certain she felt that He would not have placed such insinuations in her mind if they were groundless.

The trouble was, now that Paul was dead, the farm was Georgina's. Well, it always had been hers – legally speaking. Uncle Harry and Aunt Queenie had taken Paul and Georgina into partnership the same month Samson divined the water, on the understanding they'd buy the old folks out at so much a year – which was like their pension. So Georgina had every right to ride over the farm with Finbar, inspecting this, discussing that, planning the other. And the farm was big enough, especially with Suidhoek added in, to take them out of sight from dawn till dusk a couple of days each month. So hadn't they the perfect excuse for it – if *it* was on their minds at all!

Debbie's suspicions had started long before Paul's death, but they had, of course, gained new vigour since that tragedy; unfortunately, she could see no way of confirming them directly. She thought she saw a chance one day when a message came from some lawyers in Port Elizabeth asking Georgina to come into town and sign some family papers sent out from Ireland; if she came at once, they could catch a vessel leaving on that afternoon's tide. Debbie wasted no time in saddling a horse and riding out to that corner of the farm where they had said they'd be. But all the care she took to catch them unawares was to no avail. It was the sort of day on which even a slowly walking horse can raise enough dust to be seen a mile off – and anyway, one horse is swift to catch the sound and scent of another's approach. The pair of them were twenty yards apart and fully clothed by the time Debbie saw them – and probably had been all day, she admitted reluctantly to herself.

Again, Finbar was often out at night, checking the stock, riding the fences, fighting endless skirmishes with baboons, monkeys, wild boar, and feral dogs; but Debbie had no way of discovering whether Georgina was out at those same times, for she was most certainly not going to start making direct inquiries of the servants at Fountains. Once one of the cooks had mentioned an absence of Mrs Georgina on a night when Finbar had also been absent, but then it turned out that she had been playing bridge with friends in Walmer, a suburb of Port Elizabeth, over ten miles away.

So, Debbie concluded, if discovery was to be made, it would have to be by indirect means – a dropped hint, an unguarded word, a taunt given out in anger. She'd simply have to bide her time.

The only regular contact between the two women was during the weekly visit to Port Elizabeth, when Debbie rode over to Fountains and they both went to the city in the gig. In the week that Paul died, Georgina had not felt up to it – understandably; but by the following week the larder was running low and her hair was in a mess and two friends were moving to Jo'burg . . . so, what with one thing and another, she felt both obliged and tempted to resume her weekly habit.

Debbie rode over after an early breakfast and joined her in the gig in the usual way – the only difference between this and previous occasions being that both women were now in full mourning. Debbie watched closely, though out of the corner of her eye, as Finbar walked over to check the traces and see them off – something he had always done, even when Paul was alive. Apart from Georgina's arch farewell: "Don't do anything I wouldn't do!" – which she often said, even to the children and the most casual of friends – there was nothing untoward in their leavetaking.

"He's a tower of strength," Georgina said when they had left the farmhouse well behind. "It would all go to pieces without him. You chose a fine man, Debbie."

Debbie sighed and said it was the God's truth – which it was, too, even if it wasn't the whole of it.

She crossed herself as they drove past the little grove that marked Samson's grave – or, rather, his memorial, for his remains were never found. It stood among the gravestones of several of Georgina's relatives, the pioneers of Fountains all the way back to the 1820 Settlers. Georgina noticed that her eyes were lifted to the skies throughout the little ritual; not once did she turn her head toward the memorial itself.

"Still feeling numb?" she asked.

Debbie nodded. "Sometimes I think I'll never feel anything ever again. Had we found just *some*thing of him . . ."

"I know. I find myself looking about me in a kind of amazement that everything's going on so normally – the farm, the animals, the sea . . . you know. I'm even amazed that I get hungry if I don't eat."

"Time slows down, though," Debbie pointed out.

"But not enough. What we really want, I feel, is some way of stopping time altogether – out there, I mean – while I go on on my own. Don't you think that would be wonderful?"

It struck Debbie as odd that here she was, sitting beside a woman who might very well be committing adultery with her husband, which would make her equal with the Whore of Babylon and Jezebel and all those creatures rolled into one – which would mean, in turn, that she, Debbie, should burn with shame to be near her, never mind the jealous rage that should be consuming her every mile of this journey . . . and yet she felt nothing against the woman at all. Nor did she detect any need to judge her. It gave her the uneasy feeling that her suspicions caused her greater torment than their confirmation would ever provide.

"It was God's will," she replied.

Her tone was so matter-of-fact that Georgina, who had, of course, heard her voice the opinion before, was nonetheless shocked into silence.

"When I lost Salome," Debbie went on, "I found that hard to accept – that He had willed it so. But I have no such fears about Samson. He is in heaven already and smiling down on us."

"Of course," Georgina agreed – and then turned swiftly to the arrangements of the day, the shops they'd visit, the purchases they'd make, and, finally, the time Debbie could take off for her regular confession.

They were about a mile out along the highway, and just over a mile short of the village of Uitsdorp, when a most curious incident took place.

Georgina broke off her conversation to say, "Hark! I think there's someone there." She pointed toward the bush to their left and drew the gig to a halt.

There were traces of an old road there, about ten yards to the side of the present highway; it must have been washed out by a storm two or three decades ago, for it was deeply eroded in several places. In the silence they were able to hear a commotion some way off in the bush. A crowd was shouting. The volume surged up and down, excitably, and every now and then it was punctuated by a scream – though whether of pain or rage they could not tell.

"No dust," Georgina pointed out. "That's odd. A large crowd and no dust."

"It must all be rock?" Debbie offered, though she could discern no clearing in the bush to support the possibility.

The tone of the crowd changed to a sort of bantering, laughing whoop – as if they were chasing some animal; if so, they were chasing it toward the highway.

"Someone's coming," Georgina said, leaning half across Debbie and peering intently into the dense wall of shrub and cactus. "They know their woodcraft, too," she added. "Look – not a leaf stirring to give them away."

"And still no dust," Debbie pointed out.

By now the sounds of people crashing toward them through the bush were unmistakable – even though it was unaccompanied by any of the other signs of such an approach. The horses grew restive and Georgina took up the reins again, preparing to trot them on – indeed, to whip them to a canter if need be.

But Debbie stayed her hand. "It might be someone in trouble," she said.

"I don't think there's the slightest doubt about that!" Georgina replied. "The question is, do we wish to join them? It's probably only natives – drinking their beer and smoking dagga."

"We can't leave until we know for sure."

A moment later her caution was justified when a nun came racing out into the open and looked wildly up and down the highway – the old highway, that is. Her habit was torn and there was blood on her starched wimple.

"Here! Over here!" the two women shouted at her, amazed she hadn't spotted them immediately.

The nun raised her hand to shield her eyes – as people do when peering a long distance over the veldt – and then laughed in delight at spotting them.

"She must be extremely short-sighted," Georgina commented drily.

Debbie leaped down to help the woman up, shouting, "Come on! Run!"

The nun obeyed. The pursuing rabble was frighteningly close by now, to judge by the clamour.

The nun caught her foot in a small gully beside the gig and would have tumbled headlong beneath it if Debbie had not caught her and, using the momentum of her fall, swung her up into the seat beside Georgina. She gathered up her own skirts and leaped over the tailboard, crying, "Gitaaan!" – as much to the horses as to anyone.

The creatures needed no whip to get them going from a standing start to a canter. The poor nun, who had hardly got her balance in the seat, was flung back against Debbie – who was saved from being bounced out again only by the fact that she still had the impetus of her forward leap to stay her. She laughed as she disentangled herself, and the nun laughed, too; but Debbie was quite shocked at the powerful reek of ancient sweat from the woman – as strong as off any goat. As the shock wore off, however, and she settled herself to kneel on an old straw cushion behind the two women in front, her nostrils found it not unpleasant, merely rather strong.

The nun gave her two rescuers no more than a cursory glance before turning her attention to the road ahead. Her eyes darted this way and that, as if she had never seen it before and were committing it to memory. Not once did she glance behind to see how near her pursuers had come.

Debbie looked back once or twice but the mob must have realized it had been cheated of its quarry for it never broke clear of the bush. Nor, so far as she could tell above the roar of the gig wheels, did it continue to chant and howl.

"Had you some trouble with the Kaffirs?" she asked the nun.

Georgina, who had been concentrating on the road until then, glanced back, too, and, realizing they were not being pursued, began reining back to a trot. "Eh?" she prompted when the nun made no reply.

The woman appeared not to hear.

"*Praat jy Afrikaans?*" Georgina tried – though surely a question in any language would have commanded her attention, if not her understanding.

The nun looked at her and smiled – then at Debbie, to whom she smiled even more broadly.

"There's a doctor the other side of Uitsdorp," Georgina said, speaking slowly and distinctly, as to a child. "We'll get those cuts of yours dressed. They don't look serious to me but one never knows, does one."

The nun smiled again but did not take her eyes off the road. The other two women exchanged baffled glances. Then Debbie noticed that the nun, a woman in her twenties to judge by her complexion, had a definite moustache – not what you'd call a manly moustache but not really a womanly one, either – certainly not in one so young. She began to suspect that the nun (if, indeed, that is what she was) kept silent for a much more compelling reason than deafness or incomprehension: She was afraid of revealing she could sing in the basso-profundo range!

When the gig lurched over the next pothole Debbie took advantage of its motion to grasp the woman at the waist. In fact, she grabbed at Georgina with the other hand, just to make the comparison easier. They could have been the paired hipbones of a four-foot-wide woman; there was no doubting the sex of their silent passenger.

Georgina turned and stared at her in surprise, and then grinned. Debbie realized she had just begun to entertain a similar suspicion about the nun, and so had guessed what her, Debbie's, real purpose was in taking such a liberty.

"Lord but I'm sorry," she exclaimed. "These roads!"

The nun, who had paid no attention to Debbie's grasping her hip like that, tapped Georgina's arm urgently and signalled her to stop. When the request was not obeyed quickly enough she grasped the reins herself and pulled the horses to a standstill. They were less than half a mile from Uitsdorp now, and little over a mile from the place where they had rescued the nun.

"The doctor's is the other side of the village," Georgina explained, taking back the reins and preparing to start off again.

The nun shook her head and rose from her seat, plainly intending to get down.

"Sister," Debbie said. "Will you not bless us before you go – and remember us in your prayers?"

She intended it as another test, not of sex this time but of vocation.

The nun laid her hand on Georgina's shoulder and smiled at her. Georgina just sat there as if paralyzed. Looking up into the nun's eyes Debbie began to doubt her earlier guess that here was a woman in her twenties; those eyes had seen much, and suffered much, too. They could have been any age.

Then the nun turned to her and, kneeling on the seat, leaned over and kissed her on the forehead – a lingering kiss that somehow filled her with a sense of peace and wellbeing she had not experienced in years.

"God bless you, Sister," she said to the nun, "and keep you in His mercy."

She could not say why she chose just those words; they did not form part of any church ritual that she knew; they just rose within her from . . . nowhere. But it was almost as if the nun were waiting to hear them, for the moment they were spoken she straightened up again and, with amazing agility for one constrained by such a voluminous habit, leaped down from the gig. As soon as she felt the ground beneath her she turned her back on her rescuers and walked swiftly toward the bush.

Moved by a single thought the other two turned round to gaze back up the highway, the way they had come, fearing their pursuers might at last be in sight. But the road was empty.

Again in unison they turned to tell the nun this news, but she had already vanished back into the bush. They listened hard but could hear no sound of her. Nor did they see any telltale movement of a shrub or thorn. Nor was there the slightest stirring of dust.

"How extraordinary!" Georgina said with a baffled little laugh.

Debbie climbed back into her seat, saying, "The smell off of her!"

"Yes, I noticed!" Georgina shook the horses to a slow trot. "Not that it was offensive, mind – just rather strong."

"She must have been living in the bush a long time."

"Yes. Just look at the way she disappeared! A convict tracker would give his eye teeth for a skill like that." She smiled archly at Debbie. "And you made sure she was what she appeared to be, I noticed!"

"I made sure she was a woman, anyway!" In a more thoughtful tone she added, "And I feel sure she was a nun, too, you know. When she touched me . . . Didn't you feel it? The holy calm of her?"

Somewhat reluctantly Georgina agreed. "When she laid her hand on my shoulder, I wanted to tell her again about going to the doctor, and how she must get her cuts dressed . . ."

"They weren't that bad."

"Even so. You know how things fester in this climate, even in winter. Anyway, I was saying, I wanted to sort of cajole her into coming to see Doc Harkness, but the words just . . . dried up. Well!" She shook herself and added in an altogether brisker tone. "What excitements!"

A hand-written sign outside one of the houses in Uitsdorp said: ORANGES 3d A POCKET. Debbie nudged Georgina and said, "Look, only a tickey a pocket. Shall we get some?"

The orange grove at Fountains had been blighted by salt spray that year and the yield was poor; Suidhoek still had a good harvest but it would not be enough to provide for both households.

They bought two pockets and set off again. Georgina had wanted to tell the man that there was trouble with the natives in the bush but he was so surly – as poor whites often are with their rich brethren – that she said nothing. However, when they reached the far end of the village she realized they ought to let someone know about the commotion, so she said, "I think we'll just stop and tell old Doc what happened back there. One never knows."

They met the man just coming out of his gate with a wheelbarrow full of small tortoises. "Little beggars!" he called out jovially as the gig drew to a halt. "I carry them half a mile away and, bless me, they're back in my garden before I am! What may I do for you ladies? You both look woefully healthy."

"We're as well as can be expected, Doc," Georgina said, thinking that their black dresses should have reminded him – if he needed it – of their state.

Pungent tortoise urine fell in steady drips from cracks in the barrow.

"Let's move upwind," he suggested, putting the barrow down and striding off toward the far end of his front wall. Georgina, driving the gig a pace or two behind, called down to him, "You may soon have more patients than you bargain for."

"And divil a one with a coin to pay you," Debbie added.

"Dear me!" He halted and turned to face them, eyebrows arched in query.

They began to tell him about the incident, but the moment they mentioned the nun he threw back his head and roared with laughter. "So you've seen her, too!" he said at length.

Georgina asked what he meant.

"Dear Mrs Delaroux! That nun has been stopping carriages, dogcarts, bicycles – anything that moves – for longer than anyone can remember. She was probably stopping oxwaggons in the days of the Great Trek. She's a Familiar."

"What d'you mean – a Familiar? A ghost?"

"I don't believe in ghosts," he said firmly. "She's a Familiar. She . . . appears. She just appears."

Georgina and Debbie exchanged glances, reassuring each other that what they had seen and touched – and smelled! – was much too substantial to be any old ghost. Even when the doctor went on to describe more or less precisely what had happened (which Georgina had not even begun to tell him earlier) they still refused to accept his talk of Familiars. However, they did not tell him of the nun's response when Debbie had asked her blessing on them; he would only have laughed again.

Agreeing to differ – in their interpretation of the event at least – they parted as amicably as ever, leaving him to gather up the half-dozen reptiles that had meanwhile climbed out of his barrow.

"She was as real as you or me," Debbie said when they were alone again.

"Of course she was. He was pulling our leg, that's all."

"Still, it's a quare thing that he knew what happened before either of us said a word of it."

"He must have had a telescope on us," Georgina said. "You know how he loves a joke." She laughed. "And didn't we just walk right into it!"

Doc Harkness was known as a local stargazer and had, indeed, built an observatory platform up on his roof; less charitable people said he used his telescope to pry into his patients' houses, for, though no one had ever seen his telescope pointing at anything other than the skies, he always seemed to know a suspicious amount about their eating habits and private lives.

It occurred to Debbie, however, that though his instrument was powerful enough to show him what had happened a mile the other side of the village, he could not at the same time have gathered up three or four dozen lively tortoises like that. Mind you, one of the garden boys could have done the gathering, so that wasn't conclusive, either.

In the end she decided not to think any more about all those different possibilities. She *knew* what they had seen out there between Uitsdorp and Fountains – an angel of mercy, sent by God to assure her that Samson was happy in heaven that day and her darling Salome alive and well, somewhere here on earth.

And there was another, more surprising message in it for her, as well.

Toward the end of the afternoon she went to the Church of the Sacred Heart and made her confession. To Father O'Halloran's relief it was indistinguishable from the thousands of other confessions he had heard down the years from blameless wives of Debbie's age.

A moment later, however, he was kicking himself for his complacency. The woman leaned closer to the grill and said, "Father?"

"Yes, my child?" he responded with sinking heart.

"A woman like me – you know who I am?"

After a pause he said, "I'm afraid I do."

She laughed. "Ah, don't be codding me now! Tell me, I want to hear – how would a woman like me go about taking the veil? I want to become a nun."

34

The rising ended formally on Saturday, 29th April, five days after it had begun. Late that afternoon, Patrick Pearse handed his sword to General Lowe and issued orders to all the remaining outposts for an unconditional surrender; they were, in any case, surrounded and heavily outnumbered. The following Wednesday, 3rd May, the English shot Pearse, Thomas MacDonagh, and Thomas J. Clarke at Kilmainham Gaol. On Thursday they shot Pearse's brother William, Joseph Plunkett (roped to a chair, being too ill to stand), Edward Daly, and Michael O'Hanrahan. On Friday, John MacBride. On the following Monday, Eamonn Ceannt, Michael Malin, Con Colbert, and Sean Heuston. On the Tuesday, Thomas Kent, who, with his brothers, had held out at Bawnard House in County Cork for two days after the general surrender. And on Friday, 12th May, James Connolly and Sean MacDiarmada faced the last Kilmainham firing squad, thus completing the grisly harvest of 'traitors'.

In all, more than a hundred and twenty others were

sentenced to death for their part in the rising, but by then even the English military were beginning to see what a ghastly mistake they had made. When the last rebel shot was fired outside the GPO, Ireland had heaved a sigh of relief that the madness was over. Not a good word was to be heard for the deluded rebels who had caused so much damage to property and to the commercial life of the country. It took ten days – and fifteen executions – to transmute the base villains into golden heroes whose names would resound forever in the nation's history.

Castle Moore resounded with Richard Bellingham's fury at the brutal stupidity of the generals. Hadn't he foretold the consequences even before the rising collapsed? But then, as both the women in his life reminded him, he had predicted disaster on almost every public issue for years; the only novelty in the present situation was that he could at last say, "I told you so!" For their part they wished he would voice his opinions a little more cautiously; the Anglo-Irish no longer went about the land, denouncing all and sundry at the tops of their voices – not if they knew what was good for them.

But there Rick was on fairly safe ground. The Bellinghams had long ago fought and won their own private battle with the republicans – and had then stood up for real justice when the military had bungled it yet again. No one was going to attack Castle Moore.

Cloonaghvogue Castle was quite another matter, as Rick learned when he delivered Maisie and Salome there in person. It was a week since the executions had been halted and a numbed country was just awakening to a full sense of the outrage. No one could say where it might lead. People who had agreed to differ and who had lived side by side quite amicably for years – indeed for generations – eyed one another nervously and wondered how much longer such agreements would stand the strain. Fear stalked the land and danger lurked behind every hedgerow. Rick was overwhelmed with relief as he turned in at Cloonaghvogue gates, having covered the intervening twenty-odd miles with nothing more serious to report than a puncture at Simonstown. But it was soon countered by his dismay at the sight of the Culham-Brownes' home.

Word had reached Castle Moore that the place was 'desthroyed intirely!' – which Rick had taken to mean you could see the odd spot of damage here and there. C-B himself, speaking on the phone, had said the place was hardly touched – which Rick had taken to mean you could see the odd spot of damage here and there. So it was a great shock to discover that, for once, the luxuriant Irish version of the truth was closer to reality than the understated English variation. The lawns were littered with burned furniture, ruined carpets, and fragments of things too wrecked to identify. The windows that had not been burned out by the fire had been smashed during the attempt to get at least some of the valuables out – and the firehoses in. Anything that might possibly be repaired was under tarpaulins. C-B and Miss Kinchy were going about with clipboards, making lists.

Marion was upstairs in the newer, Georgian annexe to the house, supervising the removal of their bed from the damaged tower. This had involved taking the roof off part of the tower, removing a section of the floor (sacrificing the plasterwork underneath), and winching the hated Culham-Browne bed up, over the battlements, and down to the upper floor of the annexe, where the largest of the windows had to be removed. There, despite the most careful measurements beforehand, it proved three inches too large to pass through the opening. An argument developed among the carpenters as to which of them had the accurate tape-measure.

"I'd gladly saw the bloody thing in half," Marion murmured to Edith.

They watched the bed spinning slowly on its rope, a tempting two floors above a cobbled yard that would surely smash it beyond repair. "The number of nights I've lain there, dreaming of separate beds!"

"We'll have to lower her to the ground and see if she'll dismantle," said Tom Hogan, the Protestant head carpenter. He communicated the decision to Joe Clancy, the Roman Catholic master mason, who was in charge of the winch above.

A moment later word floated down that the rope wasn't long enough; they hadn't expected to lower the thing all the way to the ground. Could Tom not dismantle enough of it where it hung?

The aerial discussion turned lively but at that point Marion spotted Rick's car turning in at the gates and she raced toward the stairs; she called back over her shoulder, saying she didn't mind how they solved the problem as long as they got the bed indoors in one piece.

She flew down the stairs and out through the front door, taking the stone steps three at a time. Edith followed at a pace more suited to her condition but was in time to see her cousin rush past C-B and the housekeeper and on down the drive to where Richard Bellingham was bringing the car to an early halt.

"Such a fuss!" C-B called angrily after her. When she paid no heed he turned and repeated the words to Edith, who stopped and drew breath to say something in Marion's defence.

But the impulse died and she just stood there, watching all the laughter and hugging going on, fifty yards away down the drive.

C-B stared at Edith with undisguised loathing. He had little enough patience with women at the best of times, but when one of them retreated into the invulnerable ivory tower of her pregnancy – that was the worst of all times. To make herself the centre of attention for nine long months! Not to mention the weeks of sentimental coo-cooing afterwards! A whole year in which you were a beast if you crossed them, or argued with them, or told them a few simple home truths for their own good . . . and that secret, simpering smile on their lips, when you *knew* they were communing with that disgusting little bag of bone and jelly, festering away inside them . . . and the way they formed into covens around any one of their company who happened to be in that broody condition – like cattle in a field. How *could* these scientists and philosophers go about claiming they were as far up the evolutionary ladder as men? You only had to look at them.

And this Edith Woods, with her spare physique, her curly, carroty hair, her million freckles of every shape and size, her secret, simpering pregnancy – and above all, her disgraceful opinions – enraged him most of all: "Foxhunting is the pursuit of the uneatable by the unspeakable!"

How *dare* Marion bring such a creature to stay at Cloonaghvogue!

The 'creature' in question stood at his side, watching Marion hugging poor Salome half to death – *and* listening to the girl's excited account of these momentous weeks at Castle Moore, *and* trying simultaneously to take in Miss Morrell's explanations of the obscurer references.

But even Miss Morrell was reduced to shocked silence when Salome made the proudest announcement of all – that she had become Hereward Bellingham's mistress.

The laughter and the hubbub came to a sudden halt. Marion stared at Maisie. Maisie stared at Rick. And Rick goggled open-mouthed at Salome – who at last realized she had said something awful.

"Look!" she said, struggling in Marion's embrace to shed her coat and roll up her sleeve.

When they saw the last few scabs of the blood-brother ritual, and absorbed Salome's explanation of the phrase she had used, their laughter was almost hysterical. Then, to her chagrin, Salome realized she had unwittingly said one of those accidental and inexplicable things that grown-ups find so charming in children. But she *wasn't* a child any more – not like that. She demanded to know what it was they found so amusing.

"What?" she kept saying. "Tell me!"

And when they refused, her eyes filled with hot, angry tears.

But Rick saw it and, taking her out of Marion's arms, hugged her tight and said, "Well done, Salome! Well done! You put us all to shame, so you do."

And the odd thing was that, although she still had no idea what was so funny, nor what she had done that he could call it 'well done,' she felt a warm glow inside and no longer cared to know.

Marion, momentarily bereft of her child, turned to Maisie Morrell, expecting a womanly exchange of significant glances and some sign of relief that it was all a false alarm. Instead she found the woman staring at Rick Bellingham with such intense admiration that her mind started off at once along an entirely different track – though the word 'mistress' was prominent there, as well.

Rick, glancing over Salome's shoulder, saw C-B standing on the lawn, fists clenched, clipboard dangling at his side; the fearful, cowed stance of his housekeeper completed the picture. Troubled waters. It was time to pour a little oil. God, do I look as old as that? he wondered – and then recalled that C-B was fifty-one whereas he was still that magical forty-nine. The difference was a lot greater than two years.

The other woman, the one in mourning, must be Marion's cousin, about whom C-B had complained so harshly on the phone. Hard to judge her at this distance.

He put Salome down, correctly guessing that she wanted no more hugging or other signs of her childish status. "I think C-B's about to explode," he said with a wink at Marion as he walked away.

"What a wonderful man!" Maisie said under her breath,

though he was already out of earshot.

Marion smiled at her. "I see he has made a . . . a *convert* – can one say? – out of you." The guilty glance the woman shot her did nothing to unconfirm Marion's suspicions. To her amazement she found that the feeling this shocking revelation aroused within her was not of righteous indignation – which it certainly ought to have been – but a sharp and unambiguous pang of jealousy.

Edith began walking toward the little group by the car as soon as Rick detatched himself from it. He kept his eyes on her all the way. Black did not suit her figure, nor her colouring; she should be in something frilly, jade-green, and silky. She'd be a corker then. Sad eyes – understandable, really. Pert little nose. Hardly any top lip. That meant quietly passionate in his experience.

"You must be Mrs Woods, Marion's cousin," he said as she drew level. "Allow me to say how dreadfully sorry I am."

She smiled brightly – but more with her lips than in her eyes – and thanked him. "I hope you're staying for tea, Mister Bellingham," she added. "I do so want to talk with you. I've read all your books."

"How kind," he said as he resumed his brief stroll. Then, calling back to her, he added, "But I think I'd enjoy a talk with you, Mrs Woods, even if you'd never seen one of them."

It was a good thing Gwinnie and Letty had decided not to come along today. He'd had his rations for quite some time, he guessed.

"No memsahibs?" C-B called out as he came within hailing distance.

"Not today." He accelerated and closed the gap rapidly. "A woman's instinct – I always think. When the nest is threatened, stay and defend it."

"I don't know what *I* married, then," the other growled. He passed his clipboard to Miss Kinchy, saying, "You can carry on. I'll come back later." He flung an arm around Rick's shoulder and pressed him toward the house. "Come and see what the bastards did. I've decided to drink up all the whiskey."

"Today?" Rick asked in alarm.

"No!" C-B responded testily. "I mean use it all up. What's the sense in hoarding anything these days?" He waved a hand toward the gutted tower as if to add: 'when this sort of thing can happen at any moment.'

"It looks worse than I expected," Rick offered as they mounted the front steps.

C-B paused at the top and frowned in the direction of the group of three women and Salome, who were making slow progress across the lawn toward the stables; presumably Salome's desire to see Hannibal, her pony, had coincided with her desire *not* to return to the house. "That's the real problem here," he muttered.

"Say?" Rick prompted.

"Fucking women!"

So many responses clamoured for Rick's attention that he ended up saying nothing at all.

C-B flushed pink and he said, "You don't mind, I hope?"

"What?"

"My swearing like that."

"Not at all," Rick answered magnanimously. "In any case, old fellow, *women* is not a swear word in *my* vocabulary."

C-B laughed uproariously, slapped him between the shoulderblades, and led him inside.

When they had finished inspecting the damage they repaired to the drawing room, which was on the ground floor at the back of the annexe. While C-B made a ritual of pouring out the whiskey, Rick stood at the tall french windows and stared out across the lawn – or appeared to do so. In fact, out of the corner of his eye he could see into the stable yard, where Salome was petting Hannibal while the three women stood in an earnest knot near by, lost to the world at large.

How happy could I be with any, he thought, paraphrasing the parlour song, *were t'other two charmers away!*

C-B followed the direction of his gaze and said, as he handed over a good stiff tot, "Take the lot back with you to Castle Moore, dear fellow!"

Rick turned his back to the daylight and held up his glass, admiring the amber mellowness of the whiskey against the dark interior of the room. Then he sniffed it deeply; these things had to be done right.

"You'll stay on here, I'm sure?" he said, preparing to take a sip.

C-B grunted, preoccupied with his own whiskey ritual.

Rick took his first sip, swirled it round his mouth, absorbed the bite of the alcohol, let it trickle down his gullet, and breathed out an ambrosial fire. "Superb," he said, little above a whisper.

Satisfied that honour had been done to his especial blend, C-B made shorter work of his own first gulp.

"You'll rebuild?" Rick prompted.

C-B savoured it to the last fumes before he replied. "Probably not."

Rick sized up the drawing room with a surveyor's eye. "Well – I suppose this annexe is as big as most country houses on its own. You could get shot of a dozen servants and still live here quite comfortably. I'm thinking of doing the same at Castle Moore, frankly."

His host shook his head and stared awkwardly into his glass. "Thinking of going to live in England," he said gruffly. "Drink up. There's plenty more."

"Seriously?" Rick tossed his whiskey back and handed over his glass. "Not quite so much this time. I want to get home before dark."

"Think it smacks of cowardice?" C-B asked as he crossed the room to the decanters. "You can have water in it, if you like."

"Never!" He waited until the other was on his way back

before he added, "As to cowardice – certainly not!"

"You'd have every reason, old chap – you above all. Still – the bastards will never touch *you*, now, will they!"

"That was a different struggle in a different age, C-B. Resemblance to any actual persons now living is purely coincidental! Mind you, England's changed out of all recognition, too. You know Castle Bellingham in Norfolk – the ancestral family home? It's a loony bin now!"

"At least they lock the loonies up over there!" C-B responded morosely.

At that moment Salome trotted past the window on Hannibal. Rick prepared to say something complimentary about her when his host put in: "That's another reason to cut and run." He dipped his head after the retreating pony and its rider.

Rick stared at him aghast. "Has somebody threatened *her?* Surely not!"

C-B tossed back his drink and lifted an eyebrow at his guest, who showed his glass, still more than half-filled, and shook his head. The older man (by two years) stumped back across the room to fill his own. "Never should have taken her in," he said. "Should have put the old foot down at once, chop chop!"

"Will things be any different in England though?" Rick asked.

C-B gave him a curious grin but declined to be drawn any further.

35

A single yodel can start an avalanche they say. In the old nursery rhyme the lack of one horseshoe nail leads to the loss of an entire kingdom. So it is, too, in human affairs –

cause and effect may be so disproportionate that the mind can hardly put them together. The Culham-Brownes might have weathered the total destruction of the castle, Georgian annexe and all – because it would have been a single act of violence with a single group of perpetrators united in a single-minded purpose. There would have been a clear-cut balance in that situation: us versus them. Black and white.

They would know precisely how to respond to such a challenge. They'd have left the ruins as a standing rebuke to all who cared to view them in that light; and they would have added half a dozen rooms to the gate lodge, creating a sensible house for sensible, modern people, a house that could be managed with a mere half-dozen servants, indoors and out. There would even have been a kind of revenge in such a course, as the thirty or forty dismissed servants packed their bags and took the emigrant boat, never to return to that Ireland for which the republican-arsonists thought they were fighting; the satisfying irony would lie in the fact that the republicans and the new emigrants were almost certainly related, however remotely.

But black and white are the colours of *nothing* in Ireland, where all is misty, iridescent, fleeting. When C-B followed a shocked Tom Hogan, master carpenter, round to the back of the annexe and saw the heap of shattered oak and walnut that had been the Culham-Browne four-poster, he knew it was time to leave. A duel with the republicans was one thing, but a three-cornered fight with the Fates as well was beyond him. The decision to cut his losses and run popped into his mind, ready-made, as he stood there contemplating the wreckage. Such a little incident, really, and yet such huge consequences!

Only the carved head had survived relatively unscathed. In the large cartouche at its centre sat the horn-of-plenty, spilling its carved pomegranates and other fruits of Olympus, and mocking him. Every Culham since 1610 had been conceived under its benign influence – and every Culham-Browne since 1832. A chill settled on his innards as he realized he was now the last. Never again would a Culham-Browne baby spring into its privileged world from that solid four-postered citadel.

For the first time since his boyhood C-B felt the tears prickling hot behind his eyelids and he sought urgently about him for some reason *not* to cry. In all her life Marion had never picked a worse moment to join her husband, but she was not to know that.

As she picked her way over the cobbles – avoiding the outlying shards and trying not to let her elation show on the surface – Tom Hogan mumbled something embarrassed and unintelligible and left them alone. An informal circle of people, trying not to look as if they were looking, gathered around and above them – servants and retainers who knew in their bones that their entire futures were in some obscure way at stake during the next few minutes.

"Will it mend?" she asked C-B in a too-solemn voice – to counteract the ecstatic laughter she was afraid might otherwise erupt. She looked down on his head, thinking it was rare to see him hatless out of doors, thinking that the wrong bit of the Culham-Browne legacy was now in smithereens.

"No bloody point," he replied morosely. "A stall for a barren cow."

She froze. The heat of her previous elation turned to the dry ice of bitterness. "How dare you?" she asked quietly.

"I'll thank you to keep your head," he retorted. "And keep your voice down, too."

"Oh!" she laughed venomously. "I can *whisper* the news to you, if that's your wish."

"News?" he echoed gruffly. "What now?"

"News you should have been given years ago. It's no longer news to anyone else, of course – and it wouldn't be news to you if Doctor Hooke had half as much courage in speaking the truth as he managed to rustle up when naming his fee!"

A little voice within her started mumbling a warning, telling her she was within half a dozen words of wrecking their marriage as thoroughly as a combination of gravity and cobblestones had wrecked their marriage bed. But some more primitive element in her soul, which needed neither voice nor words to have its way with her, pressed onward, still ice-hot with fury.

"Hooke?" he snappeed. "What are you babbling about?"

"Doctor Pusillanimous-Hooke, Master of the Mellifluous Emptiness." She clapped one hand over her right eye and made a mock microscope tube with the other, which she put to that blindfolded eye. " 'I see nothing here that might stand in the way of a happy outcome'!" She parodied the mealy-mouthed advice the doctor had given them all those miserable years ago. " 'Roger away like gluttons, my darlings! And you, my dear lady, stand on your head and . . .' "

"Marion!" A large purple vein throbbed at his temple and the capillaries on his cheeks and the tip of his nose formed into a winter landscape of twigs. He had to fight for the control of his breath. He gazed wildly about him and became aware of the gathering throng of interested (in all senses of the word) onlookers. "Be about your business!" The words rang around the courtyard with the waspish malice of a drill sergeant's voice. He turned his face skyward and yelled, "You too! Be off with the lot of you."

It was a mistake. The presence of spectators, however dimly their presence registered on two people who spent all their waking hours under the watchful regard of servants, had restrained their tempers until this moment.

"Now!" He turned to Marion, shuffling his feet apart into an executioner's stance.

"Yes – now!" she responded before she could think

better of it. "Now is the time to tell you what Doctor Cowardy-Custard was too gutless to say in person . . . what he delegated *me* to tell you – a duty which, I may say, I have *ached* full many a moon to discharge, if you'll forgive the word in this context!"

He drew a deep breath while she spat out these words. He held it awhile before saying, almost too softly to be heard, "Go on, please." His eyes burned with ill-will; their lids no longer blinked.

She wondered if there were words so dreadful, so infuriating, so challenging to all his illusions about himself, that he would have a heart attack and die. It was not her actual purpose, but she did fleetingly wonder if it were possible. "He said . . ." Her mind raced. "He said that peering through his microscope into your . . . your *ejaculate* . . ." Thank God she remembered the correct word – the Word from which all verisimilitude would flow! "He said it was like looking at a river in spate. A regular flood, he said."

"Hah!" He stood a quarter of an inch taller – which, in him, was noticeable.

My God! she thought. *He's actually taking it as a compliment!* "You know," she went on, "teeming with life – cattle, trees, bushes, wild animals, people . . . no end to it all. Except that, when you look a little more closely, there's only one or two of them actually moving. That's what your little spermacules are like, C-B." Was 'spermacules' the right word? Never mind – he wasn't leaping in to sneer at her ignorance. "Millions of the little lads all right – but most of them haven't learned how to swim! Dead, you understand!" She laughed wildly as a common catchphrase occurred to her: "Dead – and never called me 'Mother'!"

He began to shiver as if taken with a violent ague. Perhaps it *would* be possible to finish him off with words alone! "You lying swine!" he hissed. "You stupid, ignorant, good-for-nothing sow!"

An excited calm gripped her. She had never seen him like

this before, and it would be so easy to squander the moment in an orgy of mutual recrimination at the tops of their voices. Instead, she made every muscle in her body go tense and then forced herself to move as slowly and calmly as possible into this new and thrilling territory: the land of pure, undiluted hatred. "I quite agree," she said mildly – which stopped him in mid-insult.

"A *sow* is precisely what I have been all these years – a snout-in-the-trough breeder, stupid and ignorant – too stupid to see my rutting boar as he really is and too ignorant to do anything about it. Well, the leopard may not change his spots, but this sow can certainly change hers."

Then her elation got the better of her calm as, with an almost maniacal laugh, she laid herself down on the wreckage of their bed, ignoring the splinters and the hard, jagged edges, and scuttled her feet up the drunkenly tilted bedhead – simultaneously scrabbling her skirts and petticoats above, or, as her feet climbed upward, below her knees. "Look, C-B!" she laughed. "For the last time, feast your eyes on the most pointless act since they gave the Pope balls!"

It was a phrase she had overheard him use once, in the kennels, when he felt certain that neither lady nor Roman Catholic was in earshot – and would rather have died than utter it if they were.

He just stood there, staring at her, forgetting to breathe, paralyzed by a horror too great to register. Then, driven at last beyond the bounds of civilized control, he picked up a broken bit of the mattress frame and began to thrash her with it.

Lost in a red tide of fury, some small remnant of his former self was surprised that she did not protest. But she just lay there, laughing – giving a little scream of pain at each successive blow, but laughing in between – and panting, between each bout of laughter: "Now we see him! The true Gordon Culham-Browne! Go on! Go on! Show yourself for all the world to see! Look everyone . . ." And so forth.

Her actual words finally penetrated his frenzy and made him stop; yet still he stood over her, with his impromptu shillelagh raised against the sky, and himself breathing like a dying stag – with actual foam at his lips and nostrils.

And then Salome escaped at last from the terrified clutch of Miss Morrell and raced from the concealing shadows of the stable, arms flailing like the sails of an eccentric windmill, hot tears of anger spilling backward off her cheeks. "Leave her alone!" she screamed as she ran, all gawky knees and elbows. "You beast! You bully!"

Her screaming stopped abruptly when a panicstricken C-B knocked her unconscious with a single blow of the timber he still held in his hand.

36

Rick took Marion, Edith, Maisie Morrell, and Salome back to Castle Moore that night. He was rather apologetic about it to C-B before he left with them, and tried making all the obvious excuses to explain why the old boy was 'not quite himself'. But the old boy in question brushed them all aside, saying that, on the contrary, he had never truly been himself until now, and that if he, Bellingham, wanted to saddle himself with a heifer and three stray cows, one in calf . . . why, more fool him! For his own part he'd welcome their absence as it would leave him in peace to arrange . . .

And there he bit off the rest of the sentence.

"Arrange what?" Rick asked.

His attitude became shifty. "Never you mind! I'll arrange certain . . . *things*. I'll do what should have been done years ago. Don't worry – I know my duty – better late than never, you may say. But, late or not, it will be done!"

Rick, who would never dream of saying 'better late than never', left him to his own devices. "Poor old boy!" he said to the women as soon as the car was under way; and he repeated the assurances with which he had tried and failed to pacify C-B. "This business has unhinged him more than one thought. He seemed so dismissive about the damage on the phone."

Salome, her headache still pounding furiously, fell into a merciful sleep on Edith's lap almost immediately.

"It has nothing to do with the arson," Marion said coldly. "The rebels have given him his happiest hours since the incident of the Streamstown fox. He'd gleefully have joined them in his own private war until . . ." She was on the point of saying 'until the cows come home' but then remembered how Rick always sneered at clichés. "Until Belfast welcomes the Pope," she concluded. She had to bite her lip to stop herself from laughing at this unconscious link with her previous mention of that same pontiff.

Rick chuckled. His eyes settled on her in the rear-view mirror and she relished the approval she read into his glance. Even Miss Morrell, still shocked at the violence she had witnessed – or, rather, at the raw emotions that had prompted it – managed a thin sort of smile.

"You're obviously not going to let it get you down," he said. Then, turning to Miss Morrell at his side, he added, "Cheer up, Maisie, it could have been a lot worse!"

It still shocked Marion slightly to hear him address the governess in that familiar way; he had done it a couple of times back at Cloonaghvogue, within her, Marion's, ear-shot if not exactly in her presence. And yet, thinking about it now, in these new circumstances, she realized that to hear him call her 'Miss Morrell' would be just as much of a jolt. It would be a courtesy from an age that she and C-B had just shattered into more fragments than the great Culham-Browne four-poster.

She considered the matter further and decided it would be even worse than that – it would suggest that Rick was trying to revive that vanished age and resurrect the polite complaisance that had sustained her marriage with C-B through almost a dozen years. The very thought of it made her soul shrivel.

And that, in turn, helped her realize that her relationship with the governess had just undergone a change almost as profound as had her union with C-B. She was no longer the mistress of the household – not merely for the passive reason that the household itself barely existed any more but for the more active reason that she had deliberately exiled herself from it. In the same rash stroke she had also, and unintentionally, stripped the title of 'governess' from Miss Morrell – no, from Maisie. But what had she turned the woman into, instead? She could think of no other title than 'friend of the family' – and 'family' now meant herself, her cousin Edith (for the moment), and her darling little Salome (for ever).

To Rick's statement that it could have been a lot worse, Maisie responded that she didn't see how.

"C-B and I could have kissed and made up, Maisie, dear," Marion told her.

Maisie turned round as if the familiar use of her name had stung.

Marion grinned reassuringly. "There is absolutely no going back," she said. "That man and I said things to each other that could not be atoned for in a dozen reincarnations. It is over!" She closed her eyes, flung herself back in the upholstery, and repeated: "Over! The long nightmare is over!" Then, to her own amazement as much as anyone else's, she burst into tears.

Edith leaned awkwardly across the slumbering child between them and tried to comfort her.

"Tears of happiness!" Marion sobbed. "Assure you! Relief . . . inexpressible . . ."

Maisie knelt awkwardly in the bucket of the front seat and tried to pat her hand. When Marion became aware of it she sat forward a little, gripped the proffered hand fiercely, blinked away her tears – and sniffed back those that had already filled her nostrils – and said, "I suppose you have, willy-nilly, lost your place as governess, Maisie, dear. The only position now on offer, if you're at all interested, is that of companion – to one rather light-headed, hysterical woman. No one in her right mind would blame you for thinking twice about accepting, but I'd deem it an honour if you would."

"An honour *and* a cure," Rick added.

Maisie hesitated – not that she found the offer disagreeable – indeed, every sensible particle in her makeup (which amounted to about ninety-nine parts in a hundred) would have accepted at once; but there was still that mad one-per cent which had not yet got around to suggesting to Rick that, if he would just set her up in a little apartment in Dublin, she could make her own living at this and that, and be his loving mistress, ready and waiting for him every time he visited the city.

Marion suppressed her childish disappointment that the ex-governess did not at once rush to accept. She told herself it meant at least one of them was keeping a cool head. "Sleep on it," she said. "And, as I told you, no one will blame you for saying no in the end."

Maisie's sense of self-interest now vanquished her romantic desire for nights of passion with Rick; how many nights would it amount to in a year, anyway! And what were a few more nights huggging herself to sleep against a tearstained pillow – in a life already rich in such experiences! "The only reason I hesitate," she replied, "is that I can hardly believe my ears – nor my luck. Also" – she licked her lips nervously and darted a glance at

Edith – "I can't help feeling your cousin is both a better candidate for the role and has a better claim."

Rick stepped in adroitly. "I think we're all running ahead of ourselves," he said in a firm tone. "Let's drop it for the moment, eh? Such decisions surely lie weeks in the future – by which time all sorts of alternatives may have occurred to us – and we'll all have a much better idea of what we really want in life."

"You?" Marion asked in amazement. "Surely you know what *you* want already?"

"Yes, indeed!" He laughed as if she had said something unintentionally funny – and, while turning to flash them a brief smile, he winked at Maisie with the eye the women in the back could not, at that moment, observe.

"What?" Edith asked sharply.

"More, of course!" he replied.

37

By the following morning the welt on the side of Salome's head had turned into an angry bruise whose blue and purple blotches almost shone among the roots of her raven-black hair. Henny remarked that she supposed her skin was always bruised in some place or other in the days when she had been a slave girl – which took some of the glory out of it. Salome had to pretend to a nonchalance that rather detracted from Hereward's determination to make the most of it.

"What we'll do," he said, "is we'll do this. When the car comes to take you back to Cloonaghvogue next time, Henny and I will sneak into the boot, and when we get there . . ."

"I'm not hiding in a cramped, smelly old boot with *you*," his sister protested.

"It's a matter of honour," he reminded her. "Our blood-sister has been violated. We must avenge her. So, as I was saying, when we get there, Sal can let us out at an appropriate moment and we'll take the bully by surprise, overpower him, tie him up, and give him a jolly good biffing that he won't forget in a hurry."

"Overpower him!" Henny echoed scornfully.

"I can stun him with my catapult. Anyway, we can work out the details later. The main thing is we've got to make them understand that they can't just go about doing *that* sort of thing to one of us."

Henny, who had no relish for biffing anyone, least of all the peppery Mr Culham-Browne, tried another line of evasion. "You may leave me out of your plans, thank you very much," she said. "You're not doing it because Sal's our blood-sister. You're doing it entirely because she's your mistress!"

Salome giggled at the word. She didn't know why but it was what the grown-ups had done when she used it. Hereward glanced sharply at her. "You know what it means?" he asked in surprise.

She stopped giggling. Of course, she couldn't admit she had no idea of its meaning, especially in front of Henny, so she just nodded airily. He pursed his lips in a silent whistle.

"What?" Henny looked from one to the other and repeated her question insistently. "What does it mean?"

Hereward threw in the full weight of his recent reading on the subject: "A paramour. A kept woman. A female favourite. Anyway, let's talk about something else."

"That doesn't make sense. All women are kept by someone, or almost all – even nuns are kept by the churches. And every female is almost bound to be *somebody's* favourite. And what's a 'paramour'? A female blackamoor, I suppose?"

"No." Hereward licked his lips nervously and said in as neutral a tone as he could muster, "It's either of two persons between whom illicit sexual relations exist."

"Wonderful!" Henny exclaimed. "Now we know everything, of course!"

To her, 'illicit' meant how to distil poteen; 'sexual' described those bits of flowers in which bees took an interest; and 'relations' were aunts and uncles.

Later, when the precise details of their revenge attack on C-B were shelved, Salome and Hereward went for a walk together, because, as she said, they had a lot to discuss. They followed their feet down over the lawns to the edge of the ornamental lake, where they turned along the path that led beside the outflow canal to the shores of Lough Cool.

"Uncle C-B is going to emigrate to England," she told him.

"I suppose that means you'll be going, too," he responded glumly.

"I don't know. Maybe Aunt Marion will stay here. That's what they were talking about in the car when they thought I was asleep."

"Here? At Castle Moore?"

"No. Here in Ireland. She has money of her own. She and Miss Morrell and Cousin Edith were talking about starting a school together in Dublin. For young ladies."

"Dublin's not *too* far away," he said hopefully.

"I could come down and stay for holidays."

There was a brief pause before he said, "I wish you could always be here, Sal. I know you're going to be the only girl I'll ever love."

She slipped her arm round his and hugged him tight. It felt very . . . nice. "I'll never love any other boy than you, either, Hereward. But you'll be going away to Saint Columba's this autumn, so, if we do move to Dublin, we'll actually be nearer during term time than if I got adopted here."

"We probably couldn't meet, though," he warned her.

"It's a bit like being in prison, they say."

"But we'd still be closer. And you might be let out for tea. Aunt Marion knows a lot of people."

He swallowed heavily and said, "Can I kiss you, Sal?"

"If you want." They were in the woods between the drive and the lough by now. She stopped, turned to him, closed her eyes, and lifted her face toward him. When he took her head between his hands, being so careful of her bruise, she thought it the tenderest, dearest thing that ever happened her.

"It's going to be a *real* kiss," he warned her. "A long one."

"That's all right. I haven't got a cachou this time."

"I've got a black imp," he assured her.

The moment their lips met she knew that a 'black imp' was something made of liquorice; but apart from that the sensations were a renewal of everything she had felt that night in the tent on the island – only this time there was no Henny looking on and cutting them short. They rolled their mouths against each other's, delighting in the alien novelty of the contact. He put his nose this side of hers, then moved it to that, then back to this side again. He grazed his lips against hers, nuzzling as a pony nuzzles for sugar lumps, starting at one corner of her mouth and ending at the other, and then going back again. And then she did the same to his. They broke for breath but rubbed cheekbone to cheekbone and murmured *Mmmm!* and *Oooh!* And at last they just hugged each other and marvelled that even the contact of ear upon ear was also rather nice.

"So . . . we are lovers at last," he said.

"I suppose so," she replied happily, moving the hot little liquorice pastille around her mouth.

"Duty calls," he said vaguely.

She giggled. "Not until I've given you back your black imp!"

And there followed another long, lingering kiss, which

merely cemented their new status as lovers more firmly still. Then, hand-in-hand, experiencing an amazing sense of oneness, they continued their walk toward the lough.

"D'you ever think of your mother?" he asked. "Your real one, I mean."

She was silent so long that he began to mutter an apology for prying.

She cut him short. "It's not that. The thing is . . . oh dear! I didn't exactly tell the truth about . . . all that. It's just that Henny was so . . . you know."

"Insistent?"

"Yes. I didn't lie, I just . . ."

"Embroidered it?"

"Yes." It was lovely the way he seemed to know just what she was thinking.

"That's all right, darling." He tried the word and it thrilled them both. "Anyone would have done the same. What really happened?"

"It gets faded all the time. More and more faded. It's just pictures, really. It's funny. They're so sharp, some of them. And I *know* they're somewhere in Ireland. Near Ennis in County Clare."

He pointed among the thinning trees on the far side of the canal, across the silver expanse of the lough, to the blue smudge of the farther shore.

"Yes."

"Did you ever go there?"

"No. I did ask Aunt Marion once or twice but she always said 'Soon, dear,' and things like that."

"She doesn't want to take you there in case your real mother recognizes you and wants you back."

"No. They went to the Cape. It was on my birthday in nineteen-and-thirteen and the ship they were on left without me."

He halted and stared at her in amazement. "But why didn't you ever tell us? That's *much* more exciting than being shoved up chimneys to knock down the soot!"

"I don't know. Aunt Marion doesn't like talking about it. Doesn't like me talking about it, either. Anyway, that's what happened. She was there, Aunt Marion, waving goodbye to a friend, and she . . . well, sort of adopted me."

"On the spot!"

"On the spot."

"I suppose she wrote to your parents and made it all right with them?"

"I don't know. I suppose she did. In the beginning she said I must write, too, and the ship would come back and collect me. But then the war . . . you know."

"Perhaps you'll go out and join them when the war's over?"

The possibility had not occurred to Salome, who was filled with foreboding at the prospect.

"I hope not," Hereward added fervently. "If you did, I'd ask to go, too. I'm sure the Bellingham tribe has branches out there. There's some in Patagonia so there's almost certain to be at least one in the Cape. It might be quite fun, don't you think?"

"If *you* were there, yes." She slipped her hand into his and swung their arms happily.

"And when we grew up we could buy a farm in the bushveldt. Have you seen pictures of it?"

She had, in fact, but she shook her head because she didn't want to spoil his flow.

"I'll show you. Rick's got a whole book on the place. The bushveldt goes on for ever. And we could buy a farm there and live simple lives of honest toil." A picture of the pair of them standing side by side, watching the sun set over the endless veldt, overwhelmed him for a moment.

And for that same moment Salome caught herself thinking that perhaps it wouldn't be the worst thing in the world if she did go back to her first mother in the Cape. "It's a long time since I even thought about them," she admitted ruefully.

"Had you brothers and sisters?"

"Two brothers. Samson was nine and David only a baby. Of course, they'd be three years on, now. Samson would be your age. And Martha would be seven."

"You must miss them. D'you think you'll ever see them again?"

Salome shrugged. "I don't know. I dream about them sometimes but often it's not them, really. Just people who *say* they're Mammy and Daddy and Samson and so on. It's funny. I can close my eyes and see pictures of the farm where I was born . . ."

"Was it your farm? Your daddy's?"

"I don't know. But I can see it very clearly. One corner by the pigsties. And the barn door with the hole for the geese. And the trasher."

"It's thrasher, really."

"I know, but listen! The thing I'm saying is, the pictures in here" – she lifted his hand in hers and touched her brow – "they're pictures like a dream but they're actually real. I mean they're of a real place – here in Ireland. If we just rowed across the lough here and got out the other side and kept walking for . . . I don't know. A few hours? We could find that place."

"Shall we?" he suggested excitedly. "Oh, let's! If we took a packed lunch and set off after breakfast . . ." His voice trailed off. "They'd never let us row all that way." Then he brightened again. "We could go by train! If someone'll take us in to Simonstown, we can take the train to Limerick and change there for Ennis."

"D'you think Miss Morrell will come with us?" Salome asked.

He shook his head scornfully. "I've got enough money saved up. We don't need to tell anyone. We can just leave a note to say we'll be back before sunset, so they won't fret too much. Anyway, they've got lots of other things to worry about. They might not even notice."

Salome had never considered the possibility of actually going back to Ennis and looking for the home of her birth. It didn't appeal to her much, though.

"Shall we?" He pressed the question.

"If you like," she replied.

"It's not if I like, it's if you like."

She shrugged. "I don't see the point."

"Someone there might recognize you, and they might know where your parents went to in the Cape. And then you could write to them and tell them you weren't lost after all. Your letter might come on the worst day of their lives and suddenly it would make it the best day, instead. They could be on the brink of despair and it would change their lives for ever and ever."

"And they might have forgotten me altogether," she pointed out.

"Well, then it would be like finding something you lost so long ago you'd even forgotten you lost it. Like last year I found the old Spanish doubloon my great-grandfather Hereward gave me for my christening money, which I threw out of my cradle they said. I was still very happy."

Salome, who did not really want to revive anything of her past before meeting Aunt Marion – though she had not realized it until Hereward began pressing her with these ideas – said, "What's a doubloon?"

"It's worth sixteen pieces-of-eight."

She smiled and murmured, "Long John Silver's parrot said that."

Hereward, seeing at last that he was on a losing wicket, said, "We could at least write a letter to your mother and father. Just pretend. We needn't post it. We could just keep it in case we ever found out their address. And we could buy a farm on the veldt even if we both grew up here in Ireland. So if we went out there when we're married and just happened to meet them, we could show them the letter."

"Why?" she asked.

"Well, it would prove we at least tried."

However, as with so many children's projects, the day-dreaming was the important part of it; they never got around to the actual execution.

38

Autumn in the Cape was well advanced. Debbie's cousin, Noel Breen, and his wife Mary, who had opened a livery and haulage business at Graaf Rienet, invited the McKennas for a week's holiday before winter brought the cold winds and gray skies. Finbar said the two farms couldn't spare him – which was true enough, except that he needn't have expressed it with such angry self-righteousness, Debbie thought. She took Martha and David on the overnight train.

She made sure they got the sleeping compartment immediately behind the locomotive. The train would be climbing almost three thousand feet on the journey, so the fire was kept burning fiercely all night, with the firedoor almost continually open – casting a bright light on either side of the track. The children, who had done the journey before, loved to lie in their bunks, watching the Karroo flash past in a dazzling panorama of bushes, thorn trees, and cacti, with startled duikers and klipdassies bounding among them, desperate for the relative safety of the carnivorous darkness beyond.

Finbar saw his wife and children onto the train and stayed to wave them out of sight. They had barely taken the first curve down the line when Georgina wrapped her arms around him from behind. He struggled out of her embrace at once and said, "Be all the holy, woman! Someone'll see."

"Oh, let them," she replied wearily. "I'm sick of this hypocrisy."

"Hypocrisy, is it! I used to think Catholic Ireland was bad enough, but these Calvinists!" He shook his head at the impossibility of measuring their narrowness.

"And it's all so silly," she said. "Why do we bother? We don't need them. We don't need their approval for anything. We could live perfectly well in complete isolation. The only one we might need is Doc Harkness – and he's got no more patience with them than you or I have."

"And almost no patients, either!"

"And does he worry?"

"Well," Finbar pointed out awkwardly, "there's the childer. They can't grow up knowing nobody and being shunned by the rest."

Georgina said no more until they were back in the gig. There she passed the reins to Finbar so that she could wrap both her arms around his and cling tightly to him. "I was thinking," she said.

"Dear God!" he exclaimed in an alarm that was only half-pretend.

"This cousin of Debbie's, him and his wife, they haven't got any children, have they?"

"Not so far."

"And how long are they married?"

He shrugged. "Three or four years."

"Barren, then, one or other of them. Or both. Anyway – supposing they took a liking to Martha and David, and supposing Debbie persists in this idea of taking the veil . . ."

He roared with laughter, startling the horses to a few paces at the canter. "Would you hold your whisht, woman! She has no serious intention of . . . and in any case, the church would never let her. She's a wife and mother – and that's a sacrament as holy in God's eyes as the vows of any nun."

"They accepted Mrs Gleeson."

"But only after her husband and childer died in that boating tragedy."

"Well then! If Martha and David were to get adopted in Graaf Rienet . . ."

"And I was to drown in Uman Gorge, then they might take Debbie, too!"

"No! Don't be so literal! If you were to vanish – with me, of course – the way would be open for her. Then we'd all get what we want."

"Except that I'd lose . . . two more childer. I think I've done enough in that line, don't you?"

"They're 'aisy got'," she teased.

He said nothing.

"I was only quoting you," she pointed out.

"I know. But I only said that to kind of skit Debbie out of her mood, when she got so low. Anyway, there's as much use in all this talk as there is in rubber nails. What about the land? And the oul' wans – Uncle Harry and Aunt Queenie?"

"If I sold the farms – and we'd get a good price for them now, I may tell you – we could buy a bungalow for them at Humewood, where they could walk into the city, and be near their friends, and the shops, and the bioscope – and the doctor! Aunt Queenie would go like a shot, I can tell you."

"You've discussed it with her?" Finbar was aghast at the thought of how far she'd taken things.

"Only in, you know, a sort of general way."

"You've not told her anything about . . . us?"

Georgina chuckled. "I don't think a woman of Queenie's age and sharpness of vision needs telling about things like that!"

"Oh God," he moaned. "I should have gone to Graaf Rienet!"

She clung to him, humming a happy little tune she knew would annoy him . . . until he felt compelled to ask, "Anyway, what would *we* do – you and I?"

"Start a new life," she replied at once.

"But this *is* a new life. And I like it. And so do you, if you'd only be honest with yourself. You'd be just as restless in Australia, or Rhodesia, or Timbuctoo and all those places you keep dreaming of. I'll wager Paul was happy enough in Ireland before you harried the poor man into selling up and coming here!"

"He was not!" she protested vigorously. "He'd been out to the Cape twice before I set foot here – he'd even been to Graaf Rienet."

"I know. He told me."

"There you are, then! D'you really want to know why we left Ireland? I'll tell you. Because he had an eye for the ladies that made Casanova look like a saint." She hesitated before adding, "He had his eye on Debbie, I may say."

"Sure you couldn't blame him for that," Finbar retorted mildly, suspecting she was merely trying to rile him.

"*You* couldn't, maybe. But I could!"

They crossed the bridge over the Baakens River, leaving the bright lights of the city behind; from here on, unless the moon put in an appearance later, their only illumination would be from the gig lamps, augmented by whatever spilled from the windows of the occasional bungalow along the way.

"Are you saying he and she ever . . . you know?"

"No, I think he learned his lesson in Ireland. Besides, he knew very well which side his bread was buttered. He'd leave Debbie alone to keep you happy. And he kept you happy so that he could go off philandering in Walmer and Port Elizabeth."

"Is that the truth?" he asked in amazement.

"The philosophical society and the chess society and the tennis club – they were all just a cloak. I tell you, there are some friends who won't have shed too many tears when they heard of his death – though their *wives* may have!"

"Dear God!" Finbar said again.

"That's why I say I'm sick of this hypocrisy. They sit there in church every Sunday like monuments to piety and chastity and all the other don'ts in the calendar – and the rest of the week they're at it like a hundred of bricks."

"I never knew. I never realized," he said. Then a new thought struck him. "Yourself among them?" he asked anxiously.

She grinned at him, which he could just make out in the reflected light from the gig lamps. "D'you mind?"

He thought it over before replying, "I do" – as if it surprised him, too. "Indeed, I do."

"I'll stop, then," she promised simply. "It doesn't mean anything to me."

"Why do it, then?"

"Boredom. We're all bored, Finbar – don't you feel it? We're all landed gentry here, except we haven't the breeding and the culture. So we rut like animals."

After a silence he asked, "Is that why you . . . you know . . . you and me?"

"God no!" The spittle flew from her lips as she clutched his arm even tighter and spoke to convince him. "You're the only bright light in the whole sorry picture. I'd rather spend a day riding the farms with you than . . . well, anything else I've done since we got off the *Knysna*. D'you think I'd be bothering with you otherwise?"

"Sure how do I know?"

"Well I wouldn't, so there! D'you ever think about me when we're not together?"

"Sometimes."

"D'you even *like* me, Finbar?"

"You know I do. Why must you ask such things?"

"How do I know it? Because you poke me?"

"Don't be talking like that!" he exclaimed crossly.

"Because you *do* it with me? Is that more genteel? There isn't a genteel way of saying it, you know. Because we 'perform the act of kind'? How's that for genteelness or whatever the word is?"

He laughed at last, never having heard the phrase before. "The act of kind!" He tested it aloud. "Bedad I like that. The kindness that's in it."

"And the acting!" she added with a hollow laugh. "Yes, it covers all aspects of the business. Talking of which, how far are we out of the big bad city?"

"Not far enough," he replied heavily.

She laughed and butted his shoulder with her forehead. "So you, too, are counting the miles! And calculating the risks!"

"Nordhoek is near enough," he said.

"But that's *miles!*"

"Four miles."

She grabbed the reins from him and shook the horses to a canter.

"You could run someone over," he warned her.

"At this hour? They shouldn't be out if they can't hear a gig and pair."

"You'll tire the horses."

She laughed. "They may have a rest when we get there – a long, lo-o-ong rest, the randiness that's in me tonight, my lad!"

39

Father Hines studied his visitor carefully. Culham-Browne was clearly on some kind of knife-edge. One careless word, one thoughtless gesture even, could tip the balance. Of course, it was understandable, what with the partial destruction of his home and then that murderous argument with his wife – witnessed by all his servants; only a monster of unfeeling could pass through such trials unscathed. Father Hines made a steeple of his fingertips and rested his lower lip upon its apex.

"I ought perhaps to say that I was made aware of this . . . er, little difficulty some months ago, Mister Culham-Browne."

"The devil you were!" C-B exploded, and then added, "I beg your pardon. Figure of speech."

"Quite. I have been wrestling with my conscience ever since."

"Heavens, man – why should *you* feel guilty?"

The priest smiled. "One may wrestle with one's conscience in *advance* of an action that may *later* give rise to guilt." He chuckled. "In fact, one is usually well advised to do so!"

C-B nodded. "Look before you leap, eh? That's what the memsahib should have done."

"And do you suppose she would have come to any very different conclusion?"

The visitor thought the matter over and replied glumly, "No."

"I'm sure you're right," Father Hines went on. "And now three long years have gone by – most important years in the life of a young child."

"Surely that only makes it worse!"

The other dipped his head to acknowledge the fact, but a wave of his hand dismissed it as unimportant. The breath whistled in and out of his nostrils as he thought of some way to express his next point. At last he said, "You know Mrs Williams in Simonstown – the watchmaker's widow?"

"Pretty woman with the growth on her cheek?"

He nodded. "It seems the surgeon has decided not to touch it. Two years ago – when she wouldn't hear of it – he would have considered removing it. Now he's decided that the risk of doing so is greater than the risk of leaving it be."

He watched C-B carefully. The man grasped the point well enough – that much was obvious. And he liked the comparison of Salome to a wen on the face of a good-looking woman. But he was going to reject the gist of the argument, which was to leave well alone. When he drew breath to speak, Father Hines cut in, saying, "It is something we moralists are apt to forget. We cling to our absolutes as drowning men clutch at straws. Suppose all doctors were to live by simple mottoes, like: 'See a wen and cut it out!' No argument. No two sides to the question. Snip, snip! And if it kills the patient? Ah me, how sad – but it was clearly the will of God!" He smiled sorrowfully. "How shocked we would be if doctors really behaved like that! So tell me this, Mister Culham-Browne – why are we not equally shocked when our moralists take a similar line? Why do we find it so easy to ignore the *person* behind the sin, and the other *people* involved in it as abettors or victims, and concentrate only on the abstract sin itself?"

C-B shifted uncomfortably in his seat; he remembered a Latin master at school who had delighted in asking complicated, awkward questions – questions that forced you to think – when all you wanted was some crisp, clear answer you could write down and learn off by heart. "People need to know what's what," he said. "No shilly-shallying."

"Thou shalt not kill? Full stop!" Father Hines smiled. "Plain enough for anyone, surely? Try telling it to Generals Haig and Ludendorff, though!"

C-B cleared his throat. "Bit different," he muttered.

"Of course it is," the priest conceded. "I often think, you know, what a very different world we'd be living in if only Moses had had the foresight to carry an armful of papyrus up the mountain with him. The necessity to condense the rules of life into something that could be engraved on two tablets of stone small enough for one man to carry down a goat path has bedevilled us ever since! All the schisms of the church-universal, all the struggles of each fragmented church to control the behaviour of its flock, all the torments of the saints . . . the oppression of the Holy Inquisition – all this and more is part of our unending struggle to fill out the missing lines."

C-B glanced out of the window, trying to see the clock on the chapel tower – the clock his grandfather had given to the Roman Catholics of Cloonaghvogue. Now *there* was an insurance policy whose term had expired!

Father Hines sensed the man's impatience and added, "It's what we're having to do today, Mister Culham-Browne."

"The girl was born a Roman Catholic," C-B said firmly. "There's no blinking that fact."

"She was born to Roman Catholic parents," Father Hines said, "which is not quite the same thing."

"She was reared as a Roman Catholic, too."

"Until she got left behind."

"An accident," C-B insisted.

"And your wife's being there was an accident too? And your recent loss of your own little girl – another contingent accident? The availability of an empty nursery, not to mention an empty place in the heart – accidents, accidents all around? An atheist would have to say yes, of course. According to him we are adrift in a sea of accidents. But we who not only believe but also *trust* in God can enjoy no such simplicities. We are compelled to seek His will in every seeming *accident* throughout our lives." His eyes radiated a sympathy that C-B found hard to reject. "Nobody says it's easy, but it's what we have to do. So" – he rubbed his hands briskly and leaned forward – "are you ready to discuss this business in the light of what I've said? If not, I can soon put you in touch with a priest who will belch fire and brimstone to your heart's content."

"Who?" C-B took the offer literally.

Father Hines laughed. "Almost any of them, as a matter of fact. We're still waiting for the end of the Dark Ages here! But if you're in a great hurry – try Father McDaid. Under this very roof."

C-B pretended to wave the advice aside. He let the old fart ramble on about God working in mysterious ways, and the greater good and the lesser good, and the supremacy of love over dogma – all of which was entirely beside the point. The point was that if Marion was going to leave him, she wasn't going to take Salome with her. That little madam was the cause of all their troubles. If Marion's maternal longings had been left unfulfilled, she might have been more eager to conceive another child. But there was no use talking to a bloody celibate priest about things like that.

So he let the man say his considerable say, thanked him cordially, promised to think it over, and went in search of this Father McDaid, who sounded altogether more reasonable. He caught up with him just after sunset. The priest was exactly where Willy Mangan, the head gamekeeper at Cloonaghvogue, had said he'd be: hiding behind a ditch at the entrance to the booreen that led up to Dinny Finnegan's, a notorious shebeen about a mile from the village. Word had it that 'Dinny' was short for 'Dionysus' – on account of the orgies that took place under his thatch.

Mangan had explained that McDaid would be waiting for total darkness to fall. It wasn't the drinking that worried him so much as the dancing, and he was determined to put a stop to it. C-B liked the sound of the man; there'd be no waffle from him.

He strolled along the road, as if out for a constitutional, and paused casually to light a cigar just at the start of the booreen. He resumed his walk but took no more than a pace or two before he halted again and cocked an ear.

"Someone there?" he barked.

Silence.

"By God, if you're poaching my game, I'll have your

balls for breakfast! Stand out, man! D'you know whose lands these are?"

"They were stolen from the O'Connors before they were ever given to you!" The priest stepped forward into a gap in the ditch and folded his arms belligerently – a black, forbidding shape against a crimson-banded sky.

"Oh, you!" C-B replied contemptuously.

It shook the young fellow. "You know who I am?"

"Father McDaid – who goes about inciting people to arson."

The priest gave a low whistle. "You should be careful of the company in which you say such things, Mister Culham-Browne."

"Oh but I am!" C-B laughed and waved a hand at the unpeopled landscape all about them. Then, forcing a complete change of tone, he went on, "As a matter of fact, McDaid, you're just the fellow I need to talk to. May I?"

"I can't," the other said coldly, but there was just enough hesitation there to show that he was interested all the same.

C-B said slowly, "I think Salome McKenna – did you know that's her proper name? – I think it's time she was returned to the faith of her forefathers. And I'm thinking you're the man to arrange it for her."

Father McDaid swallowed audibly. After a long silence he said, "Is this a trap?"

C-B laughed. "If it is, it's a bloody sight better than the one you're baiting here! Come on man! You've forty-five minutes to wait until it's dark enough to approach Dinny Finnegan's unseen. If you lurk about here, you'll catch no one. Walk with me awhile and give your quarry a chance to gather at the watering hole."

Still the other hesitated.

C-B walked a few paces back toward the village, to where a gate opened into the field. He climbed over it and started across the grass, saying, "You may decide for yourself whether it's a trap or not after you've heard me out."

He did not slacken his pace, not even when Father McDaid caught up with him. "Where are you taking me?" McDaid asked breathlessly.

"Where d'you think? To what your brave lads have left of my home."

"You think to shame me," McDaid sneered.

"I hope not," C-B responded cheerily. "I hope you're quite beyond the weakness of shame – otherwise you're no earthly use to me!"

They matched stride for stride in silence. Then the priest said, "You're a strange one, I must say."

C-B decided it was time to speak directly; the dark would help – and so would the whiskey waiting at the end of their trudge. "Listen, McDaid," he said calmly. "Sparring apart, I won't pretend I even understand your beliefs and principles, nor the actions to which they give rise. But I'm not going to challenge you on any of that. I'm not even going to talk about it. It just so happens that there's something *I* want badly, and something *you* want badly – and they both concern Salome McKenna. And therefore, to achieve this one common purpose, we can cooperate to our mutual advantage. I'm not going too fast for you, am I? You seem out of breath."

The other gave an awkward grunt but was too puffed to say a word.

C-B took pity on him and slowed down. "You should try more exercise," he remarked, adding wickedly: "Dancing, perhaps?" They could hear the strains of catgut and goat-skin reaching across the fields.

He thought he had overdone it. The priest stopped in his tracks and his eyes gleamed red with a baleful fire borrowed from the last of the twilight sky. But the fanatic won. The fanatic had to stay and pick at the sore, bend the unlikeliest ear, justify himself. "I cannot understand it," he said bitterly. "We arrange perfectly good dances in the parish hall, where it is warm, and well lighted, and congenial in every way – and above all it has the blessing of the church . . . and yet they flock to a dirty, dangerous, illicit house like that and expose their immortal souls to every peril in the calendar."

In the sort of dancing the church tried to promote, of course, the dancers kept their fists clenched, their arms pinned rigidly to their sides, and they never came within six inches of touching one another. At Dinny Finnegan's the arms flew over their heads and round each other's waists as they whirled around to strains that grew ever wilder . . . and girls' breasts jiggled and men's eyes sparkled and the blood of both raced hotter than the poteen that fired it. "I can't understand it either, Father," C-B said solemnly – but his 'it' referred to the fellow's myopia.

They reached the ditch at the far side of the field. A spinney of coppiced beeches stood between them and the paddocks behind the Castle stables.

"How's your night vision?" C-B asked. "Do we go around or through?"

McDaid peered into the coppice and said, "Around."

"Good man!" his host said admiringly.

After a few paces the fellow asked, "Why did you say that – 'good man'? What's good about it?"

"I like a chap who not only knows his own limitations but isn't afraid to admit to them in public. Shall I tell you mine? My greatest limitation?"

"Go on."

"Charity – or, rather, the lack of it."

McDaid laughed drily. "Are we back to talking about Salome McKenna? Where is she, by the way?"

"They're all still at Castle Moore. You know what they're plotting over there between them?"

"Plotting?"

"All right – planning. They're hoping to start a college for young ladies in Dublin – my wife, her cousin, and the Morrell woman."

"For Protestant young ladies?"

"Non-denominational, they claim." He spoke the word with contempt. "Anyway, they're all safely at Bellingham's place, so we're free to talk."

They had skirted the spinney by now and started across the paddock. A horse snickered in the stables beyond. C-B raised his voice and said, "Mangan? If you're there, it's only me." To the priest he said, "It's called shutting the stable door after the horse has bolted, you know."

Father McDaid laughed, against his will.

"Perhaps I should have started at the very beginning," C-B went on as they rounded the end of the stable block and set off across the drive to the Castle annexe. "My wife is determined to leave me. And I am equally determined that – if she does – she shall not take Salome McKenna with her. So my belief that she should be returned to the faith of her forebears does not arise from some new attachment to the Roman Catholic persuasion . . ."

The priest interrupted with a brief, laconic laugh.

"It is pure spite on my part," C-B concluded. "I'm not particularly proud of it but I'm admitting it to you because, in the first place, you're not a fool and you're perfectly able to work it out for yourself, and, in the second place, we're going to have to trust each other – and I've always found honesty to be a good basis for trust."

He tossed away his cigar, placed one foot on the bottommost step, and wafted an invitation toward the front door.

The other hesitated. "If you're hoping for corresponding confessions from me . . ." he began.

"Wouldn't dream of it," C-B assured him. "What's done is done. You can *have* the bloody country. You'll make an even worse mess of it than the English did. For myself, I'm looking to my own future, now – mine and my wife's. And as far as I'm concerned, *her* future shall be one without little Madam McKenna."

Father McDaid waited until they were indoors and himself seated beside a good log fire, before he said,

"What, exactly, is on your mind, Mister Culham-Browne?"

His host held a decanter poised over a cut-crystal whiskey glass. "A wee dram, Father?"

McDaid nodded curtly, as if he were being forced to accept, and held two fingers horizontal. "No more than that, please."

"Take you at your word," C-B said as he handed him the meagre potion. "What's on my mind?" he echoed as he poured a full measure for himself. "*Sláinte!*" They raised their glasses in an unsmiling toast. "I'm thinking there must be convents where young Roman Catholic girls of good family are boarded and educated?"

"Of course there are." The simplicity of the question surprised the priest.

"Some of them orphans?" his host persisted.

McDaid's eyes narrowed. "Ah, I begin to see."

"And some of them *virtual* orphans," C-B continued. "I mean their parents or guardians cannot, or will not, have them home during the school holidays. They remain behind with the nuns when the other girls go home?"

"Yes, yes – of course." McDaid's thoughts were now racing ahead of him. It was everything he had dreamed of! And entirely within the law – no risk! He sipped his whiskey, licked the unaccustomed sting off his lips, and said, "I suppose you *are* the child's legal guardian, Mister Culham-Browne?"

"*De facto* guardian," was the reply. "But I can certainly give you a piece of paper that will absolve you of all blame if any inquiry should later arise. Not that I think it will, mind."

"How can you be sure of that? Surely your wife will move heaven and earth to . . ."

"I think not," C-B interrupted. "You see – she kidnapped the child when she saw her in Queenstown that day. She simply took her up and carried her home."

"But – surely – you are party to that . . . er – I mean, an accessory? No?"

C-B shook his head and smiled. "I was duped by her, too. She claimed the child had been thrust upon her by . . . well, never mind the details. The fact is – she kidnapped the girl and she won't want the fact put about in all the papers. Not once she has sunk every last penny into this school in Dublin – which she will do when she signs the papers next week. So we only have to wait a few more days and then we can put our plan – *your* plan, I hope – into action."

"Why not simply return the girl to her rightful parents?" the priest suggested.

"Is that what you'd prefer?" the other asked in surprise.

"Of course not. But it's one of the first questions any mother superior will put to me."

"Well, that rather depends on how much of Salome's history you tell her – and how much you leave for her to surmise." He smiled. "A nun, I suppose, can jump to conclusions as easily as any other woman – especially if the clues are accidentally dropped where she cannot help but notice them? That's something I leave in your capable hands. But in any case, returning her to her parents just won't do. In the first place, we don't know where they are in the Cape, so it could take months if not years. But more important than that, my wife can be a very persuasive woman. And money talks, too. She might easily induce the McKennas to let her convert her kidnapping of the child into a legal adoption. And then we should, indeed, be breaking the law – you and I. No, Father McDaid, we get one bite at this cherry, and this is it! So, what d'you say? D'you know of such establishments?"

Father McDaid tugged thoughtfully at his lower lip. "I do, but they're not cheap," he warned.

"Money is no object – within reason, of course. I imagine seventy to eighty pounds a year would cover the cost?"

The priest's jaw worked furiously as temptation and caution fought for supremacy within him. "There would be certain . . ." He faltered, hunting for the precise word –

which eluded him at last. "I hesitate to call them 'irregularities'," he confessed.

"Deviations from the standard situation?" the other offered. "Special cases?"

Father McDaid laughed openly at last. "Perfectly put!"

"But I'm sure you know of convents where they are used to such *special* cases? Girls of good family who have run a little wild? Girls who need to be removed from an *over-loving* father – I'm sure you understand?"

The priest nodded.

"And I'm sure the mothers superior are well used to handling such *special* cases with tact and discretion?"

"A hundred pounds would cover it," McDaid said. "And at that I would have every confidence of finding a suitable convent."

C-B swilled the remaining whiskey around in his glass and tossed it back in one. "By today-week," he said.

"Eh?" The priest was startled.

"Perfect day for it. Salome's tenth birthday *and* the third anniversary of the day she got left behind at Queenstown! But" – he held up a finger – "better still, it's the day the three harpies have to go up to Dublin to put their life savings into the melting pot!" He chuckled and pointed at Father McDaid's empty glass. "Come on, man – a bird never flew on one wing!"

The fellow handed over his glass with a grin. "There's one bird we must make sure never flies on *any* wing," he said.

40

Culham-Browne put down the telephone and turned to Miss Kinchy. "That was Mrs Culham-Browne," he said. "She wishes you to pack all Salome's things. We'll put them on the train to Dublin. Oh, and pack one small valise of overnight things in case of delays. They can send her linen on from Castle Moore."

"Is the colleen herself not to come back here to Cloonaghvogue, sir?" she asked. " 'Twould be a pity if we never set eyes on her again."

"That's a matter of opinion, Miss Kinchy," was the gruff response. "However, I'm sure you'll be seeing her again. Dublin isn't the end of the world."

"Sure I was never there in my life," the housekeeper mumbled as she went off to do (as she supposed) Mrs Culham-Browne's bidding. She hunted all over for Too Small, Miss Rachel's old teddy, but realized that the colleen must have taken it with her to the Bellinghams.

In the bottom of one cupboard she found a stout manilla envelope, sealed, and bearing the legend in Miss Salome's neat little hand: *Lady's sketching book – to be used when I can draw proply*. She smiled and slipped it in among her other books. After all, Himself had said to pack everything.

After an early light luncheon the car set off for Castle Moore, its dickey full of trunks and boxes, the back seat piled high with suitcases, and an uncommonly happy C-B at the wheel. Miss Kinchy waved goodbye, just as if her dear little charge were in the passenger seat beside him.

She would have been surprised, not to say alarmed, if, half an hour later, she had been standing near the railway-station approach in Simonstown, for she would then have seen the motor pass by without the smallest deceleration. On through the town it went, taking the Parsonstown road out of Westmoreland Square. Half a mile out of town it approached the demesne of Catherlough House, the Irish seat of the Earls of Westmoreland – or, rather, their former Irish seat, for it had been the convent house of the Bon Secours Sisters for the last forty years.

The sight of its wall, over twelve feet high and maintained in excellent repair by the order, was reassuring. The road frontage was no more than three furlongs but the wall ran on a full two and a half miles, completely circling the home park and woodlands. The gate lodge was impressive, too; built like a castle keep, complete with portcullis, it straddled the drive like the entrance to a medieval walled city. Here at last the car drew to a halt and C-B gave an impatient couple of toots.

Annie Coen, wife of Pius Coen, the gatekeeper, came bustling out to open up for him, dusting flour off her hands before she touched the gleaming black paintwork of the ornate wrought-iron gate; the portcullis was kept raised until the Great Silence each evening. She bobbed a cheerful curtsey as the car swept onto the drive. C-B paused to thank her and remark that he'd be coming back out in twenty minutes or so if she wanted to leave it open.

"God bless you, sir," she replied. "If it was *two* minutes, I'd still fear for my skin if I was to lave them gates open!"

Better and better, thought C-B as he motored away up the long drive. The gravel was immaculate; the edges trimmed with precision. No fallings of trees and branches littered the woodland floor. Immediately inside the high outer wall, dense thickets of thorn, holly, and bramble formed an impenetrable belt, some thirty feet wide; but it stopped abruptly two yards short of the stone, to permit inspections and patrols. The Bon Secours Sisters were clearly a wealthy order, catering for the daughters of rich Roman Catholics, both as nuns and as pupils. They even had princesses and countesses and such things from Europe's RC aristocracy. No one could say he was dumping Salome in some wretched institution, little better than a workhouse.

That, of course, was what they would *suppose* he'd done – which was why they'd never come looking for her in a grand place like this – and so close to Cloonaghvogue. He drummed his fingers on the steering wheel and hummed a contented little tune.

Half a mile up the winding drive the woodland began to

thin out and give way to open park, where a herd of fallow deer were grazing; they were clearly used to visitors in big cars for they hardly stirred as he passed them by. Around the last sweep of the drive the magnificent edifice of Catherlough House itself came into view. It was built in 1840 in the Victorian style and on a virgin site – two features that made it unusual in Ireland, where the Georgian survived until the middle of the century. Most jumped-up landowners of that day had found it cheaper to slap an imposing Georgian façade on an old three-storey landlord house than to restyle it in the more Gothic and individualistic manner of the Victorians. But the ennoblement of the Fane family, the earls of Westmoreland, went back to 1624; so Catherlough House was opulent redbrick Victorian to the last crocketed finial on the smallest of its dozen romantic turrets. It was a smug, shameless display of wealth from an age when life was cheap but public esteem came rather dear. The very sight of it, every window gleaming in the early afternoon sun, made C-B exclaim aloud: "Father McDaid – you've picked out the jewel of them all!"

Two lay sisters were trimming the grass edges of the flower borders; beyond them a nun was cutting flowers into a pannier, just as the lady of the house must have done in the days when the Fanes had owned it; it was a convert Fane who had donated the estate to the Sisters of Bon Secours, together with the endowments that helped maintain it. The nun began walking toward the front door as soon as she saw the car emerge from the trees; she paused to say something to the lay sisters, who at once redoubled their efforts with the shears. C-B, who had always felt uncomfortable in the alien world of Roman Catholic mumbo-jumbo, relaxed a little; quiet, well-disciplined hierarchies of the kind he could sense about him here were quite in tune with his own domineering spirit. He liked their motto, too: *Cognitio ardor est* – knowledge is fire.

"Mister Culham-Browne?" the nun said as he climbed out of the car. "I'm Sister Boniface, Mistress of Novices."

They shook hands. 'Bonny Face' was a good name for her, C-B thought. Never known a man, and never would. Rum thing.

"We were expecting you somewhat later than this," she added rather sharply. "Is Salome with you?"

He did not envy the novice who got across her. "I'm only dropping off her things now," he explained. "Then I'm going on to collect her from Castle Moore."

Sister Boniface smiled again. "Good. We'll be ready for her then. I expect you'd like to see her dormitory – and the preparations for her birthday party! How nice to be welcomed to her new school with a party!"

He opened his jacket and reached for his watch but she forestalled him. "Come, Mister Culham-Browne, you can get to Castle Moore and back inside an hour. We shan't be ready to receive her for at least two. So you've time enough and to spare."

She put her shoulder to the huge front door and opened it. He took a step in her wake and then said, "Her trunks and suitcases?"

"I'll send two men out for them." She stepped aside to usher him into a grand entrance hall. She took a dip of holy water and crossed herself.

The hall was dominated by a central staircase of oak that rose to a halfway landing before dividing into two wings that doubled back toward the front. A statue of the Virgin and Child, standing beneath a perpetual flame, dominated the half-landing, and there were signed portraits of Benedict XV and Pius X – the present Pope and his predecessor – in the bay where she hung his coat.

Curiously enough, these elements reassured him, too, for the statue was of pure white marble and the portraits were free of gold, lapis lazuli, alizarin crimson, and, indeed, garish colour of any kind. This was a tasteful, Anglo-Irish sort of Catholicism, quite unlike the flashy, tinsel faith-and-begorrah of the common peasantry. He felt almost at home with it – which helped him feel more at ease with his plans for Salome, too.

A lay sister was sweeping an invisible moraine of dust across the marble floor. Sister Boniface had a mumbled word in her ear and she went off toward the staff quarters, presumably to summon the porters; the sister continued on up the main stair. C-B, who was used to women in bustles – though the fashion was tending to die out in this war – was amazed at the angularity of her gait and the military ring of her boots on the bare, polished oak. Until now he had thought of nuns simply as women who had withdrawn from the society of men; it suggested a passive, shrinking activity. But this Mistress of Novices shattered that illusion. She was clearly a lady, both by her speech and by her manner of giving out commands that were instantly obeyed; and, far from shrinking from men, she almost aggressively excluded them. He realized he had expected to intrude upon a company of men-starved females who would take this legitimate opportunity to fuss over him and relish his maleness; Sister Boniface's behaviour and attitude could not be farther removed from that happy little masculine daydream.

"Nuns to the east, pupils to the west," she said at the half-landing, taking the flight that led in the direction of the pupils' dormitories.

"You all live in some style," he remarked. "West and east."

"Ah, but I did not say how *far* to the east," she responded. Her face was completely obscured by that snood or wimple or whatever they called it. "In fact, the rooms *immediately* to our east are classrooms. The convent is in the new east wing – whose style *aspires* – I only say aspires – to that of the Bridewell."

"I should have known," he said apologetically.

"I don't see why," she replied. "Our trivial arrangements are surely of little interest to busy men of the world like yourself?"

She had reached the upper landing by now; there she turned to him with a smile and held a hand toward the dormitories.

"Where are all the girls?" he asked as he entered the corridor ahead of her.

"Running."

"All of them?"

"The whole school – all hundred and twenty of them. You didn't see them in the grounds?"

"No. The place seemed deserted – apart from the gatekeeper's wife."

"They must already have reached the back woods, then. It's our annual hare-and-hounds race. That's why I said we weren't ready just now – when I thought you'd brought Salome with you. A strange choice of name!"

"Extremely!" The corridor was lined on one side with scenes from the Holy Land – original oil paintings all. He slowed down and peered at them. "These are excellent," he commented.

"Of course they are," she replied. "This will be Salome's dormitory." She opened a door onto a room that was light, airy, spotless, and very spartan. "This is junior dorm," she added. "Next is middle dorm, then remove, then senior. They all have curtains between the beds."

This supposedly alien world grew more familiar to C-B with every new discovery. "And prefects?" he asked.

The nun pointed to a cubicle behind them, immediately inside the door. "We have four prefects, who do a week each in each dorm. It makes it more difficult to build up favourites and *bêtes noires*. The head girl has her own cubicle and so does her vice."

C-B suppressed an urge to ask if her vice was at all an interesting one.

Apart from the lack of washbasins down the middle of the dorm, this could have been his own prep school in Brighton more than forty years ago. Bare polished floorboards ran the full length of the room, about thirty feet in all. Some twenty beds of black tubular iron were ranged round the wall, eight each side, two in the bay at the end, and two beside the prefect's cubicle; their blankets were a uniform charcoal gray. The centre was occupied by six identical chests of drawers, in back-to-back threes, and two wardrobes, also back-to-back. On top of the chests of drawers were swivels that had once, quite obviously, held looking glasses. These had been removed and substituted by pictures of the Blessed Virgin, a rather unsubtle symbolism, C-B thought.

Sister Boniface waited until his eye took in this oddity and then said, "There is no mirror within a mile of this house."

"And does it work?" he asked.

She frowned. "I don't understand the question."

"Well, when Cicely Fordham wanted to cure her husband, Jack, of his fondness for the bottle, she tried to make sure there wasn't a drop of the hard stuff within a mile of *their* house." His tone conveyed the futility of the woman's endeavour.

But not to Sister Boniface. "And?" she prompted.

"He took every chance he could get, of course. I told her – put a bottle on the sideboard – don't mark it or police it or any of that nonsense. Make him understand it's his backbone against that bottle. She wouldn't do it, though. Poor old Jack."

"Perhaps she knew him better than you did?"

He shook his head. "No. Some women feel that unless they have control of absolutely everything, they don't have any control at all. No middle ground."

He was simply trying to score points, of course, but the sister took the remark quite seriously. "How true," she said thoughtfully. "What an interesting insight. And actually – now that I come to think of it – there *is* one looking glass within these walls. In the art room."

"Self-portraits," he said confidently.

"No." Her eyes were merry for the first time since they had met. It was almost as if she were teasing him to guess. But she supplied the explanation immediately: "It's for when they engrave or etch lettering on copper plates. It has to be done in mirror-writing so as to print the right way round."

"And I'll bet it's kept under lock and key!"

She nodded. "And will continue to be so, Mister Culham-Browne. Your advice to Mrs Fordham will fall on deaf ears here, as well, I fear."

This slight hint that she herself did not agree with the policy intrigued him. "Ye are the weaker vessels, eh," he suggested, trying to provoke her.

But all he provoked was a return to her earlier coolness. She pointed at the bed beside the prefect's cubicle. "That'll be Salome's."

He nodded, not knowing what else to say. His eye strayed back around the room. "We had *red* blankets at school," he remarked. "They helped foster an illusion of warmth in the winter."

Sister Boniface ignored the statement. "May I ask – was 'Salome' your choice of name?" she said.

He turned to her in surprise. "Do you not know her story?"

She shook her head. But before he could begin she went back to the door, where she glanced briefly up and down the corridor outside, and then closed it with a curiously slow, stealthy motion. Then she took up two bentwood chairs from beside the nearest beds and placed them facing each other, a good two paces apart, in the space between the prefect's cubicle and the chests of drawers. She sat in one and invited him to take the other.

"I should like to hear it," she said.

It put C-B in a quandary for he did not know precisely what Father McDaid had told the Reverend Mother. "Perhaps I should see the superior?" he suggested hopefully, trying to avoid her gaze, which was suddenly intense and hypnotic.

"I should like to hear it from *you*," she insisted.

41

Halfway to Simonstown, Salome began to have second thoughts about the way she'd simply walked out of the Castle Moore gates with Uncle C-B and got into the car with him. She really ought to have let Gwinnie or Letty – or anyone – know. But then, on the other hand, Uncle C-B was rarely as friendly and jovial as this, so when he just met her on the driveway and called out "Happy Birthday, Little Face!" and held out his hand and said he'd come to take her to a party . . . well, she couldn't start explaining that Aunt Marion had said she'd have her birthday party next Saturday, when they'd all be in their new house in Dublin.

All the same, she ought to have told *someone*.

"Uncle C-B?" she said cautiously.

"Yes, my dear?" He beamed down at her – although she was now almost the same height as him. He caressed the remnant of the bruise on her face as if to apologize. "What, my precious?"

"You don't think the Bellinghams will worry about me? Going off like this without telling them?"

"Good heavens!" He tousled her hair and then smoothed it straight again. "They know already. Is *that* what's been worrying you! I telephoned them to say I'd collect you."

"Oh!" Relief flooded through her. "Nobody said."

"Of course not. I asked them not to. It wouldn't have been a surprise, then, would it?"

Salome grinned at him. "But it's not really a surprise now, either – because you've told me." She was a little nervous of saying something so forward but his good humour seemed to encourage it.

"But I haven't!" he insisted. "I've told you just enough to prick your curiosity. I've kept the best bit of all a secret. I mean, you don't know *where* this party is to be, do you?"

And for the next few minutes they played a guessing game in which Salome swiftly exhausted all the friends – or, rather, the very few friends at whose houses Aunt Marion would permit her to attend a party. The only bad thing about Aunt Marion was her narrow view of suitable and unsuitable friends. "I don't *know* any more," Salome complained at last.

C-B was quick to hear the tone of regretful complaint. "You're absolutely right, Little Face," he said. "I've been telling your Aunt Marion for some time that you don't have enough friends. You'd like more, wouldn't you?"

Salome, who was equally adept at picking up unspoken nuances by now – after her years in a well-mannered household full of seething resentments – realized she was being recruited to his side in some battle with Aunt Marion. She prevaricated. "It's better now I've got to know Hereward and Henny so well," she said.

"Yes, but now you've made that start, you'd like lots more, wouldn't you?"

She could not deny it.

"Well, my dear," he said, "your dream is about to come true!"

PART THREE – 1921

In the Name of the Father

42

Sister Porphyry, the Reverend Mother, stirred her tea loudly, making spoon and delf ring out with a pretty sort of tinkle. It drew attention to the fact that she had chosen the best service – knowing that her old adversary, Sister Boniface, would disapprove. Why the Order had sent her back to this house, after five happy years of absence – happy for the Reverend Mother, at least – God only knew. And not as Novice Mistress, either. Not as anything, really. It was all rather sinister and disconcerting. "Oh, and Sister Ladislas also died," she said.

Sister Boniface continued to stare out of the window, her untouched cup of tea in her hand. "I heard," she replied. "I'm glad for her sake, of course, but we shall miss her. Our last link with the old days."

Reverend Mother had a brief vision of a hand – not her own, of course – slipping a knife between the shoulder-blades of that stubborn, vexatious back. Then she closed her eyes tight and shook her head in annoyance.

When they had informed her that Boniface was being sent back to Catherlough House, she had sworn to set aside all those ancient animosities and start afresh; but one look at that face of hers – so pale, so beautiful, so saintly, so dead – and all her good resolutions had gone by the board. It was no use. Saint Porphyry himself, for whom she was named, would not have suffered her under the same roof – and, as the guardian of the True Cross, he would surely know the symbolic value of burdens sent to try the soul.

"The old days!" Boniface echoed her own last words. "We, too, are living in the old days, Reverend Mother. Fifty years from now there will be nuns in this room, talking of the old days and meaning you and me. God send we have as good an innings as Sister Ladislas!"

"Is your tea not to your liking, Sister Boniface?"

The Sister drank it down in three unladylike gulps. She really was a most unsuitable nun to send to a school for young ladies.

"Very refreshing, thank you, Reverend Mother," she said as she set it back on the desk.

At last she sat down, facing her superior, who said, "People will hardly look back on these as the *good* old days, though, will they? I suppose, in Rome, you were fairly out of touch with events here in Ireland? The dreadful times that are in it."

"On the contrary, Reverend Mother, the Irish College was buzzing with it every day. People there cannot understand the conservatism of our hierarchy. Tens of thousands of armed raids on private houses . . . the Black-and-Tans rampaging at will . . . the constabulary out of control . . . women and children murdered – even the English are sickened by what their own forces are doing. And still our hierarchy holds back!"

The muscles at the Reverend Mother's temples were rippling with annoyance. Not a week earlier she had faced an English priest in this very room – sitting in that very chair – and her sentiments then had been the same as Boniface's, expressed, if anything, with even greater vehemence. Even so, she could not bring herself to agree with the woman now. "Bishop Fogarty has spoken out quite strongly," she said.

"He's alone in an otherwise crowded hall!" Boniface pointed out. "The rest might be Trappists."

"Well, it looks as if we're nearing a truce at last. We must continue to pray for peace each day." The Reverend Mother's tone laid the topic firmly aside. "Tell me," she went on, "have you any notion as to why you've been sent back here? You know Sister Severinus is the Novice

Mistress now? I was told you'd explain it all to me in person. All I know is that you're not back on the teaching staff here. It's a mystery."

Boniface knew very well what was agitating her superior – the thought that she herself was about to be replaced as Reverend Mother, and by the nun she most disliked in all the world. It would have pleased her to prolong the agony, for the ill feeling between them was just as strong on her side, too. But, she realized, the chief casualty of such aggravation would be the work she had been sent here to do; so she reluctantly bent her will to her conscience and kept her powder dry.

Indeed, she bent her will over backward. "I must start by asking your advice, Reverend Mother," she said. "For, though the task itself is mine, it cannot succeed without your blessing – and it would not deserve your blessing, I think, unless you were wholeheartedly involved from the start." She forced a smile – and found it not as difficult as she had feared.

The Reverend Mother, alarmed and distrustful, said, "Task? You have been sent to perform some task? Here?"

"In Simonstown. But I shall stay here at the convent, of course. It all began when the bishop paid a visit to the workhouse at Portumna – one part of which is a sort of hospital for incurable cripples. He was distressed at what he saw there. It's not inhumane. The warders do the best they can but the money they're voted isn't enough to keep even the able-bodied . . ."

The Reverend Mother's eyes narrowed. "When was this?"

"Oh, some four or five years ago – you know yourself how slow the wheels turn! In fact, it was over five years ago – just after the Easter Rising. Anyway, since then – between dodging bullets from the Tans – he has visited other places for incurables and found conditions in them no better than at Portumna. So, as soon as the war was over, he sent someone to Rome with a suggestion that one of the religious orders should establish a hospice for such cripples as are capable of benefiting from treatment. And the long and the short of it is that the Franciscans will establish three houses – in Cork, Galway, and Dublin – for cripples who might benefit from physical treatment. And we, the Bon Secours Sisters, have been chosen to start a school for . . ." She hesitated, wondering how best to put it.

"Female cripples?" Reverend Mother suggested.

"No, for youngsters of both sexes. The problem lies with those who, though severely crippled in body, are of high intelligence. They are, as it were, imprisoned inside their affliction . . ."

The Reverend Mother was aghast. "D'you mean *we* are to . . . but why was I not consulted? We are to open our classrooms at Catherlough to . . . to . . . *defectives* of one sort or another?"

Boniface held up her hands in a gesture of saintly conciliation. "Not at all, Reverend Mother! Quite the reverse."

"Because our parents would not tolerate such a . . ."

"They won't be asked to – truly. That is not part of the plan at all. The plan is to find some suitable building in Simonstown – one of the larger private houses in Fane Mall, I thought – and adapt it for its new purpose . . ."

"Adapt?" Reverend Mother was having adaptation problems of her own.

"Well, for obvious reasons, the cripples' bedrooms will have to be on the ground floor – for ease of evacuation in case of fire, to name but one. Also a lift will have to be put in. That sort of thing."

Her superior, back on an even keel, was beginning to grasp the outlines of Boniface's new mission – and its implications, too. If she carried it off, it would be quite a feather in her cap. On the other hand, if she failed, it would reflect badly on the Order in general and Catherlough

House in particular. Neither prospect was particularly happy, in her view. She was trapped into wholehearted support. Of course, Boniface had arranged it so! "You say you need my blessing?" she said.

"Blessing, advice, support, Reverend Mother . . . I am so out of touch with the district. For instance, I gather that several of the houses in Fane Mall are vacant at the moment?"

The other nodded warily. "English people mostly."

Boniface smiled. "I'm sure you'll know which of them is most keen to sell – or you can tell me who *does* know. Also which solicitors to use, which builders . . . and so on. I wish to tread on nobody's toes. *Nobody's,*" she repeated with unmistakable emphasis.

Reverend Mother nodded gravely. "And this was the *bishop's* wish – his idea, I mean?" It was beginning to occur to her that if this new venture for the Order were a success, it would be a great feather in her cap to be associated with it. If she could somehow collar the limelight and make Boniface seem the mere dogsbody . . . Well, that seemed a tall order at the moment; but the alternative – to oppose it or assist it grudgingly each step of the way – could leave her exposed and friendless.

"His idea entirely," the sister conceded. "I merely happened to be in Rome at the time the decision was arrived at. It lay between us and the Sacred Heart Sisters – as the two principal teaching orders – and we had the good fortune to have a spare nun in the right place."

Reverend Mother was still wary. "Whom did the bishop send to Rome?" she asked.

"Monsignor O'Hare." Sister Boniface was surprised to see the other start at the name. She went on, "The moment I mentioned the possibility of being based here at Catherlough, he said, 'With Sister Porphyry! Say no more!' His opinion of you could not be higher, Reverend Mother."

"Well . . . well . . ." The superior relaxed a little. Then, seeing she had betrayed her feelings earlier, added, "There must be wisdom in age, even for the likes of that one. He and I had a . . . a disagreement, shall we call it? In earlier days."

'Disagreement' was hardly in it. The old goat had been her confessor and had taken advantage of her once. Two or three times, in fact. She suppressed a shiver at the memory.

Boniface was less inhibited. "I can't stand the man. He's never learned to keep his hands to himself." She gave the shudder her superior had eschewed.

Reverend Mother, knowing how ambiguous was her own distaste at the memory, wondered if Boniface was entirely sincere – for even at sixty Paul O'Hare was still a handsome and engaging man. She enjoyed a passing daydream in which she inveigled the pair of them into a compromising situation and then unmasked them. Two birds with one stone – revenge against the monsignor and triumph over the rival nun! "I've heard he has that reputation," she said. "I've never let him hear confessions here. Except of old Sister Anskar when she was dying that time."

Boniface sat up at the news. "Is she gone, too!"

Reverend Mother nodded sadly.

"I *am* out of touch." Boniface stood up and returned to the window. "The girls are a long time on the hare-and-hounds this year," she remarked.

"They were late starting. The IRA shot an informer who tried to find sanctuary here last night. We had to call them back to take the body somewhere else. They have no consideration at all."

Mention of the hare-and-hounds jogged Boniface's memory. "Talking of being out of touch," she said, "is that orphan girl still here? The one who came just before I left. That was on hare-and-hounds day, too – we did a slap-up birthday treat to welcome her, I remember."

"Oh! Salome McKenna!" Reverend Mother waved both hands in a *shoo-off!* gesture of despair. "I don't know what to do about her. We can't even expel her."

"Really?" Sister Boniface returned to her chair and leaned forward with interest. "She seemed such a nice, quiet little girl."

"Then, perhaps. But she has become quite ungovernable. And such a bad influence." She rummaged in one of her desk drawers.

"Can't you write to Mister Culham-Browne and ask him to remove her?"

The superior stopped her rummaging and stared at her in surprise. "What has he to do with it?"

Boniface remembered then that the Reverend Mother had not been there when the man had told her his tale; she herself had left Catherlough House soon after Salome's arrival. Perhaps the school had been told quite a different story – and by someone else? She retrieved the situation swiftly. "He was the one who brought her here," she pointed out.

"Ah!" Reverend Mother smiled. "An understandable . . . er, misunderstanding, Sister. He was merely obliging Father McDaid – of Cloonaghvogue, you know."

"Well – I didn't understand that, Reverend Mother." So they still didn't know Salome McKenna's story – assuming, of course, that what Mister Culham-Browne had told her *was* her true story. "Father McDaid, then, is . . .?" She left the question hanging.

"*In loco parentis*," the superior answered as she resumed her search of the drawer.

"The child's legal guardian?"

"She's hardly a child any longer, Sister. She's sixteen years of age – this very day, indeed. Ah!" She found what she was searching for and tossed it triumphantly on her desk, immediately in front of Sister Boniface. It was a leatherbound book too large to be a diary.

Boniface picked it up.

"Most decidedly not a child," Reverend Mother said grimly. "As you will see."

Sister Boniface found the offending drawings – the sketches Lady Orden had left behind at the Royal George when she did a bolt for Paris. "Not very good," she remarked.

Reverend Mother's lips vanished into a thin line; the flesh each side of it turned pale. "Not very *good?*" she repeated.

"They're copies, of course."

"Ah . . ." It was clearly news to the Reverend Mother. "Of course," she said uncertainly.

Boniface, who knew her old adversary well enough to be sure she hadn't left this offending material lying around in her desk without doing something about it, decided to discover what that punishment might have been. "What are you going to do about it, may I ask?" She put as much challenge into the question as she dared.

The woman rose to the bait. "Do? D'you think I'd let the sun set on something so horrible? I have punished the girl already. She won't do such a thing again."

Boniface raised her eyebrows, showing a cordial interest, but said nothing.

The silence compelled further explanation. "I held the offensive material up over her head – before the entire school, of course – naturally they were too far away to see any . . . er, detail – and I made it quite, quite clear how deeply we at Catherlough House are outraged by such filthy, lewd, indecent, depraved, obscene scrawls . . ."

Sister Boniface held up one of these 'scrawls' with a questioning air – a naked man grasping a naked female around the waist and looking as if he were about to apply his lips to her right nipple.

"Just so!" the Reverend Mother exclaimed.

"It's by Raphael," Boniface said.

The superior closed her jaw and swallowed heavily.

"By . . . Raphael?" she echoed.

"It's a study for *The Triumph of Galatea*, one of the first paintings he completed after becoming chief architect to the Vatican."

The Reverend Mother took the sketchbook from her and stared again at the drawing. "But it's so . . ." She was unable to repeat her condemnation now, but nor was she willing to say anything weaker.

"The painting is in the Farnesina now," Boniface continued remorselessly. "But the sketches are in the Vatican collection. I saw them at an exhibition last year. Perhaps they were reproduced in one of the journals – and that is where Salome made this copy? For a sixteen-year-old girl, you know, they're really . . ."

The superior gave her a withering look. "No such journal would be permitted in *this* school – I'm surprised at you, Sister! And what about *this!* – I suppose it, too, is by Raphael?"

Boniface peered at it closely: a rather more competent sketch of two females sitting at each end of a marble bench, one clothed, the other nude. "Titian," she said. "*Sacred and Profane Love*."

"Ha!" The Reverend Mother was triumphant at last. "Profane love – see."

"The painting belonged to Cardinal Scipione Borghese."

The other reached across her desk and snatched the book back again. "Excuses for lewdness!" she exclaimed. "Cardinals are just *men*, after all! I can see you're not shocked by them, Sister. Well, all I can say is that your years in Rome have done little to improve your . . ."

Boniface laughed. "If one was offended by painters like Raphael and Titian, Reverend Mother, there's not a church in Italy where one could safely worship. Did McKenna not tell you herself where she had copied them?"

"You'll get nothing out of her – nothing but dumb insolence. That girl can use silence like a . . ." The breath keened in and out of her angry nostrils but she did not complete the sentence. "I expect she *did* know they were by Raphael and Titian," she concluded bitterly.

Boniface banged the final nail in the coffin: "And there are two Michelangelos there – the male nudes."

"I don't wish to hear! As I was saying – I'm sure she knew it. I'm sure she chose them for that very reason – just to show us up."

Boniface forbore to point out that, if that was, indeed, her purpose, she had succeeded rather well. Instead she said, "Why d'you say we cannot expel her, Reverend Mother?"

The older woman, annoyed by that use of 'we', was torn between a desire to exclude her from the counsels of responsibility in *her* school and a need to explain what must seem a strange lack of authority.

Sister Boniface, seeing her hesitate, gave an unobtrusive push by stating the obvious: "Surely Father McDaid has no power to say whom we shall take in here?"

"Let him just try!" Reverend Mother recovered all her old ebullience. But it did not last long. "However," she went on, "there are grave difficulties about doing *anything* with that girl." She licked her lips nervously, still hesitant to commit herself. "I shouldn't like this to go any further now, but there is *bad seed* there!"

"In Father McDaid? Oh, you mean in Salome McKenna."

"Or whatever her true name is! We've had so many tales out of her."

"Is she not really an orphan, then? You seem to be hinting there is some scandal connected with her parentage, Reverend Mother?"

The woman nodded gravely. "And there you have it, Sister. Of course, Father McDaid wouldn't – probably couldn't – quote chapter and verse but he gave me to understand that she is" – she licked her lips again – "a priest's chance-child. There now!"

"And this unnamed priest is paying her fees here?" Sister Boniface asked skeptically, for Catherlough House was the most expensive boarding school for Roman Catholic girls in the country – indeed, in the whole of the British Isles. It had more titled young ladies than any in Ireland; and if you counted European and Indian titles, more than any in Europe.

Reverend Mother cleared her throat meaningfully. "I believe he is no longer a mere parish priest," she said. "There is no shortage of money there – the price of conscience! When she had her appendix out last year, a physician was sent from London to take charge of her case. I believe her father is a prince of the church – so you see my difficulty."

Boniface nodded.

Reverend Mother continued, "And you see too, I hope, why I am taking the risk of telling you all this – because if you're going to work mainly among the lay community in Simonstown, people are bound to start asking you questions about the McKenna girl. They all know there's something odd about her. And the girl herself tells so many lies about her background."

Boniface looked quizzically at her. "For example?"

"She told some of the girls she'd been a chimney-sweep's devil – you know – sent up chimneys to rake out the soot."

The sister chuckled. "She'd probably been reading *Tom and the Water-Babies*."

"Precisely! Anything will feed her imagination. Even poor Mister Culham-Browne was dragged in. All he did was bring her here – to save Father McDaid an awkward journey by bus and rail. And you should hear the fantasy she wove around that! It was extremely convincing, I have to warn you – she can be a very convincing liar. I had to write to the man to secure his denial – and, of course, there wasn't a word of truth in it." She smiled triumphantly.

"That soon shut her up – when I showed her the letter and made her write a formal retraction to the poor man. But she never stops. She's probably thinking up some other fantasy this very minute."

"Why? Where is she?"

"In the coal cellar. I told her – if she's going to do smutty drawings, she can go where the smuts all come from. I locked her in there with a loaf of dry bread and a bottle of water."

"In the dark?" Boniface tried to keep the horror out of her tone.

"There's no light there," Reverend Mother admitted.

"How long ago – may I ask? It seems rather drastic."

Salome had, in fact, been incarcerated immediately after her public humiliation that morning, directly after Mass – some eight hours earlier. Reverend Mother had intended releasing her in time to bathe herself clean with the girls who had taken part in the hare-and-hounds. However, Boniface's open show of sympathy had given her another idea. The sister had no idea what a truly awful, ungovernable, incorrigible girl McKenna had turned into; she probably remembered a rather quiet, friendly little creature who kept saying how nice it was to have so many friends her own age and it was all she'd ever wanted. If anything could hinder her in her commission to establish this home for educable cripples, it was surely the McKenna girl. Indeed, if she could, she'd bring it down in ruin about her ears.

The trick, then, would be to get the sister to volunteer to *do* something about the girl.

"Only eight hours so far," she replied, as if it were a mere fleabite into her punishment.

The sister rewarded her with a comical mixture of deference and horror. "But how many hours are you . . .?" She could not complete the question.

"Oh," Reverend Mother answered robustly. "It's not a question of *hours* with that one! Eight hours won't even have dented her rebellious spirit. You have no idea, Sister Boniface! The question is – would eight *days* be long enough?"

Boniface could bear it no longer. She sprang from her chair, yet again, and crossed the room to the window – where the girls were at last streaming back across the deerpark on the final leg of their chase. She wrung her hands incessantly. She bit her lip. Several times she drew breath to speak but always thought better of it. At last, however, she plucked up her courage: "Reverend Mother," she said. "May I make a suggestion?"

43

For the first dark hour Salome sang. The songs of Percy French, mostly. 'Abdul the Bulbul Ameer'; she put especial feeling into the bit about the lone vigil of the Muscovite Maiden. Also 'Slattery's Mounted Fut' and 'Father O'Callaghan' and 'Come Back Paddy Riley to Ballyjamesduff', which French wrote for a bet that he couldn't work Ballyjamesduff into a song at all.

Nobody came to disturb her. Nor did the dark frighten her any more; darkness had become a friend, years before this. Then she did speeches from Shakespeare. *The quality of mercy is not strained* – analyze and discuss.

Well, you couldn't put it through a tea-strainer, Sister.

You must think you're very funny, McKenna, and very clever, too, no doubt, but the truth is we're all rather bored by you and your cleverness.

I mean, mercy is something you have to accept lumps and all, Sister. This is a serious philosophical point, you know.

We have no time for serious philosophical points, child. [I'm not a child.] We have serious examinations to pass.

We still have time to run hare-and-hounds, though. *Cry havoc! And let slip the dogs of war!* Now *that* was a more satisfying picture for you! Reverend Mother with her habit up round her knees and two Hounds of the Baskervilles after her, streaking through the deerpark . . .

Salome felt the discomfort of a large lump of coal beneath the old coat or bit of sacking or whatever it was she was sitting on; she pulled it out and flung it indiscriminately into the dark. It hit something metallic and fell in several pieces. No harm done, more's the pity.

The Sinn Feiner had put his pistol in the Informer's mouth while the man was saying, "Please, please, please . . ." But the Sinn Feiner said the mouth that betrayed Ireland was the proper target. Afterwards there was no back to the man's head. It was all in little bits spread out on the chapel wall. The nuns knew what was happening. They stood at the windows and watched but they didn't come out.

And after that, Salome had decided not to run away after all. Breaking back into the dorm was twice as hard as breaking out.

She began to lose track of time. She bit into the loaf Sister Fructuosus had given her. Dear old Fructy! She didn't agree with what Reverend Mother had done. She didn't say anything, of course. Just like the nuns didn't say anything about the Sinn Feiner. Nuns' lives were full of things they never said. But old Fructy gave out one of the best new loaves from that morning's baking.

Still hot. Or warm, now – so she couldn't have been in here long.

Panic. An impulse to tears? She laughed to quash it.

What to think about next?

Why to think about next? Why think at all? Why not lie back and enjoy the absence of everyone and everything?

She rubbed her eyes, pressing hard to make sparks and pretty Catherine wheels and coloured aurora borealis. She stopped when the pain outweighed the pleasure.

She could measure the room. Compute its area. Estimate its volume – length times breadth times height. Then she could estimate the volume of the coal pile – one third of pi times the radius cubed. Or two-thirds? You won't be able to look it up when you get into the examination room, child! [I'm not!] We have serious exams to pass here.

In measuring the room she found a box full of old newspapers. She took one back to her cushion-on-the-coal – to read, of course. What else?

"Sure ye wouldn't be lettin' a li'l t'ing like the tawtal absince of light stop ye from raydin, now, wootchya?" she asked aloud in the scullery-maid's accent. Sister Macarius might not find her imitations of people funny but everyone else did.

"Foul Murder at College for Snooty Young Ladies", she 'read' aloud. "No *Good* Looking for *Succour* from the Sisters of Bon Secours, says Ghost of Informer!"

She laughed aloud, too, but it wasn't the same. Jokes like this demanded a real audience.

"I demand a real audience," she cried. Then, "I demand an audience of the Pope!"

God, I could tell *Him* a thing or two! About gluttony and pride, for instance, and why wasn't cruelty one of the Ten Commandments? And Sister Severinus kissing one of the novices in the woods. And Sister Godric pulling a face when Father Ganley gave her the Host. And Sister Pancras spoiling a whole bale of silk for the surplices for the choir because she was too lazy to use a pattern. And *all* of them grovelling like whipped bitches in front of the rich and titled parents.

And she could tell on all of them for not believing her when she said *she* had parents, as well. Four of them, two in the Cape and two in Ireland. They just said of *course* Salome *would* have twice as many parents as everyone else! That was the sort of laughter she *didn't* welcome.

Still, it didn't make her cry any more. Nothing made her cry any more.

She had another bite of bread. Cold now. Two hours gone, perhaps.

Or four – oh yes! You'd have to have twice as many hours as everyone else!

She laughed aloud again.

Reverend Mother could heap as many hours as she liked on her punishment; she could stay here and sleep on the coal forever.

It was *one*-third of pi times the cube of the radius – she'd just remembered.

One third of a pie would go down nicely now.

She set the thought to various melodies until the actual words had lost all meaning. She took a swig of water. She relieved herself in the furnace, whose fire would not be rekindled until the new school year began in September. The cold edge of the firebox grille touched the backs of her thighs. One of the few times she would have preferred to be a boy. Hereward used to make it arc as high as his head. TE AMO. You could still see the faint traces. It also spelled O MATE if you juggled the letters. An anagram. Also TEAM O and O MEAT and O TAME. And nonsense like A MOTE – unless you meant a mote in thy brother's eye.

God, this is boring.

Whatever the words spelled, they meant nothing. 'I love you' means nothing. Otherwise why hadn't Hereward hacked his way through the thorns around this castle and kissed her sleeping lips by now? Why had she had to sneak out of the dorm last night and try to run away to find him?

Fancy being kissed on the lips by a nun – eurgh! Especially Sister Severinus with her moustache. Perhaps she was a man underneath her habit? What a lark! She-he could get away with it for years, since everyone over the age of ten at Catherlough House wore a long cotton shift to bathe in. No one would notice her-his tail. Especially the way it shrivelled in cold water, which Hereward showed her that time.

"Hereward!" She whispered his name into the dark and raised her lips to receive the ten-thousandth kiss of their long, one-sided courtship, reserved for the dark. It was as beautiful as ever.

She yawned. Usually those kisses came just before she fell asleep each night. Usually they helped, but sometimes they disturbed her and made her wide awake again. Then she'd rise on her elbows and look around the dorm, wondering how many were truly sleeping and how many were, like her, enjoying happy little dreams of ponies, pet mice . . . troubadours . . . Prince Charming. Pretending to sleep. Pretending to sigh in their sleep. And then if Ursula Legrice was dorm prefect that week and she heard a girl sighing like that she'd leap from her cubicle screaming, "Arms out! Arms out!" and cavorting up and down pinching their cheeks until they were all awake and all had their arms out rigid on the counterpane. And if you crossed your arms over your chest and pretended to be a corpse, just because it was gas, she'd report you for the strap.

One beautiful go-to-sleep dream when Legrice was dorm pre was to tie her face down on her bed and lay into her with the strap until she stopped screaming and passed out.

What are little girls made of?

Sugar and spice and all things nice.

The chapel bell began to ring. That would be Terce, Sept, and None, surely. Midday already! This would be easy. How long till Vespers and Compline?

Sometime after that, or it could have been an hour, she fell asleep.

She woke with permanent dents in her flesh. Who made your vile body? I don't know, Sister, but coal tried to *re*make it.

Actually, it's a little-known fact, but not all bodies are vile. Sister Severinus's is, of course – especially if she's hiding you-know-what down there under the wet calico. But Angela Lowndes's isn't. Leo Coen, the gatekeeper's son, told Mary Kelly, one of the Magdalens, that Angela Lowndes has a perfect body for a woman.

She ate more of the bread and took another swig of water. They'd have to feed her again sometime if they weren't going to let her out today.

When the nun came, she'd pretend not to hear a thing. She wouldn't look at the woman, nor speak when spoken to.

Or she could throw herself at the nun's feet like the Penitent in the painting on the cupboard door where the strap was hung. She could be a Penitent and pray in the chapel all night and follow the Rule all on her own, like Ursula Legrice who wanted to be a nun after leaving college. She could be more holy than Ursula Legrice. She could be the holiest woman the nuns had ever seen. Not inside, of course, but she could act it well enough to take them all in. They'd talk about her day and night, she'd be so holy. They'd all go down on their knees to her, begging her to join the Order. And then – she laughed aloud to think of it – when it came for her to take her vows, just before they took the razor to her hair, she'd rip off all her clothes and dance naked on the altar!

The sound of her laughter, echoing briefly in the dank cellar, left her dispirited. It would be one in the eye for the nuns. Reverend Mother would never recover from it. But, on the other hand, she didn't want to go upsetting God – if He existed at all, at all.

It would be a subtler revenge to go and be a Protestant nun. Becoming a Protestant was even worse than becoming . . . that other word – like Protestant – which she heard two of the Magdalens use once in whispers. They told her Reverend Mother would rather she became . . . whatever it was than a Protestant. So becoming a Protestant *nun* would be like rubbing salt and vinegar into the wound.

She said the Lord's Prayer aloud, using '*which* art in heaven' and all about the power and the glory at the end.

Then she listened to the silence for a while.

Then she said, "God! Are you there? If you can hear me, shine a light down here! Give us a sign, God!"

Nothing pierced the blackness – except unprovoked hallucinations playing tricks with the backs of her eyelids.

She fell asleep again.

She woke up when a rat walked over her. She was about to scream when it struck her that she could try to make friends with it. If she could tame it enough to hold, she could slip it into the nun's pocket who came to let her out. She spent a long time trying to find it after that.

Then she heard someone approaching down the cellar steps. A nun. They had a particular way of walking. Dotty Carter could recognize most of them from their walks.

Salome waited just long enough to see the shape of the wimple against the light beyond and then turned her back on the door.

The door closed and all was darkness once again; the nun must just have opened it, peeped inside, and closed it again. Salome strained her ear for the departing footsteps but heard none. She must be standing outside with her ear to the keyhole.

Then she heard the woman breathing. She was *inside* the cellar! Just standing there in the pitch black. But why? Sister Severinus come to kiss her? A little squirt of fear stirred in Salome's belly. She wanted to call out, tell her she knew she was there, ask her what she supposed she was doing. But she did none of these things.

Then, after a silence that must have lasted several minutes, the nun spoke at last – and in a voice Salome could not place. She recognized it – or sort of *half*-recognized it – but could not for the life of her attach a face or a name. "Happy birthday, dear Salome!" was all the voice said. "I've brought you a bit of cake."

44

For a long while Salome made no reply. Her visitor certainly wasn't one of the Catherlough nuns. She knew all their voices by now. Anyway, none of them would dream of calling her anything other than McKenna. So one of the girls must have cut out a bit of cardboard in the shape of a wimple and come in wearing it – except that she'd recognize any of the girls, as well. So she just sat there in perfect silence, which she was quite used to by now, waiting for the intruder to make some move.

But the intruder seemed blessed with the patience of Job, too. She just sat there, perfectly content to do nothing.

At last Salome could stand no more of it. "What the hell are you doing here?" she asked.

It was worth the strap – either to shock a sister or to smoke one of the girls out of her attempted imposture of one.

"I'm trying to imagine what it must have been like to spend most of the day in these conditions," the stranger said. "Hell is a *good* word for it."

It was a woman's voice, not a schoolgirl's – not even a senior's.

A visiting nun, perhaps. A travelling deaconess of studies come to discipline her?

"You haven't gone mad, anyway," the visitor added. "That's a good sign."

"If you say so," Salome said gruffly. Had the woman mentioned cake? Salome was too proud to ask.

"You don't think it is? It must require a fairly robust spirit, surely? You must be able to get on with yourself quite well."

Salome sniffed. If she wasn't careful, this woman would drag her into a ding-dong conversation. "It hardly matters, either way. Who says a whale is a bird?"

Let her puzzle that one out!

It didn't take long. "Sheridan!" said the woman after the barest pause for thought. "*The Critic*. We do it every six years here. Act Three, Scene . . . something or other. Tilburina, going mad. Is that what you'd like me to believe, Salome – that you're going mad? I shan't oblige you, I'm afraid."

Salome laughed despite herself. An equal! She'd found an equal! She didn't care whether the woman was a nun or a peripatetic deaconess of studies . . . or even a ghost. She enjoyed the same games – and she was quick! "A lot you'd care!" she said, quelling her laughter and assuming a sulky tone. "A lot anyone would care."

"Oh, diddums!" the other said sarcastically. "You're getting too big for self-pity – sixteen today! You're wrong, anyway. The first thing I'd want to know is: Are you going mad in white satin? Because if so, *I* should be obliged to go mad in white linen."

To her annoyance Salome laughed again, before she could check herself. That was from Sheridan's play, too: Heroines go mad in white satin, their confidantes go mad in white linen. The visitor was volunteering to be her confidante but without actually saying so; she added, "I'd rather not go mad at all, of course."

"What would you rather, then?" Salome was forced to ask.

"I'd rather get rid of this sticky morsel I'm still holding between my fingers – if you wouldn't mind helping me?"

Salome edged her way over to where the voice was coming from. Something brushed her knee. A hand. She bent down and took it in hers, feeling for the promised cake, but it was empty. However, it guided the other hand there – which did, indeed, contain a large slice of fruit cake.

"Happy birthday!" the woman said.

Salome took it, thanked her, and began to stuff it greedily into her mouth.

"I'll bet that tastes like manna, after all this time," said the other.

Salome munched her way steadily through it, licking every last smear of currant and treacle off her fingers.

"There's Guinness in that," the woman continued. "They know how to line their stomachs, these Bon Secours Sisters – wouldn't you say?"

Once more Salome had to laugh, still against her inclination. "What are *you*, then?" she asked.

"Oh, I'm one of them – but that's the least important thing about me at the moment."

"What's the most important thing?"

"Do you not remember me, Salome? I'm the sister who happened to welcome you here when Mister Culham-Browne left you. Perhaps you don't. I was ordered to Rome the following week."

"Sister Boniface!" Salome exclaimed. "God, I *knew* I'd heard your voice before. Are you back here now?"

"In a way. I have work to do here in Simonstown. I'll maybe take you to see it tomorrow. But that's not the most important thing about me at this moment, either. Shall I tell you what is?"

"Yes."

"The most important thing about me at this moment is that I seem to be the only person at Catherlough House – apart from yourself, of course – who knows the truth about you."

After a shocked pause Salome said, "You do?"

"About being left behind at Queenstown and being adopted by Mrs Culham-Browne. Has she been in touch, by the way?"

"No!" Salome's breath was coming in shivers now; she began to think this pitch-black conversation was all a dream. Or some special kind of hallucination brought on by so many hours in the dark.

But Sister Boniface seemed already to understand. "I didn't bring a candle," she said apologetically, "but there's the whole of God's great sky out there. And it's a fine May evening. Shall we go for a stroll and talk about this, and what it all means, where we can see each other?"

"Will I be let out?" Salome asked.

"That's entirely up to you, my child."

"I'm *not* a child," she spat out with sudden savagery.

Boniface gave a toneless whistle. "You're a kitten that's been teased too much! My *dear*, then – is that better?"

But Salome was barely mollified. "What d'you mean – it's up to me?" she asked bitterly. "What forfeit do you demand now?"

"None at all. When I said it's up to you, all I meant was that you need only walk over to the door and turn the handle."

Salome, not believing her, went over to disprove the promise. The door swung open easily on freshly oiled hinges.

To her eternal credit the sister did not say, "See!"

Salome blinked at the dim light that filtered down the cellar steps. The nun rose and came to her side. "I had a rabbit when I was a little girl," she said. "When we opened the cage door to let her go, it was several days before she got up the courage – and her with the door open all that time!"

Salome took the steps three-in-one. When she reached the top, blinking at the increasing strength of the light, she looked down at her dress, her white cotton blouse, her hands . . . and her dismay increased with each moment of her scrutiny. "God, I must go and wash myself – and change these clothes," she exclaimed. "Can you come with me and talk to matron? *Make* her give me a set of clean clothes?"

"No!" Boniface gave a quick, conspiratorial glance all around and then murmured, "Let them see you like that! Let them feel a little shame, too!"

If there was a single moment when Sister Boniface recruited Salome's spirit to her cause, that was it.

They came out into the old stable yard; it was, as Sister Boniface had said, a fine, warm evening in May. In the Fanes' day the stables had been adequate for forty horses. Now there were a dozen hacks for the girls, which doubled as draft horses for the gigs; the remaining stables had been converted into art rooms, music-practice rooms, and – the latest fad in upper-class education – a room for Swedish slojd. Also a eurythmics hall where the girls were schooled in grace and deportment, and (when the curtains were drawn) Greek Dancing. The education at Catherlough House was rather more worldly than was usually provided at Roman Catholic girls' colleges, for many of its pupils were destined to become the wives of ambassadors, presidents, and captains of industry – where worldly wisdom was at a premium. The aim was to provide knowledge without corruption. *Cognitio ardor est* – the 'fire' was the kind that purifies, not consumes.

"These are just like the stables at Cloonaghvogue," Salome said as the pair of them stood there, deciding which way to go. "Do you think they had books of plans you could buy in those days?"

"Talking of Cloonaghvogue – did you know the whole place is a ruin now?"

Salome stared at her, mouth open.

The nun nodded. "The IRA tried to use it as a stronghold and the Tans burned it to the ground. Of course the castle walls are still standing . . ."

"They're twenty feet thick at the bottom."

"Goodness! That's even thicker than the average Black-and-Tan skull! But the rest . . ." She waved her hands hopelessly. "Let's go out across the hockey field, shall we?"

It was what Salome had been hoping she'd say, though she'd never have suggested it herself because she was so used to the nuns doing the opposite of anything she ever suggested. On the far side of the playing fields, on a little rise leading up to the woodland, stood a darling gazebo, a folly of a Greek temple, which one of the Fanes must have built after a visit to Castle Moore. It was sufficiently like the Bellinghams' marble pavilion to have drawn her there many an evening during the long summer holidays, when all but a handful of girls went home. There she would sigh her heart toward Lough Cool and plan her escapes in such vivid detail it became unnecessary to carry them out.

As they entered the central arch of the stable block, which led through to the fields behind, she had a sudden memory of that first Christmas at Cloonaghvogue, when she was led through just such an arch as this to discover Hannibal waiting for her in the paddock beyond. The life she had enjoyed there seemed so remote now that it was hard, even for her, to believe it had really happened. Hannibal had been eight years ago. More than half her lifetime.

Girls peered at her as they passed, girls with clay and deer-droppings on their knees and faces; nonetheless they thought the coal that disfigured hers was amusing. They would have laughed aloud, too, had they not caught Sister Boniface's eye first. The older ones recognized her and greeted her with genuine warmth. Salome knew that she was going up in the general estimation, which was always very elastic where she was concerned – stretching from disdain among her elders to a grudging sort of admiration among her contemporaries.

She closed her eyes just before they emerged from the archway-tunnel, pretending this was Cloonaghvogue and that Hannibal would be waiting there, just beyond.

"Are you all right?" Boniface asked.

She opened her eyes and smiled sadly. "I was just

remembering Cloonaghvogue, Sister. Is it really all gone? Were you there yourself?"

The other shook her head. "You remember Father Hines? The priest there?"

Salome shook her head. "I was Protestant then." She waited for the usual shock and cries of horror but all the nun said was, "Well, I met him in Rome last month. He was leading a pilgrimage. He told me. They burned it down last year. Of course, the place was empty since . . . well, since nineteen-sixteen."

Burned down since last year! So for a whole year she'd been daydreaming about a place that was no more. "Did he say about the statues in the lake?" she asked.

Boniface shook her head. "Were they anything special?"

Salome chuckled and then spoke with a sort of histrionic exaggeration, to show she was repeating an idle fancy. "They were real people once, but those Cloonaghvogue waters have the power to petrify living flesh. So there was this young girl, bathing there in a state of nature, and turning slowly to stone without realizing it. And along comes the god Pan – the pagan with the pipes – and him playing his heart out – when he sees the wee girl in the last of her living flesh. And she turns around with her heart all on fire at his strange, sweet melodies. And he sees her face and falls desperately madly in love with her on the spot. And he plays and plays, calling her back from the waters that petrify. And she tries to turn and join him, for she has fallen for him, as well. But all her struggles are to no avail, d'you see. She's too far lost to the flesh and the marble is in her soul by now."

At this point Salome saw that the nun, who had previously been laughing along with her over-dramatic rendering of the tale, had stopped smiling and was hanging on every word, with a great, soulful stare in her eyes.

For some reason Salome's own heart missed a beat and then began hammering away at the double, but she couldn't think why. Then she tried to make as swift an end as possible of a tale that, starting out as a joke, had become an embarrassment – and all for no reason whatever. "So doesn't he plunge into the waters himself, playing louder and louder, and drawing nearer and nearer. But 'tis too late, too late! He, too, is turning to stone – which he does before e'er he reaches her. So there they stand for ever – the half-goat, half-man playing a frozen music only she can hear. And she turned to him, pleading for something her lips can no longer name, staring at him with eyes that will never see anything other than him – though they will never see the distance between them shrink by the thickness of a hair. So there!"

She laughed, trying to recruit at least a chuckle from the nun. But Sister Boniface just went on staring at her, an odd sort of sadness in her eyes. "Did you make that up?" she asked at length.

They resumed their stroll between the senior and junior pitches.

"I wove it a little," Salome admitted. "But 'twas old thread."

"D'you understand the story?"

Salome laughed awkwardly. "There's little enough to understand, surely? It's an old legend, that's all. Like Pandora and her box." Memories long dormant began to surface once again. "Miss Kinchy said we're all called Pandora and we all have our own little boxes full of troubles."

"Well, this Miss Kinchy understood one or two things about ancient legends that you have so far failed to grasp."

"For instance?" Salome asked belligerently.

"That they survive from generation to generation only because they contain some ancient message which we still find important."

Salome, who could spot a sermon ten miles off by now, waited for it: 'And the Christian message is the most durable of all, my child . . . blah-blah-blah!'

Sister Boniface said, "Still – all this is very amiable and interesting, no doubt. But it's not getting us any nearer an answer to *your* particular problem."

They had reached the end of the games fields by now. A short stretch of deer-cropped grass led up to the gazebo, which gleamed all pink and warm in the westering sun.

"My problem?" Salome prompted when the nun said no more.

In reply, Boniface waved a hand toward the marble seats awaiting them; they covered the remaining distance in an easy silence while Salome wondered precisely what form her 'problem' had assumed in the other's mind. At a guess the woman was referring to the fact that, although she, Salome, had told the truth about her past, no one was inclined to believe her. In her own mind it had almost ceased to be a problem at all. She was reconciled to their stupidity. It was enough for her to know the truth. If anything, their ignorance enabled her to feel a little superior – the only one with the True Knowledge.

"Tell me," Boniface began as they seated themselves on the marble bench. But then she broke off and lifted her face toward the sun, eyes closed, a serene smile on her lips. "We might be in Italy!" she murmured dreamily.

In that moment Salome thought she had never seen any creature quite so beautiful as this nun – this strangely composed woman who bore conviction and purpose around her like an aura. An overwhelming desire to become just such a woman herself, one day, possessed her; but it was at once cancelled out by an equally overwhelming realization that it could never be. She might have an equal sense of conviction, an equal strength of purpose – those qualities she did not doubt; but the serenity was something she would never match, the love that seemed to radiate from her. Her own sort of conviction would always have a tinge of anger; her own purpose would never be quite free of bitterness.

"Tell me!" Boniface resumed her original line. "Why do you think we humans have been granted the powers of reason?"

The question – not unnaturally – took the girl aback.

"I know what we use it for," the nun went on. "To justify cruelty and selfishness, mainly. But what d'you think the real purpose is?"

Salome played safe. "For the greater glory of God, Sister?"

"If I had more cake I'd give it you!" she replied sarcastically. "Now – if you've finished jumping through hoops – tell me what you really think."

The girl squirmed awkwardly; the marble bench suddenly felt very hard beneath her. "I don't know," she said at last.

"You do."

Salome swallowed heavily. "Is this what you called my problem, Sister?"

"It lies at the very heart of it, my ch . . . my dear."

"Well I don't think *I* ever used it to justify cruelty. Selfishness, maybe."

"There's a start! And what lies behind cruelty and selfishness, eh?" She tapped her breastbone by way of a clue.

"Feelings?" Salome offered. "Passions?"

Boniface smiled triumphantly. "I told you you knew! Feelings and passions!"

"But some feelings and passions are good in themselves, surely, Sister?"

She chuckled. "Now you're running ahead of me. They surely are – and they're the ones we should talk about – you and I – because they, too, are at the heart of your problem. *Good* feelings. *Good* passions. What has reason to do with *them*?" She breathed in deeply and continued. "Suppose you're walking down the street and you come across a young beggar woman with a child in her shawl. What do you *feel?*"

"I feel I should feed the hungry and clothe the poor, Sister."

"Good feelings, surely?"

Salome nodded and waited for the 'but' she felt must surely come soon.

"But what docs reason step in and tell you? Well, maybe not you because you're probably still young and idealistic. But a crabby old nun like me, say – what should my reason, that other gift of God, be telling me if I'm not to neglect or abuse it?"

"That she'd only spend your charity on drink?"

Boniface encouraged her with a nod.

"That, um, she could easily go to the workhouse and get food and lodging there – and care for the child."

"More?"

Salome rolled her eyes in a search for inspiration. "That if you give to one, you should give to all? That you're only encouraging indigence and mendicity . . ."

"Indigence and mendicity, is it! Where did you get such words from at all?"

Salome laughed at being caught out. "From the monsignor's sermon before Christmas last year, Sister."

"Ah! The monsignor! As he sows, so shall I reap, eh? Well – enough! You understand the beauty and the power of reason – we've established that. Reason is given us to sit in judgment on our finer emotions."

"Mostly to hold them in check?"

"I'm afraid so, my dear. Sad but true. So let's see how we might apply this understanding to *your* feelings in your present situation. What *are* your feelings in your present situation?"

"God, where do I begin!" Salome exclaimed with some fervour.

"At the beginning?" Boniface suggested. " I only know as much of your story as I managed to get Mister Culham-Browne to tell me that day. So start there."

"But he didn't stay," Salome blurted out. "He put me down and scuttled off like . . ." She faltered because the only comparison that occurred to her was mildly improper.

"Like a shot off a shovel, I know," the sister put in. "No, I saw him earlier that day – when he left your trunks and cases in on his way to Castle Moore. What I'd like to hear is your version of the story."

For the next twenty minutes or so, while the sun dipped toward the horizon, turning from gold to red as it went, Salome told everything she could recall of the hitherings and thitherings of her turbulent life. Boniface prompted her with a question now and then but her interruptions were few and Salome's narrative gathered in pace as she grew in confidence; the main thing was that she was believed at last by someone – not just Monica Dawes and Cecilia Bowen, whom you could get to believe in *anything*.

Even so, she had to have it out in the open between them – in so many words. So she had barely concluded her tale before she was asking, "You do believe me, Sister, don't you?"

"Of course I do, Salome," the nun replied. "That was never in question. But I'll tell you what is. The question is, what do we *do* about it? What are your feelings? D'you ever think about your parents in the Cape?"

Salome gave a single ironic laugh. "Like the girl in *Daddy Long-Legs* – except that my Daddy would need very long legs! Anyway, they've forgotten me – the same as Aunt Marion, the same as Hereward . . ."

Her bitterness hurt Sister Boniface. "Oh, my dear!" she murmured gently.

"Feelings!" Salome sneered. "It's not much use having those things here."

The nun tried to steer her back to less troubled waters. "You're angry that no one believes you?"

"Not any more. I was in the beginning, mind."

"I can imagine. And now you keep it all hidden away

inside you? You don't try and convince them any more?"

"Sure what'd be the purpose?"

"Perhaps you even feel a little superior? *You* know the truth and they don't."

She closed her eyes and hung her head, nodding her confirmation of this final guess.

Boniface laughed and, putting a hand on her shoulder, squeezed hard. "And now I've come along to spoil it all!"

Salome turned and stared at her in surprise. "Spoil it?" she echoed.

"Yes. I mean it's a great comfort to be able to feel that sort of superiority over others – surely? But also, wouldn't it be marvellous if a nun like me was to let them know they'd been wrong all this time and you were absolutely right!"

"Lord!" Salome's whole face lit up. "Would you?" It had never crossed her mind that Sister Boniface would go *that* far.

"Well, that's the question I want you to ponder now, Salome. We've only talked about your feelings so far. And, to be sure, *they* tell you how splendid it'd be if all your adversaries were made to look like fools. That's why I brought in the whole question of *reason*, before we got carried away in a bloodbath of grand passions. What does your reason tell you would be the effect of letting out this truth?"

Salome, unable to bear the hardness of the marble beneath her a moment longer, sprang to her feet and stamped them in an agony of pins and needles. "You mean the effect on discipline and the college?" she began.

"Ah no!" Sister Boniface laughed. "The place would easily weather a little storm in the teacup like that. Don't be giving yourself airs, now! I'm talking about the effect on you. Let's walk again, shall we? Tell me, what d'you think Marion Culham-Browne has been doing all this time?"

Salome was thoughtful as they set off once more, taking a

course that would lead them in a wide arc round the eastern side of the big house, where, since she was accompanied by a nun, she would be privileged to go in by the front door.

"D'you think she's tried to trace you?" the woman prompted.

"I'm sure she has."

Boniface noticed that Salome had become quietly agitated, pulling at her fingers and walking with an odd, jerky motion. "D'you miss her?" she asked suddenly.

"Yes, of course!" Salome almost protested the words. Then, glancing away toward the lowering sun – which filled her eyes with a lambent fire – she added, "At least, I did, at the beginning."

"And now?"

"I don't know." She gave a feeble laugh and looked at the nun, almost as if asking for support. "Will I tell you? I woke up this morning saying, ' 'Tis your birthday, colleen. You'd better be packing your bags.' There now!"

"But why?" Sister Boniface already half-guessed the answer but she wanted to hear it on Salome's own lips.

"Don't you see? I lost one mother on my seventh birthday and another on my eleventh. I'm overdue my third!"

Sister Boniface laughed aloud and then threw her arms around Salome in an effusive, unthinking hug. To her surprise, the girl stiffened at once, bristling with rejection though she did not actually struggle. "I'm sorry," she said, disentangling herself quickly. "I couldn't help it. You made it seem so comical. However . . ." She took a visible grip of herself and became serious again. "You have a point. Only there is a difference this time. *This* time it's *you* who decides whether or not you are to lose your third home in life."

After a brief, shocked silence Salome said, "I'm sorry but I don't understand."

Boniface was tempted to tell her, as before, that she did,

in her heart-of-hearts. Instead she said, "Well, just try to imagine what would happen – what *must* happen – once your story is believed. Marion Culham-Browne *kid-napped* you that day, you realize? It's not what one usually thinks of as kidnapping but that's what it actually was. And in sending you here and paying for your education in secret, Mister Culham-Browne is only compounding that crime. Again it's the very opposite of what kidnappers usually do but that doesn't change the legality of it. Legally, you still belong to your parents in the Cape, you know. So once Reverend Mother believes your story, she'll have no choice but to start making inquiries out there with a view to restoring you to your true parents. And, knowing the church as I do, and all the tentacles it has, I doubt they'd be long about it. You'd be out in the Cape by Christmas – if that's what you want."

There was another longish pause before Salome said, "The tentacles of the church didn't work very well from *their* end, Sister."

"Don't be too sure of that! They might have traced you to the Culham-Brownes – in which case, the last place they'd go looking for you would be a college for wealthy young Roman Catholic ladies only a stone's-throw away from Cloonaghvogue! And that, incidentally, is also the last place Marion Culham-Browne would come looking for you, too! That old fox she married is no fool. When she went looking for you – which I feel sure she did – I'll bet it was to every Protestant boarding school for girls in England. She'd not come in here, even if she happened to be passing the very gates with half a day to spare." She cleared her throat. "But this is getting away from the point. The point is, d'you want to stay here – with only me knowing the truth about you . . ."

"What do *they* think is the truth, Sister Boniface? Reverend Mother and the other nuns. I don't understand them at all." Her big, green-grey eyes searched the nun's face with an appeal the woman could not resist.

"Why d'you ask?" she responded.

"Because if I was in their shoes, I'd have expelled a girl like me yee-ars since!"

"You've been testing them!" Boniface only half-suppressed a smile.

Salome did not share her amusement. "It's like plunging into a pool of water and never finding the bottom, so it is."

"They think you're a cardinal's daughter, of course," the sister told her at last. "Or a bishop's at the very least.

Salome's bewilderment only deepened. "But cardinals don't get married."

The other agreed with a weary nod. "Never mind that. I'll explain all in good time. Meanwhile, just accept it from me – cardinals and bishops are men like any other men. They can father children out of wedlock as well as in. And that's what the good sisters here . . ."

"Out of wedlock!" Salome exploded. "They think I'm . . . that I'm a . . ."

"Oh no! None of that. They think your mother married *someone* before you were born but they don't believe that person was your true father. Your fees and pocket money are paid by Father McDaid – one of the curates at Cloonaghvogue. You probably don't recall him, either. But where would a poor man like him be getting the sort of money Mister Culham-Browne has been paying all these years?"

"But Reverend Mother *met* Uncle C-B when he brought me here."

"She thinks he was just obliging Father McDaid – because he happened to have the car and happened to be driving this way. It's Father McDaid who pays all your bills – as agent for Culham-Browne, of course, but he's never let on about that!" She touched the girl's arm and they resumed their walk. "Again," she said, "we wander from the point – which is: Do we upset all the present arrangements and return you to an unknown life in the Cape, or . . ."

"I just want to be shot of this place," Salome said bitterly.

"An understandable *feeling*." Sister Boniface stressed the word. "Now suppose we let Reason sit in judgement upon it for a week or so, eh?"

Salome responded with a nod, a rather unhappy nod, for she already knew what Reason was going to say. Also, she couldn't deny, Catherlough House might be a very different place if Sister Boniface was going to be around. "I'll try," she said.

Their path brought them due east of the big house, whose shadow suddenly engulfed them. The sun was within minutes of setting.

45

You'd hardly believe there was a war of liberation going on, Hereward thought as he crossed Saint Stephen's Green. The band was playing selections from *The Merry Widow* and *Princess Ida*. The gardens were thronged with people out for a Sunday afternoon stroll, and many of them, disregarding the traditional advice to 'cast ne'er a clout till May be out', were in light summer frocks and suits of unbleached linen. He strode more purposefully among them, trying not to notice those anatomical novelties that even the most respectable ladies had acquired during the war: calves and ankles.

By a habit so deeply ingrained that he no longer noticed it, his eyes flickered from girl's face to girl's face to girl's face. If they were blondes or redheads, they got no second glance; if they were his own age or older, his eye passed swiftly on as well. But dark-haired girls in their mid-teens could make him deviate from a path that was otherwise arrow-straight. He had to see their eyes. For the rest of their persons they might be fat or slender, tall or short – for who could say how Salome might have developed over the past five years? But her eyes could not have changed – those grey-green pools of mystery whose appeal to him was as fresh now as on the day he last saw them.

Near the gate at the foot of Leeson Street his heart began to beat faster. It always did on approaching that particular spot – specifically, a plane tree just inside the entrance. For there on Armistice Night, almost three years ago, a ragged little girl not yet in her teens, the very image of Salome, had stepped out from behind the tree and offered her favours for a shilling. In the dim street lighting his height had misled her into thinking him much older than his fifteen years. "Salome!" he had blurted out. A fraction of a second later, of course, he had realized it was not her. Then, after a moment during which they stood staring at each other in bewilderment, the child had laughed and said, "I can pretend!"

And he had taken to his heels and fled in dismay.

The shame of that encounter was with him still. The shame of thinking Salome could ever sink so low. The shame of his animal regret that he had not accepted her offer, closed his eyes, and pretended along with her – oh, what mortifications he had undergone to purge himself of that belated impulse! And then there was the recurring shame of hoping to find her – or, rather, the real Salome, his blood-sister – not precisely behind that tree, but somewhere nearby. For this was a mystic place, now and always, charged with some arcane *otherness* for him.

He realized he had let a number of mid-teen girls go past unexamined. He quashed an impulse to turn about and do the job properly, though a year ago he would have done so.

After all, what was so special about Stephen's Green – except that her foster-mother had a school nearby and Salome might one day escape from wherever she was being held and come directly there. Even now she might be wandering down Hatch Street, or coming up Dawson Street, or making inquiries across the Liffey in Sackville Street. Or she might not be in Ireland at all. She could be in an orphanage in Liverpool – Aunt Marion's most pessimistic theory. Or shipped out as a bond servant to Canada (Aunt Maisie's). Or returned to her true parents in the Cape (Aunt Edith's).

His mind's eye created an impossible blend of alien streets, orphanages, workhouses, prairie farms, and rondaavels in the Great Karroo – through all of which his mind wandered in less than half a second, the way the mind can, and drew the usual blank.

He straightened his tie for the umpteenth time and skipped across the road, nimbly avoiding a gun carriage drawn by a troop of horses going east and a family in a dogcart, going west and enjoying the sun. The accidental symbolism – Ireland Today, you could call it – amused him enough to make him forget his eternal obsession with dark-haired girls in their mid-teens. He was about to take up a position in publishing and Rick had recently let him into the secret about Symbolism in Literature, so he was on the QV for such things. He made a mental note to tell his father, who might even use it in one of his novels.

The Earlsfort Day-School for Young Ladies (Non-Denominational) was, as its name implied, in Earlsfort Terrace, in the grand but decaying Georgian houses beyond University College. Today being Sunday, the classrooms were silent, the benches empty, the chalk dust undisturbed. And, today being warm and sunny as well, several of the windows were open for ventilation. At one of them Aunt Maisie was standing on the sill, oilcan in hand, lubricating the wheels over which the sashcords turned.

"Hallo, Hereward!" she shouted, waving the can. She must inadvertently have pressed the lever, too, for it ejaculated a thready train of oil, frozen for an instant against a fleecy cloud – from his vantage below. "Oops!" she giggled as he executed a dance-like movement to avoid its impact on the paving stones. "Lucky it was only you!"

"Only *me?*" he asked accusingly when, a minute later, she opened the door to him.

She bit her lip. "I realized how rude that was the moment I said it. But you know what I mean."

Rick was right. There *was* something eternally girlish in her behaviour; spinsters never grow up fully, he maintained. All the same, Hereward never met Aunt Maisie without remembering what he and Salome had seen her and Rick doing in the woods that day – and what he, alone, had seen them doing in the boathouse on several later occasions. He kissed her proffered cheek; she was perfumed today. He wondered why.

She supplied the reason at once, almost as if she could read his mind. "I'll tell you before the others do," she said. "I'm going to be married next week! You'll meet him if you stay to tea."

Hereward said all the things that etiquette demanded and then asked, "Do I know him?" He couldn't recall meeting any young bachelor here on previous visits.

"I doubt it," she replied. "Your father might have met him a couple of times. His name's Andrew Fielding. He's a nephew of Fergal McIver – the man who married your father's childhood sweetheart. He's a Roman Catholic."

"They've rather lost touch," Hereward said.

"Yes," She smiled sympathetically. "One does – with childhood sweethearts. We have another bit of news – of more interest to you, I'm sure – but I'll leave that for Marion to tell you."

"About Salome?" he asked eagerly.

Her sympathy turned to sadness, dashing his hopes. "In a

way, my dear. I shouldn't have said 'news' – it's more of a development, really. Anyway, I know Marion wants to tell you. She's in the larder, doing a bit of stocktaking. I must finish oiling the sashes."

"Try and hit your man when he comes," he advised. "You came jolly close with me."

She gave him a playful punch and skipped back toward the empty classroom – a woman of almost thirty!

As he went through to the back of the house – or, rather, of the three houses that had been run together to make the school – it struck him that she was actually making an excuse to linger at the front windows and catch the first glimpse of her fiancé. That man's face would be as stirring to her as the sight of Salome's would be to him.

Suddenly the mystery of love overwhelmed him. What was it that could make one particular face out of all the millions and millions in the world so utterly special? What would keep Miss Maisie Morrell standing on windowsills in acute discomfort for anything up to an hour, just so that she wouldn't miss the wonderful moment when Mr Andrew Fielding hove into sight in Earlsfort Terrace? And, for his own part, what kept the memory of that dear, childish face, those misty grey-green eyes, those pretty dark ringlets . . . what kept it so evergreen in the deepest and most secret corners of his heart?

Sex? So Rick always said. But Hereward had a passing familiarity with that monster by now and he knew that *this* impulse was something far more profound. Rick enjoyed dragging everything noble down to the level of mechanical necessity and animal instincts; but that was because – as Letty pointed out once – he was far too romantic for his own good; the Postwar Age demanded cynicism; love was not real if it was not brutish, too. Letty was never happier than when she could prove that History was sweeping us all forward, whether we liked it or not. Gwinnie preferred to explain life as a compound of individual effort and bloody-mindedness. Between them they wrote all Rick's books, really – all he did was fill in the words.

"You know what day it is?" Hereward asked Aunt Marion as soon as their greetings were done. He liked to provoke that sadness in her eyes – to know he was not alone. Sometimes she wallowed in misery with him; sometimes she spurned his remarks and told him it wasn't natural for a young man like him.

But he knew there was no other young man like him, not in his eyes, and not in Salome's either.

"Yes," she replied indecisively.

"I bought her a little pearl pendant," he said. "It's too old for her now but she'll appreciate it one day. I've put it with all the others."

Marion closed her eyes and rested her fingertips on the scrubbed deal top of the kitchen table. "Oh, Hereward!" she sighed.

"What?" This was a new mood for her; it alarmed him.

"You must give up," she said wearily. "For your own sake. It was a fine adolescent fantasy – and I'm sure it kept you out of a lot of mischief. But you're a young man now . . ."

"I'm starting at the Nolan Press next week. Or *this* week, now, I suppose."

She smiled with delight and became more animated at once. "Oh, congratulations! I suppose Rick pulled a string or two?"

"No. He wanted me to start with the Maynard Press in London."

The gaiety deserted Marion again. "But of course *you* had to stay in Dublin!" she said bitterly.

He smiled, trying to recruit her good humour back out of hiding.

" 'Fraid so, Aunty dear. You might as well make your mind up to it – I'm not going to give up looking for her. She *must* be somewhere – and I'm going to find her one day."

Marion raised both hands briefly to the heavens. "I should have known better than to try, I suppose," she said. "You're a man now but you're still young enough to believe you're immortal. You wait till you pass the watershed of forty – and your search *still* hasn't ended! You'll see your life being corroded away by it."

"Are you really giving up?" he asked in dismay. She was his one ally in all the world – the one person he never needed to explain himself to.

She drew out a chair. The legs grated fiercely over the quarry-tiled floor. She sat down heavily, saying, "There's elderflower cordial in that brown jug." Then, with a wan smile, "I suppose that now you're a professional man I should offer you something a little stronger?"

"Perish the thought," he replied as he took down two glasses and the jug.

"Listen, Hereward," she said. "I've sent her photograph to every boarding school in England, Scotland, Ireland, and Wales. It's cost a small fortune in postage. Edith's friends in the RIC – when they haven't been distracted by Sinn Feiners – have inquired at just about every workhouse and orphanage in Ireland. I've paid private investigators to watch C-B . . . they even went through his dustbin looking for old envelopes and letters and things around the time when school reports might fly. Nothing! Well – grounds for divorce three times over, but nothing important. And that cost *several* small fortunes, I can tell you. What more can I do, my dear? I never stop looking for her, everywhere I go. But what does she look like now? I can show you school photographs of little girls who came here in our first year, girls who are now sixteen and still with us. You wouldn't recognize them! Don't you see? It's already a hopeless quest. Next year it'll be impossible. And the year after that . . . pointless!"

"It'll never be pointless," he said quietly, trying to keep the shiver out of his voice.

"She'll be nineteen then. God alone knows what sort of education and upbringing she's . . ." Her lip trembled and she waved him away, as if she wished he'd just vanish. "My little girl!" she whispered. Then she looked at him with desperation in her eyes. "Don't you understand what it costs to say I'm giving up?"

He sniffed heavily and blinked to suppress the tears that threatened to ruin the day. They both sipped their cordial in silence. Then he said, "Aunt Maisie said you have some . . . I mean, there's been some development?"

"Oh," she replied flatly. "If you call locking the door a development. I've written to those cousins of Martin Woods's – or, rather, to her, because we found his name posted among the casualties of the Easter Rising. Her letter started it all, you remember."

"What did you write?" he asked in some alarm.

"The truth. Everything – right up to the point where C-B collected her from Castle Moore and she apparently vanished off the face of the earth."

He swallowed heavily and stared at her. "But you've laid yourself open to a criminal prosecution."

She nodded but said nothing, putting the onus back on him.

"And C-B, too." he said. An admiring light filled his gaze. "That's the idea, isn't it!"

Again she nodded and said nothing.

"My God! Talk about putting the lot on red or black!"

"It will force him to say, 'No, she's alive and well and staying at such-and-such a school.' That's my last hope now. But *I* can't start the investigation rolling. It has to come from her real parents."

He looked at her in surprise. "Her *real* parents?" he echoed. "D'you remember what you said to me once when I was foolish enough to call them that?"

She nodded glumly. "I know."

"I was lucky to get out with my scalp still on!"

"Well take that as a measure of how much I've changed."

He considered this amazing new development in silence awhile. Then he said, "You know what?"

"What?"

"Her real parents lost her almost *ten* years ago. Not five."

"And?"

"Well, you'll have to pray they've got *my* stamina – rather than *your* brand of defeatism."

46

The calendar said August but the sky, as it so often does in Ireland, paraded an autumnal cloudscape that ranged from watery gray through sepia to black. Salome and Sister Boniface, well wrapped in oilskins, set off for Simonstown immediately after Mass, without even waiting for breakfast. Salome wondered why, for they usually fortified themselves quite heartily before setting out; it saved stopping for lunch, Boniface said. However, she did not question the change in their routine.

It was not actually raining but the drive was mottled with puddles, great and small, and the birds were having a field day with the worms, caught between drowning and the winged nemesis out of the sky.

"Am I not to go back into classes at all?" Salome asked as the drive became swallowed up in the woodland.

Boniface shrugged. "You're so far ahead of the others, girl, you'd only torment Sister Philibert. Anyway, you're doing the prep, aren't you?"

"Ye-es." Her tone was doubtful.

"You are, surely?" the nun insisted.

"Oh yes, Sister. It isn't that. Only it's a month now since I attended school."

Boniface relaxed. "*I* know what it is! You're enjoying it, aren't you – helping me with this work."

"God, it's the bestest thing ever!" Salome gushed.

"And you think if it's fun, it has to be wicked, too. So that makes you feel guilty! The Divil has all the best tunes, eh?"

"Well," Salome offered hesitantly, "Sister Severinus says we're not put into this life to enjoy ourselves." They were passing the glade where she'd seen Severinus kissing the novice; she wondered would she tell Boniface? There was almost nothing she couldn't say to her by now. But maybe she'd better not. Perhaps this was one of the boundaries.

"I think God intends some people to be like that," Boniface replied tactfully. "Anyway, you'll have the whole summer holidays to catch up on any studies you feel you've missed."

"Will I not be helping you teach the cripples?"

The sister pulled the horse back to a slow walk while they went through a large puddle. "We must stop calling them cripples," she said. "It's not a nice word for them to hear, coming from us. We'll call them handicapped instead – like steeplechase runners. It suggests they're in with a sporting chance, don't you think?" She smiled at the girl and clucked the horse back to a brisk trot.

"But won't I?" Salome insisted.

"Of course you will! But you'll have to keep up with your studies, even for that."

Pius Coen heard them coming and had the gate already open. As they slowed down to pass the time of day with him, Boniface caught sight of Leo, the son, at an upstairs window. She asked if he was unwell but the father assured her he was grand – just a little off his food.

"He mopes all the time," she said to Salome when they

were out on the highway. "Was he always like that? I remember him as a bouncy, cheeky little thing."

"Only since those last weeks, Sister," she replied.

The nun bit her lip. "I wonder if he saw something – that night the IRA shot the informer."

"He wasn't there," Salome said unthinkingly.

The nun looked at her with some amusement. "You say that very confidently."

"Well . . . I mean . . ." the girl stammered. "I mean what I mean is how could he have been?"

Such hesitations were so uncharacteristic that the smile faded from the other's lips – and a hardness took its place as an almost unthinkable possibility began to form in her mind. "You were, though, weren't you?" she said at last. "Oh . . . Salome!"

The reins fell slack and the horse began to wander across the crown of the road. Salome gave them a twitch and put them back into the sister's hands. Should she try to bluff it out? Or confess the least possible crime?

"I couldn't sleep," she said. "I just went to the window, you see . . ."

But Boniface had a spirit of steel. Reason, with her, never did other than sit in judgment over her emotions. "Don't try to fob me off with any old tale now, my dear," she said in a kindly but firm tone. "It's much too important for that. It's much too important for anger, too. I promise not to get angry with you but you must tell me everything. Now start at the beginning and leave out nothing."

It was little enough to tell. Salome described how she had decided to run away and had got as far as the quad by the nuns' chapel when she saw this man hammering desperately at the door – crying, "Sanctuary! For the love of God, sanctuary!"

When she had told her own story to Sister Boniface – after being locked in the coal cellar last month – the nun had listened in almost complete silence; but now she interrupted often, asking how near was she, was it bright moonlight, could she see any of the nuns at the windows of the convent? And so on. And by this means she established that Salome, lost in the shadows, had a bright moonlit view of the entire incident – and so had the nuns from the convent. "I'm sure they saw me, Sister," she said. "I thought next day I'd be strapped in front of the whole school for sure."

Boniface was thoughtful after that – wondering just how long Reverend Mother had been storing up that offending sketchbook. If she had found it that very morning, it had certainly come at a most convenient moment to enable Salome to be punished but without bringing up the business of the informer and the IRA the previous night – and to be kept out of the way of the investigating constabulary all that day.

"Will I go on?" the girl asked. "About how they shot him?"

The sister shook her head. "I've heard enough. I know how they shot him. And Godric and Lioba are still reliving their moment of glory – when they cleaned the mess off the chapel wall."

"Where is he buried, I wonder?"

"Why?"

"Someone should say a prayer over him."

It worried Boniface that Salome was so cool about the whole business. A girl of her age who had witnessed a man pleading for his life, only to have the executioner stick a pistol in his mouth and blow out his brains, ought to be more distressed than this. She could not imagine what emotional tempering must have gone into her to make her able to remain so calm. To have said nothing about it for a whole month was bad enough; but to have given no indication, either by word of mouth or by her behaviour, that anything of the sort had happened was dreadful. One read of little children – in the Balkans or parts of Russia during the Great War – who had been so numbed by horrors that nothing could distress them now. But what could have happened to Salome to make her respond so collectedly?

"He'd not have been buried in *our* cemetery," Salome said. "Not even with the Magdalens and lay sisters."

The nun winced.

"What's wrong?" the girl asked.

"Your attitude, young lady." Boniface was glad to be back on familiar ground. "Yes – young *lady*. You are a young lady, aren't you. A snob, miss – that's what you are."

"Why?" Salome was stung into protest. "You don't bury the Magdalens like the nuns, all separate and with names."

"Oh, I know – we're snobs, too. Or some of us, but it won't always be like that. Listen – there are some things we do that are part of God's ordinance; and they will never change. And there are other things we do that are part of . . . I don't know – just the way we are today. And they *will* change – believe you me! They'd better!"

"Like?"

"Like having lay sisters at all. They're just glorified servants recruited from the servant classes – and we're the ladies of the manor. We pick the flowers from the beds they weed! Well, that's got to go. Oh, don't start me now!" She waved away words Salome had not been going to say. After a silence she said, "The Tans buried him in Saint Saviour's churchyard but the people dug him up again and buried him . . . in unconsecrated ground."

"Where?"

"I'll show you. We pass it." She was still thinking furiously about what Salome had just confessed – now taking in the wider implications. With almost any other girl she'd have let well alone for a day or two, but with Salome some instinct told her the only thing to do was go in while the door stood open. That restless, questioning intellect would never 'leave well alone'. She drew a deep breath, framed herself to it, and said, "So! The brave and pious sisters of Bon Secours witness the murder of a man crying 'Sanctuary!' and not a word do they say!"

"He was a traitor," Salome protested. "He betrayed Ireland to the English."

Boniface looked at her in amazement. "So that makes it all right, does it?" Her eyes narrowed. "Or do you have a more personal grudge against the English?"

Salome grinned like a child who's been found out. "I did until that night – or the next night, rather, when you came."

The nun made a mock-severe frown and said, "I warn you, I'm impervious to flattery."

"But it's the plain truth, Sister."

"Is this your way of answering the question I put to you that night – when I said let reason sit in judgment on your feelings? You've kept me waiting a month, so I think it's high time you answered."

The girl drew breath to speak and, to judge by her smile, it was going to be a flippant answer; but then the smile faded, to be replaced by an awkward hesitancy. "There's just one thing," she said.

"Yes? Go on?"

"It's why I said nothing, then or since."

"You mean it's something that occurred to you then – and you've been mulling it over ever since? Just like you witnessed the murder of the informer?"

Salome shook her head. "It has nothing to do with that. Except it may be in the same class as the nuns all keeping silent. You won't be angry with me now? Promise?"

"So it's to do with me?"

Salome nodded gravely.

They came to a halt at a crossroads. Boniface nudged Salome and pointed her whip at a recently turned patch of bare earth in one of the angles.

Salome crossed herself. It was the first time the nun had seen her do such a thing, for she aggressively avoided it at

Mass each morning. She passed no comment though.

When they set off again she said, "I promise I'll not be angry."

Salome licked her lips, still nervous. "It's just this. You said Uncle C-B told you my story . . ."

"The barest outline compared with the details you filled out."

"But he told you Aunt Marion kidnapped me, legally speaking, anyway? That didn't come as a surprise to you?"

"No. And if you remember, it was I who pointed that out to you."

"Just so, Sister. It was you gave me the idea – when you said that if you confirmed my story to Reverend Mother, she'd have no choice but to call in the police and treat it as a kidnapping."

Boniface stirred uneasily; she already had more than half a notion as to what was coming next. But she let Salome put it in words: "You said it would be *her* moral duty. The thing I don't see is why wasn't it *your* moral duty as well, all these years?"

The nun said nothing for a long while.

When Salome could bear the silence no longer she said, "You see, the moment Uncle C-B told you, you ought to have . . ."

"I know!" the other said fiercely. "The wound is deep enough, Salome. There's no need to rub in the salt."

Salome touched her on the arm. It was the first slight gesture of intimacy she had ever volunteered; Boniface did nothing to hinder it. "It should be no surprise to you," she said in a broken, dispirited voice, "to learn that we are all human, all frail. We say it blithely enough at every office of the day!"

"But I'm glad you said nothing . . . did nothing," the girl began to assure her.

"Oh, don't go giving me absolution before you've heard the sins!"

"Honestly, there's no need . . ." She was hot with embarrassment now.

"There is a need!" the nun insisted. "There *is* a need. This sin against the Holy Ghost was also a sin against you. You have a right to understand – and I have a need to confess. Don't you ever feel a need to confess? Forgive me, Father, for I have sinned?"

"No," Salome said simply.

Boniface stared at her in surprise, and then broke into a feeble smile. "No. After this day I can believe that! Well, *I* have a need to confess, so you'll please indulge me. I said nothing because I saw a greater good coming out of the evil. I saw a Catholic soul being saved from the Protestant heresy. I saw *that* as God's will – beside which nothing else matters. Oh yes! I really thought like that in those days!"

The implication surprised Salome. "But not now?"

The other shook her head.

"What changed your mind, Sister?"

"Rome," she replied simply.

"And what d'you believe now?"

"In your case? Why d'you think I left the choice entirely to you? And in general? I believe that evil done for the greater good is still evil. The greater good is not served by it. It is tarnished. We must do what is right and good, without fear of the consequences."

"And what if all the consequences are evil?"

"We must leave them in the hands of God. After all, an evil act may have good consequences, too. Like the way they kidnapped you and the way Mister Culham-Browne has kept you virtual prisoner here – it's sharpened your wits beyond your years and given you an education second to none."

"And put me where I may help you and the cripples." Salome touched her arm briefly again. She had enjoyed the contact last time; this time she found it thrilling; she thought perhaps she was falling in love with Sister Boniface just a little.

The nun smiled at her and said, "You'll do, colleen! One day we'll be allowed to understand it all, no doubt. In the meantime . . ." She shook the reins to make the horse trot smartly through the town.

But instead of going to the house in Fane Mall, where the builders were working, she turned left beyond Westmoreland Square and went down the back lane to the workhouse. "I meant to go about this another way," she said enigmatically. "But now I think this is right. And so is the time."

One of the servants came out and took the horse, leading him round to the stables. He said you'd think it was October, which prompted Boniface to call after him, saying he was to throw a blanket over the beast. Then, grim of face, she took Salome by the hand and led her into the building.

The scenes that now passed before her eyes were such as she'd never forget. The stench, which was quite overpowering, was first to strike – the vapour from filthy rags in the laundry, the steam off boiling cabbage and other vegetables that could not be offered for sale in the town, fresh urine, ammonia off old urine, uncleared night soil, the acetone reek of rodents . . . all were distilled into one squalid essence: the fragrance of despair. The day was cool enough but the rooms, which nun and girl traversed at a bewildering speed, were colder still, as if warmth of any kind were fearful of trespass there. A steely daylight struggled through windows iron-barred against all hope and grimed beyond all normal cleansing. In one room two men lay dying, watched over by a skeletal woman with just enough strength to share a pipe between the three of them; the clouded fumes hung upon the grieving air, scarcely more substantial than the wraiths who breathed it out. At the beginning of this walk through purgatory Salome had resented Sister Boniface's proprietary clutch; now she clung to the nun as if for her very life.

Up endless flights of stairs they went and along bare-boarded corridors. In one, a gaggle of young women pressed themselves against an iron grille that spanned from wall to wall and floor to ceiling. Almost all had babies at their breast or on their hips. Eight feet farther along the same corridor, a second grille held back a crowd of men – their husbands, mostly. They were shouting at one another – recriminations, advice, fragments of unworkable plans, cries of baffled rage and love. And still the nun plucked her onward, down yet more echoing, cheerless passages, until at last they came to a door marked, ASYLUM. A handwritten card told people who had no business there to keep out.

Boniface hesitated at last; Salome wondered if the handwritten notice were new and did it apply to them. But the woman was retrieving an old memory.

"D'you remember dear Sister Ladislas?" she asked.

Salome smiled as the kindly old face popped up in her mind's eye. "Yes!"

"She used to work here – fifty years ago. Oh yes – the Bon Secours Sisters used to work in places like this – we weren't always as high and mighty as we are now."

Salome had a sudden intuition. "Is that why you're starting this school?"

"*I'm* not starting it," she replied nervously. "I've been *sent* to start it. It's an order from Rome."

The girl grinned. "It's your idea, though, isn't it? I'll bet it is."

Boniface compressed her lips against a smile. "You may think what you please," she went on. "I have my orders. Anyway, what I was going to say was that Sister Ladislas told me they used to charge people money to go where we're now going. Yes! It used to be considered a pleasant recreation on a Sunday afternoon – to come down here and gawp at the loonies. Just remember that. No matter what you think – we *have* progressed."

Later Salome was to realize how wise Boniface had been to issue that reminder, for the horrors she had witnessed so far were as nothing to the horrors that lay ahead. The wretchedness, the squalor, the utter hopelessness that attended the able-bodied in the main part of the workhouse were here compounded by mental and physical afflictions that beggared all belief. One child she saw, a little boy no more than eight, had a head the size of a prize-winning pumpkin. A girl around her own age had no arms, and her face looked as if it had passed through a colander. Another, beautiful in her features, had her head in a kind of cage and saw nothing but flickering shadows. A boy of about ten, unblemished, stood on one foot against a wall – an attitude he had adopted at every free moment for the past two years. Another youth . . . but why go on? The mass was more piteous still than any individual. They drooled. They shouted words in nobody's dictionary. They laughed at nothing, cried at nothing, smiled at the empty air. They whimpered to be helped and snarled when they were.

Salome kept waiting to be taken through this antechamber of horrors – to meet the children whom the new school was intended to help. And then at last it dawned on her and the flesh crawled, all down her spine – these *were* those pupils-to-be!

Boniface waited until she saw the penny drop. Then she leaned forward and asked, in a quiet, unchallenging tone, "Now d'you understand?"

Salome did not understand. Here was nothing – nothing she would ever be able to understand. How could a loving God permit such suffering to exist? But she nodded and smiled at her questioner.

And again Boniface said to her, "Do you understand?"

Behind her, somewhere, a cripple laughed – which Salome did not understand. But she smiled as before and nodded with even greater vigour.

And yet again the sister asked her, "Do you understand?"

And then she understood – or, at least, she caught the first intimations of things that might one day be clear. One fact had already struck her. Never again would she feel despair; never again would she think of herself as hard done by; never again would she grumble at her lot – or not without immediately recalling in shame what she had witnessed here today.

And this time, when Boniface saw that her smile was genuine and the nod wholehearted, she let the question lie. "Now we can go and eat some breakfast," she said. "I was afraid you might not keep it down."

47

When Georgina appeared at Suidhoek early one September morning, Debbie said, "It's Monday surely?" And Georgina, slightly awkward in her company, as always, replied, "Yes, but there's something that can't wait."

Debbie was intrigued. She was quite certain that the 'little fling' between Finbar and the woman who was still, for a few more weeks, anyway, their employer, had ended years ago. In any case, she chiefly blamed herself for that little episode. All that nonsense about taking the veil! Of course, they had never spoken about it, not face to face; all their communication had been through Finbar. But it *was* over; a woman could tell things like that.

Apart from which, there were all those stories about Georgina that filtered out from the city. The founder and owner of the Gay Widow nightclub, with its notorious 'jass' band, its cavalier attitude to the liquor laws, and those little parlours in the back where unmentionable things took place, surely had much bigger fish to fry than a simple farm manager who lived twenty miles out of town!

So what could be urgent enough to bring her out here on a Monday, which she always called her 'hangover day'?

"Can *I* help?" Debbie asked. "Come in and have a cup of coffee, anyway. I'll run up the flag – there's a good chance himself will see it. He's in the eastern section today."

Georgina hesitated. "I don't want to take him away from anything important. You don't know exactly where, I suppose?"

"I do, but I couldn't describe it to you. You know how alike one bit of bush is to another." She stepped aside and wafted an inviting hand indoors. "*Daar is kaffie in die kan.*"

A somewhat reluctant Georgina accepted the invitation. Whatever it was, it couldn't be desperately urgent, Debbie surmised, otherwise she'd have asked her to saddle up a couple of horses and lead her to the place.

Unless it was some business Georgina didn't want her, Debbie, to know about!

"*Can* I help?" She repeated her question as soon as she had told the girl to bring the coffee.

"Er . . . no . . . thanks all the same. Just some tedious business with the bank. They claim to have discovered an error in our favour, made last year but only now detected. I just wanted to make sure it *is* an error."

And it couldn't wait until Wednesday? Debbie wondered.

The maid came with the coffee.

Georgina must have been thinking along similar lines. "They close the August books tomorrow, Tuesday, so I want it sorted out before then," she added.

Debbie thought it must have been an enormous error to bring her out here so early on a Monday morning, but she pressed the point no further. "Well, if it's that urgent," she said, "I could saddle up and fetch him. That would be quickest."

Georgina almost accepted the offer, but the relief that

began to show in her expression was swiftly effaced by some other realization. "No," she replied off-handedly. "Thanks all the same, my dear." She glanced out of the window. "Actually, it's such a spiffing day, perhaps I'll ride out myself and take a chance on finding him." She took out a packet of Orient Sobranies, black with gold tips, and offered one to Debbie, who, to her surprise, accepted. Her lighter, however, refused to light. She smiled ruefully and said, "The spirit is willing but the flash is weak." She took out a little book of matches, which said *Gay Widow* in gold on black, and soon the air was heavy with the tang of Turkish tobacco smoke. Debbie called back the maid to open the windows.

Georgina sipped the coffee, relished it, and sat back in greater ease than she had so far shown. She smiled an arch, naughty-girl smile at Debbie and said, "You wouldn't have a drop of gin to liven that up, I suppose?"

"Whiskey?" she offered. "It's Paddy's, Finbar's favourite tipple."

" 'Twill do," Georgina told her.

She sipped the laced coffee as if it were nectar. "Oh, the day looks better already," she said.

Debbie hesitated and then poured herself a little 'snifter', as Georgina liked to call it.

Her visitor, now in expansive mood, wagged a finger at her. "Careful! You'll have to confess that to Father O'Halloran."

"G'wan!" Debbie slammed the cork back in the flagon and raised her cup, adding, "*Sláinte!*"

"Or do you prefer young Father Myers? I must say I would." She almost added, *And the things I could tell you about that one!*

"Mock on! Mock on!" Debbie grinned. " 'Tis yourself will burn in Hell one day."

"Yes, I shan't need this lighter there! Still, I'm sure you'll put in a good word for me. The thing about being a

Protestant, you know, is that we're all destined for the Eternal Flames, anyway – according to your lot. So we may as well be hanged for a sheep as for a lamb."

"Or a whole flock?" Debbie suggested daringly.

"The more the merrier."

Debbie realized the woman was trying to work around to something – as if she wanted certain information without letting Debbie know she was extracting it. She probably only asked for the liquor so that she could get onto the subject of sin . . . and thus religion. She decided to make it easy for her. "Are you starting to be bothered by doubts, Mrs Delaroux?" she asked.

Georgina tilted her head and raised a hand as if she were about to deny it; then she had second thoughts. "I'm beginning to doubt – how can I put it – extremes. Extremes of piety, and extremes of . . . well, everyone knows my reputation nowadays – though I do little enough to deserve it, I may say. All you need do here is cut your hair short and dab on a bit of rouge and you're the original Scarlet Woman."

She took a further gulp of coffee and brightened. "Still, every whisper at the Mothers' Union Bridge Club is worth a guinea in the bank to me, so who am I to grumble?"

Debbie, still stepping briskly down the proffered path, replied, "And extremes of piety are no answer, either. Take it from one who knows!"

Georgina's smile was slightly bewildered – as of someone who has started out to explore a fearsome maze and is surprised to find herself at its centre after only three or four turns. "That is all over, is it?" she asked, anxious not to let the topic slip away.

"Utterly. We never yet spoke of it, I know, but . . ."

"Well . . . it was very personal . . . all very understandable, too."

"And I never yet said how grateful I was to *you*, Mrs Delaroux."

"To me?" Georgina's surprise was genuine – and tinged with alarm, too. They surely weren't going to discuss *that* after all these years?

"A hard time of it I gave poor Finbar – and yourself so patient with him then, when he neglected your business to tend my . . . my . . . well, it was a sort of illness, wasn't it?" She tapped her forehead.

"Hardly as bad as that." Georgina laughed awkwardly.

"It was every bit as bad as that. Me – a nun! I ask you. Me with children to rear – and a husband to mind. He could have strayed anywhere. Anywhere! And who'd have blamed him?"

Georgina was not altogether sure she liked this gloss on her affair with Finbar – that she had simply made herself available to him to prevent him from 'straying'. Men were always telling her that the girls in the little parlours behind the Gay Widow helped them not to 'stray'; so she was hardly pleased to be put in that same category! However, she was within an ace of the subject she most desperately needed to talk about so she did not demur. Instead, she decided it was time to grasp the bull by the horns. "You really are over it all now?" she asked, immediately adding, "Forgive me if you'd rather not discuss it . . ."

"No, I'm over it all, Mrs Delaroux. I accept what has happened. I accept I may never see my little girl again – and she's hardly a little girl now, in any case!"

"Sixteen or seventeen?" Georgina offered.

Debbie nodded. "I was two years in service at sixteen, so Lord alone knows where she is now. Good luck to her! We remember her in our prayers each day – and that's all we can do now."

"And you also accept that it was . . . the will of . . . you know."

To her surprise Debbie shrugged. "It may have been. Once I was more sure of that than I was of my own existence."

"But no longer?"

"No longer. It could have been just an accident. Why not? So many things are."

"Goodness! D'you know – I had no idea these were your feelings, Mrs McKenna."

She licked her lips uncertainly, Debbie noticed. She was turning something over in her mind.

"What does Father O'Halloran have to say to this change in tune? I shouldn't think he's too pleased."

"God but he's only delighted," Debbie replied. "Didn't I have that poor man by the ears, morning, noon, and night!"

Georgina finished her coffee, sipping at it more thoughtfully this time. "May I ask," she said hesitantly, "what happened? How did it change?"

"Sure 'twas like any bush fire," Debbie told her. " 'Twas like a bush fire in here." She tapped her breastbone. "And what happens to any bush fire in the end? Whether we beat at the flames or pour on water – or just leave them in peace – don't they all burn out in the end?"

Georgina smiled at this happy conclusion. Then she looked at her watch and said, "Good heavens! I must press on." She laughed. "I've been tipped off about a police raid this evening – my third this year. So I must be there to welcome them! Can you get the boy to saddle a horse while you tell me roughly where Mister McKenna is, today?"

"Listen," Debbie told her, "if it's about our offer to purchase the two farms, Mrs Delaroux, you may speak to me as freely as to him. There's no distinction between us as to . . ."

"No. I told you – it's to do with this bank oversight. He'll have to come into town with the papers before noon tomorrow. As to your purchase – well, you know I'm amicable enough. It's all with the lawyers now."

"We're as keen as you to secure Uncle Harry's and Aunt Queenie's rights."

"I know. But the lawyers have to consider every angle –

including the possibility that people do go off their rockers and start doing things quite out of character . . ."

"Ah, you mean like wanting to become nuns!"

Georgina laughed awkwardly. "Please! I wouldn't dream of including that in the same category."

"You're about the only one south of the equator who wouldn't, so! But still, I understand the delay, and 'tis all for the best, I'm sure." And she went on to describe, as near as she could, how her visitor might track down Finbar in the eastern section.

It proved a lot easier than the rather complicated sequence of minor landmarks Debbie had suggested, mainly because the wind was from the balmy north and the sound of the hammer and boring bar, which began some five minutes after she left Suidhoek, carried clearly through the spring air. Obviously Finbar had decided to start blasting some of the rock out there to make a raised bed for a galvanized-iron reservoir.

She reached him just before the first stick of dynamite was placed.

"That's a bit of luck," he commented, pulling a face. "I was going to fire without warning. I didn't think there was anyone within a mile."

Some of the galvanized sheets had been raised lean-to a thorn tree. They all took shelter behind it – Finbar, Georgina, and half a dozen Kaffirs – while he wound up the magneto and pushed down the plunger. The explosion was sharp and brief; she had the impression she could hear the rock cracking. It shattered into tiny fragments, several dozen of which rained down on the iron sheets. One of them made a small cut in the ear of one of the Kaffirs, who had not been far enough under.

The charge had sheared the rock neatly horizontal for about a quarter of its upper surface. "Three or four more should do it," Finbar said happily.

"Can you leave them to get on with the boring while we

have a little talk?" Georgina asked.

"Sure." As they strolled away he gave a little preparatory laugh. "You know Tim Maloney who runs Dodds's wool warehouse in PE? You know he has a glass eye? Whenever he leaves the boys to work unsupervised, he takes it out and leaves it on the balcony railing, just outside his office door. Watching over them, you see, while he slips out for a drink or to place a bet."

"I should think they'd soon tumble to that," she said as they strolled away from the site. "They're not fools, these town Kaffirs."

"Ah, well, the first time he did it, he hid in his office and kept a lookout with his one good eye. And of course one of the boys tested the glass eye – came up to it and stuck out his tongue . . . thumbed his nose at it – that sort of thing. Well, old Maloney slips down the fire escape and comes rushing in by the main door – miles away – sjambok in hand, and beats that Kaffir black and blue! He's never had any trouble since, the old fox. Anyway" – he rubbed his hands eagerly – "what can I do for you, today?"

He expected her to make some flirtatious remark, which was their way of handling ancient embarrassments, but she remained solemn as she drew Marion Culham-Browne's letter from her pocket and said, "You can read this and tell me what the hell we're going to do about it."

Finbar read it slowly, once he saw what it was all about. Then he read parts of it again.

"I jolly nearly didn't show it to you," Georgina admitted when he finally looked up.

"And here's half of me wishing you hadn't," he replied dourly, adding at once, "Not the better half of me, though." He closed his eyes and breathed out, as people do when a pain or a threat subsides. "Lord, but isn't it great to know *something* at last!"

"Yes – that she wasn't just dumped in some foundlings' home. Or worse."

"Salome with her own pony!" He laughed feebly. "And riding to hounds with the master himself. God, I'd have loved to see that!"

"Yes. Well – talking of your 'better half' – in the usual meaning of that phrase – she is the real problem here, of course."

He looked at her in sudden alarm. "You didn't . . ."

She gazed back with weary accusation. "As if I would! Credit me with a little savvy." As his eyes fell to the letter once again she added, "What d'you think she'd do if she were to read this news?"

" 'Tis hardly news, is it! Five years ago we could have walked into Cloonaghvogue Castle and claimed her back. But now?"

"You could put this into the hands of the police. This Culham-Browne woman is as good as confessing that she kidnapped Salome. God, when I think back to all we went through on the *Knysna* and all the torment of waiting, waiting, once we arrived . . . I could *kill* her! One anonymous letter care-of the Algoa Line is all it would have taken. 'Do not worry. I rescued Salome and took her home with me. She is safe and well and living in the lap of luxury. But I love her too much to give her up. Please try to understand. Will let you know her progress. Recently bereaved mother.' What would that have cost compared to the torment it would have spared us! She could have got it sent anonymously from London or anywhere."

"But sure she knows that herself. She as good as says it in the letter." He began hunting for the place.

"I know. That only makes it worse, don't you see! She knew damn well what agony you and Debbie must be in. She *knew*. And she did nothing! I'll tell you – I'll kill her if ever *I* see her." She reined in her anger. "Still – I didn't come here just to let off steam. The question is, what are we going to do about it?"

He raised a hand to his brow and massaged it with the

tips of his fingers, leaving clay smears in the perspiration there. "God I need to think."

"Oh, I didn't expect an answer now. I told Debbie we had a muddle at the bank." She explained her white lie in detail. "I said I wanted you to bring the papers in before noon tomorrow."

"And she believed it?"

"Completely." Georgina hesitated before continuing. "I stopped for a coffee, as a matter of fact, and a chat. And the conversation got around to . . ."

"Buying the farm?"

"Yes." Georgina took the easy way out. "She wondered why it was being delayed all this time. And I explained how lawyers always have to draw up an agreement so that, even if all the parties to it went stark staring mad, it would still hold. And she sort of grinned and said, 'You mean, if one of them wanted to go off and become a nun or something?' *She* said it, not me!"

"Just like that?" He didn't believe it.

"Not *just* like that. I'm summarizing. But, essentially, that was the way it came out. So, of course, I took the chance to talk about it – how she felt now – about Salome and all that. Not even hinting at . . . this letter, of course. Just in general. And I must say, she seemed pretty balanced about it all now. Accepting it for what it was – a ghastly accident, no more. D'you think that's all put-on?"

He shook his head. "No. I think she's come round to it at last. The trouble with *this* letter" – he handed it back to her as if it were corrupting – "is that it makes *me* – even me – feel like getting on the next boat back to the oul' country and finding out what this Culham-Browne bastard did with her."

"His wife seems quite convinced he's put her into some very posh Protestant girls' school in England."

"Yes, I saw."

"I mean, she must know the man. And if he's as sly and

as cunning as she says, it's a very reasonable theory. Because if he were ever caught out he could get all high and mighty and say his wife was spoiling the girl and he put her where she'd be beyond harm. I mean, no one could say an expensive boarding school was *depriving* Salome of anything, could they?"

Finbar nodded agreement. "Except she's tried every school in the register."

"The school might simply have agreed to treat all inquiries with a negative. He was paying the piper – he'd call the tune. We just don't know."

He mopped his brow on his rolled-up shirt sleeve. The streaks of clay became a general smear. She smelled the sweat off him as he raised his arm and had to quell an impulse to suggest another assignation. She'd never get over him, she knew that; what she didn't know – and was too fearful to find out – was how much, or how little he had got over her. She still saw a hunger in his eyes – but that was true of almost every man.

"That's my point," he said. "We *don't* know. And, as I said, it makes me want to get on the next ship and go and find out. If I showed a copy of this letter to *Mister* Culham-Browne, and threatened to take the original to the police, he'd cave in soon enough." A faraway look came into his eye. "It'd be so easy!"

She stuffed the paper away hastily in her breast pocket. "Perhaps I'd better get rid of it," she said, rolling her eyes upward. "I want to be rid of this farm as much as you want to buy it – now that Aunt Queenie has realized I'm never going to make a go of it. Can't have you going back to Europe!"

"That's not the point, though," he replied. "I might *feel* like doing it, but there's too much to hold me here." His eyes dwelled ambiguously in hers for a moment, making her shiver. "But what is there to hold Debbie?"

"Her husband?" she suggested feebly. "Her children?"

"Oh, she'd come back to us, all right. But what's to stop her visiting the oul' country? Sure she'd only be away six months!"

Their eyes met and they knew how impossible it would be; discreet little visits to the parlours behind the Gay Widow would never satisfy Finbar.

"We daren't take that risk," she said bleakly.

"There's your answer, then – tear the letter up and say no more." Then he had second thoughts. "No – keep it somewhere safe! In a few years' time we may be able to go back to Ireland – for a visit. It could come in handy then."

"I shall have to reply. This confession from Mrs Culham-Browne is simply begging for absolution."

He nodded at the truth of that. "What'll you tell her?"

Her level gaze met his. "I thought *you* might write the letter – when you come into PE tomorrow."

"Me!" The suggestion astonished him. "Why not just say we've lost touch? Tell her we were distressed for a bit but soon reconciled ourselves to the loss. Say you're sure we'd be delighted at all she did for the colleen. Say anything that'll ease her conscience."

But Georgina began shaking her head before he was even halfway through his suggestions.

"Why not?" he asked.

"Because you're thinking like a man – legalistically. Don't you understand what's going through this woman's mind? She's as good as confessed to a serious crime. Why? Why has she risked her all?"

"To spite her husband?" Finbar suggested.

"Exactly! She wants you to do precisely what you suggested just now – go and beard the lion in his den – threaten him with the police. Because if she has committed a crime, he's doubled it in spades! If she gets the sort of letter you suggest – from me – she'll only try again. She'll start looking for you through the church. She'll get Father O'Halloran's name out of some register and write a similar letter to him.

And then the fat will be in the fire!" She patted him on the arm. "There's only one thing for it, my lad – you have to write the sort of letter that will make it abundantly clear to her that you're entirely satisfied with what she did . . . that one brat more or less is neither here nor there to you and Debbie. You *and* Debbie – make that crystal clear. Make her understand she's flogging a dead horse if she thinks she can rely on you to mount a charge against her estranged husband."

For a while Finbar continued to hunt for other ways out but he knew in his heart she was right. He was going to have to do as she proposed. "Tomorrow at noon, then," he concluded glumly.

"Good," she said. "I've already written a rough draft, so it won't tax you much."

48

The risk Sister Boniface took in throwing Salome in at the deep end proved worth it – and in several ways. First, the girl never again had the temerity to complain about her own situation, or even to think of it in self-pitying terms; and second, no subsequent visit to the handicap school in Fane Mall could hold the same horrors for her as she had experienced in the workhouse infirmary on that grim grey August morning.

But the good it did her went even deeper.

Such a traumatic encounter exercised the same power over her developing character as a straight religious conversion would have done. The girl who had spent all her time and energy thinking up ways to subvert the prescribed order at Catherlough House now devoted the same ingenuity and that same energy to helping Bessie and Tom and

Carmel and Immaculata and John-Joe and Seamus and Mary.

Bessie, who was twelve, had a large head and great staring eyes, but she was good at most school subjects and especially good at sums.

Tom was around eight or nine; no one was quite sure. According to Boniface, he was something called 'autistic'. She had a book by Professor Bleuler, all about people like Tom, and she said he was their greatest challenge; Salome agreed. He was the one who just stood staring into space most of the day. The change from the workhouse to Fane Mall upset him, even though his life was materially better in every way.

Carmel, at sixteen, was blind and had the smallest bottom jaw you ever saw. None of her lower teeth fitted anywhere near the ones in the top jaw. She also had a harelip and a cleft palate, so it was hard to tell what she was saying. About a year ago her parents had left her standing on the workhouse steps with her ankle tied to the railings. They must have been quite well off, though – rich enough to possess a piano – because she could play beautifully by ear and Boniface said if they could get braille music she could go on to great things. When Salome looked doubtful at that, she laughed and said, "Well, dear, all my geese are swans – as you'll find. Even you."

Immaculata, also sixteen, had been born without legs and had one withered hand. She said it was because her daddy hit her mammy when she was expected; she never knew her daddy. Otherwise she was beautiful to look at and could paint little water colours as good as any artist. Boniface said her prospects were also very good. Or quite good. Or not as bad as you'd think.

John-Joe, who was fifteen, really had nothing wrong with him most of the time, except that he had seizures every now and then. One or two a week. First he'd scream, then he'd fall in a faint. He had to wear a helmet, like aeroplane pilots, only more padded and without the goggles. Apart from that, he was quiet, withdrawn, and rather studious. He was the only one who still saw his parents; they paid the Bon Secours Sisters something toward his keep.

Seamus was the oldest at seventeen but you wouldn't think so to look at him. He had some kind of wasting disease and his muscles were getting weaker by the month. He looked like a walking skeleton. He just sat in a corner with half a dozen sharp pencils and wrote stories all day – and smiled when anybody did him a kindness.

Mary had pulmonary stenosis, which meant that some bits of her heart were glued together and the blood had a hard job getting round the obstruction. She was only twelve but the doctors said she could live another sixty years if she just took it very easy and never exerted herself too much. And never married or had babies. Boniface said she'd only been in the infirmary a couple of weeks so nobody knew much about her; they'd have to find something sedentary that she'd be good at and could earn her living by.

And these were the people who had wrought such a startling transformation in the Bad Girl of the school.

Sister Porphyry, the Reverend Mother, was both pleased and irked. The rescue of a lost soul pleased her and she had no quarrel with the new Salome McKenna who was suddenly revealed; but it irked her that her old adversary and rival, Boniface, was instrumental in bringing it about – especially as her purpose in 'giving' Salome to the woman had been been quite to the contrary.

Also there was the worrying fact that Salome had witnessed the execution of the informer and had possibly seen the sisters looking on, doing nothing – and saying nothing afterwards. Obviously the girl had not mentioned it to Boniface, yet; or sparks would already have flown, she felt sure. Perhaps it was one of those things the educational press was full of these days – *repressions* – where people forgot awful things that had happened to them, just blotted them out of their minds, but whatever it was went on distorting their behaviour for ever. It even occurred to Sister Porphyry that Salome's behaviour had been so distorted before the traumatic night of the execution that her new tractability might be the distortion of a distortion! After all, if you bend something that's already bent, you stand a chance of making it straight again. All the same, she felt it would be prudent to mend a fence or two with the girl, and generally see which way the wind was blowing.

Salome's mind had not been idle, either. Since her discussion with Boniface on the day they visited the workhouse, she had been thinking over the consequences – and even more the potential consequences – of what she had witnessed that fateful night. Her conversation with the nun immediately after being let out of the coal cellar – when Boniface had pointed out that one's best course is often to let sleeping dogs lie – had as much to do with the new moderation in her behaviour as had the more obvious dedication of her time and spirit to the unfortunate youngsters in Fane Mall.

So when Sister Porphyry sent for her after school one day, she was mentally prepared for what was to follow, even though she could not guess what, in particular, it might be; that is, she was ready to be reasonable and accommodating on *any* subject the superior might have in mind.

By the same token she was not as surprised as she might earlier have been when the Reverend Mother's first action was to hold aloft the lewd, disgusting, obscene, etc. sketchbook with the words, "On looking into this business further, McKenna, I learn that my immediate reaction may have been a little hasty. It seems that these . . . these . . . er . . . these are copies of sketches by painters of impeccable virtue and sanctity . . . works commissioned by popes and cardinals, no less. They are not very *good* copies, which is why I was misled, of course, but copies they are – of sketches, as I say, by Raphael and Michelangelo and Titian, to name but three." She smiled, lowered the book, and put her head on one side. "Why did you not tell me, child?"

Salome lolled awkwardly, until she realized she must look like Bessie. "I didn't know that, Reverend Mother," she said.

"But surely . . .? I mean, when you copied them, didn't it say? Where did you copy them from, by the way?"

"It wasn't me who drew them, Reverend Mother. I mean it wasn't I."

The nun nodded her approval of the self-correction but the implications of the reply disquieted her. Was the girl going to accuse some other pupil of making the copies? "Who did them then?"

"I don't know, Reverend Mother. They were in the book when it was given me."

"Given by whom?"

"It was the day I . . ." Salome began; but a great weariness overcame her, born of the many times she had tried to tell this tale before – and had always been punished for it. "I forget, Reverend Mother," she said. "All I know is I was given the book when I was very young and the sketches were already in it."

"And you saw nothing . . . improper in them?"

"I was seven, Reverend Mother." Her eyes pleaded for them to move away from this dangerous ground.

"I see. Well, it shows a commendable purity of thought. However, not all our girls are so blessed, I fear. So – although you and I may know they are works of the most sublime spiritual nature – others may take a more profane view. I have therefore taken the precaution of removing the drawings." She passed the book, a sort of peace offering, across the desk. "As for the rest, it is a beautifully bound little sketchbook and excellent quality paper. I'm sure you can fill it with wholesome images, more in keeping with your own purity of thought, to celebrate the splendour of creation. 'To see all heaven in a grain of sand,' as Blake put it. 'And eternity in a flower!' you know."

Salome knew that Blake did not put it *quite* like that, but she was so keen to be over and done with this grisly interview that she merely simpered and said she'd try her best.

"And no more trying to run away?" Sister Porphyry suggested archly.

"Not after what happened me last time!" the girl replied with feeling.

"Ah!" The sister settled in her chair. "I wish you'd tell me about that, child. Do sit down, by the way. Would you like a cup of tea?" She rang her little silver bell without waiting for Salome to answer, and when one of the novices poked her head around the door, she said, "Tea, please!" without even loking at the woman. Reverend Mother could get tea in an instant, by day at least, for a little kettle was always kept on the simmer, over a methylated-spirit wick in the office-anteroom to her study. The novices called it 'the eternal flame'!

Salome sat down, having no other choice. She had had no direct discussion with Boniface on this matter but their conversation in general had prepared her to think it over. She could have pretended she entered the quadrangle – the site of the execution – after it was all over. Reverend Mother would know she was lying, because the nuns were watching the shooting and must have seen her there at the same time. So she wouldn't be deceiving the superior; she'd just be saying that that was her story and she'd stick to it, no matter what – which would please everybody all round.

However, she thought she saw a way in which she could stick to the truth, and still please them all. "There's little to tell, Reverend Mother," she said. "I thought I'd run away but I only got as far as the quadrangle, where I saw that man hammering at the chapel door and begging for sanctuary. And then the others shot him."

"All of them?"

She was looking for inconsistencies with the known facts, of course. Salome realized that. It was known that the informer had been killed by a single shot through the brain, from a pistol fired inside his mouth.

"Only one of them, Reverend Mother," she replied. She pointed at her own open mouth. "Like that."

"You *saw* it?" the nun asked, being both horrified at the thought and fascinated by the girl's calm demeanour.

Salome swallowed heavily and nodded. Three months ago she would have played the memory for a lot more sympathy but she had new standards of awfulness now.

"It must have happened very swiftly?" the superior suggested. Almost casually she added, "None of the *sisters* saw it happen. By the time they arrived in that corridor, where the windows overlook the quadrangle, as you know, all they saw was the IRA running off."

"It was over in a hack," Salome agreed.

The novice returned with the tea. When she had withdrawn again, the Reverend Mother continued – for she was not going to leave the point hanging vaguely in the air, "I'm surprised *you* didn't look to the sisters for help, child." She filled Salome's cup and passed it to her. "Especially at such a dreadful moment. Are you sure you didn't cry up to those windows at all?"

This was the point where Salome had prepared herself to switch from one truth to another. Speaking of a different night – a night on which she had simply tried to go for a moonlight walk (after reading the poem, *Slowly, silently now the moon / Walks the night in her silver shoen . . .*) – she said, "I looked up at the windows, Reverend Mother, but all I could see was the moon shining in them, the reflection, you know. And then I got scared someone might come and see me, so I turned tail and ran back to the dormitory." She gave an apologetic smile. "And I wasn't seen, was I!"

If she had been brought to this interview in order to rehearse a lie, she didn't see why she should be alone in it. In any case, hers was only lying-by-implication, which you could get off with three hundred indulgences. When Reverend Mother would be forced to say, "No, child, you weren't seen," she'd be lying-direct, which was bearing false witness (the Ninth Commandment), which was mortal, which meant a certain time in purgatory and *no* indulgences!

"No, child, you weren't seen," Reverend Mother said – and completely misinterpreted the girl's triumphant smile. She thought it a smile of victory – that she had 'got away' with a lie. Still, it suited her own purpose as superior of Catherlough House. Whatever the truth of the matter might be, Salome was now committed to a version in which she alone had witnessed the murder and not one of the nuns was implicated. Amen.

She sipped her tea with relish and said, "All's well that ends well, eh? Try to forget it. Try to put it right out of your mind. We live in horrifying times, but one day there'll be peace again."

"Will they ever exhume him, I wonder, and give him a decent Christian burial? That would surely be a sign of peace."

Sister Porphyry stared at the girl with something of her former suspicion: How new was the 'new' Salome, under the skin? Or had the leopard merely learned the trick of changing its spots? "You mean the informer?" she asked.

Salome nodded. "He's buried at the Kilfedder crossroads. We pass it every day, Reverend Mother, or every day I go to Fane Mall. I say a prayer for the repose of his soul."

"And Sister Boniface? Does she . . . well, of course, it's our duty to pray for *all* sinners. But what that man did to Ireland – his own country – was a wicked, grievous thing." She frowned, wondering how they had doubled back so swiftly to a topic she had hoped to put behind them. Then she forced herself to smile. "But enough of all that," she said. "Speaking of Fane Mall, tell me, how are you getting on there? It is rewarding work, is it not?"

"Oh yes, Reverend Mother! Though, when I first set eyes on them, I thought I'd die, but now . . ."

"Yes?" She encouraged Salome with her eyebrows.

Seeing that elderly face move in ways she had never seen it move before – animated, friendly, eager – Salome had a sudden glimpse of the girl that Sister Porphyry must once have been, before she was even called Porphyry, when she was still Agnes or Concepta or Bridget, still thinking about taking the veil, still open to all possibilities. She had never thought of the woman in that light before – indeed, had hardly ever thought of her as a woman, at all. Reverend Mother was just one of the world's many fixtures, a rock you had to navigate around. The realization that she had once been a free-floating vessel herself was rather frightening, for, if she was now a fixed point in life's navigable waters, her analogy was not so much a rock as a wreck! And the corollary – that any other free-floating vessel, Salome herself, for instance, might one day become a similar wreck – was also disturbing.

How could one avoid it? Keep on the move, something told her.

But she was now becoming sufficiently self-aware to realize that a girl who had begun life as the daughter of a small County Clare farmer, and had turned into the pampered child of Anglo-Irish landowners, only to become an orphaned convent girl, *would* reach such a comforting, self-confirming conclusion.

"It's hard to express, I'm sure," Sister Porphyry said when Salome's silence had persisted uncomfortably long.

"The thing about them is . . ." Salome stumbled over every other word, for the thought was shaping itself even as she spoke, and, uncharacteristically for her, she was speaking without preparation. She began again from another angle. "The thing about most *other* people, Reverend Mother – ordinary people, you know – is that it's hard to love them. The way the church says we should, I mean. And I thought it'd be easy to love the cripples." She smiled and her words gathered speed as the thing she was trying to say took firmer shape in her mind. "I thought they'd be only desperate for our love. Because most normal people don't really want to be loved too much, do they? We don't seem to, anyway, the way we behave most of the time. But the cripples are just the same as us. There's no difference. It's just as hard to love them as it is to love anybody else!"

Sister Porphyry was so bowled over by this rush of ideas she hardly knew what to reply. She threw the ball back into the girl's court, saying, "You seem almost to be glad it's so?"

"I'm glad it's like normal, Reverend Mother," Salome agreed. "Like normal *life*, you see? I thought the easy part would be to love them and the difficult part would be teaching them and tending to their special needs. But it's the other way about. Teaching them is easy – well . . . *fun*, anyway."

"Ah!" Sister Porphyry's feet were on familiar ground once more; this territory was called *Careers for Girls*. "You enjoy teaching, then? D'you think it's what you might like to do when you leave this college?"

Salome nodded and smiled shyly. "Of course," she added modestly, "I've an awful lot to learn yet, myself. But it's like a light ahead of me."

"Lead kindly light," Sister Porphyry murmured. She wondered whether to ask Salome about taking the veil as well but thought it a little premature, perhaps. Still, half a loaf being better than no bread, she said, "A lay teacher? We shall have six lay teachers here at the start of the Michaelmas Term, you know? That's more than we've ever had before."

Salome finished her cup of tea and declined a second.

She wanted to ask Sister Porphyry what she had done with the drawings she had removed but did not see any way to reopen that old topic. They chatted on in a desultory way for another ten minutes or so. Salome told her all about the handicapped children, the subjects they were good at and the things they couldn't master. Sister Porphyry was especially interested in Seamus and the stories he spent all day writing. She said she'd like to see one or two. Salome said they were all about smugglers and young people going on camping holidays and crooks getting their just deserts. Sister Porphyry said she'd certainly like to see one or two.

On her way back to the remove-girls' common room Salome was waylaid by Boniface, who wanted to know everything that had gone on between her special charge and the superior. Salome showed her the purified sketchbook and gave a word-for-word account of all that had taken place, as near as she could remember it. Boniface, who had been quite concerned at the beginning, became more and more relaxed as the account continued.

Salome explained how she had told two separate truths as if they had referred to the same occasion, but she did not explain how she had forced Reverend Mother into spending God alone knew how many thousand years in purgatory.

When the whole account was finished, Boniface, completely at ease again, looked at Salome rather intensely and said, "How grown-up do you feel now, young lady? D'you think you're ready for another big revelation about yourself?"

Salome drew a deep breath and said, "I'm sure!"

Boniface, a merry smile on her lips, looked swiftly all about them and said, "You're Bishop Harte's daughter!"

Salome frowned.

Boniface drew her into the alcove beside the main entrance, which was little used. There they could not be taken by surprise, and they could also pretend to be observing something or other through the window. "That's what they all believe here. D'you know why?"

Salome shook her head.

"You have no inkling?"

Again she shook her head.

Boniface seemed puzzled but continued with her tale. "Three years ago, in nineteen-and-eighteen, Sister Porphyry somehow acquired a copy of your birth certificate. She must have put a private agent onto it. Anyway, it's there, in your folder, in the locked filing cabinet in the bell room. Salome McKenna, born third of July, nineteen-and-six, to Finbar and Deborah McKenna of Cloghran Farm, Kiljordan, near Ennis, County Clare . . ."

"Kiljordan!" Salome repeated the name in a kind of wonder. How could she have forgotten it? All the times she'd heard the name Jordan and never once thought of Kiljordan! Mind you, she'd never thought of McKenna when they sang 'D'ye *ken* John Peel?' Polly de Souza, who was always making punning connections, was the one who pointed it out.

"Shh – keep your voice down!" Boniface warned her.

"But I told them my father was Finbar McKenna and my mother was Deborah. So they know I was telling the truth! And they've known it ever since nineteen-eighteen."

A sad-eyed Boniface shook her head. "They think your parents agreed to foster the priest's child."

All Salome's joy drained out of her. "But why?"

"Because . . . that parish priest was – or later became – Bishop Harte, Bishop of Kinnity and Coole, our own diocese. And he's a patron of this college! *Now* d'you see?"

Salome shrugged. She supposed she did sort of *half*-see it, but it was really beyond her; she still didn't understand how a bishop could have a daughter, but when she'd edged toward asking about that last time, the sister's response had been cool. It was obviously one of those things one never talked about.

Disappointed at her lack of animation, Boniface went on.

"Father McDaid pays your fees here – and a generous allowance for your keep in the hollyers and your clothing . . . and other extras. Everyone knows he's a poor Redemptorist without two pence of his own to rub together – therefore everyone knows he's acting for someone high-up in the church. The moment they saw you hail from the parish where our present bishop was once the PP . . . well – say no more! They realized you were telling the truth about being reared by the McKennas – but they also saw why they had to leave you behind when they emigrated to the Cape. Our dear bishop obviously takes his responsibilities seriously! And he has great hopes for you." Her anxious eyes scanned Salome's face for some response. "Or so, at least, they all believe."

The girl stared glumly out of the window for a long moment before she said, "Actually, Sister, why are you telling me all this?"

Boniface smiled ruefully. "One can't conceal anything from you for long! I don't think I really had any choice, my dear. You see – Bishop Harte is paying us a visit next month and a lot of eyes are going to be trained on him . . . and also on you."

49

Sister Boniface's disturbing revelations left Salome with plenty to think about and it was a long time before she fell asleep that night. The false history that the nuns had concocted down the years was so neat that Salome herself began to wonder whether it wasn't actually the truth. That scene on the quay at Queenstown – perhaps she had imagined it so often it had taken the place of . . . whatever had really happened there that afternoon. And what *did* really happen? How might it have been?

A representative of the bishop, her father, would have come to the dock and taken charge of her. She tried to cast her mind back to see if this imagined scene rang any bells in remembered reality. Fragments of potential history stirred her imagination – the black soutane, the ancient biretta, the bristly chin shaved at some godly hour that morning . . . the knowing smiles and handshakes . . .

She couldn't absolutely rule it out.

But then, would he have handed her over to some Protestant Anglo-Irish family to bring up?

Well, come to think of it, that would be a great disguise!

A parish priest might be piously concerned to have his daughter brought up a good Roman Catholic – especially in his own parish. But a bishop had more to lose. He might be worried that people would start to connect the child with him. Where better to hide her than in a family of the *other* faith! Not any old family, of course; his lordship's conscience still wouldn't allow that. It had to be one that would do her proud. A family like the Culham-Brownes. And they'd agree, of course, because of losing little Rachel so recently.

The hair stiffened on the back of her neck as she realized the whole thing could have been planned in advance – with Mammy and Daddy as part of it! They could have told Samson to play a game that would get her back on the quayside – then get Mr Punch to frighten her – then Aunt Marion would come along and 'rescue' her! That would explain why Aunt Marion had promised to write to the Cape and never did. And why no one ever came looking for her, though she still had her name – the only Salome McKenna in Ireland. And there were all her relations in Kiljordan. But they weren't her relations at all, of course – so no wonder Mammy and Daddy never wrote to them or sent them looking.

But what had gone wrong with that plan? Why had they

suddenly changed their minds and put her in here as an orphan?

Thinking back, she remembered it happened in the weeks after the Volunteers or the Sinn Feiners or someone – patriotic Irishmen, anyway – had burned Cloonaghvogue Castle. That's when the bishop must have seen it was never going to work. Or maybe he got a conscience about his daughter growing up a heretic? There must have been some meeting between them at which the Culham-Brownes had agreed to hand her back. And, of course, she'd go to a posh convent school like this, where he was patron . . . and of course, Father McDaid would pay the fees and things from Cloonaghvogue, so it would look as if Uncle C-B was really behind it.

That was why Aunt Marion had never come looking for her, either. And the Bellinghams must also have been told, or Hereward would surely have traced her here by now.

The only trouble with all this 'it could be' and 'that would explain why' was that it fitted much too neatly together. Even in her limited experience of life, nothing ever fitted quite that neatly unless some devious person had honed and polished it.

She decided she'd suspend all judgment on the matter until she'd seen this Bishop Harte for herself. He'd surely give something away – *if* there was anything in it at all.

50

Seamus Joyce sharpened his five pencils carefully, making sure every little shard went into the hearth. It was difficult because his arms weren't as strong as they used to be and he couldn't hold things very well. Sometimes when he looked at himself he thought he must be looking at someone else, until he remembered. His writing was deteriorating, which meant getting worse, too, which was why sharp pencils were important. Also his memory. He had to keep re-reading what he'd written because he'd forget it and think he was writing something he'd actually finished weeks ago.

He showed the pencils to Miss Salome because he himself couldn't see the points too clearly any more. She said he'd done it beautifully. *She* was beautiful. She was also nice, which didn't always go together. She was the nicest girl ever and he was in love with her. When he got better he'd marry and protect her. For the moment all he could do was put her in his stories.

She helped him to the window with one arm over her shoulder. It embarrassed him because the way she held his hand, the back of it grazed against the plump curve of her bosom. She didn't seem to notice but he did, and it made him blush. Of course, when they were man and wife, he'd be able to do that without blushing.

She eased him gently into the chair by the window bay and arranged his blanket and the cushions, the way he wouldn't get bedsores, which you could get even out of bed. He asked her would she like to read the story so far, and she said she already had – didn't he remember? She said she was going to try and find the name of someone who'd print it for him. Then he remembered: He'd get his name printed in *The Writers' and Artists' Yearbook* – or was that where the printer's name would be? He asked her had it happened yet and she said soon. Then she left him to go and try to get Silent Tom to speak.

He read the bit he'd written yesterday, it must have been yesterday:

> Then came their first casulty. Skin-the-Goat got a slug in his sholder and said a naughty word. Curley took over and Skin-the-Goat tryed to get to the tent where

Brady was waiting to treat woulds such as his. Susan saw him and went to help. Brady was angry and pulled out the pin of a hand-grenade and tossed it stright at the charging Tans and it went off with a lould bang. It killed 3 or 4 of them. Salome came out of the tent when she saw Seamus get a sort of flash in his face so she went to help him.

"I'm alright Salome. Go back to the tents and keep your pretty head down."

The next casulty was Caffrey himself. He was relod-ing his hand gun when there was a small explison outside the wall and two of the tree trunks fell on his leg and he yelled. "Let me out!"

Seamus read his story through twice, just to make sure it was really as good as it seemed the first time. It was. He had to put his fist to his heart to make it calm down. This was one of the most exciting stories he'd ever written! Salome made all the difference, of course. Ever since he'd started putting her into them, they'd come alive. He licked the tip of his pencil, even though it wasn't indelible, and continued: "He couldn't move an inch below his wast and to make him more angry still a slug nicked his ear . . ."

Before the end of the day he had finished the entire story. He read it through several times, just to keep his sense of wonder alive, and then handed it to Salome, hoping she'd read it overnight, all the way through, and give him her opinion in the morning. So far she'd only read it in bits, now and then during the day. Perhaps this one would be good enough to make a fair copy of it on Sister Boniface's typewriter and send it to *The Writers' and Artists' Yearbook*.

Salome was no longer the only girl at Catherlough House to help at Fane Mall, though she was the only fifth-former. Boniface had never explained the reasoning behind the new establishment to anyone – mainly because nuns did not need to have things explained to them; the whole point of being a nun was to obey without explanation. Many of them would not have liked the reason, anyway, which was to bring them down a peg or two.

Catherlough House had always been intended as a moderately superior school for young ladies, the daughters of rich Roman Catholic families, mainly Irish, with perhaps a sprinkling of English to season the mix. But the revolutionary upheavals in Europe at the end of the nineteenth century and the open warfare of the twentieth had made the place an attractive haven to a much wider – and wealthier – circle of parents. And so the school had gained a reputation as 'the Eton of Roman Catholic girls' schools' – which, in turn, had tempted some of the nuns into the sin of pride. The establishment of Fane Mall, where the sisters at Catherlough House would teach by rota, was intended as a corrective.

A simpler logic applied among the girls; the habit of charity was something to be encouraged. But the Fourth were too young, the Remove too rebellious, the Fifth and Sixth too busy with School and Higher Certificate exams, respectively – which left only the girls of the Lower Sixth. They, facing exams that were almost two years away, were prone to idleness and introspection. For them, attendance at Fane Mall was a compulsory alternative to games, and only first-team members were exempt.

Thus Salome, though only a fifth-former, was usually accompanied by two or three girls from the year ahead of her during her almost daily visits to the handicapped school. They, of course, resented her as 'Boney Face's pet' and did nothing to hide the fact. One of them, Ursula Rolle, saw Seamus pass his laboriously written manuscript to Salome and began teasing her about it on the way back to college – trying to make Boniface believe it was really a love letter.

But Boniface, who knew everything that was going on at

Fane Mall, usually before it even happened, told Salome to read it out as it would help to allay the tedium of the drive. (She added that the drive was not *inherently* tedious but some girls could make it seem so!)

Salome began to read aloud – her mind racing ahead to the point where her own name and Seamus's would be romantically linked. Should she change each occurrence as she came to it? No. Ursula, who was at her side, would surely notice and make great play with it. Better to brave it out and try to make them look petty-minded if they giggled. The other possibility would be to slight the story itself – emphasizing all the misspellings and making the most of each awkward sentence. But she remembered Seamus's big, limpid eyes in his skull-like face and just couldn't bring herself to do it. Indeed, she tidied up the tale as she went along.

The girls did giggle, of course, especially when 'Seamus and Salome' (so close in sound to 'Venus and Adonis'!) first began to pursue their chaste amours amid a hail of slugs and hand-grenades; but then a curious silence fell – a silence that, by the end of the tale, could only be described as *rapt*.

At first Salome supposed it was because they were overwhelmed by the strength and innocence of 'Seamus's' love for his 'Salome' – or, perhaps, by the love of the real Seamus for the real Salome, which vibrated through every line he wrote. But Boniface put her finger on it when, as the last Tan bit the dust and Salome comforted the dying Seamus in her arms, she said, "Well, girls – that's what I call a rattling good yarn, eh?" And the murmurs of agreement were more than dutiful.

As they dispersed to prep and supper, Boniface took Salome aside and said, "You made an excellent story of it, my dear. But how much was you and how much was in the original?"

"Sure all I did was not say the spellings the way he has them – and make proper sentences where he just runs things on without thinking about them."

"Well, if you could do the same to a neatly typed version of it, your idea of sending it off to a publisher isn't just an act of vain charity. D'you think it might be worth a try?"

Salome said she needed typing practice, anyway.

Boniface grinned at her and said, "You'll never utter a word that might raise your *own* hopes, will you!"

The girl pulled a rueful face but made no other reply.

That evening and the following day she hunted and pecked at Boniface's typewriter, transcribing *The Battle of Westmoreland Square* into a form suitable for publication – with double-spaced lines and broad margins, the way it said in the *Yearbook*. She reformed the spellings and tidied up the construction, just as when she had read it aloud. Then she typed a covering letter, which she got Seamus to sign in ink; and, finally, she showed Boniface the list of Irish publishers and asked her which one she should pick.

The sister was about to close her eyes and use a pin when one of the names caught her attention. "Send it there," she said with jovial grandeur. "They'll surely take it."

When Salome asked why, she went on, "Didn't you know my baptismal name? Margaret Nolan. Mind you, when I was a child 'the Nolan press' was the place where we tried to hide when my father took down the strap!"

51

Reverend Mother wrote a tactful letter to Father McDaid. She began by speaking of Salome's recent and most welcome reform, ascribing it all to the charitable work she was doing at Fane Mall. She then went on to say that, as Father McDaid probably knew, Bishop Michael Harte, a patron of the college, would be paying them a visit next month – on

Wednesday, 14th December, to be precise – and she wondered if Father McDaid, as Salome's sponsor at the college, would raise any objection to the girl's spending the entire day in Simonstown, away from Catherlough House.

At first the priest was completely bewildered by the question. If the Reverend Mother considered it appropriate for the girl to spend that day at Fane Mall, that was surely a matter for her to decide. Why should she care what he thought about it?

But, as the answer to that quite different question dawned on him, his confusion turned to amusement. He had often wondered what explanation the nuns might have devised for the fact that he, a poor curate, paid over such relatively large sums each year for the education and maintenance of an apparently orphaned girl. They must have known from the start that he was a mere agent for another, a person of real wealth. Indeed, he had dropped vague hints from time to time that it might be Mr Culham-Browne; hadn't the man himself been the one to bring her there in 1916? But how the good nuns had reached the conclusion that this shadowy 'person of wealth' (and thus Salome's true father) was the bishop of the diocese baffled him – naturally, for, though he knew Michael Harte had once been PP at Kiljordan, he knew nothing of Salome's connection with the place.

However, the more he thought about the implications of this error, the less amusing he found it. Suppose Sister Porphyry were to drop an arch hint or two during the bishop's visit! The man was nobody's fool; he was the youngest of that eminence in the entire Irish hierarchy and he hadn't achieved his rank by simply waiting for dead men's shoes. He'd sniff a rat as quick as any terrier. He might not say anything at the time but he'd start a few inquiries . . . and it wouldn't be long before the trail led to Cloonaghvogue.

So Father McDaid wrote a carefully worded reply,

stressing that what the college did with *any* pupil on that day was entirely a matter for the Reverend Mother; as far as he himself was concerned, Salome should be treated like any other pupil, neither singled out for the bishop's attention nor kept hidden from it.

Then he tore it up and wrote an even more carefully worded letter – which he also tore up.

His problem divided into two insoluble halves. One half was that *any* letter from him should allow the sisters to read between the lines and to understand that they were on no account to *mention* Salome McKenna to the bishop; the other was that such a letter would be filed away in some cabinet, where it might, with luck, moulder for ever; but it might also surface again one day and provoke demands for him to explain this astonishing warning. A dozen subtle theologians might devise a suitable document between them, but it would take another dozen at the other end to tease out the infallible interpretation of their words.

There was nothing for it – he would have to visit the Reverend Mother in person and convey his message without leaving a trace of it in any file. Or not in his own hand, at least. He replied accordingly and paid his visit on the last day of November, a fortnight before the bishop was due.

He made no bones about it from the beginning. He was answering her inquiry in person because 'certain things' could be stated verbally that would be hazardous to leave behind in written form.

Reverend Mother understood his meaning at once – and pointedly laid her pencil and notebook aside, though she was otherwise an assiduous recorder of minutes and memoranda of all occasions.

He then told her that the bishop, being fully aware of Salome McKenna's story, would not respond at all favourably to even the vaguest hint that it might be known to others.

Sister Porphyry said, "Quite." Twice.

"On the other hand," Father McDaid added, "a *total* silence about a pupil who was doing such outstanding work might also be construed in the wrong light. So, Reverend Mother, though I would never dream of suggesting any particular course of action to your good sisters, may I – in general – urge you to ask yourselves what you would do if Salome were any other girl in the school? And, whatever your answer might be in these or those circumstances, let it guide you in your treatment of her."

Sister Porphyry understood perfectly; their conversation was already forgotten. "And now, I suppose you'd like to see the girl herself, Father?" she concluded.

There was no particular reason why he should, of course. She was no more to him than she was to Hickson and O'Dowd, the solicitors who administered the small 'arm's-length' trust fund C-B had established for her. However, he supposed that even they, if they had occasion to visit the school, would not spurn such an offer – and he was, in any case, curious to see how the colleen was turning out.

So the dog cart, instead of taking him directly to Simonstown Station, carried him a short detour to Fane Mall.

A lay sister was polishing the first of two brass nameplates, on either side of the front door; the one to the right said SCHOOL FOR THE HANDICAPPED and the other, SISTERS OF BON SECOURS. Sitting on a bench beside the second plate was a good-looking girl in college uniform; she was hugging a boy of about ten tightly to her and murmuring something in his ear. From what Sister Porphyry had told the priest, he already had an inkling that this might be Salome herself; she certainly had the pale eyes and the dark hair he remembered. All the way up the path he watched her closely for any sign that she might recognize him, too.

"Pardon me?" He addressed the lay sister, who bobbed a curtsey. "I'm told I may find a Miss McKenna here?"

The girl was, indeed, Salome. She sprang to her feet and extended a hand toward him. "You're home in one,

Father," she said cheerily. "But you have the advantage of me." She kept her other arm around the boy's shoulder, holding him to her.

The visitor shook her hand, thinking he did not know many girls of her age who'd be so much at ease, socially. In fact, he knew none. "I'm Father McDaid," he said. "Do you not remember me?"

Her eyes narrowed. "The name rings a bell," she replied uncertainly. "Forgive me."

The boy looked up at her, his face seemingly contorted in pain. He gave out something like a snarl. She put a finger to his lips and said, in a warm but decidedly firm tone, "That's quite enough out of you!"

"You've grown wonderfully," the priest said. "Last time I saw you, you were as tall to Miss Kinchy as that lad is to you."

It was a moment before the name registered. Then, to his amazement, she stared at him in a kind of shock, which was swiftly tinged with fear. "Miss Kinchy at Cloonaghvogue," he added, thinking there must be a more recent Miss Kinchy in Salome's life to provoke such a response. "I'm the curate there."

Salome, still holding the boy to her side, turned from him and took a pace or two toward the door; she poked her head inside the lobby and called out, "Sister Boniface? Would you ever come outside?"

He stepped toward her, saying, "Now what's all this?"

But she spun round and faced him. "Sister Boniface will explain everything to you, Father."

The boy began to whimper. This time, instead of telling him off, she picked him up and hugged him to her, saying everything was all right and she'd finish her tale in a while.

"God be with you, Father," came the cry from the lobby. "I'm Sister Boniface."

"And with you, Sister." He stepped past Salome to shake the nun's hand. "Father McDaid, CC at Cloonaghvogue."

"Ah!" The nun's tone suggested that all was now plain to

her. "Let's take the air," she suggested – and then immediately contradicted herself. "No. Let's make young Tommy here comfortable, first. Come away in, do. You'll be wishful to see Salome's star pupil, I'm sure."

It wasn't a question and he had no choice but to follow her in. Salome, still hugging Tom against her, brought up the rear. "I'll tell you the rest of it when I tuck you up for the night," she promised him.

He began again to whimper, more fiercely than before. But he shut up at once when she told him any more of that and he'd get nothing.

He let himself be led off to his tea by one of the other girls.

"He understood you!" Boniface said in surprise.

"He understands every word we say," Salome replied. "It's just that there aren't many to which he feels a need to respond."

Boniface chuckled. "Well, *you'd* be the one to understand that!" she told her.

They went through to a room at the back, where Seamus was busy writing his next great epic, *Salome McKenna – a True Irish Heroine!*, part of which he proudly showed to Father McDaid. While the priest wondered what he might say that wouldn't sound too patronizing, Seamus scrabbled awkwardly in his satchel and eventually produced a piece of board on which he had mounted a postcard that had come the previous week. It was headed *The Nolan Press* and read:

> Thank you for your ms. 'The Battle of Westland Square' which we shall read with interest. If it should happen not to accord with our present publishing schema and you wish us to return it to you, please fwd. s.a.e. 4d.

The signature was of one Heather Nolan and the whole was

penned in the same fair hand. Seamus turned it over so that the priest could see it was written to him, personally; he had cut a portion out of the board so that the address showed through. And he had decorated all round the outside of the card with flowers, drawn entirely with pencil and compasses and coloured in seven different inks. The address began: '*Mr* Seamus Joyce, c/o Miss Salome McKenna . . .'

"C/o means *care of*, Father," he explained.

The priest, seeing a way out without making a direct comment on the drivel the youth had shown him, smiled broadly and said, "You're proud of that, eh? Being in *care* of Miss McKenna? And lucky you are that it's so, say I!" He smiled at Salome, being keen to bridge the gulf his earlier remark had inadvertently opened up between them.

"She's the apple of my eye," Seamus told him.

Boniface suggested they take advantage of what was left of the day's sunshine and go for a brief stroll up the Mall and back. They wandered toward the front door, leaving Seamus happily scribbling once more. "God be good to him," Father McDaid murmured as he turned for a final glance from the door.

"In what little time he has left here below," Boniface said in a near whisper when they were safely in the hall. She saw the shock of the words register in Salome's face and went on, "You didn't realize that? I've been wondering." She smiled briefly at the priest and then returned to Salome, adding, "It's as well you know, my dear."

"How . . . many . . ." Salome faltered.

The nun squeezed her shoulder, taking care not to outstay her welcome. "He won't see Christmas, I fear."

Salome swallowed heavily and sniffed away tears she was determined not to allow fall until she was alone that night – or as alone as any girl ever got at Catherlough House.

Boniface led the way outdoors. Father McDaid was surprised to find Salome following them but passed no open comment. Boniface spoke at once, as soon as they were out of earshot of the lay sister, who was just starting on the second brass plate. "Well, Father, we meet at long last!"

"Eh . . . ?" He fingered nervously behind his collar. "I was not aware . . ."

"This is in connection with the bishop's visit the week after next, I take it?" she persisted.

"Well . . ." he replied uncertainly.

"Don't worry. We don't believe that oul' tale. In fact, we know the truth of Salome's story. But there's no harm if Reverend Mother and the rest of them continue in their . . . well, continue in this tale they've concocted among themselves."

She was delighted at the speed with which he cottoned on to her meaning; he was, she felt, the sort of man she could do business with – and there was one bit of business she was very keen to do with him, once she'd got Salome safely back indoors. But first the man had to realize that the girl was no immediate threat to him, no matter what might happen when the bishop paid his visit.

"How *could* they!" he exploded. "I couldn't believe my eyes when I read between the lines of Sister Porphyry's letter. What in the name of God put *that* idea into their minds at all?"

"Salome's birth certificate," she replied.

He stopped in his tracks and stared at them both. "But she never had one," he objected.

"Everyone has a birth certificate, Father," she replied.

"Well, I know that, Sister! But, I mean . . . one was never forwarded."

"Precisely!" Boniface smiled. "We are an orderly order, the Bon Secours – as you ought to have realized. We do not like a mere ninety-nine-and-a-half per cent of our girls to have copies of their birth certificates in their folders in the bell room. So we sent for a copy for Salome, too."

He raised a fist to his brow and rolled his knuckles back

and forth over it. "Aiee!" he sighed. "So simple! So obvious!" He smiled wanly at her. "And I suppose something in it gives grounds for this extraordinary assumption?"

She nodded. "Tell him where you were born, Salome. The parish."

"Kiljordan, Father," she said.

"Ha!" Father McDaid raised both hands briefly level with his shoulders, as if conceding one round to God. Then he turned to Salome, saying, "I'm sorry my child – all this must pass far over your head. I hope so, anyway!" He smiled a benign and priestly smile.

But Salome stared solemnly, as if she were watching a mere ritual that required no response from her. Then, just when he was feeling reassured, she said, "I don't know *whose* child I am any more, Father. And that's the God's truth. For all I know, Reverend Mother may be right and it may be the bishop after all."

Father McDaid rounded on Boniface. "Be all the holy!" he exclaimed in a fury. "What sort of convent school is this – where an innocent colleen of sixteen can even *hear* such things spoken of a bishop, let alone believe they may be true!"

Boniface was every bit as surprised at Salome's outburst, though for quite a different reason – she thought that Salome found the notion merely ridiculous. But she kept her nerve in the face of the priest's anger; she was wonderful, Salome thought. She just said, "Never mind about that, Father McDaid. Just you ponder this: I doubt our convent would ever believe what *really* happened in the case of this young lady. And if we did, I know we wouldn't be party to detaining her here one minute longer."

Her level gaze, cold and pitiless, made it impossible for him either to brush aside the rebuke in her first remark or to ignore the threat in her second. He merely sniffed and said, in a more measured tone, "At least *your* conscience seems to bear it lightly enough, Sister."

"It tells me what to do for the best, Father – which is its trade, when all's said and done. But we'll come to that in a moment. Incidentally, I hope you understand now why the knowledge of the truth is confined to Salome and me? She enjoys it here as much as I enjoy having her here." Before he could reply, however, she turned to Salome and, searching her face eagerly, said, "Were you serious just now, my dear? Are you truly in a quandary about it all?"

The girl nodded.

Boniface turned back to the priest and said, "Very well, Father McDaid, you tell her. She'll believe it from you."

Had it not been for her earlier threat he might have refused. If he could arrange the world exactly as he would have it, Salome alone would believe the bishop was her true father; then she'd be no threat to him at all. However, Boniface's words, together with his fears of what folly Salome herself might commit during the bishop's visit, led him, reluctantly, to disabuse her of any such notion.

The sister watched Salome's face intently all the while the priest was speaking. She could see how disappointed the girl was to realize that she was just any old tenant-farmer's daughter from County Clare, after all. When the recital was over, she asked the priest if he'd kindly wait a moment as she had one more crow to pick with him. Meanwhile she took Salome by the arm and steered her back toward the house. "Shame on you!" she exclaimed as soon as they were alone. "To be so disappointed when you learn you're not some bishop's by-blow! D'you think God would cherish you the more if you were? What you've done here in Fane Mall is ten thousand times more seemly in His sight."

"I know, Sister," she admitted, adding with a rueful grin, "but to be honest with you, being a bishop's daughter is a lot more seemly in *my* sight."

"And how much sleep will it cost you – to learn you're no such thing?"

Salome laughed then. "None, I daresay."

"Away with you, then!" Boniface joined her laughter and gave her a push toward the house. "Go and finish telling Tommy his story."

She had, in any case, achieved her main purpose, which was to send the girl home in a goodish humour – and completely unaware that she, Boniface, was about to hold a conversation with the priest that would, in the fullness of time, affect the entire course of the young girl's life. *Cognitio ardor est* – well, she had knowledge that would light fires beneath this priest *and* his Anglo-Irish paymaster. And those fires would raise enough steam to carry Salome all the way through university, too.

52

Seamus Joyce's latest effusion, *Salome McKenna – a True Irish Heroine!*, ran to about thirty pages. Heather Nolan read no more than two of them before she decided to reject it; she continued to read to the end, however, because, in its own ghastly, uncommercial way, it was quite a gripping yarn. As she read each page she turned it face-down on her desk. Two pages were left when she heard her father returning from lunch. The sound of his tread upon the stair made her realize how many other unread (and probably uncommercial) manuscripts were still waiting to claim her attention. Guiltily she turned the two remaining pages of Seamus Joyce face-down, tidied up the stack, and slipped an elastic band around it. She was just reaching for the next when in walked . . .

"Hereward!" she exclaimed. "Your tread is just like my father's."

He grinned. "Is that good or bad?"

She dramatized her palpitating heart. "In the present instance, bad. You should whistle a little tune or something to warn me."

"Office boys whistle tunes," he said. "Are you ready to go?"

She thought of pointing out that that's all *he* was, really – except, of course, he was the son of the great Richard Bellingham and it was already clear he'd stop being an office boy soon enough.

"More or less," she replied. "I must wait for Daddy to get back – any moment now." She fiddled with the stack of unread manuscripts. "I should have got through more of these."

"I'll develop a portly publisher's wheeze," he suggested, and gave her a couple of stertorous gasps by way of demonstration.

"Don't!" she screamed. "That's even more like Daddy."

He lifted three or four envelopes from the top of the pile. "May I lighten your burden?" he asked.

"Take the lot!" she said with feeling.

"These'll do to be going on with. Don't you think it's exciting? I mean, *someone* must have been standing – just like me, here – in Murray's office when the first manuscript from a completely unknown Lord Byron stood in a pile like this. Think of it – to be the *first* person to recognize a poet of that stature! And" – his tone changed from rhapsody to censure – "someone in the old Browne and Nolan office must also have been sitting at a desk – just like yours – when the first manuscript from a completely unknown James Joyce turned up in the pile! Except that *he* turned it face-down!" He pointed to the pile of rejects on the far side of her. "Think of the horror of that!"

She laughed and reached for Seamus Joyce's manuscript. "It's funny you should mention *James* Joyce . . ."

The street door below opened and slammed. A decidedly portly wheeze accompanied the heavy tread upon the stair.

"Daddy!" she whispered in a panic and, grabbing the three or four unsolicited manuscripts that Hereward held in his hand, she plonked them on top of the one she had been about to show him. She cleared her throat and, raising her voice, said, "Well, just three or four, Mister Bellingham!" as she thrust another handful at him.

Really she had no idea why she behaved like this – as if her father were some kind of office martinet. Mostly to encourage some kind of respect for him among the rest of the staff, she supposed. They admired him already, of course, but it wasn't the sort of emotion that kept the nose to the grindstone. Also she did it because she was 'only a girl' . . . only playing at being in publishing until Mr Right came along. So she had to show more willing than anyone else.

Joe Nolan poked his nose, which was large and red, round the door. "Breaking the back of it, are we?" he inquired jovially. "Jaysus but it's cold outdoors today – there's a stepmother's breath on the wind, as they say."

"Only nine hundred and ninety-nine to go," Heather told him – with a martyr's breath on her voice. "Mister Bellingham is being a brick."

"Good, good," he said vaguely. "The subscription from Mudies' for *Touch of the Tarbrush* is four thousand. We're back on the baker's list. Your mother can start buying butcher's meat again soon!" He turned to continue waddling along the passage to his own office at the end.

"Actually, sir" – Hereward went to the doorway – "I don't know if you recall, but I did ask to leave a little early today? I'm invited to tea with my friends in Earlsfort Terrace." He hefted the manuscripts in his hand. "I thought if I took these home . . . ?"

"Of course, my boy!" His employer turned uncertainly and smiled at him. "When teatime comes . . ."

"It's half-past four now, sir."

Ponderous with disbelief the other fished out his pocket

watch, studied it, and exclaimed. "Jaysus! Off you go, then!"

Hereward cleared his throat again. "They asked me to bring Miss Nolan, too?"

Heather appeared in her doorway, already dressed for the street. She pushed Hereward out into the passage. "We were only waiting for you to get back, Daddy."

He wafted them away; there was a comfortable chaise longue in his office where he could lie down and work up an appetite for supper.

Heather took the manuscripts from Hereward and put them back on the pending pile. "We can come back and pick those up after," she said. "No sense in weighing ourselves down."

Outside in Dawson Street, when the cold blast hit them, she said, "Thank heavens it's just across the Green. Is it one of those Protestant, keep-'em-frozen schools? I hope not."

"Aunt Marion likes her creature comforts. I don't know about the school part but their domestic quarters are snug." He wondered if he should offer his arm, just for the warmth.

She took it anyway, saying, "D'you mind?"

"Not at all. I shall feel no end of a swell with *you* on my arm. It's a pity I don't know anyone in Dublin yet to flaunt you with a swagger."

Their footfall, and that of passers-by, sounded crisp and harsh on the frosty pavement; the breeze was slight but people sank their necks deeper into their collars and scurried for home, or cafés, or the warmth of the next shop on their round; they loomed out of the misty dark and vanished back into it. Trinity was invisible at the lower end of the street; the gaslights round Saint Stephen's Green at the other end were mere pinpricks in the gathering fog, which also muted the clatter of the trams.

"You know lots of people in Dublin," she told him. "All

those extraordinary people in your boarding house, these three spinsters in Earlsfort Terrace. And me."

He wanted to say something about not knowing her very well yet but hoping . . . et cetera, et cetera; he also wanted to point out that none of the ET ladies, as he called them for short, was strictly a spinster. One was widowed; one almost divorced; and one a fiancée. Or affianced. Could one also say divorcée? In America, probably. So, trapped between linguistic, social, and factual imperatives, he ended up saying nothing.

"Well, that fell flat on its face!" she remarked.

He laughed and then tried to explain the whole thing in a rush. She put an end to it by suggesting they should buy a bunch of roses for their hostess – whether widowed, divorced, or affianced. He said he'd never done such a thing before. She said that was why he should start now. He followed her suggestion, though he was unable to do the same with its logic.

They took advantage of a gap in the traffic to dash across to the Green. He cradled the roses in one arm and offered her the other. "Round the Green or through it?" he asked.

She chuckled. "Are you in a hurry, Miss, or shall we take the short cut through the woods!"

"Oh . . . nothing like that," he said awkwardly, turning to take the long way round, along the perimeter pavement.

"Why not?" She tugged him back, toward the dark – or feebly lighted – walks among the viburnums and laurels of the Green. "We *can* just use it as a short cut if we want."

They walked a short way in silence, until limestone pavement turned to gravel path. Then she burst out laughing. "Oh dear, Hereward, I suppose you think I'm awful!"

"Not really," he said, without much conviction.

"Well, I am," she went on. "But at least I'm not *serious* about being awful."

"What are you then?"

"Frivolous! You must study your antonyms if you want to get anywhere in publishing. I want to enjoy life. I can be serious in that office eight hours a day – or six out of the eight, anyway. But when I leave it, it's hi-diddly-dee, an antonymous life for me!" She skipped a couple of times, forcing him either to let go of her or pull her back, since he did not wish to skip around with the roses on his arm. He pulled her back.

She deliberately misinterpreted the gesture and pressed herself against him on the recoil. However, she didn't stay long enough for him to recover from his astonishment, much less make use of the opportunity. "It *is* short-cut weather!" she exclaimed by way of an excuse.

"Your father . . . ?" he began.

". . . has given me up long ago," she replied.

"No, I mean, when he talks like that – about being back on the baker's list and being able to afford red meat again, you know . . ."

"I know!"

"It's a joke, of course?"

"It's a serious joke. If you want *me* to be serious for a moment, Hereward, it's the sort of joke that sometimes cuts very near the bone. We were a thriving house in my grandfather's day. He's the one who built up the business. But he made the mistake of sending Daddy to Winchester, and . . ."

"I don't see why that was a mistake," Hereward objected.

"No? Just look at him!"

"Well, I presume he wasn't quite so . . . er, portly when he was . . ."

"I'm not talking about his figure, man. It's his attitude. They managed to teach him a love of literature – I grant that much – but a love of literature without a corresponding grasp of pounds-shillings-and-pence is a lethal combination in any publisher. And," she added, digging him heavily with her elbow, "in anyone who *aspires* to be a publisher, too!"

"I see what you mean by 'a serious joke', then," he commented.

They emerged at the farther corner of the Green, where the homegoing traffic was making the crossroads hazardous in all three outward directions. They waited until a tram forced its way through to Earlsfort Terrace and crossed in its wake.

"That's enough seriousness for one day," she said when they were back on the pavement. "Except that I'm serious about wanting a good time while it's there for the taking."

An army lorry trundled past them full of regulars, each conspicuously minding his own kitbag and rifle. They stared incuriously at the populace, who hardly bothered to stare back.

"Remember how the stomach used to sink at the sight of them?" Hereward commented. "I wonder when the last of them will go? D'you think this treaty-thing will hold?"

"Probably not," she replied cheerfully. "The other thing Winchester did for my father was to leave him with the feeling that Ireland isn't quite real. It's just a stage where brilliant, witty people can strut around, imitating real life."

"But he's Irish himself, surely?"

"I know. But he's not the only one with that taint."

Hereward wondered who else she might mean – including, perhaps, himself. He did not pursue it. "Remind me again about your three harpies," she said.

He complied eagerly. When he came to tell her about Marion he was on the point of mentioning Salome when something held him back. If Heather hadn't made that flirtatious offer back there on the Green, he probably would have done. However, as he had no particular desire to begin a flirtation with her, and as he was sure she'd renew the offer before long, he thought it best to say nothing. He did not trust himself to be casual about

Salome; indeed, he might even over-compensate for his feelings and be *too* casual. Either way a bright young busybody like Heather would be onto it like a travelling rat, and she'd tease him to death for ever after. All he said was that she'd lost a daughter before the Great War, when the little girl was only seven, and it was still a topic best avoided. Also Edith, the widow, had suffered a miscarriage when they first set up the school in Dublin – so the topic of children in general was probably best avoided.

The meeting went very well, and their high tea proved a most enjoyable meal. Later, when it was almost time to go, Heather became involved in an intense discussion with Marion on some of the finer points of English grammar – on which subject she, like everyone who has worked almost twelve whole *months* in publishing, felt herself to be a world-class expert. They were down to the use of commas in defining and non-defining relative clauses when Maisie asked Hereward if he would ever slip upstairs and have a go at opening a locked trunk that no one else had been able to manage.

The locked trunk proved a ruse, as he had suspected from the start. As soon as they were alone in her room Maisie handed him an envelope, saying, "Marion asked me to let you see this, just in case she didn't get the opportunity herself. It's a reply to her letter to Edith's cousin in the Cape – or cousin-in-law, if there is such a thing. You know who I mean, anyway."

It was, of course, the letter Finbar had written, almost at Georgina's dictation – making it quite clear that too much water had flowed under the bridge and that, as far as he and Salome's mother were concerned, it was best to let sleeping dogs lie after all this time.

"I suppose they've littered another dozen brats between them by now," he said harshly as he handed it back to Maisie.

Privately the three schoolmistresses had concluded that

the letter smacked of some hand other than the one that had written it. The words had been concocted in the brain; they had not risen from the heart. However, it made the fact abundantly clear that Marion could not hope for support from the McKennas in any action she might undertake to force C-B to reveal what had happened to Salome. And, since that was Marion's sole interest in the McKennas, she, for her part, intended to let the matter drop. For the same reason, Maisie mentioned nothing of these suspicions to Hereward.

Instead she clucked a few words of sympathy and, brightening, said, "So that's that, eh! On with the new! Talking of which – what an exceptionally pleasant young lady Miss Nolan is! Are you and she . . . er, 'doing a line', as our girls say? Or shouldn't I ask?"

Hereward laughed awkwardly. "I don't know."

Maisie remembered Rick telling her how, when he was a young man – he must have been around Hereward's age, come to think of it – he was desperately in love with a girl called Judith or Julia . . . something. His childhood sweetheart, he called her. Anyway, sweetheart or not, he lost her. Gwinnie and Letty came along – two very determined young women who saw in him exactly the man they were looking for and, quite simply, they overwhelmed him. From what little she, Maisie, had seen of Miss Heather Nolan today, she could easily believe that history was about to repeat itself. Another childhood sweetheart would be swamped out of existence by another determined young lady who knew exactly what she wanted. "What d'you mean, you don't know?" she asked. "Surely a man would have to know a thing like that – since the initiative lies with him. A woman can do nothing until he makes the first move, you know."

"Hah!" was all Hereward said to that – but it was all the answer Maisie needed.

"Have you mentioned Salome to her yet?" she continued.

"I hope you notice how tactful we all were at tea just now – though, naturally, it was the one question to which we were simply dying to know the answer."

He smiled wanly. "You're all such cynics, Maisie!"

"It comes from working exclusively among the female of the species, dear. We do need a dose of your masculine altruism from time to time."

"Ha ha! But you won't shake me – and nor will Miss Nolan. She can throw herself at me all she wants . . ."

"Is *that* what she's doing! Poor you!"

". . . but she won't deflect me. I shan't ever stop loving Salome. And I shan't give up looking for her until I've found her. So there!"

53

The Sisters of Bon Secours searched their hearts and decided that, in all conscience, they would in any case have placed Salome McKenna at Fane Mall on the day of Bishop Michael Harte's visit – regardless. No matter whose daughter she was. And for the whole day, too. After all, wouldn't Magella Crosbie be at her loom all day, weaving beautiful patterns of her own design; and wouldn't Teresa Wilson be at the potter's wheel; and wasn't it a fact that the choir hadn't attended a regular lesson for two days – good works all, and all for the sake of the good bishop's visit? Salome's devotion to the cripples was, they reasoned, in a similar class; so of course she'd pass the day attending to *her* particular good work. And if it should turn out that, at the end of his visit, what with so many set-piece demonstrations to entertain him, the bishop had no time to spare to cry in at Fane Mall . . . well, worse things happen at sea.

Boniface, who had been accidentally excluded from the

decision, approved of it, nonetheless, greatly to the sisters' surprise. But the sisters had forgotten – as she herself had not – that the principal architect of the scheme for helping the handicapped (after herself) was Monsignor Paul O'Hare, one of the bishop's closest advisers. She needed no second sight to be sure that, whatever other treats Bishop Harte might forgo among the sisters and young ladies of Catherlough House, a visit to Fane Mall would be indispensable to him.

Salome spent much of the morning with Seamus, discussing their forthcoming marriage – agreeing with all his plans and promising to be faithful unto death. Neither of them had a precise idea what 'being faithful' might mean, but it seemed a reasonable enough thing to promise – in his case because it filled him with a virtuous glow, and in hers because it kept him happy and he hadn't long to go, anyway. She no longer needed Boniface to tell her that. He now lived permanently between bed and a bath chair, for he could not even stand. He was just about able to hold a pencil and, if someone sharpened it for him, he could draw wiggly horizontal lines in which he, but no one else, could discern whole words and sentences. This deterioration had come about in less than two weeks, so Salome denied him nothing, crossed him in nothing, and resigned herself to the inevitable. Fortunately he was in no pain and could still remain cheerful.

As if to counterbalance this impending loss to the little community, Tommy, the withdrawn boy, was emerging from his shell in a most satisfying way. On the day before the bishop's visit he actually started a conversation with the lay sister who was cooking their breakfasts that day – the first time he had spoken to anyone without having Salome there to cajole him into it. He said, "I don't like mushrooms." True, he refused to add to this statement or to carry the conversation one word further, no matter how hard the sister pressed him. But, to those who had known him down the years, it was still a minor miracle that he had spoken at all.

Salome put on all her best linen, trimmed her cuticles, scoured her ears inside and out until they were sore, brushed her teeth twice, and covered three disfiguring pimples on her face with a mixture of naples yellow and chinese white powder paints, mixed with a little glycerin to stop the daubs from cracking when she smiled. And she was able to smile with more confidence after making these efforts. Then there was nothing to do but to keep the handicapped youngsters happy – and control her beating heart.

For, although she *knew* the man wasn't her father, there was a strange sort of what-if possibility still hovering around the notion – just as there was with Seamus's absurd dreams of marriage. She knew such a marriage was pure daydream, and yet marriage itself – the *state* of being married – was not. She couldn't explain it but the idea kept flitting through her mind. The man at the other end of her fantasy bargain, however, was just a shadowy figure. She wished it would turn into Hereward but she also knew the futility of relying on anyone or anything, outside herself, by now. Even Boniface would disappear one day. The Bon Secours would send her onward, somewhere else, and she'd be under discipline to go. And then all the love and warmth between them would have to be packed away, just like her love for Mammy and Daddy, and Aunt Marion and Miss Morrell, and Hereward and Henny . . . and even Hannibal, her pony.

Shortly after breakfast the bishop's Armstrong Siddeley came nosing up the immacuately raked drive to the college. His purple cassock was like a shout of joy in the winter sunshine. The nuns fussed around him and made a lordly tour of his progress around the classrooms and dormitories. He was a youngish man, still in his forties, and his keen eye missed nothing. He also said little – which said much for the means by which he had reached such eminence so early.

He told Jeanne deLisle, winner of the Galileo Prize for Mathematics, that Christ was in every quadratic equation. Consuela O'Kelly, who made the best egg custard, learned that the bishop's mother had once nursed him back from death's door with that very dish and that he always gave it up, among other favourites, for Lent. And Fenella McKeon, who had gained the best marks for deportment the previous year, learned to her delight that people who walked upright with their heads held high spent less time in Purgatory than those who just slouched around and scuffed their heels.

He applauded the choir and asked for an encore, then another.

When he saw Teresa Wilson throwing a pot on her wheel, he told her he'd been foolish enough to try it once and had only made a hames of it; he said it gave him renewed respect for the potter's craft.

He threw the bobbin through a few shed changes at Magella Crosbie's loom and said that, though the actual process of weaving was simple, devising the pattern was a skill of the highest order. When he had gone Magella reversed the sheds and pulled the warp out again, muttering, "Simple, my foot!" And then, around mid-afternoon, he announced that he would pay a brief visit to Fane Mall. Reverend Mother and the sisters were thrown into consternation, but the bishop had whizzed round the show-pieces so quickly they had nothing left to detain him with. They suggested a further choral concert . . . a hockey match . . . an equestrian display, all of which could have been laid on at the drop of a hat. But to no avail. He left most of his entourage, including his chauffeur, at Catherlough House, in order to take command of the wheel himself, and he drove the monsignor and Sister Porphyry the few miles into town. He enjoyed driving and did it with such panache that Sister Porphyry was in a fair state by the time they arrived;

as Boniface, a student of art history among other things, put it later, after the drive back to the school: "The bishop is obviously a follower of Hogarth, who taught that a *straight* line cannot possibly be beautiful."

The brief drive seemed to change him, too. The avuncular cleric who had managed to be both cheerful and remote while touring Catherlough House – descending from a great height, as it were, to try his hand at this and that – was now replaced by a man much closer to his subject, keen to learn the nuts and bolts of the business. He was more critical, too, though not in the sense that he set out to find fault with what Boniface was doing. He wanted to know what she had found easy and what had been difficult or even impossible to achieve. He required a week-by-week summary of the previous four months. He asked if any of the present arrangements or procedures of the diocese had hindered the work – or proved helpful; and he would not be fobbed off with bland assurances. And all this was in Boniface's office, before he had seen a single room or talked to one of the handicapped youngsters. Porphyry, who had thought him a bit of a cypher during his tour of the college, changed her opinion entirely during the visit to Fane Mall.

Something of the benign uncle returned when they went out to tour the building and meet its residents. Salome was in the playroom with Tom, pushing him on a swing that hung on chains from a ceiling joist. They had only just got the hole plastered over again, that very morning, in a last-minute panic – so she was taking a chance that it had hardened enough by now. The alternative, to deny Tom his daily go on the swing, would have been far worse; every day had to follow its own set of unvarying rituals – he even resented the random changes in the weather.

Bishop Harte was a little surprised when the boy took no notice of him; the young lady helping him was as respectful as anyone could wish, but she, too, soon turned all her attention to the lad once more. The lad did nothing but stare into space – not even helping himself to swing by kicking his feet in rhythm.

"As far as we know," Boniface told him, "Tommy never spoke a word until a few weeks ago. We couldn't even be certain he understood what anyone said – though we now know he did." She bent forward and grinned at the lad, adding, "Didn't you, you scallywag!"

Tommy continued staring into space. But, when Boniface straightened up and turned again to the bishop, he murmured, "It's Wednesday."

"That's right!" Salome's tone was bright with encouragement. "And what's the date?"

But he wouldn't tell her that.

She smiled apologetically at the others and resumed her gentle pushing.

"And what has brought about this change?" the bishop asked.

Sister Porphyry answered: "This young lady, my lord."

"Salome McKenna," Boniface added, ignoring the Reverend Mother's panic-stricken stare.

"Salome!" The bishop seemed amused at the name. "One of the women at the foot of the Cross. I hope you take after *her*, Salome, and not the other one – the daughter of . . . d'you know? Who is Salome the daughter of?"

Porphyry looked in alarm at Boniface. The bishop was onto it at once but, of course, mistook its origin. "Do they not know their Bible, Reverend Mother?" he asked. "Surely?"

Salome answered while the superior was still gathering her wits. "She's not named in the New Testament, my lord – not the Salome who asked for the head of John the Baptist."

"They *do* know their Bible," he said approvingly. "To know what *isn't* in it is almost harder than remembering what is! And whose daughter was *that* Salome?" he asked.

"She was the daughter of Herod Philip, my lord, who was the son of Herod the Great by his third wife, Mariamme. And Mariamme was the daughter of Simon, the high priest. Salome's mother was Herodias, who divorced Herod Philip and married his brother, Herod Antipas . . ."

"Goodness!" The bishop raised both hands. "A genealogist, no less! You've taught her well!"

Porphyry's surprise showed they hadn't taught her at all – or not those particular facts.

The bishop added, "I could name you one man – who is now a brother bishop – who was asked that question in a viva (before his ordination, let me add): Who was the mother of Salome? And instead of 'Herodias' he answered, 'Herodotus'!"

They laughed dutifully, though only Salome among his female hearers could have said for certain who Herodotus was; ancient history was fast becoming her favourite subject.

Tommy began his curious howling whine and Salome gripped him fiercely by the wrist, saying, "Enough!" in a vehement whisper.

He stopped at once and resumed his staring into space. "He wants to own me," she told the others though her tone implied she was really speaking to the lad. "And he must learn that he can't."

"Good girl, yourself," the bishop told her. "Is he your only charge here, may I ask?"

She replied that she tried to be of help to them all.

"Pay no heed to her modesty, my lord," Boniface said. "She's brought Tom out of hell and she's turned Seamus Joyce into an author. Will we show you him?"

Salome tried to signal that she didn't think it would be such a good idea but they were already turning away and Boniface was explaining all about Seamus to their visitor. Salome half-crouched and stared Tommy straight in the eyes, saying, "Hark now – I *have* to go with them. I'll be back the minute they've left, I promise. You may come, too, or you may stay. But I'll be back." And then, without waiting for his response – which would probably be forthcoming, if at all, only after she had repeated herself many times – she raced after the bishop and his entourage.

They were already in the back room where Seamus was working that afternoon. The moment she entered it, she knew something was wrong. The bishop was standing above Seamus's chair, muttering some incantation. Reverend Mother was on her knees beside him. And Boniface was turned toward the door with an anguished look on her face. The moment she saw Salome she ran to her and clasped her tight.

As for Salome, an icy calm descended on her. "Seamus is dead," she said in a flat, numb tone.

"Yes." Boniface pushed hard down on her shoulders, forcing her to her knees. She knelt beside her and joined in the last rites, which the bishop was administering. Salome clasped her hands in prayer but remained silent.

When it was over she rose at once and crossed to where Seamus was lying face down on the table; she behaved precisely as she would have done if there had been no one else in the room. Even the bishop stood aside and watched her in silence.

She picked Seamus's pencil up from the floor and laid it with the others in the little coffinlike box in which he had kept them so lovingly. She put his eraser and penknife on top of them and closed the lid. She lifted his head and drew his penny exercise book out from underneath him. She removed the slip of paper on which he used to rest his palm so as not to smudge the writing and get pencil lead all over his hand – his wasted, almost skeletal hand. She folded the book and laid it at the centre of the table. She put the slip of paper upon it and then the pencil case on top of that. She performed all these actions with a ritual grace that held the others spellbound.

Then she touched Seamus's head – ran a gentle finger through the tight stubble of his hair, cropped short in case of nits. All that love he felt for her – all going cold inside there now. Cut short at its very height, the way love always was.

In despair she turned to the bishop and, slipping her arms around him, hugged him tight, crying in a loud, formless wail and weeping a flood into his fine purple cassock.

The bishop just stood there, hands raised in accidental benediction, horrified. And then he melted. Like the skins of an onion, his personalities, some actual, others merely potential, sloughed off him – dignified bishop, austere priest, example-setting superior, even, fleetingly, the sinful man he thought he had long since vanquished, the man who would relish the embrace of a nubile young girl, weeping her eyes out in his arms – all these melted away until at last there stood the elemental human, neither man nor woman but all that is immortal in both, a being of infinite sympathy. Then, with his fine silk cassock forgotten along with his dignity and gravitas, he hugged the girl to him and gave her grief its scope.

And when Tommy joined in, one arm around Salome, the other around the man in the coloured skirt, howling his eldritch howl but now with real tears to ease it, Michael Harte simply lifted one hand and let him in, too.

PART FOUR – 1924

The Name of the Mother

54

By the Christmas of 1924 the Gay Widow had been raided so many times that Georgina really ought to have been used to it. So everyone was surprised, especially Georgina herself, when she was struck down by a heart attack in the middle of one such raid. Fortunately it wasn't fatal, but it shocked the police, who called off *their* attack at once, put everything back where they found it, and even washed up the glasses. They also banked that night's takings the following day – and in her name, too. They had intended nothing more serious than the usual evening of mild harassment – to keep the books straight and the watch committee happy. All the while she remained in hospital someone from the station visited her every day, bringing flowers or chocolates and numerous messages of encouragement. Life in PE, they said, wouldn't be the same without her.

She bade the doctors and nurses goodbye after a fortnight, having made a complete recovery. But they said she needed another couple of weeks' convalescence before she could return to the nightclub; and even then she'd have to learn to take life easier and to delegate more. Aunt Queenie said she and Uncle Harry would look after her at Fountains, but Georgina knew that they really were rather elderly for that sort of thing. True, they had servants to do all the physical labour, but even so it would be a disruption and a worry to have her in the house after such a close shave with death. Anyway, Debbie put her foot down. She said it was out of the question for Georgina to stay anywhere other than Suidhoek. Martha and David had gone to stay with their relations at Graaf Rienet, so there'd be peace in the house. Georgina could ride over to Fountains each day, which would do her good, and her aunt and uncle could enjoy her company without feeling responsible for her day and night. In a week or so – on the twenty-first of December – it would be midsummer, something the weather was already anticipating. When she wasn't visiting Queenie and Harry she could bathe in the lagoon and tan in the sun to her heart's content. So, with some trepidation, Georgina yielded to these blandishments and moved in.

The arrangement worked surprisingly well. Finbar behaved himself and the fears Georgina had that Debbie knew what had happened between him and her began to recede, though they did not entirely evaporate. Christmas Day came and went. They all agreed how insane it was to be eating roast goose and ham and the flaming plum pudding in such a heatwave – but they gobbled it down nonetheless . . . and pulled crackers and put on funny hats and tried to eat the jelly before it melted, just as if the children were at home . . . and finally they sank into a pot-bellied stupor from which it took all of St Stephen's Day to revive.

A week later Georgina said she really must be getting back to work. The business would go to rack and ruin without her. Doc Harkness looked her over and said another week would do no harm – and anyway, from all he'd heard, business at the Gay Widow over the holiday had been as brisk as she could have wished for. The whole world was booming as never before, now that the great incubus of the war was off their backs; a one-eyed baboon could run the nightclub at a profit. Another week's rest would do no harm.

Debbie said she had to go into town anyway. The storehouse was low and there were all the sins of Christmas to confess. She offered Georgina a lift (she now drove a Model-T Ford) so that she could satisfy herself that all was well. But Georgina looked at the lagoon, looked at the clear, azure sky, looked at her almost-there suntan, thought of the sweltering city, the dusty, bumpy car ride . . . and said she was sure the Doc was right. She asked Debbie if she'd kindly go to her apartment, which occupied the entire floor above the Gay Widow, and bring a couple of her favourite books and a few items of clothing. She gave her the keys to her wardrobe, which she always kept locked.

About twenty minutes later, when Debbie must have been well beyond Uitsdorp, Georgina gave a loud cry of "No!"

Finbar, who was about to set off for a round of the fences, came running to her, thinking she must at least have been bitten by a tarantula, some of which were as big as kittens and had bites that could be very painful. He found her standing at the front door, beating her forehead with her fist.

"Be all the holy!" he exclaimed. "I thought you'd collapsed on us, woman."

She shook her head. "It's worse. It's far worse than that. It's the end."

"What? In the name of God!"

"My keys – I gave them to Debbie."

"I know. I saw you. What of it?"

"*All* my keys. I never thought! I should just have given her the wardrobe keys and my dressing-table ones."

"So what else is there? The keys to the bar? You're safe enough there. The safe itself? . . ." His voice trailed off.

She was pressing her forehead against the doorjamb, rolling it so hard it must surely hurt. "The keys to my bureau," she said at last.

"What'll she find there?" he asked scornfully. "Not that she'd dream of prying, mind – but what'll she find? That Lizzie Longlegs can earn forty pounds a night? So what? Anyway, like I say, she'd never pry."

Georgina stopped hurting herself and leaned disconsolately against the door, staring out through the flyscreen, screwing up her face against the pitiless sun beyond. "She will,

Finbar. She knows *something* happened between us. Don't ask me how – and I'm not blaming you, because it's just as likely to be something *I* said or did that gave us away. And don't ask me how I know, either. I just do." She turned her eyes upon him, quite calm again, and said, "She'll pry. She'll want to know for absolute certain-sure. She'll look for diaries . . . notes passed between us . . . anything."

The blood drained from his face, making his tan look gray. "You didn't keep a diary!" His tone was both shocked and accusing.

"Of course I didn't. But you know what I did keep – and it was at *your* suggestion. It'll give us a hold over this Culham-Browne lad, you said."

He closed his eyes and swayed. "Mother of God!" he whispered. Then further horrors assailed him: "And my reply to that woman – his wife – I suppose the draft you wrote for me is there, too?"

She could not bear to answer aloud. She simply nodded.

He rallied, but she could tell it was bluff and bluster. "Sure she'd never go prying at all. She's not that kind, I'll swear."

She smiled, as if he'd given her some hope; but made no direct reply.

Later, on his round of the fences, it occurred to him that Georgina's 'fatal slip' might not have been entirely accidental.

A little later still, he wondered why that possibility did not make him as angry as it surely ought to have done. Indeed, it did not make him angry at all.

55

Debbie lay on Georgina's bed and wondered how many assignations the gay widow herself had conducted there – just as she had often lain in her own bed at home, wondering if Finbar had ever brought her up there. She felt the pressure of men, unknown men, alien men, in this room as she felt them nowhere else; it was an antechamber to another life. Not a life beyond – for the life-beyond was ancient and familiar to her – but a life beside. A parallel. Parallel lines never meet.

Never was the vilest word in the language.

Never was the word that had come between her and Salome. She would be twenty now. Or nineteen? A moment of panic . . . twenty, of course. And why 'would be'? She *was* twenty. Married, no doubt. With a baby at her breast and another on the way – just like her mother at that same age: Samson at the breast and Salome on the way.

A daughter she'd never see – and now grandchildren she'd never see.

Never.

Where had all the tears gone?

She raised one arm above her, dangling the keys like a bunch of grapes. She had fingered them while waiting outside the confessional, like rosary beads. That's when it had struck her that she must be holding the keys to Georgina's entire life. This was the wardrobe key – she remembered Georgina saying it. And that's the dressing-table key for her face cream and nail polish and the comb with the bobbly bits halfway down each tooth. She only needed those two, really.

So what about the rest? Why hadn't she asked what the rest were for?

And why hadn't Georgina said, off her own bat, something like not to bother about them. She hadn't said a word. She'd just handed over the lot, oh-so-casual.

Was it some kind of complicity between them – Georgina and herself – that neither dared acknowledge, even in their own minds? Was Georgina saying, 'This tiptoeing around has gone on long enough. Take the keys. Ransack the place. Discover everything. Let's have it out in the open!'

With something of a shock Debbie realized *that* was the only thing keeping her back – the thought that she might be dancing to Georgina's tune; otherwise she'd have been through half the drawers and files by now.

And it *was* a shock. Before today she'd have been certain enough of her own virtue to swear nothing would ever make her pry into another's private papers and diaries. Now she was certain of nothing.

Nothing and never. Life was all noes and they were all closing in.

There was a laugh, a woman's, from the courtyard below – the infamous courtyard behind the club. That had been the first place she looked, of course – never having seen it before, except a million times in her imagination. Not surprisingly, it had been empty, the hour being two of the afternoon. She rose and went to the window again. The courtyard was empty still, the hour being but half-past two. How innocent it looked, silent and deserted under the savage sun – like a row of beach huts. The stone-terraced courtyard was where the beach should be, and the nightclub stood in for the ocean itself. People were jetsam, of course, but the tide wasn't in yet.

Beach huts fascinated Martha and David. Friends in town rented one at Humewood; no need for such things at Suidhoek, of course. Beach huts had bits of ordinary homes in them – shelves, cups, a stove of kinds, washing-up bowls, threadbare rugs, bamboo chairs and tables, and so forth. A stripped-down life was possible there, confined to the bare elements – that's what fascinated the children. It was life at a level that they could comprehend.

In a way, an adult way, it was the same with these . . . hoor huts, or whatever you'd call them.

The woman laughed again – more of a giggle this time. Debbie realized she had been looking in the wrong place. The woman was immediately beneath her, concealed by the canopy of a grapevine. Through chinks in the leaves she could see a swaying movement. Something pale. The giggle turned to a crooning, a formless song, provocative. Then it erupted into a giggle again, which ended this time in a little scream.

There was a sudden flurry, maddeningly invisible beneath the leaves. The scream turned into words. "No! No! You dare!" all spoken on a rising wave of laughter. A wood-slatted chair fell over. Something streaked diagonally away under the canopy and emerged beyond its fringe – a young Chinese girl, naked but for short white socks and tennis shoes. And bangles. A moment later a man ran after her, big, fat, and old; he, too, was naked, not even socks and boots. His fat trembled at every slap of his bare feet on the paving. The girl looked over her shoulder, gave a shriek of apparent delight – of unambiguous welcome, anyway – and slipped into one of the beach huts, wiggling her bottom very crudely.

It was too hot to close the blinds – and anyway, who would see them at that ungodly hour! Debbie saw it all. They remained standing because it was the only way to avoid heat stroke. The man was so fat the girl had to bend double and back herself onto him, wriggling her lithe little body under the overhang of his paunch. To Debbie, they ceased to resemble two human beings – which accounted for her lack of shock, her failure to experience the slightest horror.

She watched until she realized it was pointless. Then she turned away from the window, thinking that any woman tempted to that way of life should be brought up here and made to look on. All the same, it now felt much less sinful, in the universal scale of these things, for her to select one of Georgina's keys and see did it fit the bureau.

The key and the hole – it was like marriage – the very opposite of what was going on out there. Here only one would fit.

She found Marion's letter rather quickly, which no longer

surprised her. It was, as far as she could tell from a cursory glance, the only document of that age near the top of the heap. She was dancing to Georgina's tune, all right, but at least she knew it. She could see where the conga was leading, and she could step out of the line at any moment if its direction no longer suited her.

The contents of the letter, however, took her completely by surprise. Down the years she had – or so she supposed – imagined every possible fate that might have overtaken her little girl. Most brought a happy smile to her lips and let her drift off into a calm and contented sleep; some fetched her bolt upright in horror, crying "No, no no . . . !" with her eyes clenched tight and her palms sweating. A few were so absurd she indulged them as a kind of humorous byplay when more serious fantasies had exhausted her. But even in this latter category there had never been one that began: "So along comes this rich Protestant lady who's just lost a little girl of her own, who'd have been the same age as Salome if she'd lived – *exactly* the same age, in fact, because she was also born on the third of July . . ."

One can only accept things like that when real life serves them up; in a daydream, they're just too fantastical.

As she read on, her eyes filled with tears, mostly of happiness, because, if God so willed it that she *had* to leave Salome behind, she could not have wished for a better home – materially, anyway – than Cloonaghvogue Castle nor a kinder foster mother than this Marion Culham-Browne. Even the fact that they were Protestants did not distress her; that, too, must form part of God's inscrutable purpose – because if He wanted Salome brought up a Roman Catholic, He'd surely have put her on the *Knysna* with the rest of her family.

The role of Marion Culham-Browne worried her slightly, though. The woman was undoubtedly confessing to a kidnap. But then Debbie realized that, just as she herself was not to blame for leaving Salome behind – it being God's will – so Mrs Culham-Browne was not to blame for what she had done. You couldn't call it kidnapping because that, too, was the will of God.

The same unshakeable conviction sustained her through the distressing news, right at the end of the letter, that Salome had once again vanished without trace – at least as far as her adoptive mother could ascertain. Marion Culham-Browne might say it broke her heart, but then she was a woman of little faith – and even that faith was heresy. Debbie, for her part, just knew that God would not have allowed all this to happen simply in order to abandon Salome to her fate at the age of ten. She was still in His hands, and He had hidden her somewhere safe – somewhere just as good in its way as Cloonaghvogue Castle.

Salome with her own pony, riding to hounds with the master!

No, she mustn't let herself be led astray into those pleasing byways. She must concentrate on what to do next.

The letter was dated Sunday, 26 June, 1921. Written on the sabbath, see! God's day. God's work. He leaves these little clues around for those with eyes to see them. Three and a half years ago. Of course, Georgina had said nothing about it at the time. What time? It would have arrived around September that year, with spring turning to summer. What had happened in 1921 around September? They completed the fence at Suidhoek, right down to the cliffs. They built the shelter beside the lagoon, where they could get out of the sun on days like this. And water – the history of the McKennas' upward climb to prosperity was measured in gallons of water; 1921 was the year they brought water to the eastern section, when that Kaffir nearly got killed in the accident with the dynamite – Shadrak. The one who found Samson in the other dam, Samson's dam. "Shadrak got no luck with water, madam," he said when she dressed his wounds.

Then she remembered Georgina had driven out to

Suidhoek that day, not her usual day. Her hangover day. It began to come back to her. A story about the bank making an error . . . Finbar wanted urgently in PE . . . straighten it all out. My foot! That was all malarkey. *This* was why he had to be fetched into PE that time – to answer Marion Culham-Browne.

But what had they concocted between them? Why had nothing further happened in three and a half years?

With little hope of finding anything she began to scrabble through the heap of papers in the bureau. It was just possible that Georgina had kept a draft – or simply forgotten to throw it away. She was looking for something in Finbar's hand, which was why she missed it the first time; it had to be his hand because if Georgina had simply replied in her own right, she wouldn't have bothered to haul him into town.

Salome with her own governess!

She closed her eyes and shook her head angrily. Stick to the business, she told herself, there'd be time for all that gloating later.

She was just about to give up her search when she saw a sheet of paper that ended, *Yours sincerely*, *Finbar McKenna* – but in Georgina's hand!

Halfway through the first paragraph the significance of it dawned on her. Georgina had, indeed, replied in her own right, saying all the things *she* wished to get over; she had merely roped in Finbar to copy it out in his own hand. She had dictated it, right down to his very name at the end – she couldn't even trust him to do *that* for himself!

And what did she write in his hand? That Mr and Mrs McKenna were very grateful and relieved to know the truth after all these years. That they were sorry to hear Salome had become a pawn in the struggle between Mrs Culham-Browne and her husband (Finbar using phrases like 'a pawn in the struggle' – imagine!). But they felt sure Mr Culham-Browne was a man of honour and would not have harmed the girl. Circumstances on the farm – and in Ireland – prevented them from leaving it just at this moment but Mrs Culham-Browne may rest assured that as soon as it was propitious (*pro-pish-us* – would you hark at the man!) they would return to the old country and take up the search where she herself had drawn a blank.

She let out a hoot of laughter. "Lord love us, Finbar – but you never wrote a truer word!" she cried in exaltation. "The only difference between us is that *you* never thought the pro-pish-us moment would come. Well it's come *now*, so it has!"

For the next half-hour she sat at the bureau, making a fair copy of the two letters. It was rote work and her mind went on grinding away independently of what her eye and fingers were at.

When she had finished her copying, she knew exactly what she was going to do – not just next but for the rest of her life, probably.

She put the originals back in the bureau and locked it again. Then she picked up the telephone and asked the operator to get her the farm at Suidhoek. Violet, the half-Indian maid, answered. She told the girl the car had broken down and wouldn't be repaired until tomorrow, so she'd stay at the club and Mrs Delaroux and the master weren't to worry.

Then she took one of Georgina's cigarettes and went to the window to smoke it, something she had never done in all her life – or not straight out like that, without being offered one. It was, she felt, the first of many things she'd now start doing, never having done them before.

The fat old man was lying fast asleep on the divan, diagonally across it, as if he were afraid its middle would not bear his weight. He was naked but his thing was so shrivelled he could have been a fat old woman. The Chinese girl, dressed in a thin cotton slip, was standing in the open doorway, leaning her head against the jamb, smoking.

Inscrutable, they were supposed to be. It wasn't the word Debbie would have applied to her. Weary, sick-to-death, bored, dejected . . . there was a fiddler's notebook full before she'd even think of 'inscrutable'. She blew out a cloud of smoke, which the girl noticed; she looked up and waved, thinking it was Georgina up there. Debbie withdrew from the window before the girl could realize her mistake; she didn't want them coming up here to investigate. The manager fella knew she was here, of course, but they might not go to him first. She went back and lay down again on Georgina's bed, in the dents she had already made there.

She tried inhaling the smoke, the way Georgina did it, gasping inwards sharply and pulling down the corners of her mouth so fiercely that the strings in her neck stood out.

The whole world swam around her.

She'd give Georgina and Finbar until gone midnight. They'd be sure then.

Salome being friends with the children of Richard Bellingham, the great writer! It was certainly the will of God.

The brief transition from daylight to dark, with hardly any twilight in between, no longer surprised her. She fell asleep soon after. When she awoke it was nine o'clock. Still too early. She rose and took a shower; then she sat at the window and used the open vee of her blouse as a bellows to keep cool. She smoked more cigarettes and tapped her feet to the jass music from the club below. She watched men and girls, all covered in sweat, stagger across the courtyard into the little pavilions or booths, most of which were now occupied. The Chinese girl was still among them. Now they drew the blinds, which must make the interiors like little ovens; they were sweating even more when they came out again. It took about twenty minutes by her watch.

She stopped looking at her watch because it only made the second hand crawl. It probably crawled even slower for those poor creatures down there, though.

Marion Culham-Browne had obviously been barking up the wrong tree from the start. If her husband had been the cunning sort of rat she said he was, then the last place he'd have hidden Salome would be the first place his wife would go looking – all those Protestant girls' schools in England. Sure they were all listed, the way she said, and she'd written to them all – and, naturally, she'd drawn a blank.

Mind you – fair dues to the woman – the fact that she *had* drawn a blank made it easier for her, Debbie, to consider the alternatives. Without knowing that fact, she, too, might have been tempted to start her own search using the same futile list. But, knowing it *was* futile was a great lepp forward. It forced you to consider the man himself – the way such a creature's mind might work.

Suppose you had a rat's cunning, the way Marion Culham-Browne described him – surely you'd hide Salome in the very *last* place that the likes of herself would go looking. That meant, if you were Protestant Anglo-Irish, you'd put her in some Roman Catholic school. If you were going to live in England, herself would assume you'd bring the child with you and hide her where you could keep an eye on things. Therefore you'd leave her in Ireland!

Herself knew you detested the girl and would therefore guess you'd throw her into some institution like that place Charles Dickens wrote about, under Mr Wackford Squeers. So instead you'd send her where all the Roman Catholic aristocracy sent their little girls. Therefore – granted that Salome wasn't in a Protestant girls' school in England – she must be in the best equivalent that Ireland could offer.

Would he go to that expense, though? In time of war nobody counted the cost; and that was as true of marital wars as any other – as Finbar was about to learn!

Or would he have sent her to France? Or Italy? Or Switzerland – Georgina had gone to a finishing school there, where they had Roman Catholic countesses and even one princess.

No – she didn't want to consider that possibility. Remember, this was all part of God's plan, really. Mr Culham-Browne was only His instrument. God *wanted* her to find Salome now, so He wasn't going to make it impossible.

Ireland it was, then. *Somewhere* in Ireland. As far from Cloonaghvogue Castle as possible – or right on the very doorstep? That'd be the bold, brave thing to have done – and the very, *very* last place herself would go looking.

On the other hand if Salome were hidden *too* close to Cloonaghvogue, an awful lot of people would recognize her, and – the way it is in Ireland – word would soon spread. So she was probably at the other end of the country. Or lost somewhere in the great, anonymous crowds of Dublin.

The truth of it was, she couldn't tell. She'd just have to wait until she got there. She'd start at Cloonaghvogue village, anyway, even if the castle was empty those many years. Start with the priest. He'd know the high-tone girls' schools if nothing else. She'd write to him tomorrow.

Shortly before midnight she rose again, took another shower, and then went down to her car. She could have driven the whole way in the dark by now. In fact, when she came to the farm gate, although she was still several miles from the house, she switched off the lights. The moon was bright enough for her to read the crudely painted sign: MAAK TOE DIE HEK. As she obeyed the instruction she thought, *Ja, Mynheer – but the horse has already bolted!*

She cut the engine at the top of a long, gentle slope, about a mile from the house, and let the car coast as far as it would go. It came to a halt about a furlong and a half short. She took nothing with her, except her handbag, and began walking as silently as she could, picking the softest sand for each footstep. In that way she did nothing to rouse the dogs until she reached the gate, whose catch undid all her good work.

They came bounding toward her but ceased to give

tongue as soon as they saw who it was. The Kaffir dogs in the kraal didn't take up their noise. She didn't think that brief disturbance would have roused anyone in the house – certainly not Finbar and Georgina if they had danced according to *her* tune that night! The dogs barked like that – and stopped as swiftly – a dozen times a night. A baboon, a wild pig, even a snuffling little porcupine, would set them off; you only roused yourself if they persisted.

She crouched low and cuddled the dogs until she was sure the sleepers were still sleeping. Then she rose and slowly walked toward the house. The stoep was glazed against the antarctic blast on the southern side of the house, but here on the northern side, where the bedrooms lay, the arches were open to the elements. She slipped off her shoes and, risking the scorpions, went tiptoe along the waxed quarry tiles, past the empty children's bedrooms, past the nanny's room and guest room (which she did not bother to check), to the only one where the windows were wide open. She shielded her eyes against the flyscreen and peered within.

They were there, of course, naked, side by side; the mosquito nets lent them a fake allure.

She continued on tiptoe to the end of the stoep, where she put her shoes back on and went down to the beach, to the shelter beside the lagoon. There she slept fitfully until about seven, by which time the sun was well up. Then she walked directly through the straggly coastal bush to the point where she had left the car. She started it and drove slowly all the way to the farm, toot-tooting every ten yards or so.

She had timed it well. Finbar was already up and shaven. He came out onto the stoep and waved cheerily. A bleary-eyed Georgina opened the guest-room window and waved, too.

For the rest of the week Debbie said nothing, giving no clue that she had found the letters and seen the pair of them *in flagrante*. In the end, even Georgina was forced to admit she had been wrong: Debbie had not gone prying in the bureau – or if she had, she had somehow missed the incriminating letters; the phonecall about a breakdown had not been a ruse; and Debbie suspected nothing.

Debbie, who did not need to *suspect* anything in that line, suspected that Georgina had reached those conclusions. That was when she announced she'd like to go back to Ireland, just for a visit.

When Finbar got over his shock he said they couldn't afford it.

She just looked at him with a little smile on her lips and said, "Oh, you will. The time is propitious now."

Then Georgina knew.

He asked did she want him to come, too.

She smiled again and told him not to be absurd.

He bit his lips and asked when was all this going to happen. And she said it wouldn't be for months and months yet. "I just wanted ye to know in good time." She used the plural 'ye' rather than 'you' so they wouldn't misunderstand. "There's letters to write and replies to gather, and replies to those replies . . . and Lord knows what before I set off," she added.

Later, when Finbar had gone out to the fields, Georgina said, "You know, don't you."

But all Debbie would say was, "I know I'm getting what I want at last. And I think I'm not the only one."

"And Finbar?"

Debbie laughed. "Begod but that's the *price* of him!"

56

Salome was at Kingsbridge a good quarter of an hour before the Cork train was due – which was just as well, since she was five minutes *later* than the time stated in the timetable. Again and again she saw its smoke plume out beyond Inchicore, only to realize it was some local goods train or a shunting engine, fussing around. Soon, however, the monster itself would arrive, and then the platform would be bustling with people, and there'd be twenty nuns among them, and she'd be desperate to see which one was Boniface.

Dear Boniface! So much to tell her! She hadn't seen her since the day they parted at Trinity's gates – a century ago last September, after all the screaming and no-no-I-shan't! and phone calls to lawyers and Uncle C-B himself saying, "I'm on my bended knees, Salome . . . I'm begging you – please accept!"

God – suppose she'd still refused! What a fool she'd have been. Boniface was right. For all the distinctions she'd got in her papers, she was a stupid, ignorant, wild, and wilful colleen who didn't deserve one iota of the love and effort and money that had gone into the nature and nurture of her.

"Boniface – dear Boniface – you were so right and I was so wrong!" Those were to be her opening words.

She was so certain by now that she could tell a shunter's plume from an express that the monster was pulling into the platform before she came out of her umpteenth rehearsal of the rest of her little speech of welcome.

There were not twenty nuns; there was only one – for the first time since the station was built, probably. Salome threw decorum to the winds and raced, arms spread wide, toward the one solo nun, fit to bowl her over. As it was she spun her round almost a full circle, and, if they hadn't been hugging each other so tight, they would both have gone sprawling.

"Child! Child!" Boniface said, struggling to hold her off.

Salome laughed and relaxed her grip.

The nun managed to get the length of her arms between them then. "I suppose I may call you that now?" she asked.

"Especially if you behave like this!"

"Oh but I've missed you!" Salome exclaimed. "How's the school? How's Tommy? And Carmel – did the false teeth work? I've met a dental student who says they can rebuild jaws and everything now."

"Wait, wait, wait!" The nun turned to point out her suitcase to the porter. "First things first. Now tell me – was I right or wasn't I? I'm referring to the little fracas at our last parting, of course."

"Oh!" Salome, reminded of her prepared opening speech, but afraid she might break down in tears if she tried to deliver it now, contented herself with a shy smile and a contrite hanging of the head.

"Well done," Boniface said, patting her on the arm. "That's enough humble pie – I know it's not your favourite dish. Though by God, the last time I stood on this platform, waiting to go back to Simonstown, I swore I'd force a ton of it down your throat before I was through! But enough, as I say. You're looking grand."

"And so are you, Sister. You are, so."

"Oh – 'Sister' is it now?"

"Boniface, then."

"That's better."

They grinned at each other and breathed out steam, momentarily at a loss for words. The porter emerged with her case and asked would he get a taxi. Boniface gave him a shilling and said would he ever put it in a cab for the Bon Secours house in Glasnevin. To Salome she said, "It's such a fine day and we see so little of God's sun this time of year, I thought we'd take advantage of both and walk down the Liffey to . . . well, wherever you think yourself, now. Dublin's your city these days."

"Well, gladly, gladly," Salome replied. "But I wish you were right. The girls of Trinity see less of Dublin, I may tell you, than the girls of Catherlough House ever saw of Simonstown – and I mean before Fane Mall was even thought of. I had to get an exeat just to meet you here."

"I'm sure?" Boniface said in surprise.

They began walking toward the station entrance.

"We're locked in at half-past six," Salome complained. "We're not even allowed in the library in the evening – mustn't mix with the men, you see. Worse than that – we can't even keep the books out overnight, the way the men can. We have to hand them all back in by six. I think I'll tell Uncle C-B I'd be happier at Cambridge."

Boniface chuckled as they emerged into the frosty sunshine. "D'you think you'd be any more free there?"

"At least they have their own library at Girton – and a very good one, too. And they can keep books out of the varsity library overnight. Stella was there and she says it's much better. Stella Maybrick, that is – did I write about her? That's another thing – d'you know, they read our letters!"

"You did – and I'm sure they do. She sounds the perfect feminist rebel and you and she get on famously, I make no doubt."

They paused while a tram crossed the forecourt. A taxi went by with Boniface's suitcase on the luggage pad; the driver gave them a toot and a wave. They crossed the bridge to walk down the north bank of the Liffey, partly to avoid Guinness's gate but mainly to take advantage of the sun.

"You approve, of course," Salome said accusingly. "Of them reading our letters, I mean."

"Well you're not yet twenty-one," Boniface pointed out tactfully.

"Stella's twenty-four and they still insist on reading hers." She giggled. "She copies bits out of Boccaccio and Rabelais, in the original Italian and French, which aren't on the approved list but which they can't say aren't great literature, and she underlines all the rude words just to show the censors she knows what's what."

Boniface tut-tutted and shook her head. "Treat them like children and they'll behave like children – isn't that what I always said?"

"It's not children we want to behave like at times," Salome said darkly. "But . . ."

"What?"

She bit her lip and shook her head. "No matter. We have a plan to shake them, anyway."

"It makes you want to strip off all your clothes and run naked through the quad – I know," Boniface said.

Her assurance goaded Salome into blurting out what had actually been on her mind. "It makes us want to put on short skirts and go whoring in Merrion Square – if you want the truth, Boniface."

The nun stopped in her tracks and turned away from her, facing the Liffey and leaning heavily on the sun-warmed capstone of the balustrade. "You know what that means, I suppose?" The question filtered around the side of her wimple.

"It's what the men do," Salome replied defensively, wishing she'd bitten her tongue off instead of babbling the words out like that. "I've heard them talking about it."

"You know what it means, though?" Boniface persisted.

"Yes."

The nun turned and stared at her – smiling broadly, Salome was surprised to see. "We didn't do very well with all that sort of thing at Catherlough House, did we," she said.

Salome shrugged awkwardly. "As well as most parents," she replied. "Judging by what some of the other girls say."

"You do talk it over then, among yourselves?"

Salome grinned at her. "And you're going to tell me nuns don't?"

Boniface shook her head. "Never in my time. Not even in the first years of my novitiate."

"Well, I'll bet they do now! Is Severinus still Novice

Mistress? You ask her. Get her tiddley one day and ask her."

To Salome's surprise Boniface blushed. "No," she said awkwardly. "She's not Novice Mistress any longer. In fact" – her eyes rolled uncomfortably – "she's left the Order altogether."

"Broken her vows?" Salome was shocked.

Boniface shook her head. "She was released. Let's talk about something else. It was a very distressing time for all of us. She was one of those women who never ought to have become a nun."

"Just because she used to take the novices into the woods for a kiss?" Salome asked.

Boniface's jaw dropped. "You *knew* all about that?"

"We all did. It was a joke."

"Mother of God!" She looked wildly to right and left as if for a rescue party. "Am I to believe my ears?"

"Well, we never thought much of it."

"*Sancta simplicitas!*" Boniface resumed their walk. "Do you, er, 'think much of it' now, may I ask?"

"Well, I know what it's all about, now. As to what I think of it, well, I suppose I think it's rather sad. I'd sooner have a gay old time with a gay young man – though chance'd be a fine thing, as Stella says." After a brief pause she went on, "Talking of Uncle C-B, have you been in touch with him since . . . you know. All that brouhaha?"

"Only by letter. He says he'd like to see you now. I think he's genuinely ashamed of what he did all those years ago."

"I think he's ashamed it turned out for the best," Salome replied scornfully. "I must be an enormous disappointment to him."

"That's unworthy, dear," Boniface told her. "If he came over for the horse show, would you see him? Or run away?"

Salome thought it over and said, "Neither." The sadness in the nun's eyes made her add, in a softer voice, "I can't,

Boniface. It's past. It's over and done with. I can't . . . the past is . . . I just want to . . ." She put her open hand above her head and pushed some invisible cloud away. "If my own *mother* were to stand before me now," she said . . . but she didn't complete the thought. Instead she added, "I haven't even tried to find Hereward, you know – even though I really would *love* to see him again. I'm sure he's in Dublin – and it would be so easy to write to his father and find out. Sometimes I get a tingly sort of feeling when I'm walking down the street – as if I'm going to bump into him round the very next corner. But I haven't even tried . . ." Her voice trailed off.

Boniface said nothing. The chance to say something about Salome's mother had gone again, but there was time. Another would show itself before the day was out.

After a while Salome said, "D'you understand it?"

"With some reluctance, yes."

"Reluctance?" The word surprised Salome.

"Well, I'm part of it in a way, aren't I – your past."

"Oh no!" Salome laughed cajolingly. "You're my present – look, you're here!" She tapped her playfully on the arm. "And my future, too. I'll never willingly lose touch with you."

Boniface smiled gratefully but stuck to her line. "That still leaves the others. Marion Culham-Browne thought she was doing her very best for you . . ."

"I almost went to see her the other day, you know." Salome giggled naughtily. "They advertised for a maid and I thought I wonder if she'd recognize me? D'you think she would? I thought I'd pretend to apply for the post."

"Why didn't you?"

The blunt question surprised her.

"Were you afraid?" the nun persisted. "What of? That she *would* recognize you or that she *wouldn't?* Which would be worse?"

In a subdued voice Salome said, "I was afraid she *would*

recognize me and say nothing."

Boniface shook her head. "She'd never do that."

"She might. If she thought Uncle C-B had put me in some workhouse or in a convent among the Magdalens and I'd been trained up to be nothing better than a skivvy? That sounds snobbish but you know what I mean. It's the way *she* would see it anyway. She'd believe it was too late to rescue me. Think how sad she'd be then."

"Very noble!" Boniface said drily. She realized that this self-glorifying answer, involving a most unlikely scene, was far from the truth but she was wise enough not to pursue the point directly. Instead she asked an apparently unrelated question – as a way of getting round to the back door. "Are you the only Roman Catholic girl at Trinity just now?"

Reluctantly Salome, who had been stung by the jeering tone of the nun's reply, said, "I'm not a Roman Catholic girl, Boniface. God, you were *there!*"

The nun laughed aloud at the memory of the occasion: Salome on registration day. When the man asked her her religion, she answered, "Atheist, sir."

And the man had looked her up and down, and then turned to her, Boniface, with a suspicious glint in his eye – suspecting a rag from Dublin's *other* university, UCD, the Roman Catholic crowd.

And she had said, "You heard the girl, my good man. Mark her down as an atheist, so."

And 'her good man' had written *Protestant*, muttering that since Protestants were as good as atheists in Roman Catholic eyes, atheists might as well be Protestants when they didn't have a column to themselves.

So now, here on the Liffey's banks, when Salome repeated the claim that she was an atheist, Boniface said mildly, "That's like getting rid of your past, too."

"Everything I ever loved," Salome said, almost tonelessly, "has vanished, just when I began to love it most, and need it most – except you." She slipped her arm through the nun's and hugged her tight. "I thought I'd lost you, too, that day – especially when we had to go and telephone Uncle C-B."

"You did try very hard, I must admit," Boniface replied solemnly, giving her arm a squeeze in return.

"I just didn't want to be beholden to that man any more – I mean, I never realized he'd be paying for me at Trinity, too."

"We've buried all that, Salome – I hope."

"I know. And yes, we have. I'm reconciled to it now, and . . ."

"Reconciled? Is that all?"

A Guinness boat went by, tooting at a small rowing boat to get out of the way. The two women watched to see would it manage it time – which, of course, it did. But the oarsman brandished his fist at the skipper of the much larger vessel.

It occurred to Salome that it was rather like her – shaking a fist at the Roman Catholic church. And next week she was going to shake her fist at Trinity, too. Was God telling her to call it all off?

"You were saying you're reconciled?" Boniface prompted her.

"More than reconciled, then."

"Content?"

"Even happy, you could say. Actually, I wouldn't mind seeing Uncle C-B. I could cope with that. I mean there's little danger I'd fall in love with him or come to depend on him – emotionally, I mean. I couldn't ever *need* him in that way."

"Could you forgive him?"

"Oh I did that a long time ago. In fact, I don't think I was ever aware of a hurt that needed forgiving."

"If you say no more to him than that, whenever you meet next, it'd be . . . well, I won't pollute your atheist ears with the thought."

Salome chuckled, but some glint in her eye told Boniface it was not at the words she had just spoken; she asked what was so amusing.

"D'you remember," Salome said, "one time when we were talking about me being the Bad Girl of the school? That was after we started the work at Fane Mall, of course . . . by the way . . . you didn't tell me about Tommy and Carmel and the others."

"Tommy got a distinction and two credits in his School Certificate. At Catherlough House we still sit the English examinations, of course. Carmel's new artificial palate means she can speak properly – or, at least, that we can understand her properly for the first time. She read from Saint Matthew at our carol concert. Anyway – I'll tell you all the news later. What about when you were the Bad Girl of the school?"

"Oh – you asked me why and I said I didn't know. And then there was an embarrassing pause. And then you said, 'D'you realize, Salome, I think God *intends* some people to be like that.' And I felt . . . eeurgh!" She clenched her fists against the azure sky and gave out a restrained scream. "And I know it's what you're thinking now – about my being an atheist. You're thinking God intends me to be like that – aren't you!"

"Well, of course I am. God intends *everything* that happens. Not a sparrow falls from the sky but He intends it."

Salome looked at her with kindly pity. "You've never been free, Boniface," she said. "You've never walked abroad under a sky like this" – she raised her face once more, but this time grinned at the bright, cloudless vault above – "and said to yourself, 'There's no one there! There's nothing there! I'm alone! I'm myself! I'm free!' You've never felt the sense of relief that goes with knowing all that."

Boniface took her arm again and almost frog-marched her down the quay, past the Four Courts building, which still showed signs of its near-destruction in the civil war. "I can understand the desolation, the sense of betrayal, that must make such a bleak prospect seem enticing," she replied. "But we'll get nowhere by prolonging this discussion. Just let me know when you start your Jewish phase. I have an idea that'll be more interesting than this. To be candid, I find atheism rather arid. Meanwhile, will I tell you one bit of news that I only heard yesterday?"

Salome laughed. "You see!" she said. "We'll never fall out, you and I – not for long. Religion's like beauty between us – it's only skin deep. Anyway, what did you hear only yesterday?"

"You haven't a weak heart, I hope? No tendency to fainting fits?"

"Go on!" Salome shook her arm vigorously.

"All right – you asked for it straight. It seems that Father Hines – you remember Father Hines, the PP at Cloonaghvogue?"

"Vaguely. Anyway?"

"It seems he's received a letter from a Mrs Deborah McKenna, near Port Elizabeth in the Cape."

She gripped Salome's arm very tight, not just to sustain her but to be sure of missing none of the involuntary muscular tics people make on hearing such news as she had just given out. But she might as well have saved herself the trouble. Salome needed no buoying up, nor did she make the slightest jerk.

She simply walked in silence, a good hundred paces, and then said in the calmest voice imaginable, "How would she know to write there?"

"I don't know," Boniface replied, equally calmly. It seemed absurd to be discussing this news like Sherlock Holmes and Doctor Watson but that was apparently Salome's wish. "I heard it from Father McDaid, of course. He hadn't *seen* the letter, only heard of its arrival. There's no love lost between those two, I can tell you! But he's worried, of course – McDaid. It's dawned on him that his Redemptorist zeal in restoring one straying lamb to the RC fold, whatever its religious merits, has the disadvantage of being plain kidnapping – or aiding and abetting the same – in the eyes of the law. Even in our brave new Irish Free State!"

"*Someone* must have written to *someone* out in the Cape," Salome said. "But who? Aunt Marion? Did she know my parents' address all along? How can one tell?"

"You could go and ask her. I'm not one of your betting nuns but if I were, I'd lay six to four she's somewhere behind all this. If even C-B is developing a conscience, perhaps she is, too. Anyway, it doesn't really matter, does it – the important point is that Father McDaid is wondering whether it wouldn't be more prudent to confess the truth."

"Surely he's done that already?"

"I mean in a civil sense, not sacramental. He's thinking he ought to tell Father Hines at least."

Salome was silent again, not so long as previously. "And will he?" she asked at length. "What odds are you offering on that?"

"Evens," Boniface replied. "He's just as likely to write privately to your mother. Or wait and waylay her if she ever comes back to Ireland. Or, of course, he might funk it and do absolutely nothing. Anyway, I thought I ought to tell you because, if he does let the cat out of the bag, your mother's going to come walking through Trinity gates, six to eight weeks from now."

57

There was a knock at Salome's door; she was far away at the time – with Schliemann on the slopes of Troy, digging through the layered remains of Agamemnon's city without realizing it, sacking it yet again as Menelaus had done . . .

there was surely a poem in it somewhere: *As Menelaus through Troy's ruin raced* . . . Too many r-sounds.

The knock was repeated. They called her name – Stella's voice, then Carrie's.

Her stomach suddenly vanished inside her, to be replaced by a great, yawning nothing. Was it today? Oh, please let it be not-today!

"Are you all right, Sal?"

"Yes," she called out. "Come in!" She slipped markers in her books and stacked them neatly. Ancient Troy buried once again, this time under layers of scholarship.

They didn't come in. They stood in the doorway, eyes bright with the gleam of battle, two brave Helens of Troy. No, not the right image at all. Two Joans of Arc, two Boadiceas, two Amazons with the scent of battle on the breeze. "Aren't you ready?" Stella asked.

"Today's the day," Carrie added.

"Today's the day," Salome repeated woodenly. "I don't know how one gets ready for something like this. I've just mislaid my stomach, that's all I know."

The others exchanged a nervous glance.

"You're not funking it?" Carrie was contemptuous.

Her face looked more horselike than ever, Salome thought. Carrie was Stella's warhorse, with her pugnacious nostrils and red-gold mane. And Stella – silver-blonde, shingled and bobbed, eyes bright, tongue sharpened, larynx gritted, and features specially honed that very dawn no doubt – Stella smiled her recruiting sergeant's smile and said confidently, "She's not funking it, are you, Sal."

With something like cold-molten lead in her veins Salome rose and put on her coat. She was shivering already, though her chamber was sunny and warm. "I still feel there must be a better way," she said.

"Such as?" Carrie seized one arm, Stella the other. They were taking no chances.

"It seems so petty. We can't eat in their dingy, smelly

dining hall. So what? Our own dining room is light and airy and has floral curtains. And the food . . ."

"It's beside the point," Stella interrupted.

They let go of her to negotiate the narrow stair, but Carrie went ahead and Stella behind.

"Yes, it's beside the point," Carried echoed.

"What is the point, then?" Salome challenged her.

Carried turned round and looked at Stella, who drew breath to reply.

"No – let her explain," Salome said.

"The point is," Carrie said wearily, "we don't see why only bits of the college should be ours. We pay the same fees as the men, the same lodgings, the same subs. Why should we be barred from parts of the college they can just stroll into like lords of creation?" She checked this reply with Stella.

Stella said, "Spiffingly put, if I may say so."

They reached the bottom of the stairs. Salome bent to retie a shoelace. "So we demand the right to walk into that grease-dungeon and sit cheek by jowl with a crowd of oafs who don't want us there. Is that it? When we could be sitting in our own beautiful . . ."

"They've got to be *made* to want us," Stella said. "It's nothing to do with personal likes and dislikes. I don't *like* the men here, but . . . I say, are you going to be all day tying that shoe?"

Salome stood again; she dragged the pace as much as she could on the brief walk between their house and the dining hall. Stella continued: "I don't like the men. And I detest that squalid piggery of a mess hall. I adore our own little dining room. But all that is by the way. It's a matter of principle. We pay for the facilities and we ought to be able to enjoy them – by right."

"Well, we certainly couldn't enjoy them by inclination," Salome said.

Carrie flared her nostrils for a specially deep inhalation.

"It's a right," she said. "And we're going to assert it – now."

Now! The word echoed in Salome's mind like the manic threat of some Wicked Fairy in a pantomime. "I'd far rather protest for the right to keep library books out overnight."

"Who'd notice?" Stella replied scornfully.

"No one!" Carrie put in.

"They would if we simply walked out with as many books as we could manage."

"Oh *they* would," Stella agreed scornfully. "But no one else. *They'd* just stick whopping great fines on our bills. Who'd notice that? Only Mumsie and Dadsie – which isn't the sort of splash we're trying to make, at all at all. But they can't ignore us in the dining hall. We're going to be famous tomorrow. And next term, when they give way to the inevitable and open the place to *all* undergrads, the women will remember us three as the pioneers."

"We'll be gated and rusticated, you'll see," Salome said morosely.

"We're as good as gated already. Anway, we can't call it off now because" – she checked her watch – "Rodney and Simon will be just . . . about . . . ready!"

She quickened her pace, suggesting they were now running seconds late – and that every second counted.

"You told them to get a table as near the entrance as possible, I hope," Carrie asked nervously.

Salome's other shoelace came undone but they wouldn't let her stop to do it up again.

"No," Stella replied. "I said slap-bang in the middle. We're going to score a bullseye!"

The men knew something was afoot – or a good number of them must have done, otherwise the silence would not have fallen so quickly, almost the moment the three of them slipped into that sacred dining hall.

And a strange sort of silence it was, too. It was not the

sort that asked, 'What the hell is going on here?' It was more like, 'So they *did* mean it after all!"

The three young women – one with slovenly shoelaces that made an annoying little tintinnabulation on the old stone floor – hardly dared to breathe as they ran the gauntlet of that merciless hush; a hundred pairs of eyes, hostile, curious, disdainful, amused, followed them every step of the way.

Stella, Carrie, and Salome! Their hearts were beating fit to leap right out of their breasts; they looked neither right nor left, for their eyes were fixed on that pathetic little haven of a table, reserved for them by Simon Pockett and Rodney Fitzergerald, two stalwarts of the TCD Feminist Society. They, too, looked as if they'd rather be fishing their favourite trout stream today. Or helping to carry out the night soil.

This is a big mistake! Salome told herself as she followed miserably in the wake of the other two. But, curiously, the words acted on her as a much-needed encouragement. *After all*, the cynic within her pointed out, *big mistakes are quite a speciality of yours, aren't they!*

She glanced at a group of men at a nearby table and smiled; one of them was brave enough to smile back. The rest fingered their bread rolls as if wondering whether it was time to start throwing them yet; the women were prepared for that. They were going to stand up and take it until the men's innate sense of shame got the better of them.

She stepped out with a lighter spirit – and almost tripped over her loose shoelace.

Somebody tittered.

But somebody else – a man who didn't want this occasion to be bathed away in laughter – began to hiss.

S s s s s . . . ! It was like the escape of gas, a foul, poisonous fuming. It was taken up at other tables: *S s s s s !* until it rose like a miasma all around them. By the time they joined the two men it was loud enough to make ordinary conversation impossible.

Rodney and Simon waited until the last minute – so as not to give the game away to men at the nearby tables – before they rose and assisted the women into their chairs. Three tepid plates of overcooked beef, mushy carrots, and potatoes whose lumpiness vied with the gravy awaited them.

"Just think!" Salome said bitterly as she raised the first unappetizing forkful to her lips, "those other poor women are being forced to eat *gigot de mouton à la Soubise* with *fèves au beurre!*"

"Oh shut up, Sal!" Carrie almost screamed.

With some shock Salome realized she was close to tears. She laid down the forkful again and patted her arm. "It's all right," she shouted. "At least it's taken my mind off my shoelaces!"

Carrie laughed, but that, too, bordered on the hysterical. *We shouldn't fight these battles*, Salome thought, *until we've mastered our tearducts*.

The hissing stopped – not suddenly but as if something new was happening out at the periphery and the realization of it was spreading inward table by table.

"Don't look up!" Stella whispered vehemently. "We shall behave like ladies."

Salome wondered why ladies wouldn't look up in such circumstances but she obeyed nonetheless. She raised the fork again to her mouth but found its contents quite uneatable. She forced it down her throat and then just played with the food on her plate.

"I thought it looked like rain earlier this morning," Rodney said miserably.

"What's happening?" Stella whispered out of the side of her mouth. "Why have they all gone silent?"

"Miss Klugen is coming this way," Simon said, even more miserably.

Salome risked a glance to her left and saw it was so. Miss

Klugen, who had never been given a first name, even as a baby, was a nine-headed ogress who ate little boys and girls for breakfast. She was also, in her spare time, the refectory manageress. The men's misery was not merely explained by this development, it was justified.

She was a little barrel of a woman, swaddled in thorn-proof tweeds. Her steel-gray hair was not simply gathered into a bun, the bun itself was then screwed so tight that it stretched the skin – or hide – of her body right down to the soles of her feet, which made it easier to polish to such a high and menacing shine. It also made her eyes pop out, 'like a scorpion's on stalks', Salome thought.

She dropped her fork with a clatter; Carrie was shivering like a leaf. But curiously enough the bracing effort of that one brave smile Salome had received on their nightmarish walk from the door to this table was with her still; she now felt as calm and as cool as she could have wished.

Unfortunately for her, she should have wished to be as upset and frightened as the other two women, for she was now the only one in a fit condition to speak.

"Ladies!" Miss Klugen exploded in a restrained sort of whisper – as if to suggest that the men might not yet have noticed their grave lapse in decorum and the three of them might, with luck, creep out again and save the day for respectable womankind.

"Good afternoon, Miss Klugen," Salome said amiably. Then, to fill the shocked silence that followed, she added, "We're still a little unfamiliar with the rules here. Are we allowed to go up for seconds?"

A titter went up from the nearest tables. Then came a sussuration of whispers as others wanted to know what she had said. Someone shouted, "Oliver Twist!"

But none of it could survive Miss Klugen's glance, which would surely have won the day for Napoleon had she been at Waterloo. The hush that now fell was more deathly than before.

"You know you are not permitted in here!" she said, throwing all attempt at secret diplomacy to the winds. "This is the dining hall for gentlemen undergraduates. The *ladies*, if such you are, have their own arrangements."

Salome, still with her engaging smile, said, "If our status as ladies is as uncertain as all that, Miss Klugen . . ."

She got no further. Miss Klugen stepped right up to the table, leaning her thighs against it and revealing, through her prickly tweeds, curves and things most ladies prefer to hide. "Please get up from this table and leave quietly," she said.

Salome was tempted to jab a fork in that mound; she hadn't felt so angry with the world since . . . well, since before Boniface came back to Catherlough House. Any minute now Miss Klugen would grab her by the ear and drag her off to the coal cellar. "If you will just go back and do the job for which you are *paid*, Miss Klugen," she said, "– out of *our* fees, too, may I point out – there will be no fuss." She raised her voice. "These men are in a state of shock but they are decent fellows at heart and . . ."

She got no further. Spitting bile, Miss Klugen said, "The job for which I am paid, is it! Well I am paid to manage a respectable, orderly dining hall, Miss . . . Miss – whatever your name is. What *is* your name?"

"Salome McKenna." She offered her hand.

It was ignored. "You are a *disgrace* to your sex," she thundered.

Salome glanced at Stella, inviting her with a lift of the brows to take over. Stella just continued to stare at her, open-mouthed with admiration.

She turned back to the manageress, only to find her walking away. "You have not heard the last of this," she shrieked over her shoulder.

Salome grinned at the other four. "I never imagined it would be so easy," she said, and pretended to tuck into her now cold meal with relish.

"You were magnificent, Sal!" Stella said breathlessly.

"Magnificent!" Carrie echoed in a voice that wavered up and down the register.

There was a surly muttering all around them. The men wanted to express their disapproval, but they had already done the hissing bit and it would be an admission of weakness to return to it. Someone booed and a few others took it up for a while but somehow Miss Klugen's appeal to the finer points of civilization had put *them* on their best behaviour, too. It was damnable. All they could do was mutter their disgruntlement at one another and wait to see what happened next.

That *something* would happen next they had no doubt.

The triumphant spirit that had enabled Salome to actually swallow three morsels of the disgusting meal evaporated. She copied the other two women and contented herself with small, ladylike morsels of bread. That at least was edible.

"*You're* the brave ones, really," she remarked to Rodney and Simon. "They're going to give you hell after this."

"Thanks," Simon said flatly.

"We do appreciate it, though," Stella assured him, "don't we, Carrie?"

Carrie agreed. "I think I'm going to be sick," she said.

A man at the next table laughed, more in embarrassment than contempt. Salome turned to him and said, "She's right, you know. How can you eat this slop, day after day? It's enough to make anyone sick."

"No one asked you to come barging in here," the man beyond the first fellow said.

"You should welcome us," she replied. "We wouldn't stand for *this!*" She plunged her fork into the mashed potato – at an angle, but it didn't fall down. "We'd use this for patching ceilings. If you'd let the women in here, you'd have good, edible food inside a month."

The men at the table glanced uncertainly at one another.

"But that's not the point," Stella put in suddenly. "It's a matter of *principle*, you see?"

The man who had begun this conversation by laughing now waved contemptuously at her. "We've heard all that," he sneered.

"You may have heard but you haven't listened," she retorted into a forest of dismissive waves.

"Boring, boring, boring . . ." began the chant. But that, too, petered out – this time because the *something* they had been expecting was now nigh.

It took the shape of the proctor and two of the college porters. Men at the peripheral tables rose to their feet – not so much out of respect for the internal forces of law and order but because their arrival promised a showdown at last. They soaped their hands and said among themselves, "This is going to be good!"

"Ohmigod!" Simon murmured. He and Rodney rose to their feet; in their case it *was* out of respect for the internal forces of law and order.

"Now let's be having no trouble," the proctor said crisply. "I shall ask you ladies to leave this hall just once, and then, if you refuse, I shall have you forcibly ejected."

He folded his arms and stared at them.

Everyone looked at Salome, who heaved a sigh and said, "You are asking a great deal, sir – and we are asking for so little." She waved a hand around their table and repeated: "So little."

"Very well," the man snapped, and gave a curt nod to the beadles.

One of them advanced on Salome and clutched her arm, hard enough to hurt.

She did not flinch. She put a finger to his nose – actually pressing it like a button – and said, "You are committing a criminal assault, fellow. A *criminal* assault. And be assured – I *shall* report you for it. To the polis."

The man let go and glanced uncertainly at the proctor,

who made no effort to conceal his fury. The muscles on his temples rippled and the breath howled in his nose like the banshee. But, as a professor of jurisprudence himself, he knew she was right. "You are digging your own grave, Miss McKenna," he warned her in his most ominous tone.

"They're a disgrace to their sex," Miss Klugen repeated, having returned to the scene of the crime.

"Even worse than that," the proctor said. "They're a disgrace to Trinity!" He returned to the assault on Salome. "If we're going to turn legal," he said, "*you* are trespassing."

Salome, who knew no more law than the average convent girl might pick up at haphazard in her nineteen and a half years, doubted it; but she saw no point in taking the sort of hair-splitting path that only lawyers relish. She simply murmured, "Civil law!" with, she hoped, enough ennui in her voice to imply she knew all about that, too.

"Very well," the proctor said. "You've had your chance. It is no assault, let me tell you, to carry the *chairs* on which you are seated outside – which is what I now propose to do. If you are still seated in them . . . that is your choice." He nodded again at the beadles, one of whom looked at him and said, "It'll have to be one at a time, sir."

He dipped his head angrily. "So be it. Take the ring-leader first." He pointed at Salome, of course.

The moment they lifted Salome's chair, Stella rose to her feet, saying, "Well I think we've made our point." Carrie rose, too, and the pair of them walked at their new leader's side, or as close as they could.

For her part, Salome tried her best to keep her skirt well tucked between her knees while looking as much like Joan of Arc as possible.

There were boos all around, and jeers and catcalls, too. But there was also applause, here and there, and they heard several cries of bravo!

The porters put her down unceremoniously just a few

feet beyond the door, which they then barred with their bodies, arms folded, brows beetling – as if all the mysteries of the male universe lay behind it.

The three young women made a silent and dignified progress back to Salome's chamber.

"It's a start, anyway," Salome said disconsolately as soon as they were safely inside. "I suppose."

They all burst into tears at once – and then cried until they laughed.

58

Heather had her father's office these days; it had become increasingly awkward for her to run the firm from the 'little cubbyhole' (as she now called it) where she first made her office on joining the firm. That room was now her father's, though he hardly ever used it since he was so often out, 'lunching' (as he now called it) 'my authors' (as he still called them). In point of fact, Hereward was now more often to be found there than the old man himself; his assigned office really was a cubbyhole.

Anyone else would have moved on months ago, if not years. But the situation was complicated. Heather didn't love him, and he didn't love her – at least, he didn't think he did and he rather hoped she didn't. She *said* she was a career woman with no time for marriage or children, or even romance. But she was quite modern about it all. She said she recognized she was a *normal* woman with *normal* appetites and so she did what any normal man would do if he had a business that demanded all his time and there was no money left over for a home and all the usual livestock.

Not that she went out and picked them up on street corners, of course – the way some men would. But there could be discreet arrangements. In fact – as she once pointed out to Hereward in her best editorial style – since he came along, 'discreet' had become 'discrete' and the arrangements, plural, had dwindled to the singular – 'a discrete arrangement' – quite separate from their relationship as mistress and servant. But the ambiguity of 'mistress' amused her.

Hereward was always most discreet anyway. He always finished like a gentleman – no smuggled devices in plain wrappers, but no risk, either, of *squeelies*, as Heather called them. It wasn't until he edited the *Nolan Home Doctor* that he realized she was making a semi-pun on *sequelœ* – the aftereffects of an injury.

He stood at his window – or, rather, the window of Nolan *père* – that raw February evening, wondering why his way of life didn't make him quite as happy as it should have done. Rick said he ought to count himself in clover. No young man in his early twenties wanted to settle down; few even wanted a steady girlfriend. Heather might be four years his senior but in every other respect she was a young man's dream: good looking, a superb figure, a libido as strong as any man's, no false modesty, and not the slightest desire to commit herself to anything more permanent. Didn't he realize she was saving him a good hundred pounds a year?

The figure was suspiciously identical to the allowance his father had made him – 'as a matter of prudence' were the accompanying words – when he first went to work in Dublin. So he had complained no more to Rick, for fear of losing the bounty; and he had thrown himself into his nightly amours with Heather, full of renewed vigour and gratitude.

And yet something was missing still. He had tried not to think of Salome since beginning his . . . whatever one might call it with Heather. Or, rather, he had tried to ignore the fact that she would be growing with him and would soon be a beautiful young woman of twenty; he tried to focus his mind only on the remembered eleven-year-old, as a form of self-ridicule for hankering after her still.

Two trams passed each other in Dawson Street outside – place names now in Irish, too. CITY CENTRE said one sign, with VIA AN LAR beneath it. City centre via city centre? Well, you can't deny it's the God's truth. Tautology. Keeping the populace ignorant in *two* languages. God save us.

A tart linked arms with a man and flounced off; they were both laughing.

Wouldn't it be almost worth it? That tart wouldn't be calling him back tomorrow – "I want you now. We've got twenty minutes before I have to go and see Smythe."

Still, it would be five shillings down the drain. Five shillings he couldn't put by. A few dozen encounters like that and he wouldn't have two hundred pounds in the bank by his next birthday. Then he'd not be able to give in his notice and start his search – the search that would begin when he no longer had to force himself to think of Salome as an eleven-year-old.

Better stick with the present arrangements, so.

"Good night, Miss Nolan!" Hazlitt, the chief accountant – in fact, the *only* accountant. The last to go each day, not being of the literary cast.

Slam of door.

Stairs two at a time – a profitable day, then.

Slam of front door.

Ten, nine, eight . . .

"Hereward?" Heather called. "Are you there?"

He opened a gap between the flat of his belly and his waistband. "Are you there?" he cooed softly.

Squelch of hormones. Lilt of heart. Litesomeness of tread. Here we go again!

Shriek of floorboards.

"Actually, I've got the curse," she shouted, as if the

floorboards had protested the agony of his long, long wait – all of twenty-three hours since the ferret last saw the coney.

He swam into her open doorway, crestfallen – at least, up where he would have borne a crest if he had one. The rest of him had most decidedly *not* fallen.

"Are you terribly disappointed, darling?" she asked, as if she might change her mind.

But he knew her better than that by now. She got it when she wanted it – *tout court*. If he wanted it when she didn't – *tout* bad!

"We shall be brave," he assured her. "*It* and *I*."

"Good!" It was the identical word – and tone – that she used when ticking items on her dreaded lists at editorial meetings. Often it meant the very opposite of good.

"Well then . . . fancy a bit of supper? We could catch a show?" He grinned to show her he appreciated her for more than just *that* – which was, in fact, quite true. If anything, he appreciated her even more as a supper partner than as a way of saving five shillings a day.

She was reaching for her jacket when her eye fell on a heap of files in the corner. "I'm running out of space," she said. Then her eyes lit up. "I know – we can fill the same time with something really useful." She pulled a guilty face. "I've only been meaning to do it for about a year! You haven't put anything valuable on the top shelves in Pater's room, have you?"

"How could I? You couldn't even fit my salary cheque in, sideways."

She ignored the hint. "*I* filled them," she said, "when that was my room. Now what can we use?" She drummed her fingers on her forehead. "I know! There's a teachest at the bottom of the back stairs. Go and get it, there's a brick. I'll make a start clearing the decks."

The stairs were narrow and he had a job avoiding snags in his suit but he made it finally. Heather had already cleared several feet of the top shelf. The air danced with dust motes though she had the window wide open. The desk was piled high with old folders, envelopes, box files . . .

Coughing, he went over to the window and drew the curtains even wider, as wide as they'd go. The tart was already back on her pitch. A quickie. Or couldn't agree a price, more likely. Could ask her later.

Further clouds of dust billowed up as Heather dumped an armful in the teachest.

He came back to her. "Aren't we going to store them more neatly than that?" he asked.

She grinned. "Who said anything about store? We'll just dump them in the dustbin. You carry on. I'll start bringing the files from my room. Don't fill it more than half or it'll be too heavy to lug downstairs."

"But what are they?" he asked. "Why have we been keeping them all this time?"

"Laziness. No-time-to-do-that-now disease. They're just old galleys, ancient letters to printers and booksellers, unsolicited manuscripts, office memos . . ." She was already halfway down the passage.

"Unsolicited manuscripts? Shouldn't we return them at least?"

She called from her office. "If nothing has disturbed the dust on them for two and a half years – and much longer in most cases – I've got no qualms about scrapping them all. We always told people to send an s.a.e. if they wanted it back."

"And we always *did* send it back – if they sent an s.a.e.?"

She emerged again with another armful. "Go through them if you wish. I bet you won't find one."

She walked past him and dumped her load on the emptied stretch of shelf. "Only don't be all night," she added as she went back out again. "I'll take you up on the supper invitation – *if* your salary will run to it."

She was right – of course. He found a hundred old manuscripts without coming across a single attached s.a.e.

Indeed, not a single *un*attached one, either. He was just about to give up and dump the lot in the teachest when his eye fell on one that made the whole universe rock. *Salome McKenna – a True Irish Heroine!* it said on the first page – in red, violet, green, blue, and purple inks.

He looked at the name again and again, expecting it to change into . . . whatever the real name was – for he was sure his eyes were playing tricks, just as they had when he first came to Dublin, turning every dark-haired fifteen-year-old girl into *her*.

But *Salome McKenna* it stubbornly remained. He was still staring at it when Heather returned with her next armful.

"Found something exciting?" she asked casually.

It made him jump. He had to think quickly.

She spread her load loosely on the shelf and came over to him. "Salome McKenna a true Irish heroine by Seamus Joyce Simonstown County Keelity," she read in one long gabble. "That's not far from you. D'you know him?"

"No. Not at all. It's just that . . ."

"Take it from me – a manuscript with the title in five different coloured inks? You don't even need to open the first page. Come on – I'm getting hungry."

"No, it's just the name," he said. "For one awful moment I thought this might be one of my father's."

"*He* wouldn't use different inks," she said scornfully. "Anyway . . ."

"I know that! It's just that he used the same name – Salome McKenna – in *The Dastard*. I couldn't believe the coincidence. It's not exactly an everyday . . ."

"But the heroine in *The Dastard* is called Delilah . . . something."

"Gosh! I know that, too, actually. But in the *first* draft she was called Salome." He chuckled that he had managed to hit on a correspondence so apt. "I think I'll keep this to show the old man." And he slipped the manuscript into his desk drawer as if it had no more importance for him than that.

Later, having seen Heather home, he returned to the office and retrieved the manuscript from his drawer. While he was folding it to fit his pocket, he saw the note in the corner: *Please address all correspondence to Sisters of Bon Secours, Fane Mall, Simonstown, Co. Keelity.*

As a Keelity man himself, he knew of the Sisters of Bon Secours – and the connection between their cripples' school in Fane Mall and that most expensive college for young Roman Catholic ladies at Catherlough House. And then the penny dropped.

"C-B," he murmured. "You cunning old bastard!"

59

Hereward was so used to seeing young women who looked like Salome McKenna – or like the woman he imagined she might be after all these years – that he paid scant attention to yet another manifestation at Kingsbridge Station that Saturday morning. When he first set eyes on her she was making sure the porter put her trunks in the luggage van the right side up. She was Irish, anyway, judging by her speech. Then, walking rather disconsolately, he thought, she went to the rear of the train and sat in the Ladies Only. So that was that. Just as she was getting in, however, her eyes fell upon him, standing there, watching her – and she hesitated. Something about her gesture made him go on thinking about her . . . wondering . . . hoping . . . long after he would normally have given up.

His common sense told him it was impossible – or, at the least, so unlikely as to be almost impossible. But his hopes – those absurd harpies that had never slept for long in all his years of pining for her – kept spinning round two facts: She was taking the right train for anyone going to Simonstown; and she had looked at him in that odd way, as if she, too, found him vaguely familiar. However, she was also going the right way for Cork, or Kerry, or even – if she changed at Portarlington – Galway and Sligo. The whole west coast of Ireland, in fact. Also, a lot of girls who vaguely resembled the Salome of his imagination had looked at him oddly down the years – only, in their case, it usually meant, 'Who d'you think *you're* staring at?'

There was one other fact that his mind deliberately avoided: Salome McKenna would now be past school age; she was, however, perfect for the novitiate. So if she were travelling all the way from Dublin to Catherlough House, it might be the death knell of his hopes, anyway. In finding her at last he would lose her for ever.

Wait until we get to Maryborough, he told himself. *Or Port Laoise, as we must now learn to call it. If she gets off there to wait for the stopping train to Ballybrophy, I'll ask her.*

At Port Laoise the enigmatic young lady got off and stood beside her two trunks, waiting for the stopping train to Ballybrophy. She glanced his way several times but he failed to pluck up the courage to carry out his self-promise.

If she goes all the way to Ballybrophy, he re-promised himself, *and changes onto the Roscrea train there, I'll definitely speak to her.*

Between Port Laoise and Ballybrophy, however, he played the scene so many ways in his mind – with the possibility that she was intended for the novitiate looming ever more starkly – that he once again held back. While they waited on the branch-line platform at Ballybrophy, she yet again glanced at him, more than once. If she was intended for the novitiate, she had a stony path ahead of her, he thought. Women who glanced at men like that weren't exactly thinking of giving them up for good.

Indeed, it was doubtful if *good* were in their thoughts at all!

Once more, however, he fought shy of an open approach to her.

His cowardice plagued him all the way to Roscrea. He knew very well why he was behaving so absurdly: He was afraid she would turn out to be some other woman after all; he wanted to preserve for as long as possible the slim possibility that she was Salome.

At Roscrea she would have a choice between two local trains – northbound for Parsonstown (or Birr, as one must now learn to call it) or westbound for Simonstown.

If she takes the westbound local, he yet again promised, *I'll absolutely-definitely-certainly-positively speak to her*.

Now she looked at him with almost feverish interest. *And* she climbed aboard the westbound train – in an ordinary second-class compartment this time!

He twitched. He realized he was desperate to use the gents – and the local train had no corridors. Whistles were blowing and flags were waving as he emerged onto the platform again. The train, however, remained stationary as the driver was telling one of the porters how to build a clock, or something equally absorbing. Taking his courage in his hands Hereward ran across the platform to the compartment where *she* was seated.

She stared out at him in what he thought was alarm – except that the window was so misted he could hardly see her expression at all.

It was even worse when he drew close, for now he could make out her expression – and it seemed to him very frightened indeed. At the very least she was under the stress of some powerful emotion.

He noticed that the condensation was all on the outside of the panes. In desperation he wrote on it: TE AMO, knowing that on her side it would read OMA ƎT.

At once she tried to wipe it away – but, joy of joys, she was smiling now. Smiling fit to split her face in two. He wiped it off on his side and stared at her in disbelief. Salome! Of course it was Salome! How could he have doubted it for one minute!

The train started to pull away from the platform.

"Hereward?" she shouted through the plate-glass pane.

"Yes!" He struggled with the door.

The train gathered speed.

She, on her side, struggled with the door, too, but it would not budge. He gestured for her to lower the window. By the time she managed to get it down six inches, the coach was pulling away from him. He had about four seconds to leap into the next one behind it, whose window was wide open.

"Are you going to be a nun?" he shouted, maintaining his sprint while the carriage continued to inch away from him. His own suitcase was battering his knees at every step.

She stuck her head out of the gap and shouted. "No!" She cheered when he managed to open the door of the carriage behind. And then she shouted, "You absolute *eeejit*, Hereward!"

"I know!" he yelled back. And those were the last possible words between them for the next twenty minutes.

They were the longest twenty minutes of his life but he relished every one of them. He sat in a stunned sort of euphoria, saying, again and again, "Salome! . . . Salome! After all this time!"

And Salome sat in the next compartment, twelve inches away from him, she guessed, telling herself he was married, engaged . . . intended for another . . . that it would be absurd to have any hopes after all this time . . . and anyway, she hadn't exactly hankered after him . . . couldn't she have discovered his whereabouts quite easily, any time she liked since she came up to Trinity . . .

But now that he was *there* again, she knew full well it hadn't been a case of not bothering. She hadn't *dared* to bother. And all this nay-saying now was merely her way of coping with loss and betrayal even before it happened. How could she know these things about herself – how could she analyze them so clearly – and still be so powerless in their grip?

She would leave it all to Hereward, she decided. If he leaped from the carriage at Simonstown and swept her in his arms and covered her face with kisses, she'd take that as their new beginning. If he behaved like a childhood friend, happy to see her again after all this time – well, that would be another new beginning, too.

Still, it was nice that his very first question – asked in some anguish, too – had been about her becoming a nun.

During the final minutes of their journey, sobriety returned to Hereward as he began to think of all the questions he wanted to ask her . . . and how the answers might embarrass her . . . and how he might assume things that were no longer the case . . . and how that might insult her . . .

And so at last the truth – the awful truth – dawned on him: that his feelings down all these years were his alone; at least, he dare not, must not, would not assume she shared them. If she did, she must reveal them in her own good time and in her own unprovoked way.

In short, he must behave to her as if they were no more than childhood friends who were happy to meet again after so many years.

Still and all, he was glad his first blurted-out question – as to whether or not she was going to be a nun – was out there in the open between them; it was a sort of marker toward which they might gently drift . . . given time.

Time! How could he make that time between them? Once she vanished among the Bon Secours Sisters – even if she wasn't to become one of them – he'd be measuring his privileges in minutes, and every one of them chaperoned. Only one way out: She *must* come and stay at Castle Moore instead, at least for this weekend.

He meant it to go so much more smoothly. A few minutes of suave conversation leading up to the casual invitation, which she could casually refuse if she wished. Instead, the very moment he was out on the platform – while she was still having trouble with her door – he pulled her window down full and said, "Don't go back to Catherlough House! Come and spend the weekend at Castle Moore instead!"

It was the one possibility that had not occurred to her – for she had heard that the house was burned down in the civil war. But before she could dream up all the objections that Boniface would undoubtedly put in her way she said, "Oh well – yes – all right, then."

"Really?" he asked, surprised out of his wits.

"Yes!" she laughed. "Really. Open this door and give me a hug. I can't believe it, can you? After all this time!"

There was a lot more talk of 'can't believe it' and 'all this time' before they reached the Stag Hôtel, where Hereward telephoned Rick to tell him the wonderful, amazing, heart-stopping news . . . also to say he needn't hurry in to collect them as they'd remain at the Stag for a bite of lunch.

"I thought Castle Moore was burned down," she said when he returned. "During the civil war."

"It was, but they've moved into the old castle keep and made quite a comfortable home there. One cook, one tweeny, and Rick's valet. When you think there used to be twenty-four servants in the big house! Rick says it's marvellous not being spied on all the time. I'm talking too much. Shall we ask for a menu? They do very good roast beef here."

"Not roast beef!" she said heavily. "I'm *never* going to eat roast beef again."

And so the whole Trinity saga – the Battle of the Men's Dining Hall and her subsequent rustication, with effect from this morning and for the rest of the term – came out. Fortunately the term had only a few weeks left to run.

Hereward's grin became broader and broader as the story unfolded. "What are you going to do?" he asked.

"Study like hell and get a first. I'll show them! It'll be the best first they've ever awarded."

"In? What are you reading?"

"Ancient History."

He laughed. "How symbolic! Er, d'you think ancient history is still relevant today?"

She reached out a hand and stroked his forearm a couple of times with one extended finger. "Let's find out," she said.

The waiter came and told them their table was ready. It was Saturday, so the dining room was fairly busy, but he found them a nice table in a secluded alcove away from the entrance and the doors to the kitchen. They ordered mulligatawny soup and baked ham.

"I wish I'd been there," Hereward said when the man had gone.

"Why – what would you have done?"

The question took him by surprise. "I don't know. Just watched, I suppose. And applauded, of course."

"You wouldn't have leaped in and biffed the porters?"

"And spoil your show? Anyway, I'd just like to have been there because *you* were there. I don't want to lose touch again, not ever."

She smiled but said nothing. Her gaze strayed around the room, looking for people she might know.

Hereward could not take his eyes off her. She was far lovelier than he had ever dared imagine she would become; but there was a sadness in those pale grey-green eyes. And it brought a sadness to him as well, for it hinted at all those unknowable, unreachable parts of her, all those experiences she might speak of but could never share. From now on he would have to yield up that intimate Salome he had carried within him all these years, a Siamese twin to him, infinitely accessible; and in her place he'd have this other

Salome with her own ambitions, her own needs, her own timetable. He had a fleeting intimation that he had not even started on the business of life as yet – that he was getting his first operational orders this very minute. Heather had spoiled him for sex and his dream-Salome had spoiled him for love – making it far too easy in both cases. The long upward climb was beginning now.

"Where are you going to do all this studying?" he asked.

She shrugged. "At Catherlough House, I hope. It all depends on how Sister Boniface responds to this." She patted her handbag. "The letter from the Dean of Studies, explaining – no, setting forth the circumstances of my rustication."

"The nuns aren't expecting you today, then? I should have asked that first, I suppose – before I invited you to Castle Moore. But I mean, they know nothing of your rustication yet?"

She shook her head and bit her lip. His eyes asked why. She said, "I tend to *do* things like that. If I just turn up, trunks and all – *fait accompli* – they're much less likely to turn me away."

He frowned. "And d'you think they would – if you gave them more warning, I mean?"

"I'm always afraid people *will*, you see. Just when I'm most in need of them."

He closed his eyes and his lips moved a little; for a moment she thought he was praying. He murmured, "Yes, of course – thoughtless of me." Then, forcing a bright smile, he asked, "How d'you *think* this Sister Boniface will take it?"

"Inside? I think she'll laugh and be proud. A little bit, anyway. I'm sure she'd have done the same in my shoes."

"Except that *she* would have ensured that the laces were properly done up first?"

"Yes!" Salome laughed delightedly, making his heart turn over in his breast. She reached across the table and squeezed his hand. "Oh, Hereward! It's so . . . I don't know. It's *nice*, isn't it!"

It was his turn to smile and nod – and look around to see whether anyone he knew might have noticed.

"So tell me all about *you*," she said. "What have you been doing all this time? Have you got a . . . a job?"

He was sure she had been going to say 'a girl'; he told her about his work at Nolan & Co, mentioning his friendship with Heather. He was tempted to tell her the complete truth but he remembered his father on the subject: "Women will beg you to be honest and sincere and truthful with them but you'll get more kicks than ha'pence if you take them at their word. Just look at the books they read! It's Sheila Kaye-Smith for them, not James Joyce."

So he kept his talk of Heather on an entirely professional plane. His account lasted through the soup and into the main course.

By way of rounding off this fragment of autobiography – for he had seen her start and almost interrupt him at the name of Nolan & Co – he said, "And you'll never guess why I was on the train today. I wasn't coming home – I mean, that wasn't my reason. I was going to the Bon Secours in Fane Mall to get news of you!"

He could not understand why she turned so pale. "Salome McKenna," she murmured. "A true Irish heroine!"

"Yes!" he laughed, desperate to provoke her back into a lighter humour. "In five different-coloured inks!"

He produced the paper and began to unfold it but she reached across the table and took it from him. She pressed it to her bosom and closed her eyes.

Hereward, appalled that his little squib had distressed her so, said, "I'm sorry . . . oh, my dear – I'm so sorry," over and over.

Now it was her turn to force herself to be determinedly bright. "It's in my handwriting, you know," she said. "Not the first page, but inside." She looked at the multicoloured title and said, "Poor Seamus, God be good to him." Then, even more brightly, she turned to him and said, "You ought to go to university, Hereward. You needn't bother about a degree. It's just . . . I don't know – the *ideas* that are floating around and the discussions you'd have. I can think three impossible things before breakfast now without even trying. Surely Rick would pay?"

He said that would present no difficulty; then he asked who paid her fees – the nuns?

And so she told him about Uncle C-B and all those machinations; and they laughed at the misunderstandings surrounding poor Bishop Harte.

And that, in turn, led Hereward to mention Marion, a subject he had thought of introducing much more gently, probably toward the end of this weekend. Things between them were going so much more quickly than he had anticipated; he just hoped they wouldn't trip up and fall flat on their faces.

She surprised him by saying she knew all about the school in Earlsfort Terrace. She saw the obvious question taking shape behind his eyes. But she knew he was not going to ask it, so she saved him the trouble. "I know. It's like I didn't tell the nuns I was coming today. I feel that if I do nothing, just let the past fade into" – she smiled – "ancient history, just go forward into the future, then people can't . . . I mean, I can't . . . you know."

"People can't betray you yet again and you can't be hurt."

"That sounds awful – selfish and melodramatic. People didn't *mean* to betray me."

"Marion has never stopped looking for you, you know."

Salome became tense but did her best not to show it. "You still see her from time to time, do you?" she asked lightly.

"Practically every week."

"She wrote to my mother in Port Elizabeth," she added in the same casual tone.

His amazement was all the answer she needed. "You *know* about that?" he asked. "Has your mother . . . have you . . .? Well, I'm flabbergasted."

"I guessed it had to be Aunt Marion," Salome confessed, and went on to tell him of the letter Father Hines had received, and how news of it had reached her.

"Just in these last few weeks?" Hereward asked in surprise. He then told her how Marion had learned that Mrs Delaroux was the widow of her parents' first employer in the Cape and how, after years of fruitless searching, she, Marion, had finally written to Mrs Delaroux, confessing all. "But that was back in nineteen twenty-one," he added. "In the summer, I think – getting on for four years ago."

"Did this Mrs Delaroux reply at all?" Salome asked.

He tilted his head and said reluctantly, "Your father did, sometime that autumn."

"And?"

"Well, there was a lot about how he and your mother were establishing a farm – twenty thousand acres or something quite incredible . . ."

Her eyes went wide.

"Yes!" He chuckled. "You're probably the daughter of quite rich people by now, d'you realize? Little orphan whatever-her-name-was meets Daddy Long-Legs – life imitates art, eh! Anyway, he sort of implied they couldn't leave the place at that time – and also all the troubles in Ireland – the Tan wars and the civil war, you know . . ."

"They couldn't be bothered," she summed up dejectedly. "So much for Daddy Long-Legs!" She remembered making the same comparison herself once, to Sister Boniface, but she couldn't remember the context.

"To be fair," he pointed out, "if Marion, who was on the spot and must be presumed to know her husband better than most – if she had drawn a blank after five years or whatever it was, then your parents must have seen it as pretty hopeless. And we don't know how many other mouths they have to feed out there . . ."

"All right, all right," she cut him short. "It's all perfectly true."

"And your mother, at least, *is* doing something about it now."

"I know." She grinned at him. "Sometimes I wish Boniface hadn't started the school for handicapped children. It would be so nice to be able to bemoan one's own fate with a clear conscience – just once!"

He wanted to suggest that she should go to Earlsfort Terrace and meet Marion again but he felt it could wait.

They both chose spotted dick and custard for pudding. Hereward took out his cigarette case and offered her one. She hesitated and then took it, saying, "I do, occasionally. Even Boniface smokes now. She says quite a lot of the nuns have taken it up – in private, of course."

"A lot of priests smoke," he pointed out. "Like chimneys."

"Yes, but nuns! A nun with a fag in her mouth!" She blew a cloud at the ceiling and removed a stray shred of tobacco from her lip. "Did *you* ever go looking for me?" she asked teasingly.

"Every day," he said, meaning his reply to be chirpy, in keeping with the humour her question had set. But the memories overwhelmed him and he repeated, in quite a different tone: "Every day, Salome. I've never been able to forget you. It's ridiculous – when you look at me now, and you now – but it's true. You've been in my thoughts every single day for the past eight years, eight months, and I don't know how many days." He choked and swallowed heavily. "And you?"

Her eyes were brimming with tears. All she did was nod, and whisper, "I'll tell you."

He sniffed inelegantly and drew a deep breath. "And

there was I – wondering if I'd *ever* get around to confessing it!"

The pudding arrived and they stubbed out their gaspers; the activity allowed them to gather their feelings. "You don't have a boyfriend, then?" he asked before he could think better of it.

"No!" She was wonderfully positive. "And you?"

He shrugged. "I've tried."

"Not even Miss Nolan?" she persisted. "She's very pretty."

"How do you know?"

"She gave a talk to us feminists before Christmas."

"Oh yes." He shut his eyes and shook his head. "Think how close we've been – without knowing it. I mean, think of that manuscript lying on that shelf, two feet above my head, for the past three years!"

"Am I . . . I mean, do I look the way you expected?"

"Yes, except for being a hundred times more beautiful. What about me – no, don't answer."

They ate in silence awhile, a happy sort of silence, then she said, "I used to have a daydream about you. I used to dream we'd meet again and I'd recognize you but you wouldn't recognize me. And you'd fall in love with me all over again, except that for you it wouldn't be *again*. It'd be like the very first time for you. Then I'd know, you see, that it was genuine on your side, not just dying embers reddened with a forced draught." She giggled at her own childishness.

He took it up as a kind of game, pretending to feel wounded. "But you *would* know – that I was me, I mean. You didn't have much regard for *my* feelings in your daydream. It didn't matter that I might suspect your love was just old embers reddened up!"

"Ah, but I knew it wasn't," she told him. "I knew it had never died down like that. You're the only man I've ever loved and dreamed about like that. But listen, Hereward – to be serious. Now that we've admitted these things to each other, we *can* start again – as if it really was something quite new. We must, don't you agree?"

He nodded vigorously. "Absolutely."

"But at least we know where we're starting *from*."

He lifted his tumbler of water and toasted the proposal.

"It makes quite a change for *me*," she concluded as she raised her own glass to join him.

60

When Mrs McKenna had finished her interview with Father Hines she walked through the village to the ruined gates of Cloonaghvogue Castle – or what was now the ruins of that place. After a moment's uncertainty she went in and started up the drive. The priest sent Miss Kinchy after her, not knowing that Father McDaid had intentions of his own in that line. The pair of them met, by chance, at that same unhinged and rusted gate, just a moment or two before Mrs McKenna passed out of sight beyond a bend in the drive. Benjy Moran kept his threshing engine in the ruins of the castle, so the drive was maintained free of undergrowth at least.

Priest and ex-housekeeper looked at each other and then turned to stare up the drive. She waited respectfully for him to speak first.

"Ah," he said vaguely. "I was just wondering who . . . er . . ."

Miss Kinchy, who remembered well Father McDaid's nighttime visit to the castle, only a week or so before Salome's disappearance – and his strange complacency when she reported it at the presbytery – had never overcome her suspicions that he was somehow implicated in the business. "You'll recall the little colleen, Father," she said guardedly. "Salome Culham-Browne."

"Or McKenna, Miss Kinchy," he replied.

"She was called both," she conceded. "Well, that's Mrs McKenna, her real mother. Father Hines is after saying I should tip up to the castle and have a word with her myself."

"Her real mother, you say. How interesting! I remember the little girl now you mention her. Are they reunited at last then?"

"It seems not, Father." Miss Kinchy fired a shot at hazard. "But by God I'll tell her all I know of C-B and his capers. Isn't she the one who could summons him and make him say what he'd done with her!"

She turned on her heel and left him to think it over.

She found Debbie standing on the top step, wondering how safe it was to walk beneath the roofless portico. "Mrs McKenna!" she called out.

Debbie took a step back and turned toward her.

"I'm Concepta Kinchy," she cried, still some way off. "I was housekeeper here at Cloonaghvogue Castle – in the days when there was any class of a house to keep."

Debbie tripped down the steps and went to join her. "You obviously know who I am," she said, holding out her hand. "I'm delighted to meet you."

"I knew Salome, too," Miss Kinchy replied, shaking hands warmly. "Like a daughter to me, she was, those few years before . . . ah well."

"Tell me about it?" Debbie asked. "I want to hear all. I know I'm going to find her. And when I do, I want to know everything there is to know."

It was an average April day. For the next couple of hours – between sunshine and rain – Miss Kinchy took her all over the demesne. Neither the old castle keep nor the Georgian house was safe enough to enter, but she pointed out the window of Salome's nursery and described it in such detail that Debbie could have walked across it blindfold. She showed her the stable where Hannibal had been kept – and said he was still alive, living in a field in the next parish, if she wished to see him. There was the walled garden where the swings had been, the croquet lawn (would you ever believe it!), the bridle path where they'd watched the hunt spreading the foxcubs, the ditch where she'd lepped and fallen and hurted her elbow, and the lake, of course, where she'd tickled trout and gazed in fascination at the statues. "The colleen had a head and arms then but the lads knocked them off in sharpshooting practice in the troubles," she explained.

She described Miss Morrell and the Bellinghams and the children who came to the parties and the parties Salome had gone to in return. By the time their wanderings had brought them back to the ruins of the castle, Debbie felt she probably knew more about her little girl's early years than grown-up Salome herself would now remember.

"The one person you haven't said much about, Miss Kinchy," she remarked, "is Marion Culham-Browne herself – the woman responsible for it all."

"Ah, well now, ma'am – there you have it," she replied evasively. "Sure she never meant you harm."

"Whether she meant it or not, she did it. She caused our family a great deal of harm."

"Wasn't she desthroyed with the grief, herself, ma'am."

"Oh I'm sure. And when I say she did us so much harm, I hold no grudge against her for it now. She had the courage – and the decency – to write and let us know what she did. I know it's come half a dozen years too late – but still, she wrote."

"Is she over the water now, ma'am – like himself?"

"Indeed she is not. Did she never come back here at all?"

"Divil a sight of her did we see since she left – in the time of the Easter Rising in Dublin that was."

"Well that's where she is now – in Dublin. She has a

private school for girls there, just off Saint Stephen's Green. I'm going to visit her, of course. Tomorrow afternoon, in fact. I began my search in Queenstown – or Cobh as they call it now."

"Cobh and Port Laoise and Dun Laoghaire and County Offaly – God, you wouldn't know what land you were in half the time!" Miss Kinchy said with feeling. "You'd think Dublin would leave Ireland alone!"

"Anyway, I shall be going to Dublin tonight and calling on Mrs Culham-Browne tomorrow afternoon, as I said. But if you're worried I might do her harm or summons her to court, you may rest easy in your mind. From all you've told me – and from what I've seen here, overgrown and ruined though it is – I believe I should be more grateful to her than angry. When you think of the sort of fate that might have overtaken a little seven-year-old waif all alone in the world!"

These words set Miss Kinchy's mind at rest and she occupied the rest of their stroll, back toward the village, with her own memories of Mrs Culham-Browne and the wee colleen.

As they went out by the gate Miss Kinchy's sharp eye caught sight of Father McDaid, lurking in the ditch a fair way up the road.

Meanwhile Mrs McKenna was saying, "Before I go, Miss Kinchy, may I ask you *your* opinion of what happened? People here must have talked about it when Salome vanished like that – what sort of thing did they say? And what do they say now?"

"Lord, ma'am, you'd find her on the far side of the moon to hear them tell it. There's not a workhouse in Ireland she hasn't been seen in by one or other of them – with their very own eyes! I stopped sending word of it to poor Mrs Culham-Browne, so I did. Wasn't she seen in Simonstown, ten miles up the road, one time! Wait till I tell you – that oul' divil, C-B, as they called him – he's put her where you'd never think of looking. 'Tis himself you should be talking to, not the missus."

"Oh I will. Indeed I will. All in good time, as the man said. But I want to know what's to be gleaned here before I get to him, else he'll dance rings round me, wouldn't you say."

Miss Kinchy chuckled. "Well you weren't behind the door when brains was giving out, ma'am – I want to tell you that. And d'you know what I'm going to tell you now?"

"What?"

"There's a spalpeen in the form of a priest creeping in our shadow – don't look round. His name is called Father McDaid. And of all the men and all the women in Cloonaghvogue, the one that'd know the most of what became of your Salome is that oul' divil. But whether he'd tell you or no, well, that's a calf from another cow, as the man said."

Debbie accepted the old woman's invitation to a sup of tea, mainly to see whether Father McDaid would continue to hang about. He did. So when she went outside again to find the driver whose taxi had brought her here from Simonstown, she gave the priest the chance he was obviously desperate for.

She knew that curates always suspected their priests knew more about them than was actually the case – guilt being part of their trade, so to speak. So she stepped up to him, holding out her hand, and said, "Father McDaid? I'm Mrs McKenna, the mother of the little girl the Culham-Brownes fostered just before the war. I'm glad to meet you before I leave Cloonaghvogue. Father Hines mentioned your name to me."

She said no more than that but the shock in his features confirmed all that Miss Kinchy had said about the man.

"Ah yes," he replied. "Her disappearance was a great mystery. We were all very sad."

"Sadness, is it! Well, I'm no stranger to that emotion myself, Father," she said.

"To be sure, Mrs McKenna. And it's a sad pilgrimage for you. Tell me – have you any word of her at all? Has anybody written to you with news?"

"Well, it was a letter from Mrs Culham-Browne herself that brought me here to Cloonaghvogue."

"Ah – well, I was wondering about that."

He became a living monument to uncertainty, biting his lip, cracking his knuckles in a manner she found intensely annoying. Since time was getting short if she was to catch a reasonable connection to Dublin that evening, she took a chance – most unusually for her. "Listen, Father," she said in as pleasant a voice as she could muster. "You should understand that I have no intention of returning to South Africa until I have found Salome. And when I do find her, I shall know everything. Mrs Culham-Browne has been courageous and frank with me. She has confessed her part in keeping Salome from being reunited with her proper family. As I've just been explaining to Miss Kinchy, I bear that woman no grudge and would not dream of pursuing her further. But listen till I tell you – it will be quite another matter with those who have obstructed my search. So if you know anyone in this parish – anyone in all the world – who could be spared the shame of exposure by helping me now, you'll do him or her a kindness by passing this on. I'm staying with a cousin in Donnybrook for the next week or two – however long it takes – so if you have e'er a slip of paper about you, I'll give you the house and road."

The revolting clicking of his knucklejoints came to an end at last. "It won't be necessary, Mrs McKenna," he said quietly. "Will we step into the church while I tell you?"

Twenty minutes later Debbie found her taximan but decided he was no longer in a condition to drive her. She told him to move over into the passenger seat while she took control of the car. He didn't demur. All he said was, "Will you find your way back to the station, missus?"

"I'm not going to the station," she said triumphantly.

"You'll have to show me the way when we get to Simonstown. I'm going to the Bon Secours house in somewhere called Fane Mall."

61

Salome behaved impeccably until they were halfway across Saint Stephen's Green. Then she stopped and said she couldn't possibly go through with it. Hereward put his arms around her. "Listen, love," he said patiently. "D'you want to go as yourself, instead?"

"No!" she exclaimed, giving a theatrical shudder.

"Well what, then?"

"I don't want to go at all."

"But now your rustication's over you *can't* stay in Dublin and be my girlfriend and *not* meet Marion. We keep going round this same old . . ."

"Well, not *today*, then. Tomorrow."

"We've been through that, too. Listen – d'you remember going down to Simonstown by train that time – when I wasn't sure if it was you, and couldn't pluck up the courage to ask? First I was going to ask at Maryborough. Then Ballybrophy. Then Roscrea . . . And at each place it just got harder and harder. Honestly, one more stop and I wouldn't be here now. Or you wouldn't be."

Salome said nothing – until he relaxed his hug. Then she said, "No, don't let go!"

He sighed and relented. "If you *really* can't face it, we will call it off. We'll go and see what's on at the Grafton, instead. I didn't telephone so Marion's not expecting us. No one'll know. But I can tell you now – it'll only make it ten times harder when you *do* decide."

Silence.

"It will," he repeated.

"I know," she agreed unhappily. "I just feel that – from the way Boniface sounded on the telephone last night – I ought to see my mother first – now we know she's here in Dublin. When I agreed to come and see Aunt Marion, my mother was still just a distant threat."

He coughed at the word. "I don't think she'd like to hear you call her that!"

"You know what I mean. I just feel it's wrong."

"And I just feel you should go through with it – it'll only be half an hour – cup of tea – bit of madeira cake – what lovely roses! – snish-snish! And then you'll know whether you still like her or not and want to reveal your true identity."

"I won't. You know I won't. Anyway, can we be sure my mother *is* in Dublin? We only have Boniface's word on it – and that alleged cousin in Donnybrook was very evasive."

He chuckled. "That's the kindest description – slamming the door and shouting through the letterbox like that! You've got a weird family!"

"Ho ho! Who's talking!" She pulled away from him to make this accusation. Once their contact was broken she found it easier to say, "Oh, all right then! You'll give me no peace until I agree – and don't talk about going to the Grafton! You'd only sit there snapping your fingers and breathing like a grampus through your nose. So come on!" She stepped away from him impatiently and dragged him after her.

"That's my girl, Sal!" he said.

"If you slip and call me Salome, I'll . . . I'll . . ."

"Laugh and pass it off, I hope?"

"I was going to say something very rude."

He raised shocked eyes to the heavens, muttering, "You convent girls! Everything I ever heard about you is true!" – still trying to keep her cheerful.

But they had barely entered Earlsfort Terrace when she

got cold feet again – this time about her appearance. "Are you sure she won't recognize me?" she asked.

"Darling girl!" He mastered his impatience, for he truly sympathized with her agonies; he only kept her at it because he knew how dreadful she'd feel if she gave in to her own fears. "Even I didn't recognize you – bobbed and shingled like that."

"D'you think I look awful?"

"I think you look spiffing."

"You're only saying that."

"You'd still look beautiful with your head shaved. Except . . . I don't know?" He surveyed her critically.

"What?" she asked in a panic.

"If it were *completely* shaved, one might then be able to observe how *thick* and *obtuse* your skull is."

"Aargh!" She lashed out at him with her handbag.

"Steady the buffs!" He caught it in mid-flight and moved in to pacify her again. "Listen – we *will* call it off. We'll go to the zoo instead – and I promise not to click my fingers or breathe like a walrus."

"Grampus."

"I won't breathe at all – all right?" He inhaled deeply and held it.

She glowered at him until he showed signs of distress, then she flung her arms around him again and said, "You!"

He exhaled with enormous relief.

"Come on!" she snapped, as if *he* had been finding endless petty excuses for delay.

When they mounted the steps to Marion's house and he pulled the bell knob, she said, "Actually . . . Hereward . . ."

"Too late," he replied at once. Then he added, "Sal."

To his surprise Marion answered the door in person; what's more, she seemed none too pleased to see him. "Oh it's you," she said woodenly, staring over his shoulder and completely ignoring Salome. "I was expecting it to be someone else."

"Oh, I'm sorry," he replied in his most placatory tone. "I should have phoned. Miss Dolan and I were on our way to . . . we were going to stroll up the canal to Portobello. I just thought we'd cry in in the passing. But if it's not convenient . . ."

All this while Marion continued to peer anxiously past them, down Earlsfort Terrace, and then up, and then down again. Then at last she appeared to hear what he had said. She gazed intently at Salome, who suddenly remembered all the nice things she had ever felt about Aunt Marion and was on the point of giving everything away when Marion said, "Miss Nolan? Is this *another* Miss Nolan? How many have you got?"

Hereward coughed awkwardly and said, "No, Marion – *Dolan*. Miss Sally Dolan. You haven't met her before. She's a bit of my ancient history. I thought you might like . . ."

"Ancient history!" Marion laughed near-hysterically. "How appropriate! Do come in." She smiled affably at Salome then. "I'm sorry I'm such an *awful* hostess. Only it's all rather fraught just at the moment. Actually, come to think of it, I'm really rather *glad* you've called." She led them down the passage toward the private quarters at the back. "And please *do* stay to tea – it'll certainly help break the ice – especially you, Hereward. But don't think I'm rude if I wander off halfway through – with my guest, I mean. The one I'm expecting?"

By now, of course, both the visitors had a very good idea which 'guest' was expected – which would also explain the evasiveness of the cousin out in Donnybrook. The penny dropped with Salome a moment before it did the same trick with Hereward, so that he had to run a few paces to catch up with her. "Stay!" he hissed. "It's fate!"

"Not for all the tea in China!" Salome replied, her face as white as snow.

The doorbell rang again.

"She must have come up Hatch Street," Marion said angrily as she bustled past them. She only got a pace beyond Hereward, however, when she stopped and turned. "Listen," she said in a low, urgent whisper. "You've got to help me! That's Salome McKenna's mother at the door now – we meet at last! Please stay and help out? Do say you will?" She glanced briefly at Salome and flashed her a wan smile. "I'm sorry for you, my dear – pitchforking you in like this. But if you tangle with this fellow" – she waved a hand at Hereward – "*this* is the sort of thing you must expect."

Her anguish touched Salome, who then decided, on the spur of the moment, that Hereward was right – it *was* fate.

"Well?" Marion hung on Hereward's reply.

The doorbell rang again.

"I'm not sure . . ." He looked at Salome.

"Of course we'll stay!" she said, more confidently than she felt. She laid a hand on Marion's arm. "And we'll do our very best to jolly things along – won't we, Hereward?"

"Jolly," he replied flatly.

Marion hastened on toward the front door, calling over her shoulder. "Don't stand there like a couple of bodyguards – even if that's what you are, suddenly. You know where to take her, Hereward."

As soon as they reached the parlour Salome gave way to her agitation. "Paper! Paper!" she almost shrieked. "Any scrap – quick!"

"What for?" He pulled an old tram ticket out of his pocket.

"Bigger! And blank!" She found an At Home card on the mantelpiece and tore it in two. "Pencil!" she snapped.

"Here, you can't do that!"

"I've done it! Give me a bloody pencil or I'll scream!"

He gasped at her language and handed over his propelling pencil without a murmur.

She scribbled on the back of the card: *Do not give me*

away to Mrs C-B – PLEASE – Mammy darling. I'll explain later. Salome.

"Just in case she recognizes me," she said as she handed him back his pencil – and the other half of the torn-up invitation, which he slipped guiltily in his pocket.

There were voices in the passage now. Salome said, "I never thought I'd ever do *this* again" – and she put her hands together and prayed.

"And this is Hereward Bellingham," Marion said. "Richard Bellingham's son, you know. He was a childhood sweetheart of Salome's so I invited him to tea as well. It's a pity Maisie Fielding, her old governess – Maisie Morrell, as was – isn't here, but she's having a baby in Westport. Oh, and this is Hereward's friend, Miss Sally Nolan . . ."

"Dolan," Hereward put in.

"Dolan, I'm sorry. Oh dear! I'm afraid we've only just met, so I can't tell you anything about her."

Mother and daughter faced each other at last – after the best part of twelve momentous years.

"Good afternoon Mrs McKenna," Salome said.

"Good afternoon, Miss Dolan." The polite smile froze on Debbie's lips.

It wasn't telepathy.

It wasn't some mystic knowledge that flowed through the contact of mother-flesh and daughter-flesh.

It was the sheer panic in Salome's eyes – plus, to be sure, what Sister Boniface had told Debbie about this same Hereward Bellingham only last night.

Anger flashed in her eyes. What sort of fools did these people think she was? She began to count it down, knowing she must not speak until she had mastered it somewhat better than at the moment.

"Yes, well," Marion said awkwardly, "I'll just pop out and see if the tea is . . . yes."

The moment she was out of the door, Debbie turned to her daughter and said, "What d'you mean by all this?"

She would have said a great deal more but Salome put a finger to her mother's lips and, with the most desperate plea in her eyes, handed her the piece of card. She nodded urgently over her shoulder, hoping to indicate that the butler's pantry was only just outside.

Debbie had to read the message twice before the meaning was clear. She looked up in amazement and whispered, "You mean she doesn't *know?*"

Salome shook her head violently.

"Why?"

She pointed to the card and repeated its message: "I'll explain later." She stretched out a hand.

Debbie, still in a daze and thinking she wanted the card back, handed it to her. But Salome took her hand and gave it a firm squeeze. "Thanks."

"Well, here we are then!" Marion came in with a two-tier plate of cakes and biscuits. Behind her the maid pushed the tea trolley, cups rattling.

"Do sit down, all of you," Marion urged. "Well now – I'll be mother, shall I?"

"Why not!" Debbie laughed.

Marion looked at her askance; the other two stared at their feet.

Debbie apologized and said she was feeling a little light-headed. "You see, Marion dear – I may call you that, mayn't I? We're very informal out in the colonies, I'm afraid."

Marion only just managed not to drop the teapot. "Please do," she said, "er, Deborah?"

Debbie nodded. "Or Debbie. Anyway, as I was about to say, I'm feeling a little light-headed because, you see, I found Salome – last night."

This time Marion did drop the pot – or set it down very heavily on the tray. "You do it, Charlotte," she said to the maid. Then, turning her huge eyes on Debbie, added, "I beg your pardon?"

Hereward, realizing he had no choice but to play along, leaned forward with interest and said, "But what wonderful news! Here in Dublin? How is she? Gosh! Did you recognize her at once? I wish I'd been there to see it!"

Debbie held up a hand against this barrage. "I didn't actually meet her," she confessed. "What I mean is I discovered where she's been living all this time – ever since nineteen-sixteen. And I talked to the people who took her in and brought her up."

"Oh!" Marion snatched a handkerchief from her sleeve and dabbed it to her eye.

Watching her, Salome felt dreadful. Half of her wanted to lay aside the deception at once; but the other half was wiser. It knew she could not cope with all the emotions that would then be unleashed. Nor, indeed, would it be fair to face both these splendid women with the choices that would follow. She glanced at Hereward, begging him to do something – though precisely what, she couldn't have said.

He caught her gesture, made a hopeless movement with his eyes, but then trained them keenly on her mother. If Debbie McKenna now wanted a little sport with Marion, who could blame her? All the same, he was going to do his best to stop it.

Salome, her mind racing along similar lines, thought of pretending that the name Salome had just jogged her memory. She could then say she was studying Classics at Trinity and there was a Salome McKenna reading Ancient History. Could that be her? The convent girl . . . et cetera. It would allow her to butt in if her mother went too far with poor Aunt Marion.

But the appropriate moment passed – and, anyway, her mother seemed to be having second thoughts.

"It wasn't so very clever of me, though," she said in a gentler tone than before. "I wanted to see all the places where Salome had been before, you know, nineteen-sixteen. I started in Queenstown, of course – or Cobh. And the Royal George club, which you mentioned." She smiled. "I could just picture Salome's wonder on being taken inside a place like that!" She smiled genially at 'Miss Dolan' – who gave her a guarded smile in return.

"And then, naturally, I went to Cloonaghvogue."

"But it's in ruins," Marion said.

"All the same . . . I had the good fortune to meet Miss Kinchy, and . . ."

"Miss Kinchy!" Marion clapped her hands and smiled at Hereward. "D'you remember Miss Kinchy?"

"Vaguely," he replied. "Wasn't she your housekeeper?"

"And she's still living there!" Marion exclaimed.

"The church would grind to a halt without her. Anyway, she showed me over the place – the window that had been Salome's nursery . . . the rocking horse . . . a doll of some kind called Too Small – by the way, I still have her dolly – Maggoty Meg! I brought her with me – she'll probably laugh!"

Salome realized she had been holding her breath far longer than was wise. Her eyes were brimming with tears.

Hereward fidgeted angrily, but felt himself constrained in every direction. At last he said – just to give Salome breathing space – "Someone ought to explain all this to Miss Dolan. You see . . ." And he turned to Salome and summarized her own story to her, allowing her time to gather herself once again. It occurred to her that her mother was paying off old scores all round – not just against Aunt Marion. A few years earlier it would have raised her hackles to the point where she could no longer see reason; she would just have struck blindly back. But now she realized she was mature enough to take it – not as one of the nuns would take it, as a matter of spiritual discipline, but for the equally humble though more personal reason than she had no idea what her mother must have suffered to make her capable of behaving like this.

However, it put her on her guard and she was determined

not to be caught in such an easy emotional trap again.

Also she blessed Hereward for bringing her in like that, for it now enabled her to say, "Poor little girl! She must have felt . . . I mean, we don't think rationally at that age, do we! She must have felt that the world – the grown-up world – was a place that always let you down. Just when she'd got used to it and felt loved and wanted – bang! Down came the shutters again!"

She saw that her mother had taken in her remarks and so she smiled apologetically all around, saying, "Sorry! I shouldn't have interrupted." She looked at Hereward. "I think we really ought to go, darling. We're only intruding on . . ." She waved a hand vaguely between the two older women.

"No, no!" Marion protested. "Please do stay. And please do say whatever comes into your mind. I mean – you're the one person here who is completely detached from the whole story. So what you say is especially valuable, as you've just proved. We three all loved Salome in our own way. Perhaps I shouldn't tell you this, but Hereward pined for her for years, didn't you dear!"

He scratched his neck awkwardly and said, "Well . . . you know . . . puppy love and all that!" He turned with relief to Debbie and said, "I'm sorry. I interrupted. Cloonaghvogue, you were saying?"

"Oh, well, I saw all her old haunts."

"The swing in the walled garden?" Marion said.

"I saw where it stood."

"And the statues in the lake?" Hereward asked.

Debbie nodded. "The girl has lost her head and arms – target practice in the civil war! And Hannibal – her old pony – is still alive, would you believe!"

Hereward leaned forward and said, "Could I be terribly rude and ask for some more tea?" – mainly to give Salome a chance to assimilate this news.

But Salome was well armoured by now. She just said,

"Hereward!" in an embarrassed but peremptory tone.

Debbie heaved a sigh of relief, as if she had been waiting for her daughter to reach that pitch of self-control. Then she resumed her tale, telling them how Miss Kinchy had taken her home for tea and, in passing, advised her to pursue her inquiries with Father McDaid.

"I'm afraid I . . . well, the only word is *blackmailed* the man. Imagine! A Roman Catholic priest, and I threatening him! Wonders will never cease."

Marion frowned. "D'you mean he was involved in Salome's disappearance? But he was so kind and considerate to me, after, you know."

"Well – he never liked the idea of a Roman Catholic foundling being brought up a Protestant. And that's the top and tail of the man."

Marion blushed. "We would have encouraged her to make her own choice later," she said lamely.

"Well, he didn't like that, either. Tell me, Marion, can you imagine your husband . . ."

"My *former* husband. We have an English divorce." She turned to Hereward who was staring at her, open-mouthed. "And that's to go no further than these four walls, young man! This is a respectable ladies' school, remember!"

"Can you imagine your *former* husband buying the best possible education for Salome?" Debbie went on. "The most expensive in Ireland?"

Marion laughed at the very idea.

"Alternatively, can you imagine him sending her to a Roman Catholic school?"

The laughter redoubled.

"He was relying on that, of course," Debbie told her.

The laughter stopped. The smile faded. "You mean he did? Which?"

"Both – and not ten miles from Cloonaghvogue, which is also the last place you'd go looking."

"Catherlough House!" Hereward could bear the tickling

no longer. "The Bon Secours Sisters! The crafty oul' divil!"

Marion's face was pale as could be suddenly. "Simonstown?" she asked.

Debbie nodded. "All these years."

"She's not . . . not a nun? Or a novice she'd be, still. She's not a novice?"

Debbie shook her head. "That was my hope, of course – when I went to see one of the nuns. Sister Boniface."

"And she told you where Salome is now? Please! I can't wait much longer to hear."

"She's here in Dublin."

Marion's face lit up.

"At Trinity."

"At Trinity!" Marion stood up suddenly and paced about, saying, "Oh . . . oh . . . oh! We must . . . we must . . . what can we do? Have you been to see her? What does she look like now? Oh! To think she's only half a mile from here!"

"*Stop!*" Salome, unable to bear it a moment longer, rose to her feet, too, and shouted at her mother: "I begged you not to! I begged you!"

"It was wrong of you, child," Debbie said calmly and then waved a hand toward Marion. "Go on," she said.

"What . . . who . . . I don't understand . . ." Marion's voice was barely recognizable.

Salome just stared at her mother; somehow all her anger had faded. "You don't mind?" she asked in surprise.

"Would I have forced you to it if I did?" was the reply. "Go on."

As in a dream, Salome drifted across the carpet and wrapped her arms gently around Marion's neck. "Dear Aunt Marion!" she whispered, giving her a big, wet kiss on her cheek. "Forgive me! I wanted to be a new friend, not an old millstone – don't you see? I meant it for the best."

Marion made a few choking sounds and then said, "Salome?"

She wrenched herself free and held her visitor tight at both arms'-length. "Salome?" she shouted.

"Yes."

"And it's really you?" She looked at Hereward, then at Debbie, then at Salome once again.

"Yes! Yes! Yes!" And Salome broke free and threw her arms around her once more, shivering like an aspen, howling her eyes out.

Then at last Debbie rose and went to join them. Marion saw her coming and tugged one of Salome's arms off her, ready to put round her mother.

Salome resisted until she felt her mother's body at her side. Then she hugged her tight, almost cracking their heads together. They all burst into tears then and cried the salt from their eyes – for a long, long time.

Hereward hardly dared move. He dabbed at the crumbs on his plate, transferring them to his mouth, one by one. At last, when the weeping subsided and he feared they might start to feel ashamed of themselves – especially if they saw him still sitting there, calmly hogging crumbs – he rose and began to tiptoe from the room.

But Salome, who was facing him, cried out, "No you don't!"

He spun round as if she'd stung him. "Don't what?"

She released her two mothers at last and took a step toward him. "You don't get away so easily! I have a crow to pick with you."

"Oh?" He grinned and pretended to look guilty.

But the grin faded and the guilt intensified when she said, "Yes. What did Aunt Marion mean when she asked you *how many Nolans* you were courting at the same time?"